1A   2

W9-CFJ-534

DESTINY *of the* WOLF

TERRY SPEAR

sourcebooks
casablanca

Published by Sourcebooks Casablanca, an imprint of Sourcebooks, Inc.
P.O. Box 4410, Naperville, Illinois 60567-4410
(630) 961-3900
FAX: (630) 961-2168
www.sourcebooks.com

Library of Congress Cataloging-in-Publication Data

Spear, Terry.
  Destiny of the wolf / Terry Spear.
      p. cm.
  1. Werewolves—Fiction. I. Title.
  PS3619.P373D66 2009
  813'.6—dc22

                  2008037086

                  Printed in Canada
            WC 10 9 8 7 6 5 4

I dedicate *Destiny of the Wolf* to the memory of my father, who believed with all his heart I'd be published, but died of a fast-spreading cancer before that day came. He was a true hero, who survived numerous near-death catastrophes—from a dwindling sandbar in the incoming rush of tidal waters of the Duwamish River when he was four, to a typhoon in the Persian Gulf, to a sunken sailboat in the shark-infested Sea of Japan, and many, many more such adventures—yet always maintained a wonderful sense of humor and lived life to its fullest.

Chapter 1

WHY HAD LARISSA, HER LOVING SISTER, ENDED UP DEAD— here, of all the godforsaken places in the States? Maybe that was the reason—off the beaten path, surrounded by wilderness, a place to hide from the harsh realities of the forced marriage, safe from Bruin's retaliation should he ever have located her. But she hadn't been safe. And now she was dead.

Out of the corner of her eye, Lelandi Wildhaven thought she saw her cousin, Ural, slink into the woods in his wolf form, but she had to be mistaken. He wouldn't be angry enough with her to shapeshift this close to Silver Town and risk alerting the gray *lupus garou* pack that a couple of reds had slipped into their territory.

Ignoring her gut instinct telling her this was a very bad idea, she pushed open the Silver Town Tavern's heavy door, the squealing of the rusty hinges jarring her taut nerves.

Five bearded men sitting at a table turned to stare at her, and at once she feared the worst—they saw straight through her disguise.

She shoved the faux eyeglasses back into place, hating the way they kept sliding down the bridge of her nose. The weather-beaten cowboy hat she'd picked up at a resale shop half swallowed her head, making her look like a little kid wearing her dad's Stetson.

Amber glass lights hanging from brass rods high above softly illuminated dark oak tables and a long, polished bar. Slow-spinning wooden fan blades circulated the air, impregnated with the smell of gray *lupus garou.* Her nerve endings prickled with fresh awareness. Dingy antique mirrors covering the back wall behind the bar bore mute witness to the goings-on in the place, as she suspected they had for decades. If they had captured all the images of the bar's existence what a story those mirrors could tell.

Another bearded man crouching beneath the lip of the bar suddenly stood to his full six-foot-four height. The glass and dish towel he held nearly slipped from his grasp as his appraising glance took in every inch of her. His lips turned up at the corners slightly. Deep laugh lines were etched in his tanned skin and shaggy black hair extended to his shoulders, giving him the appearance of a rugged mountain man, unused to civilized trappings. What disturbed her most was that he was a gray, like the men drinking at the table. She'd anticipated it would be a human-run establishment frequented by *lupus garous,* like the bar back home.

"What'll you have, miss?" he asked, his voice warm and welcoming.

Expecting a chilly greeting—their kind didn't welcome strangers venturing into their midst, especially if she were human and this was an exclusively gray *lupus garou* tavern—she hesitated.

"Miss?"

"Bottled water, please." She'd meant to sound tough, to match the look of the place. She'd intended to be someone different, with her red hair dyed black and the high-heeled boots giving the impression she stood taller, more like *them.* The blue contacts she wore hid her green eyes sufficiently, but she still felt like Lelandi, triplet to Larissa, with barely any visible difference in appearance, except her eyes were greener and her hair more red and less golden than her sister's had been. Had her voice betrayed her?

The small smile on the bartender's face was more likely because she was a stranger who'd walked into a wolves' den without protection than because she'd given herself away. She cursed herself for not disguising her voice better, but the barkeep's warm demeanor gave her a false sense of security, which could be the death of her if she wasn't careful.

The bartender handed her a chilled bottle of water and tall green glass. "New in town?"

"Just passing through," she said, paying for the water.

"Sam's the name, miss. If you need anything, just holler."

"Thanks." Hollering for a drink was definitely not her style.

She chose a table in the farthermost corner of the room, half-hidden in shadows. Although any of them could see in the dark as well as she could, this location would keep her out of the main flow of traffic. She hoped she'd seem inconspicuous, not worthy of anyone's scrutiny, and most of all, human.

Lelandi glanced at the door. According to her information, Darien Silver—Larissa's widowed mate— should be here soon.

One of the men got up from his seat and gave Sam some cash. The man cast Lelandi a hint of a smile, then returned to his chair. Small for a gray, stocky, hair a bland brown, eyes amber, his clothes carrying a coating of dust, he had a soft, round baby face. Looked sweet, a beta-wolf type. Smudges of dirt colored his cheeks, and he wiped them off with the back of his denim shirtsleeve. His eyes never straying from her, he smoothed out his raggedy hair and took another swig of his beer.

Sam joined Lelandi and handed her the cash. "Joe Kelly paid for your drink, miss. He works at the silver mine, which explains his slightly rough appearance. But he cleans up good." Sam gave her a wink, and returned to the bar.

Should she turn down Joe's offer? On the other hand, if he was interested in her, maybe she could discover the truth quicker.

"Thank you," she mouthed to Joe Kelly and his chest swelled.

The other guys started ribbing him in low voices. The tips of Joe's ears turned crimson.

Her stomach clenched with the notion that Larissa had had the audacity to mate with a gray, especially when she had a mate already. She'd said she wanted to find herself, and she did. Six feet under. Yet, Lelandi couldn't help feeling it was her own fault, that if she'd taken Larissa's place back home, or even run away with her, she might have kept her safe. But what about their parents? She couldn't have left them behind—not with her dad so incapacitated—but hell, she hadn't been able to protect them either. They had been murdered anyway.

She tamped down a shudder, hating that she hadn't stopped any of it. But once she learned what had happened to Larissa and put the murderer in *his* grave, Lelandi was going to locate her brother and their uncle— damn both of them for leaving the family behind.

The barkeep clinked some glasses, his gaze taking her in like a crafty old wolf's. He probably was on the younger side of middle age but due to the beard, he seemed older. The smile still percolated on his lips. Trying to figure her out? Or did he realize what a phony she was? Hunting in the wild was nothing new, but hunting like this...

She twisted the top off her bottled water and glanced down at her watch again. Only four twenty-five.

"Waiting for someone?" Sam asked, one dark brow cocked.

She shook her head. Her hat jiggled, her glasses slipped, and the annoying earrings danced.

Two men appeared in front of one of the dingy tavern windows and then the door jerked open. Her heart skittered.

"Hey, Sam! Bring us a pitcher of beer," one of them called.

About six-foot—as tall as her brother—with windswept shoulder-length dark hair and a newly started beard, his amber eyes hinted at cheerfulness and good-humor rang in his words. Both men wore leather jackets, plaid shirts, denims, cowboy hats, and boots, and they appeared to be twins. Multiple births abounded among *lupus garous,* so no surprise there. They looked like they were mid- to late-twenties and walked into the place like they owned the joint.

"Jake, Tom." Sam glanced in her direction, alerting them to the presence of a stranger.

She stiffened her back and gripped her glass tighter.

Tom—his hair the lighter of the two, longer, curling around his broad shoulders, his face smooth as silk—fastened his gaze on her and raised his brows, tipped back his Stetson, and grinned.

Self-conscious, her whole body heated and alarm bells rang. *Keep a low profile!*

Tom took a deep breath as if he were love-struck. "The place looks a might better tonight, Sam. Done some nice redecorating."

The bearded one furrowed his dark brows. "Didn't you tell her it's a private club and no matter what, *that* table is reserved?"

"Bending the rules today. First come, first served." Sam grinned and winked at Lelandi.

Damn. Was this where Darien normally sat? She thought he'd sit in the center, so everyone could see their leader. That's the way Bruin did it back home.

Now what? Move? To where? If she moved to the table across from Darien's, she feared she'd draw too much attention. Not that she expected anyone to hurt her here, but she had thought she'd be able to keep a low profile. The tables situated on the other side of the bar sat in front of the restrooms. Anywhere else was too near the front door or in the middle of the floor, and no matter what, she wanted to have her back to the wall. She wasn't leaving until she'd had a chance to observe the leader and as many of his pack members as she could, any one of whom might have murdered Larissa.

Tom grabbed the pitcher of beer and a glass. "Come on, Jake. Change is good for the soul." He stalked over to the table opposite her and sat where he could see both the front door and, most of all, her.

Immersed in a goldfish bowl, she wondered what had made her think she could enter the wolves' lair without arousing suspicion.

Jake sat with his back to the wall to have a better view of the door. If he wanted to look her over, he'd have to turn his head and be pretty obvious about it. *He did.* The expression on his face was dark and foreboding. Gone was the humor his features had held when he first walked into the place.

Laughing and boisterous, three more men barged into the tavern, glanced to where Jake and Tom sat, then shifted their attention to Lelandi. Which meant what? That Jake and Tom normally sat with Darien at the table where she was now sitting?

Terrific!

"Howdy, boys," the older bearded man of the group said, nodding a greeting. The other two were nearly as old, gray streaking their brown beards, their gazes pinned on her. "Bring us the usual, Sam." He turned to Jake and pointed his head at her. "*He* know about this?"

"Still giving orders at the factory, Mason," Tom said.

The bearded man grumbled, "Fourth of July's coming for a second time this year."

Figuring she'd be better off sitting next to the restrooms to lessen the chance of creating *fireworks,* Lelandi grabbed her purse.

The door banged open again. The chatter died.

As soon as she saw him, she knew it was *him*—not only because silence instantly cloaked the room and every eye in the place watched Darien Silver's reaction. His sable hair curled at the top edge of his collar. Brooding dark eyes, grim lips, features handsomely rugged, but definitely hard, defined him. Wearing a leather jacket, western shirt, jeans, and boots, everything was as black as his somber mood. He looked so much like Tom and

Jake, she figured they must be triplets, and he was the leader of the gray *lupus garou* in the area. Had to be, the way everyone watched him, waiting for the fireworks.

Something about him stirred her blood, something akin to recognition, yet she'd never seen him before in her life. It wasn't his face, or clothes, or body that stimulated some deep memory—but the way he moved—commanding, powerful, with an effortless grace.

He glanced at the barkeep and gave a nod of greeting—sullen, silent, still in mourning for his mate? If he discovered why Lelandi was here, he'd be pissed.

A shiver trickled down her spine. She released her purse and kept her seat, for the moment. Everyone was acting so oddly, she imagined *that* was the reason he quickly surveyed the current seating arrangement. When his eyes lit on her, incredulity registered.

Crap! He recognized her; she just knew it. Didn't matter that she had dyed her hair this horrible color that didn't do anything for her fair skin, or that her eyes were now blue. Didn't matter that the heavy padded leather jacket gave her broader shoulders and made her appear heavier, or that she wore her hair straight as blades of uncut grass, compliments of a hair straightening iron, when her sister's and hers was naturally curly. She couldn't hide the shape of her face or eyes or mouth. All of them mirrored her sister's looks.

Then again, his look was puzzled. The hat and glasses appeared to confuse him. Maybe the fact that she wore the faux pierced earrings that looked like the real thing did too.

She broke eye contact first, her skin sweaty, her hands trembling. God, he was more wolf than she was used to dealing with—broader-shouldered and taller. His eyes locked onto hers with sinful determination, no backing down, no compromise. No wonder Larissa had fallen for the attention-grabbing gray. Lelandi couldn't help wondering how a romp with a virile wolf like him would feel. But damn if it hadn't gotten Larissa killed. Stick with your own kind, that's what her father would have said. No humans, *lupus garou* only… the red variety.

Everyone remained deathly quiet—no one lifted a mug to take a sip of a drink, no one moved a muscle. Swallowing hard, she forced herself to look at Darien, to see what he was doing now.

Still staring at her. She wanted to sink into the floor like mop water on a hot day. She gritted her teeth, lifted her glass of water, and took another swig, hoping she wouldn't inadvertently choke on the icy drink out of nervousness. But she wasn't leaving Silver Town until she avenged Larissa's death.

Darien glanced at Sam, who shrugged a shoulder and handed him an empty glass. If Darien wanted her out of his chair, *he* would have to move her.

Macho gang leaders had to show they were in charge, particularly when it came to their territory, and no one, especially women, upstaged them. There were none more notorious for this than *lupus garous.* No one challenged them and got away with it, unless another *lupus garou* was trying to take over the pack, and won.

She wasn't part of his pack. She wasn't a male. And she wasn't a gray. What's worse, she looked like his dead mate. On the other hand, it appeared he wasn't sure of what he was seeing.

The eyes that latched onto her again were cold, yet sorrow was reflected in them, too. He jerked the glass off the counter and headed to where Jake and Tom sat. He forced Tom to move to the chair with his back to the door, giving Darien a better view of both her and the entrance.

How could she observe the pack members if the leader kept an eye on her? Even now, she was certain he could smell her fear. She told herself she wasn't afraid of him, but any *lupus garou* who was worth his pelt would take heed when confronting a pack leader.

Frozen with indecision, she remained seated. What the hell, let him think she was too afraid to move from her chair—*his* chair, whatever.

The first woman she'd seen tonight entered the tavern dressed in short shorts and a turtleneck shirt, with leather boots mid-thigh, her sable hair piled on top of her head in whirls of dark curls.

"Hey, Silva," one of the four men seated at the bar said and whistled. "Looking hot."

She gave him a flashy bright red-lipped grin, then glanced in Lelandi's direction. Astonishment was reflected in her expression. Silva's gaze shifted and she spied Darien nearby. Bending over the bar to give the guys a better look at her ass, she whispered something to Sam. He looked over at Lelandi. Yep, she was sure to be the topic of conversation tonight.

Sam shrugged. "Drawing a real crowd tonight, Silva. Why don't you see if the boss needs some more beer?"

Tom lifted the empty pitcher. "Need a refill. Looks like the lady could use another drink."

Desperately wanting out of the limelight, Lelandi melted into her seat.

Silva gave her a simpering smile. "Well, well, looks like the word has gotten out to some far-reaching places. Guess it won't be long before the place will be crawling with—"

Sam slammed a pitcher of beer on the counter. "Take care of the customers, Silva, and play nice."

She sneered at him, then grabbed the pitcher. "Yes siree, boss, that's what you pay me for." Swinging her hips, she carried the beer to Darien's table, and then gave him a big smile. "Here ya go, boss. Just whistle if you need more."

Darien didn't say a word, just leaned back in his chair and looked over at Lelandi.

Silva made a face and headed for Lelandi's table. "Need another… *bottled water*?"

Time for a drink. "Got margaritas?" Lelandi spoke low, only it wasn't low enough.

Tom choked on his beer. A couple of the men at the bar chuckled. Sam smiled and poured whiskey for one of the men.

"I don't know, sugar." Silva turned to Sam. "Hey, Sam, we got fancy drinks for an out-of-towner? Like a *margarita*?" She said the word as if she was speaking of a woman's cute name.

More chuckles ensued.

"I can whip up anything the little lady would like."

Little. That described her all right. Five-four, and the size of a red *lupus garou* female. She sat taller.

"Is that what you would like, *Miss…?*" Silva asked, drawing it out, searching for a name.

"Yes, thank you."

Tough, damn it. Lelandi wanted to present a tougher image in front of the grays. She'd practiced and practiced and so what did she do? Acted like a squeaky damned mouse. Used to being around her own kind, she'd never felt intimidated—much. Having earned double black belts in jujitsu and kung fu helped boost her confidence around human brutes. But these people were neither human nor her own kind, and a whole pack of them could devour her alive if she gave them the opportunity.

The woman leaned closer and Lelandi was again sure she was about to be found out. Silva breathed in the air, and her brown eyes narrowed. Despite wearing a ton of fancy human perfumes, and of course the stench from the fresh dye job—although Lelandi had washed her hair in strawberry shampoo trying to cover up that odor—she hoped no one could smell that she was a *lupus garou,* and not one of their own kind, either. Looked like it didn't work.

"Well, well, well." Silva straightened her back. "Make the lady a margarita, Sam."

"Put the first on my tab," Tom piped up. "Wouldn't want the lady to think we're a bunch of unfriendly old coots."

"The second one's on me," Silva said.

The miner, Joe Kelly, looked disappointed that he hadn't spoken up first, but as much of a beta wolf as he appeared, he probably wouldn't say anything to tick Darien off. Darien's brothers would be the exceptions, and Silva seemed able to do as she pleased.

Darien didn't say a word. He exuded control with just a look—dangerous, not the kind of man to rile. His actions, or lack thereof, spoke louder than any words. Bruin would have blustered all over the tavern in Darien's place. Proving he was the pack leader and no one would disobey him, Bruin would have taken her to task immediately, belittled her, thrown her out of the joint bodily if she'd taken *his* seat. But just a glower from Darien conveyed a world of threat, and she'd do well to heed it.

Everyone seemed fascinated with the reason Silva had taken an interest in Lelandi. They had to figure Silva had discovered something about her. Silva seemed amused Lelandi was a red *lupus garou* masquerading as a human. At least Lelandi assumed the woman had found her out.

"Where ya staying, darlin'?" Silva's tone was much more appeasing, the sweetness faked.

Lelandi cleared the sudden frog in her throat. "Just passing through."

Silence. The woman's eyes darkened, and she quickly glanced at Darien. His eyes had widened, and he was staring at Lelandi. *Shit.* Her voice must have sounded similar to Larissa's this time, the way she spoke, the inflection, something.

Low conversation took place at the table next to Darien's and among the grays at the bar while Sam whipped up Lelandi's margarita, but no one at Darien's table spoke a word.

More patrons entered the tavern, all looking to greet their leader, then, finding a dead ringer for his dead mate sitting at his regular table, turned to see Darien, and the scenario repeated itself until the place was crowded and noisy. But no one dared sit at her table. *Thank god.* The more important conversations were conducted low so she couldn't hear the gist of them, but she only had to guess what was being said. Dead sister's clone arrives at grays' hangout, seeking revenge. They'd all be shaking in their boots. *Right.*

After finishing her margarita, Lelandi was dying to go to the bathroom, and the place had grown so warm, she shrugged out of her jacket. *Big mistake.* As soon as they saw how petite she was, the whole room grew quiet again.

Silva hurried over with another margarita for Lelandi, although she intended to get another bottle of water.

"On me, sweetie," the woman said, this time with real affection. Standing nearly five-foot-ten, in her four-inch heels, she was small for a female gray.

"Thanks." Lelandi stood, and the woman's face dropped, probably thinking Lelandi meant to leave, snubbing her for the drink. "Got to use the little girls' room."

"Oh." Silva's lips turned up slightly. "Back that way." She motioned with her hand.

"Thanks." Lelandi hadn't considered what it would feel like to walk through the tavern to the ladies' room, until everyone acted so interested in her. With her shoulders straight back, her chin tilted up, and her body ten degrees hotter than normal, she made her way to the restroom.

Several men nodded their heads in greeting. Respectfully, a couple of them took their cowboy hats off. None smiled though, not even Joe this time, which would be typical. Until their pack leader made her welcome, most would look her over, but wouldn't make any move to be overtly friendly. Darien would probably take Joe to task if Sam told him the miner had paid for her first drink.

Sitting with some men at one of the larger tables, three women glowered at her as if they wished her dead. Had any of them wanted Larissa eliminated and carried out the threat?

Ignoring them, Lelandi walked into the restroom, but after entering a stall, she heard the outer door squeak open. Her skin chilled. Too late to circumvent the trouble headed her way.

When she exited the stall, the three women were waiting for her, their expressions slightly amused in a sinister manner. All brown-haired, around mid-twenties like her—probably each vying to be Darien's new mate and fearing she was new competition.

When she'd come up with this scheme of looking for her Larissa's murderer, Lelandi had never considered anyone would think she'd be interested in pursuing the pack's leader. The idea of mating with a bigger gray for real… She mentally shook her head.

"What's your name?" the woman in denims and a cowl-neck sweater asked, her voice softly threatening, her western boot tapping on the tile floor. Her amber eyes narrowed, she took in a deep breath—trying to smell who or what Lelandi was—and curled her orange-painted lips up in a nasty way. The notion her face could hideously freeze that way briefly crossed Lelandi's mind. "You're not from around here, and you're not one of us."

"Hey, Ritka, what say we give her a nice send-off?" the shortest one asked, still towering over Lelandi by several inches.

Lelandi brushed past her to wash her hands.

"Don't plan on staying, bitch," a meatier one snarled, whipping her waist-length, muddy-colored hair about as she spoke, crowding Lelandi. Bulkier than the other two, she would make a hefty wolf and hard to beat if she craved being Darien's bitch and fought the others to have that role. But no female *lupus garou*—well, of the red variety—crowded Lelandi anymore and got away with it, and she was having a devil of a time maintaining her cool.

"Don't intend to stay long. Just taking care of a little family business, if it's any of your concern."

Ritka whispered close to her ear, her whiskey breath invading Lelandi's breathing space, "We know who you are, and you can't have him, Red. You know what happened to the other one. Get out of Dodge, honey, before it happens to you, too."

Her blood sizzling, Lelandi attempted to wash her hands as if the women didn't exist.

The short one yanked at her purse and the leather strap bit into Lelandi's shoulder. "Tell us who you are."

"As if the bitch would say, Angelina, when she's wearing this fool disguise," Ritka snarled.

Lelandi's temple pounded with frustration, but she rinsed the soap off her hands and bit back the feral part of her wolf nature clawing to get out. Beating up three female grays wouldn't help her cause.

Ritka bumped into her, probably triggered by the other pulling at her purse, each leading the other on, escalating the situation. Lelandi clenched her teeth against retaliating. Nothing they did was important enough to provoke her, she reminded herself.

The heavy one grabbed a handful of Lelandi's hair and yanked hard. "Guys don't like dyed hair, didn't you know?"

The pain ripped across Lelandi's scalp, and she counted slowly to ten, hoping to avoid physical contact, but planning swift retaliation if anyone did anything else.

"You got that right, Hosstene," Ritka said with a sharp laugh and reached for a handful of Lelandi's hair.

Enough! With a quick well-placed jab, Lelandi elbowed Angelina in the gut, judo-chopped Hosstene in the throat, then swung around and slammed her fist into Ritka's eye. While they were choking and cursing, Lelandi grabbed a paper towel, dried her hands, and left the restroom, her heart racing.

She'd asked for trouble now.

Chapter 2

No, *DAMN IT*. THE BITCHES HAD ASKED FOR TROUBLE AND as much as told Lelandi that someone had murdered Larissa for being a red.

She opened the restroom door and slammed it behind her, shutting out the women's curses. The men who were sitting with the women looked from Lelandi to the ladies' room. *Sorry, boys, the girls need to tidy up a bit.*

Lelandi retook her seat and when the women still didn't emerge from the restroom, Sam motioned for Silva to check it out.

Maybe now would be a good time for Lelandi to go in search of her rogue brother and uncle. Forget that Larissa had run away and gotten herself killed, leaving Lelandi to deal with Bruin's pack alone. Or, she could stay and face the wrath of a bunch of angry grays.

As a matter of pride and a good deal of stubbornness, she stayed. All eyes remained on the restroom while Lelandi coolly drank her second margarita. No one spoke. No doubt the whole lot of them would murder Lelandi in her sleep tonight. She hoped her time here wasn't totally wasted. But she wasn't giving up.

Silva came out of the restroom, her lips turned up, her eyes sparkling with amusement, head shaking. She raised her brows at the guys who were with the women and strolled past. Her attention turned to Darien, waiting for a report. Her smile broadened, then she spoke to Sam.

"Next margarita's on me, Silva, for the young lady." Tom offered Lelandi a grin and a wink.

Lelandi shook her head. "Water will be fine."

The three women crowded out of the bathroom, Ritka scowling, her swollen right eye already turning black and blue. Angelina was still clutching her stomach, and Hosstene's face was dark with anger—Lelandi was pretty sure her jab to the gray's throat would preclude her talking much for a while.

Everyone looked the women over, then Lelandi. No, she wasn't fighting to be the pack leader's new bitch.

She guessed it was time to come up with a new plan. This one damn sure wasn't working.

Darien Silver watched the defiant young lady who had to be his mate's twin. Had to be. The voice clinched it. At first, he thought she was some ditsy human sitting in *his* chair at *his* table, and he couldn't understand why Sam hadn't thrown her out of the place. At least he'd thought she was human. *Lupus garous* had exceptional visual acuity. Only humans wore glasses. And the pierced earrings. No *lupus garou* would get caught dead with pierced earlobes in their wolf form. Or wear a watch, for that matter. The straight black hair looked nothing like his dead mate's, and the blue eyes had stopped him cold. The perfume she'd drowned herself in, he figured, was some ploy to get all the guys in the tavern hot and bothered, but for *lupus garous,* the smell was overwhelming, burned their eyes, and had the opposite effect.

Her voice was all it took to send shivers exploding across his skin.

He swore he was seeing his late wife sipping margaritas, which she never would have done. A wine lady was what she was. And the way this woman had handled the ladies from his pack? His mate would never have managed.

Taking a steadying breath, he reminded himself the woman wasn't his mate. She only looked like her when he scrutinized her closely, her small face dominated by the oversized Stetson and the bug-eyed, rose-colored glasses, but personality-wise she couldn't be more different from his beloved Lelandi. Except his people already seemed to make up their minds. Lelandi had returned, and he would have a go at her again.

Not in a million years. She'd killed herself, unstable, unable to deal with the stress of being a pack leader's mate, and not being one of them in the first place... Nope, wouldn't happen again. Next one would be a gray, except not from his pack. Except for Silva, the eligible women had resented Lelandi, and he couldn't forgive them.

He finished his third beer and set his glass aside. He tried to watch his people to take his mind off his dead mate, but the woman sitting at his table distracted him something fierce. What the hell was she doing here anyway? Come to claim her sister's body? Scream at him for pushing her sister over the edge? Condemning himself enough for her death for the past three weeks, he didn't need anyone else's help. Not enough beers in the world could make him forget the look on Lelandi's face, at peace finally in death.

He shook his head. Although he usually stayed until closing, tonight he wanted to get away. How would it look if the pack leader couldn't deal with the image of his late wife sitting at the next table?

Growling deep inside, he poured himself another beer.

"Twin sister, don't you think, Darien?" Tom, his youngest triplet asked, his brows raised.

"Yeah. Lelandi said she didn't have any family left. Apparently she lied." Which didn't set well with Darien, but it was too late to be angered about it.

"What do you think she's doing here?" Tom rubbed his hand over the sweating glass.

"Something to do with her sister, no doubt."

"Think the woman suspects Lelandi was murdered?" Jake asked.

Darien looked sharply at him. "What the hell makes you say that?"

Jake shrugged. "Why wouldn't she meet with you and state what her business is here? Why try to conceal her identity? The only conclusion I can come up with is she doesn't think Lelandi's death was an accident. And she's looking into it herself."

"Hell." Darien glowered at the red, wondering what her hair would look like if it wasn't that hideous black color, way too harsh for her light creamy skin.

"Looks like she gave the ladies hell who meant to mess with her." Tom grinned.

"Which means there'll be more trouble." Jake's voice was as dark as Darien felt.

Darien turned to Tom. "I want you to—"

Jake interrupted, "She's leaving."

All conversation in the tavern instantly died.

Her boots clicked on the wood floor as she walked toward the door, her back stiff, her hands clenched in fists—her whole body language saying, *Don't mess with me.*

As much as he didn't want to admit it, he craved chasing after her and laying claim to her, just like he'd done with her sister. He felt an overwhelming urge to kiss those pursed lips, feel her soft skin naked beneath his, make love to her like he'd made love to her sister. He was definitely losing it.

With the utmost restraint, he remained seated and observed her open the door. "Follow her, Tom. Watch where she goes, and… hell, stick to her for the night."

"You sure? You really mean it?" Tom asked, his voice too hopeful.

"Just don't let anyone get to her, all right?"

"He means," Jake interjected, "don't let anyone screw with her and that includes you."

Tom looked at Darien for confirmation. If his brother wanted her and the woman was agreeable, who was he to say no? Their kind wasn't into casual sex, so if she wanted a mate and Tom was interested, fine. Darien wasn't about to go down that road again. "Do whatever it takes to make sure none of our people bother her."

Tom gave Jake a look like he had him there. "Thanks, Darien. I'll take care of her." He hurried after Lelandi's sister as the door slammed behind her.

Sending Tom after the woman signaled to the rest of his people in the tavern, and the word would quickly spread to the others, Darien wanted her left alone. If any stepped over the line, he'd hold them accountable.

Jake moved his glass over the wooden table, scraping it back and forth.

Darien glowered at him. "What, Jake?"

"Don't you think you should talk with the woman? Find out what she's doing here?"

"Why do you think Lelandi was murdered?"

"You've buried your head in the sand on this one, brother. Several believe someone murdered her, but when they spy me, the talking stops. No one will tell me or Tom what they suspect."

"A conspiracy?"

"No. At least I don't think so. Unless they're protecting someone, or are afraid you'd be too mad if you learned the truth."

"Most of the pack believes I'd be happier thinking she committed suicide?"

Jake twisted his head to the side. "Yeah. If we have a murderer in our midst, it could shake up the whole pack. If she committed suicide, everything would be a lot cleaner."

"She left a suicide note in her own handwriting. She killed herself. End of story." Darien took another swig of his beer, but this time it tasted sour.

"Then why don't you tell her sister the truth? Why send Tom, who's bound to botch the whole thing?" Jake's mouth curved up, the first truly evil smile Darien had seen him offer in a while. "If he gets fresh, he's liable to look like Ritka with a colorful new eye."

Darien ignored his comment. "If a twin sister is looking into what happened, Lelandi must not have had any brothers."

"We didn't know she had any family, period."

Darien rubbed his forehead, trying to ease the tension pooling there. The gnawing pain of her death would never fade away, but now seeing her look-alike sister brought it all crashing back tenfold. Yet, he was furious with his mate for killing herself. Doc said it was part of the grief process, but Darien hated himself for not controlling his feelings better. Remorse, that's the only feeling he should allow himself. "I'm beginning to assume I didn't know a lot about my mate."

Jake glanced back at their usual table. "If it were me, I'd tell the woman what I thought and send her packing. Things could get out of hand if she hangs around. It appears the other women think she wants to be your mate to replace her sister."

"That would be the damned day," Darien growled, yet a twinge of need wreaked havoc with his feelings, and his brother looked like he didn't believe him one bit.

Not far from the tavern, Lelandi heard the door creak open and shut. Glancing over her shoulder, she saw Tom taking great strides to reach her, his eyes and mouth lit in a smile.

Great. Just great. How in the hell was she going to put Plan B into effect and break into Darien's house to search for clues about Larissa's death while he was drinking at the tavern if one of his brothers shadowed her?

She cast him an annoyed look. His lips curved up even more and his eyes sparkled with way too much interest. She headed for the Hastings Bed and Breakfast, figuring she'd slip out the window of her room if Tom took up residence in the lobby.

Before she reached the brick building, Tom joined her, standing so close that the heat of his body reached out to her. "You're Lelandi's sister, aren't you?"

"Larissa's," she corrected.

He bowed his head slightly. "I wasn't certain until I heard you speak. You sure shook Darien up. But he needed to be rousted from the pit of hell he's been wallowing—"

The familiar sound of danger, a clicking sound made when someone switched the safety off on a gun, caught her ear, and she whipped her head around. In a heartbeat, she wished she'd brought her gun in her purse. But it was hidden under the mattress until she needed it. And she was afraid she needed it now.

Tom seized her arm. "Wait," he whispered.

Her skin prickled with fresh concern. He'd heard it, too. She'd hoped she'd been mistaken.

"Nine-millimeter," he warned, his voice hushed.

Before they could move, a shot rang out, Tom yelled and shoved Lelandi behind him, but collapsed to his knees. "Run! Go back to the tavern!"

Ohmigod, the bastard had shot Tom! Seizing his arm, she tried to move him, but he was dead weight as he slipped to the asphalt, passed out. Blood streaked down his face. The bullet had struck him in the temple.

The shooter moved out of the shadows, blocking her path to the tavern. A pleasant face to look at if the murdering bastard weren't wearing such a scowl. His scruffy black beard, unkempt hair, and rumpled clothes made it appear he'd been living on the run for a few days. Amber eyes looked almost wolflike, but being upwind of him, she couldn't tell if he was human or *lupus garou.*

He aimed his gun at her. *Silver bullets or regular?*

"What do you want?" Her heart racing, she tried to buy herself time.

Had anyone in the noisy tavern heard the shooting? She couldn't tackle the gunman from this distance. If she dashed for the inn, he might shoot Mrs. Hastings, or the twin girls who kept hanging around the lobby, although Lelandi sure wanted to get her gun.

Where the hell was Ural, now that she could use his help? If he was in his wolf form like she suspected, his wicked canines could take care of the menace. Taking time to strip and shapeshift into the wolf herself wasn't an option.

Out of choices, she did the only thing she could think of to rouse help for Tom and maybe scare off the hesitant gunman. She screamed.

The shooter's eyes widened, his lips curved down, and he pulled the trigger, firing once, twice, three times. The impact of the bullets ripped into her chest, throwing her against the brick building, and she nearly collapsed. At first, no pain registered as she struggled to stay on her feet. When she didn't immediately expire on the spot, he stared at her as if she was the devil incarnate.

Then the pain struck hard and for an instant, her thought processes threatened to shut down. When he raised his gun, her brain caught hold.

She dashed toward the forest skirting the town, intending to double back as soon as she could and get help for Tom. She'd give the shooter a real run for his blood money. Thank god the bullets didn't burn like silver ones would. She'd live, if she could find refuge and allow her body time to heal.

"Bloody hell!" Her assailant took chase.

Stabbing pain streaked through every inch of her now, and she could feel the hot blood seeping from the wounds. Every second her heart pumped more blood out, and she felt her legs weakening.

Run, damn you, Lelandi. If ever she had to push herself, this was the time.

Branches broke several yards behind her as she dove around trees, scrambled over fallen, rotting trunks, clawed through thick brush. As much noise as the gunman was making, she again assumed he was human. *Good.* He couldn't see the trail of blood she was leaving, nor could he smell her scent. Then again, the breeze was shifting so much, it would help to disguise her location. Oh hell, as much perfume as she was wearing, probably even a human could follow her. She tried to remain downwind of him.

Tried—was the key word, because her senses were failing—one by one.

She no longer heard the birds singing in the trees, or the wind whistling through the firs, just her heavy breathing and the blood roaring in her ears. Her eyes blurred and she misjudged the lay of the land. The ground seemed to give way. And she fell.

Striking branches and brambles, she grabbed for anything to stop her tumble down the steep incline, skinning and cutting her hands. She lost her hat first, her glasses next. A branch scraped off one earring, then the other. Her hair tangled on every branch in her path, yanking at her scalp, the branches and twigs giving up their hold as she rolled. Downward... downward, banging against rocks and stumps, her whole body bruised and battered, she gritted her teeth against the pain.

For a second, she worried about the damned disguise and the trail she'd left behind for the attempted murderer. Then her back struck something rock hard, unforgiving, massive. The pain shot straight up her spine, all the way to her brain, short-circuiting it.

Blackness enveloped her as her night vision and all her senses shut down.

Chapter 3

REACHING A DULL ROAR, THE CONVERSATION AT THE TAVERN centered around Lelandi's sister's appearance in town when Darien's cell phone rang. He wasn't surprised to see Tom's cell number and assumed Lelandi's sister was causing trouble. He sure as hell hoped she hadn't slipped away from him. "Yeah, Tom? What's up now?"

"Got to come quick!" Tom yelled into the phone, his voice breathy.

"Tom?" Darien leapt from his chair. "Where are you?"

"Gunshots fired. Hastings Bed—" The phone died.

"Gunfire at Hastings!" Darien's heart hammered his ribs as he and Jake bolted for the tavern door.

From the thunderous roar of boots tromping down the street behind him, everyone from the tavern must be on his heels. While he raced toward the hotel, his muscles tensed for battle, concern for the woman and his brother's safety swamped him.

Although the insidious thought flashed across his mind that *she* might have shot Tom.

"Hastings Bed and Breakfast," he hollered to Jake, clarifying it wasn't Hastings Hardware.

"Crap, Darien, what now?"

"Gunshots were fired. Hell, I don't know." Darien berated himself that he'd put Tom's life in danger, when he should have gone instead.

His cell phone rang, and he jerked it off his belt. "Tom, what the hell's—"

"I've been hit."

"Where are you?"

"Behind…" Tom quit speaking.

In the eerie silence, Darien held his breath in anticipation as he and Jake stopped dead. "Tom? Tom!" Silence. "Armed gunman somewhere near Hastings. Get Doc Oliver. Tom's been shot," Darien shouted to his men.

Gray-haired and bearded Mason, still wearing his gray suit—the usual attire for Silver Town's bank owner—yanked out his cell phone. "Got it, boss."

"Silver bullets or regular?" Jake asked.

"Phone went dead."

More shots sounded in the woods farther away. Darien cursed and quickened his run toward Hastings. "Careful, men. Not sure what kind of bullets the shooter's using."

He motioned for some to skirt around the front of the B&B. Then he, Jake, and several others headed around back.

"Where the hell is Tom?" Jake asked under his breath.

"Passed out maybe."

"I'll kill whoever the son of a—"

Groans came from behind a Dumpster. Anger blazed through Darien's veins as he and Jake bolted around the green trash bin.

Tom lay on his back, holding his bloodied head, his eyes dazed. "Where'd she go? Odin's beard, my head hurts like a—"

"Tell the others we found Tom!" Darien shouted to some of the men as they drew closer. One of them handed him a handkerchief. Crouching next to his brother, Darien lifted his head in his lap, then tied the handkerchief around the bleeding wound. "Silver or regular?"

"Not silver. My body's rejecting the bullet, but it hurts like hell." Tom closed his eyes. "Where's Larissa?"

Two more men came running toward them.

"Doc Oliver's on his way." Mason shoved his phone into his pocket. "No sign of the girl or the gunman." He arched a gray brow in question. "Sure they aren't one and the same?"

Hoping it wasn't so, Darien looked at Tom for an answer.

"Thor's thunder." Tom's gaze drifted and he squinted his eyes closed. "He shot Larissa, too."

Darien swore under his breath. The notion the maniac threatened Lelandi's sister's life twisted his gut. Issuing the next order took all his strength, when he wanted more than anything to take care of the matter himself. "Find her, and get that damned gunman."

Any other decision would sound like he cared more for the red's safety than his own brother, or a pack member—not a leadership quality. Applying pressure to the wound, he hoped Doc Oliver would hurry, because no matter how much he told himself otherwise, the woman looked too much like his dead mate to deny his feelings for her. Even in death, she held his heart captive.

Unable to contain his impatience he shouted, "Where the hell is Doc Oliver?"

❖ ❖ ❖

Three more shots rang out, reverberating through the forest, and Lelandi cringed. The gunman must be shooting at shadows. She hoped.

Survival of the fittest. That's what ran through her mind as she lay in the underbrush nestled at the base of a stand of spruce, her back wedged up against a moss-blanketed boulder. Her mind drifted when the pain from the three bullets lodged in her heart intensified. Her back didn't feel too swift either. She'd survived worse. Hunter's wounds when she was a wolf, an attempted rape, a near drowning, now this. Her guardian angel sure worked overtime for her.

The pain grew hot, but the perspiration on her skin, refrigerated by the cool breeze and the blood soaking her turtleneck chilled her further. Something moved toward her. Intently, she listened to the sound of its scurrying and smelled the scents. Cold, crisp autumn, a hint of moisture in the air, a time when she baked apple pies, made special soups and hot spicy chili, decorated with pumpkins, squash, and colorful mums, the colors complementary to her fiery red hair and green eyes. Autumn, her special time of year.

Darien was a winter, sable hair, dark eyes, cold, brooding. North wind chilled. Winter.

The scurrying stopped, bringing her drifting mind back to her current set of circumstances. The creature's blood rushed through its small heart and veins, and she got a whiff of its unique smell. *A rabbit.* She closed her eyes and hoped Darien had found his brother and was easing his pain, like she wished someone could do for her.

A wolf howled. *I'm here, where are you?*

Ural? He'd find her, come for her, eliminate her assailant.

The gunman couldn't kill her with regular bullets, but she had to heal up some before she could move again. Getting the gunman away from Tom had helped him, but now she didn't have the strength to move an inch in the direction of Hastings Bed and Breakfast. Worse, she had no idea where she was.

Footsteps crunched on fallen leaves maybe a half mile away. The gunman's or Darien's and his men? She made out only one set of footfalls, most likely the gunman's.

Her chest hurt like it was on fire, and she stifled another groan. *Don't pass out!* If the gunman found her, she'd make a horrendous racket, but if she passed out, he could move her somewhere else and kill her. Snapping her neck would do the trick, when regular bullets wouldn't.

Her thoughts shifted to the tavern, and she could imagine Darien racing out with half his people or more in hot pursuit if Tom had been able to call for help. Too late, she'd seen the gunman hiding in the shadows of Hastings, and she berated herself again for not being more alert.

Would the grays waste their time searching for her if they discovered Tom was hurt? Maybe not, but they'd continue to look for the gunman who'd shot Tom.

She tried to concentrate on the bullets seated in her heart. Tried to envision her body working miracles to expel the foreign substances, stop the bleeding, and seal the wounds. But she'd lost too much blood and felt weak, nauseous, disoriented. It would take some time to rebuild her blood. She groaned again.

Footsteps trudged closer, stopped, moved again.

No one spoke any words. *Friend or foe?*

She looked up through the tree branches shuddering in the wind. A sprinkling of twinkling stars littered the dark night sky. *Star light, star bright…* Sharp pains coursed through her body, down her arms and legs, and up again, sending blinding pain into her skull. Her vision blurring, she clenched her teeth to keep from fading away.

Where was Ural? Originating from one of the purest lines of the first *lupus garou,* she was a royal like him and could change into the wolf despite it being a moonless night. Being a wolf in this condition wouldn't help, however. *Except* the gunman wasn't looking for one. *Yes!* Then she could howl and return Ural's call. He'd come to her then and protect her.

She fumbled with her jacket buttons, but didn't have the strength to unbutton even the first one. As weak as she was, she wasn't sure she could even shapeshift.

Where the hell was Ural? He could rip away the gunman's life in a flash. She'd be safe—or safer. But she didn't trust Ural's motives either. If he found her weak and unable to resist, he could return her to the pack. *Damn him.*

Wincing, she closed her eyes, trying to will away the pain.

Had the shooter targeted Lelandi because she looked like Larissa? Or did he assume she was here, trying to discover who had killed Larissa?

She swore a gray had murdered Larissa, angry that the leader of the grays had mated with a red. Or had her ruthless pack leader Bruin located Larissa, pretending that he hadn't? Now Lelandi wasn't so sure.

Then she thought she smelled Ural. *Please, Ural, come and bite the bastard!* But he didn't show himself, didn't attack the gunman. Maybe it was powerful wishful thinking.

"Larissa!" Darien shouted from a good half mile away.

Here! No, not Larissa... Larissa was dead. Lelandi! Here.

Lelandi closed her eyes. A whisper of a breeze caressed her face and strands of hair tickled her cheek, but she couldn't gather the strength to shove them away. And the pain. Oh, god, the pain.

Someone shuffled only feet from her. She squeezed her eyes tighter and barely breathed. How had he gotten so close without her hearing? Her mind drifted. Keep alert! If he was wolf and downwind of her, he could smell her spilled blood. He could hear her heart pumping at a furious rate.

She heard his beating rapidly, his heavy breathing, the grinding of his teeth, his fingernail scraping the metal of the gun. Then he moved farther away from where she curled up in a fetal position, trying to conserve energy and the heat of her body, trying to make herself smaller and unnoticeable.

Others took up the call, shouting Lelandi's name as they spread out and drew closer. She frowned. How would they know her name? Larissa would have kept her family a secret so the grays wouldn't learn she already had a pack—and a mate.

The gunman tromped farther away, stealing her attention, but he was still too close.

The breeze suddenly shifted and Darien's brooding brother Jake shouted, "This way!"

She watched for them, nearly quit breathing in anticipation, not to mention the pain grew so sharp she could
barely focus on anything else.

But her rescuers didn't come.

Darien paced back and forth in the thick of the woods in
front of thirty of his men, every one of them now armed.
Although normally they hunted in their wolf coats, the
pack had always kept guns—their way of dealing with
human troublemakers over the last one hundred and fifty
years in the area.

"We thought we smelled her perfume several times,
but the damned wind isn't cooperating! So where the
hell is she?" Darien asked.

"We need to turn wolf," Jake said.

"Can't for three more days," Sam reminded him.

"Hell, I know that, Sam. I was just saying…" Jake
didn't say anything more, just poked the toe of his boot
in the pine needle–covered dirt, his hands shoved in his
pockets, his face dark with a mixture of concern and
annoyance.

"We've searched for hours. Where the hell is she?"
Darien asked again, voicing his own irritation.

They hadn't found anything—her hat, glasses,
nothing—as if she'd vanished in thin air like a puff of
mist on a hot, sunny day. He rubbed the pounding in
his temples, the thought stirring his blood that she was
Lelandi, wounded, hurting, waiting for him to come to
her aid, and not her sister. For now, she was one and the
same, and he'd protect her with his own life. *For now.*

Once he found her and she'd healed, he'd send her home to her pack and out of his life for good.

"She doesn't know these woods. She could easily get lost without her wolf senses," Jake warned.

Darien stared into the wilderness, remembering a time when he dashed with his mate through the woods as wolves, running until they were exhausted, mating, then collapsing like two half-spent dogs. He shook free of the immobilizing memories.

"What if he got her?" Jake asked, a question Darien was sure everyone else was thinking. "What if he took her body in a vehicle and planned to dispose of her somewhere else?"

Darien *wouldn't* consider that scenario.

Mason rubbed his bearded cheek, his hair whipping in the breeze. "We've searched all night. We're dog-tired. If they're just regular bullets, she can't die from them. Why don't we get some rest and try again in a few hours?"

"She saved Tom's life." The muscle ticked in Jake's jaw like it did when he was on the verge of striking someone. "I'll keep looking until some of you get rest and relieve me."

Having every intention of hunting for her until he dropped from exhaustion, Darien slapped his brother's shoulder with approval. "We'll do it together."

If she'd been one of the pack, his men would have continued searching for her. Without her being one of them, he couldn't ask them to give up any more of their energy without getting some rest. He was glad his brother had offered, despite the fact he had distanced himself from Darien the last couple of weeks. Probably because of the foul mood Darien had been in since his mate died.

The smell of Silva's feminine scent wafted in the air, and the men turned to see her stalking toward them dressed in tight jeans, hiking boots, gloves, and a short-waisted corduroy jacket. "I'll help ya." Her expression and tone of voice were as determined as Darien felt.

"No women," Darien said, his voice harsh, annoyed she'd offer to join them.

"Why? Think I might want to kill her, too? Or maybe you're a tad worried about little ol' me? But I can handle myself." Silva smirked. "The woman's got spunk and she deserves our help."

Considering his options, another body that would fill the gap couldn't hurt. "Stay with one of the men at all times."

"Jeez, Darien, I would almost think you have a thing for me." She blew him a kiss and sidled up to Sam. "Want to be my team mate?"

"Okay, those who want to continue the search, do so. The rest get some sleep. Let's get moving." Darien took off with a lengthened stride, determined to find her before the night was over.

"What do you think is going on?" Jake ducked under the branch of a spruce.

"Gunman's human."

"Why go after our brother? Why go after the red?"

"Your guess is as good as mine." Darien stopped to sample the breeze. The scent of other grays, a deer, a rabbit, pinesap, fall, nothing else. "He wasn't after Tom, I suspect. Just the red. Except Tom was following her and would have protected her."

"You still think your mate committed suicide?"

Yeah, and it was his damned fault. Whirlwind romance, although she'd seemed uncertain about becoming his mate, worried his people would revolt over her being a red, but anxious about something deeper that he could never get her to reveal. Maybe if he hadn't pushed her to be his mate. But hell, she *was* his soul mate, the one he'd dreamed about for months. And she'd finally revealed she'd had the dreams about him, too. How could he let her go?

He shook his head. "I don't know what to think." Darien still harbored the same deep-seated feelings— that she'd committed suicide. He finally admitted, "She'd tried before."

Jake's mouth dropped. "When? Why didn't you tell me?"

"She was sorry. Told me she wouldn't try again and begged me not to tell the others."

"A pack leader has to have a strong mate, Darien, pack rules. You should have at least told me."

"I promised her."

And it got her killed. Maybe if he'd deep down listened to what was bothering her. Sleepless nights, medicine to aid her sleep, but still she kept waking, fearful, exhausted, out-of-sorts. Hell, when she managed to kill herself this time, he never doubted it was for real.

"Why did she try before?"

"She wouldn't say. She was a private person. She was overly tired, distraught—"

"Pregnant."

Darien's face heated, anger and regret warring with his emotions. Yeah, pregnant with their triplets. Which made the whole damned thing even more of a travesty.

But if she couldn't deal with life before the triplets were born, how would she have been able to handle the stress afterward?

"I understand why you think she might have committed suicide then, but don't you think this business with her sister sheds a different light on it?"

"Maybe."

Although he couldn't see that it did. Unless someone coerced Lelandi to write the suicide note. She hadn't been enthusiastic about having the babies, in fact seemed even more depressed about it. If anyone had coerced her, he didn't think it took much convincing, yet if anyone had, they'd die at his hand.

Shots rang out a mile away, and Darien cursed under his breath. He charged in the direction, but Jake quickly caught up to him and grabbed his arm. Darien whirled around in fury, but saw Jake's concerned expression. "What?" he whispered.

"Listen."

He stood as silent as a frozen lake in winter and listened with his wolf's hearing.

A heart beating farther away, slow, too slow, and then a groan.

"Lelandi!"

Jake glanced at him.

Darien gave him a feral look and yelled, "Larissa!"

They searched the area again, Darien and his brother in closer proximity to each other this time, trying not to miss her. He paused. "Larissa!"

Chapter 4

THROUGH A FOG-FILLED HAZE, LELANDI FELT PRESSURE ON her throat as if a snake encircled her neck, squeezing tight. She struggled for breath, her mind blackening. She tried to smell the snake, but all she sensed was the strong odor of decaying leaves.

Then a gruff, impatient male voice shouted for Larissa, nearer now.

A low, threatening growl sounded.

Ural?

The pressure on her throat ceased, and she gasped for air, unable to catch her breath. She couldn't focus on anything, where she was, who he was, what had happened to Larissa. The snake moved quickly away, slithering through the brush, hiding from imminent danger. The pungent odor of humus departed with it. But a new scent drifted in the air. Her cousin's.

"Ural," she tried to say, but his name stuck in her throat.

He slunk close to her, licked her cheek—warm, wet, welcome. She wanted to hug his neck, but she couldn't move.

"Larissa!" the male voice shouted, growing closer, his footsteps sending a sliver of a tremor through the ground, and another, not far away.

Lelandi, she corrected him silently. Even her parents, her brother, and the pack members constantly mixed up their names, to her utter annoyance. She swallowed hard, her throat sore, the pain in her chest radiating throughout her body, agonizing, punishing. Where was she?

Ural nudged her face, then backed away.

Was he behind her? Protecting her?

Cold numbed her joints, her skin, her bones. She couldn't sit or lift her head. But the darkness was beginning to grow light.

"Larissa!"

She opened her mouth to speak, but the snake had stolen her voice. She squeaked out something inaudible. Taking a deep breath, she shut her gaping mouth, and stared in the direction of the footsteps.

Small rocks, twigs, and leaves slid down the hill in advance of the marauders, hurrying down the steep incline toward her, nearer and nearer. They'd found her! But the elation was overshadowed by what they'd want to do with her next.

"Over here!" Darien's rich baritone voice sent shivers of expectation through her torn-up body.

His hair was tangled by the wind, his brown eyes nearly black, his mouth grim and set.

Then she remembered. Larissa—she was... was dead. And Tom—shot. Was he all right? And Ural! *If the grays catch him...*

"Over here!" Darien shouted again, and soon another man crashed through the thick brush. Darien jerked his leather coat off and wrapped her in it.

Jake appeared, yanked a phone off his belt, shouted coordinates into the phone, and gave orders to keep searching for the gunman. "Shit." Jake paused as whoever he spoke to must have finally got a word in edgewise. "Sam was shot."

Darien stopped unbuttoning his shirt. "Is he..."

"Hit in the arm. He'll live."

"What about Silva?" Darien removed his shirt and started to unbutton Lelandi's jacket.

"She's shook up, but fine. The gunman's dead."

Darien looked up at Jake. "Anyone question him?"

"He's dead."

"Hell, Jake, I know that. But did anyone question him before he died?"

Jake shook his head and hung up the phone, then he lifted his nose and sniffed. "Do you smell a hint of a red?"

"Can't as much perfume as she's wearing." Darien pulled up her turtleneck.

The cold air chilled her already frozen skin. He muttered an ancient wolf curse, then tucked his body-warmed flannel shirt against her wounds—smelling of him—all hot and spicy male.

Her mind drifted until he spoke again. "Who killed him?"

She stared at his bare chest, lightly haired, muscled, bronzed, beautiful. Who said men's bodies couldn't be beautiful? Every inch of him looked incredibly lickable, kissable, real.

"Not sure who killed him, Darien."

"Damn it. The gunman should have been questioned." Darien pulled her shirt down with tenderness, warming her, and then he used the same gentleness to close her jacket. "First off, who the hell are you?"

So much for the tenderness.

Through clenched teeth, she tried to growl, "Lelandi, and you know who the hell I am," but her voice was too hoarse. Her eyes were so heavily lidded, she could barely keep them open, except to stare at his magnificent chest.

But why was the rest of him dressed? Naked, that's the way he appeared to her in the dreams, his corded muscles rippling as he moved, every part of his sculpted anatomy ready to pleasure her. And why was *she* dressed? When she was always bared to the skin, waiting for his hungry touch?

He cursed. "God of thunder! My mate's dead, so what the hell do you think you're trying to pull?"

She lifted her gaze from his chest. Darien's stern face shook her loose of her fantasy. Unable to fathom what he was talking about, she knew his mate—Larissa—was dead. She choked on a sob.

He lifted her off the cold ground and the sight of his naked chest, square set jaw, darkened eyes—everything—faded away.

"Woman," Darien called out to her from a million miles away, his steely voice cloaked in concern.

She heard him, but couldn't focus, couldn't open her eyes. Her body floated, jostled over the rough terrain while the big gray carried her.

"How many times did he shoot you?"

Too, too many.

"What did he look like?"

Who? Her eyes fluttered open briefly, then slammed shut.

"Speak to me. At the tavern when you went to the restroom, what did the ladies do to upset you?"

Crowded me. Not since she had martial arts training had anyone messed with her. Took a near human rape to convince her she needed a way to protect herself as a human. Too bad she couldn't have used it to disarm the gunman. But he hadn't been close enough. If only she'd had her gun.

With a ragged sigh, she soaked in the heat of Darien's body, the strength of his arms wrapped securely around her, the smell of his masculinity, the smell of his sex. No matter how harshly he acted toward her, no matter how disinterested he pretended to be, he couldn't restrain that part of himself. He couldn't hide the telltale signals that he wanted her, like any alpha male *lupus garou* craved a female. The sexual chemistry between them sizzled, sending a volley of heat sliding through her. She moaned and he tightened his grip on her. Larissa must have delighted in mating with such a rugged figure of a man, much, much bigger than a red.

"Larissa," he said, commanding her to respond.

She frowned and opened her eyes. Jake gave her a look as grave as Darien's as they climbed up the side of the ridge.

"*Lelandi*," she said on edge, with barely the breath to breathe.

Darien's grim lips scowled further.

She wrinkled her brows in concentration. "Three."

Darien stared at her. "Three what?"

"Maybe she's answering your previous question, how many times had she been shot?"

She nodded her head limply.

Jake ran his hand over his scruffy whiskers. "She's pretty out of it."

"That's why I'm trying to keep her talking. Ask her something."

"Where are your parents?" Jake's voice was as demanding as his brother's.

She swallowed hard, tamped down the pain in her heart, in her brain. *Dead.*

"We need to send her to her own people, let them take care of this," Jake said.

"Whoever tried to kill her came into our territory. It's our jurisdiction, our matter to handle."

"But what if this had nothing to do with Lelandi?" Jake asked.

"*Larissa,*" she said, correcting him, this time angry. Couldn't they get their names straight?

Darien ducked with her underneath the branch of an oak. "What if this *does* have to do with Lelandi?"

"*Larissa,*" she said again, her voice becoming unduly agitated.

Hugging her closer, Darien climbed over a fallen log. "She's sure not following the gist of our conversation."

The aroma of bacon, sausage, and ham cooking in houses at the edge of town wafted in the air, and a rush of voices and footsteps headed her way. A hawk glided on the wind in search of its own breakfast that morning, and clouds were building. A hint of an early snow on the breeze added to the chill in her bones, while the pain in her chest and back spiraled out of control.

Coveting the heat of the gray, she wanted to lean further into him, but she felt as limp as a rag doll, unable to control her destiny. Taking another deep breath, she tried to smell his sex again. Every man's was different and most she never paid much attention to, but his was driving her mad. Virile, strong, musky, hot as a heated oven in summer, tantalizing. Had his special scent caught Larissa's attention?

Lelandi never figured she'd be drawn to the same male as Larissa. Must be the gunshot wounds screwing up her sense of smell.

"Hold on, Larissa," Darien said, his voice darkly soothing. "Doc will fix you up."

The look he shared with his brother cast doubt on his words.

"Get Doctor Weber," she managed to croak out.

The silent glance that passed between Darien and Jake meant they had other plans. But Doctor Weber was one of the reds. He'd know what to do. He'd removed bullets from her flank when hunters had shot her as a wolf, resuscitated her when she'd nearly drowned.

"They're bringing Sam in," a guy said, crowding in with several others, hurrying to join Darien.

Sam? Oh, the bartender, devious smile, rugged, mountain-man type.

"Is he wounded badly?" Darien sounded gloomy.

"Not as bad as the little lady appears to be." The man's beer breath made her wince when he squeezed in close to get a look.

"Sam was shot in the arm, nothing vital struck," another said. "But you know him, he'll be serving drinks by this evening, boss."

"*Lupus,*" she whispered and Darien's eyes grew wide.

Before she uttered another sound, he leaned down and kissed her, but the kiss didn't stop at silencing her words. His lips pressed deeper, promising more, willing her to agree, and then his warm mouth tantalizing hers faded away.

"Larissa," he called out, drawing her forth from the darkness.

Darien's dark eyes gazed at her, pensive, pained.

Several of the men chuckled.

"The ladies will be clamoring for a kiss that would make 'em pass right out." Silva's voice was silky soft, dreamy, wistful.

Vehicle doors creaked open, and Lelandi closed her eyes, wanting to say something more to force the gray to kiss her again, but she couldn't come up with anything, her mind focusing on the way his lips touched hers— hungry, desirous, feral.

"Sure they weren't a *special* kind of bullet?" someone asked, his voice hushed.

"No. She's lost a lot of blood. The cold's taken a toll on her, too. Riding with her, brother?" Jake asked.

Darien released her and she reached out to him, wanting his warmth, his comfort, another of his mind-numbing kisses. He seemed torn about showing any further affection.

Lying on something long, flat, and hard, she felt the blankets covering her, but the bone-chilling cold renewed after losing the heat of the big gray's body.

"Meet you over there." Darien's voice sounded gruff and unreal, like he was trying to put on a show for his pack, trying to distance himself from her. "Got to check out Silva and Sam's story."

Feeling rejected, she wanted more of his touch, scowling at her, paying attention to her, anything. Yet, on another level, she shouldn't feel any of these things.

"I can give you a report," Jake offered.

Again, there was a prolonged hesitation. "No, I'll check on her later."

Darien's rejection cut deep, and she turned her misty gaze away so she couldn't see the hardened look in his eyes.

"I'll go with her, Doc." Jake climbed in beside her and the vehicle rocked like a boat adrift in turbulent water. He smelled different, not as sexual as Darien. Maybe because he wasn't attracted to her like she sensed Darien was.

Heaven forbid. A gray. Her dead sister's mate. And torn emotionally because of losing her. Yet, Lelandi couldn't stop craving his touch.

"Wait up!" Silva said. "I want to ride with her."

Darien put a hand on her arm, stopping her. "I need to talk to you first, Silva."

"Can't it wait, boss? Sam saw everything anyway. Uhm, as much as there was to see."

Again, there was a long pause before he responded.

"Got to take care of the little lady," a white-haired man said.

"All right, Doc. But I want to hear what happened out there soonest, Silva."

Pack business. Nothing else counted. Certainly not Lelandi. Only the shooter who killed the gunman mattered. She gritted her teeth against the pain in her heart.

"Yes, siree, boss," Silva said, her voice like cotton candy.

The ambulance jiggled some more, and Silva's slight feminine fragrance scented the air.

The doors slammed shut and the woman smiled at Lelandi, her expression wistful.

"You sure shook that big gray out of his doldrums, sugar." Silva turned to Jake. "So what in the world happened out there?"

"I could ask you the same, Silva. Why the hell did the gunman have to die before he talked?"

Lelandi croaked out, "He had to die. No witnesses."

Chapter 5

As soon as Lelandi's look-alike sister had invaded his favorite Friday night getaway since the death of his mate, Darien knew there'd be trouble. His men were sure he wanted *her* to replace his dead mate. The women were already jealous he'd be interested in another red. *Despite* the fact he'd made every effort to show no interest in her.

Except for the kiss. Hell, he'd only done it to silence her words. Yet, the kiss hadn't *just* stopped at prohibiting her from speaking, nor had he wanted it to, which was absolute madness. Worse, he made her pass out, not because of his passionate kiss either. She was severely injured for Odin's sake. What the hell was the matter with him anyway?

Letting his breath out in exasperation, he stood in front of Hastings Bed and Breakfast and examined Sam's flesh wound, seeing where the bullet had grazed his upper arm.

Sam was telling his story again, probably for the fiftieth time, relishing every second of his moment of glory while the townsfolk crowded around, listening in. "The gunman was following us, but Silva was chattering as usual and must have distracted me. He fired before I could get a shot off. Whoever killed the man hid in the trees on a ridge. Have no idea why he hasn't joined us to get a pat on the back."

"Probably worried Darien would be pissed at him for not hitting the gunman somewhere less fatal." Mason slanted Darien a look.

Humans, curious about what had happened, mingled with his people, so Sam and the rest of Darien's people were cautious about what they revealed. Which made Darien think *again* about the kiss. Hell, he couldn't have the little red wolf, half out of her head, talking about *lupus garous*.

"Let's get you to the hospital," Darien said, breaking up the show.

"I'll take him." Mervin still wore his old-time barber clothes, vest, red band around the arm of his white long-sleeved shirt, red bow tie, and the straw hat seated on his nearly black hair. "The sheriff's cutting his vacation short and headed back here, Darien."

"Good. I want a meeting at two this afternoon with my team."

Once he'd seen the injured transported to the hospital, Darien returned to where the dead gunman lay. Two of his men rifled through the man's clothes. His black eyes were lifeless, a scraggly two-day growth of black beard covered his face and his long hair was unkempt.

"No ID." Mason removed his hand from the guy's jacket pocket.

Not that Darien expected he'd have any. Not a local, but a human, and a good shot with a gun. A hired gun? Or his own job?

Mason jerked his thumb at the dead man. "The shooter killed him with one fatal shot to the head. Sure knew what he was doing. This guy used a 9-mm; powder residue on his hands and jacket, proving he fired the gun, silver bullets in his right side pocket."

Darien shifted his perusal of the gunman to Mason, who shrugged. "The bullets in the chamber are regular. The ones in his pocket would have killed your brother and the little lady."

"He didn't believe." Swamped with relief, Darien realized how lucky the woman and his brother had been.

Mason handed the bullets to Darien. "So a *lupus garou* killed him. How much you want to bet the silver's from our mine?"

"Might tie into the missing silver." Darien's attention shifted north where two of his men headed in his direction, John Hastings, owner of the hardware store and B&B and one of the founding fathers of the town, and Deputy Peter Jorgenson.

They both shook their heads, confirming they hadn't located the other shooter.

Deputy Jorgenson's amber eyes were nearly black, although he was never easily riled. "We found gunpowder residue and took pictures of where he'd stood and tramped down the grass."

"Any trace of his scent?" Darien asked.

"So many of us were in the area, it's hard to tell. Even Sam's and Silva's scents were drifting on the breeze up that way."

Darien motioned to the gunman. "Take him to the morgue. I want Doc Featherston to conduct an autopsy and give me a report ASAP. Have a ballistic test run on the bullet and a comparison made on every *lupus garou*'s gun out here today."

"I'll get right on it," Deputy Jorgenson said.

Mason walked back to town with Darien, his face scrunched up in thought. "You think the shooter was a red or a gray?"

"I think he was one of us or the shooter would have left a red scent. Easy to detect."

"I smelled a red scent," Hastings said, half of his gray hair, loosened from the leather strap, now whipping about his shoulders in the breeze. "Faint, but it was there."

Darien glanced in the direction of the dead man and the deputy organizing a party to carry him. "Now that you mention it, Jake said he thought he smelled one near Lelandi. And we heard a couple of howls. Why didn't Peter mention smelling any?"

"I was the only one who caught a whiff of it in the breeze. He discounted what I smelled. Said my sniffer wasn't as keen as it used to be. I'll give him that, but I know what I smelled." Hastings shook his head. "Young whippersnappers."

"Darien, wait up, boss!" Deputy Jorgenson shouted, chasing after him. "We've found evidence a red was in the area."

Darien gave Hastings a knowing look.

Hastings snorted. "Yeah, my sniffer's out of whack."

Deputy Jorgenson handed a patch of red fur to Darien. "Found it stuck to some brambles and definitely smells like a red *lupus garou*."

Darien looked up at his men. "It's fresh. Hell, he's got to be a royal."

"Same one *I* smelled." Hastings gave the deputy a pointed glower.

"Post guards for the woman around the clock," Darien said.

"Yes, sir." Deputy Jorgenson took off running toward town.

"That young man's got what it takes to be sheriff some day," Mason said.

"Only if he listens to his elders," Hastings clarified.

Darien continued toward town. "Another sixty or so years, I'm sure Uncle Sheridan will give up his job."

Hastings shook his head. "He'll want to retire once he learns all hell broke loose while he was on vacation for the first time in ten years."

Mason snorted. "He'll be in hog heaven—ordering folks around. We haven't had this much excitement since that mental patient broke out of a loony bin, killed his family, then hid out here."

"One reason not to allow humans to live in our town," Hastings said.

Darien didn't agree. "Keeps us on our toes. Otherwise, we'd get careless."

A large gathering of men at the edge of town were talking about the crimes committed. Most *lupus garou* societies blended with human-run towns. Silver Town was different—run and controlled by *lupus garous* since its inception when the first settlers moved west, and Darien's family had opted to keep it that way.

When they reached them, Mervin spoke to Darien. "The red sure stirred up this quiet little town. Don't imagine it's going to settle down none for a time, either."

"The lady's going home, soon as I explain how her sister died."

Several cast sideways glances at each other.

"As soon as she's well enough to travel," he added.

Some nodded, but he could tell they didn't believe him. The only way to prove his word was to send her packing, and he would, just like he said.

"See you boys later."

Darien stalked up the street to his SUV. Lelandi hadn't been in her grave three weeks, now this. But another thought puzzled him. If she'd cut ties with her family, how had Larissa learned about her sister's death?

If she hadn't been his soul mate, he would never have gotten involved with a red who had family, not without her parents' and the head of her pack's permission. He damn well suspected now she hadn't been a loner, giving up her pack, like she'd said.

Climbing into the vehicle, he took a deep breath and smelled the new car leather. The vehicle was supposed to be perfect for a family, this one having four doors to accommodate the triplets. He squeezed his eyes shut and gripped the steering wheel hard. Several had warned him not to take the red for his mate, yet he couldn't get her out of his system, vivacious and spirited as she was. But he should have known she wouldn't have been strong enough to be a pack leader's mate.

When he parked at Silver Town Hospital, he noted the large number of vehicles there. Probably some of Sam's kin come to check him out. And Uncle Sheridan's sons, the twenty-four-year-old quadruplets, were there, too, probably looking in on cousin Tom. Darien blew out his breath. Keeping the community calm after the incident was going to be some job.

He stalked into the hospital. With some reservation, several of the women and men greeted him in the waiting area. He could see he was going to be in the doghouse until he settled the matter.

Wearing hearts and flowers–decorated scrubs, Ritka glowered at him with her good eye. The other was half-shut and turning green and yellow. "That bitch is in room four. If Doc wants someone to take care of her, he'll have to hire someone else."

"What about Cecilia?"

"Off today."

"Call her in."

Ritka's jaw dropped. "But—"

"Call her in, or I will. You don't want me to have to do it."

Snapping her mouth shut, Ritka shoved her brown hair behind her ears. "All right, but she's not going to like it."

Ritka grabbed the phone and hit a button, then tapped her long nails on the check-in counter. "Cecilia? It's me, Ritka. Get your butt in here. We've got three patients with gunshot wounds, and the boss is calling the shots." She tilted her head to the side and gave Darien another dirty look. "Yeah, no shit. Three gunshot wounds and Darien said to get in here now." Ritka hung up the phone and folded her arms. "You can put up with her next, and believe you me, she won't treat your new fancy any better."

"Keep a civil tongue where the woman's concerned, Ritka. She's a patient under my protection," Darien growled.

Her brown brows jerked upward.

"Yep," he said for her ears only. "She's one of ours until I can send her home to her own pack, so mind your ps and qs. I won't have anyone treating her poorly. You can tell your friends I said so."

"Well, well," Silva said, slipping in on the conversation. Darien swore she had hearing that beat anybody's. "So she's an official member of the pack already."

"Unofficial. And you can spread the word." If anyone could, it was Silva.

"Will do, boss." Silva winked. "She doesn't look too good. Been asking for a Doctor Weber. Figure it's her pack doctor. Kind of out of it. I don't think she realizes she's not back home, wherever that is."

"Where's Doc Oliver?"

"Stitching up Sam." Silva glanced at Ritka. "Doc says if you want to keep getting a paycheck you'd better get into exam room number three, now."

Cursing under her breath, Ritka shoved past her and stalked down the hall.

Darien shook his head. Silver Town wouldn't be considered civilized by big town standards. He headed for room number four and glanced over his shoulder when Silva followed behind him. "Don't need an escort."

"Is that an order?"

Ignoring her, Darien walked into the white room, where the smell of antiseptic was overwhelming. Larissa blinked her eyes. The railings were locked in place to keep her from falling out of the bed. Her wrists were restrained. Her face was ghastly pale in stark contrast to her black hair, stretching down to her waist over the white sheets. How could one little red *lupus garou* walk into town and turn it upside down?

"Why is she restrained?" Darien drew closer to the bed, wanting to touch her, to assure himself she was real and well on the road to recovery.

"Ritka said she tried to climb out of bed, but she might have restrained her out of spite."

"Nope," Doc Oliver said, walking into the room. "Little lady tried to leave when I showed up instead of some Doctor Weber." He folded his arms and observed her. "She's Lelandi's twin, isn't she?"

"Yeah," Darien said. "By the name of Larissa."

"She's got tenacity. Even as bad off as she is, four of us had to restrain her. She's on heavy-duty medication, and even so, she's fighting it."

Her eyes were no longer blue, not as amber as Lelandi's but more green. "She must have been wearing contacts."

"Took them out," Doc said.

"Can you do anything about the hair?" Darien asked, half-joking.

"Melba can strip the color, try to make it more like the color of her eyebrows. She does human hair all the time," Silva said.

"I'm not serious."

Silva touched Larissa's hair. "The dye won't hold anyway once the change takes place. Hmm, there's your solution, boss. In three days, she can change into the wolf, and it'll zap that hideous dye job from her hair."

"She won't be here that long, if I can help it."

"Three days." Doc stroked his whiskerless chin. "Not sure she'll be ready to leave that soon."

"She's that bad off?"

"She's pretty weak. Doc Mitchell gave her some blood. So did Jake. Three days is pushing it."

Darien shook his head. The longer she stayed in Silver Town, the more trouble she'd be.

Doc cleared his throat. "No one knows what this is about. Is there another gunman? Just the one? Did someone hire him? Will there be another hit? Lot of folks are pretty angry that the gunman wounded two of ours and no word why or who is behind the whole thing. Sending her away isn't the solution, until we know what's going on. What if Lelandi didn't commit suicide?"

In disbelief, Darien stared at Doc. "You said she'd committed suicide, and Doc Featherston certified it. Besides, my uncle said the same thing. As sheriff, he investigated the matter and—"

"*And* came to the same conclusion. But, Darien, you're pretty persuasive when you want to be, and you were so hell-bent on believing she'd committed suicide we went along with it."

"For Odin's sake, Doc, if the three of you believed it was murder, you would have said."

"Well, yes, but—"

"Then don't blame it on me!" Darien glanced at Silva to see her take on it.

Her dark brows raised a notch.

"Don't tell me you had reservations, too."

"I'm just the barmaid." Silva threw her hands up in an exasperated gesture. "No one listens to anything I have to say."

"Well?"

"Truthfully?"

He growled.

"Hell, Darien, truthfully, I don't know. But something's not right, now that her sister comes along and gets the whole town shot up."

His mate's twin sighed deeply. She blinked a couple of times, but didn't focus on anything.

"She's got to be here for three more days, then, eh, Doc?" Darien asked.

"In town, yes. She shouldn't travel a great distance. But she can stay somewhere else for the next couple of days. Tonight, I want to keep an eye on her. She'll need someone to look after her once she leaves here."

"You're the boss, boss," Silva said, "but Sam can do without me a couple of days. I'll look after her. I'm just about the only female in town who liked Lelandi, so maybe I can do her sister a favor."

"What if someone's still aiming to get Larissa?" Doc asked.

Darien considered her groggy state. "Peter's making sure she has around-the-clock protection."

"Have Trevor do the inside surveillance, won't you?" Silva winked.

Uncle Sheridan stormed into the room, looking like a stuck bull. "What in the Sam Hill is going on?" His voice boomed, though at six-four, everything about the man seemed overbearing and loud.

"You're in my hospital now, Sheriff," Doc said. "Keep your yelling down to a low roar."

"You haven't heard yelling, Doc. Gone two days of a ten-day vacation and what happens? Where were those two worthless deputies of mine?"

Silva cleared her throat. "Trevor was busy overseeing

the clearing of a landslide on the highway, Sheriff. Don't know what Peter was doing."

"Peter was with us," Jake said, walking into the room. He glanced at Larissa. "Should we be discussing this here?"

"She's the cause of it, Ritka told me," the sheriff countered, motioning at Larissa.

"She'd certainly say so." Silva folded her arms and gave the sheriff a disgruntled look.

"Well, isn't she? The woman started stirring up trouble at the tavern. Next thing you know, three people are shot. I want to know what the hell's going on."

"It's your job to find out." Darien didn't bother to curb the acid in his voice.

Doc put Larissa's chart back in the folder. "Got some other patients to see to. Need to speak to you when you can spare a moment, Darien."

"My…" Larissa paused. "My sister… was… murdered," she stammered, then shut her eyes.

Everyone stared at her in stunned silence.

Darien had figured that's what Lelandi's sister must have thought. "Since she doesn't have any family here, I want you to sit with her for a couple of hours, Silva."

"Sure, and miss out on the fun stuff." Silva pulled a vinyl-covered chair next to the bed. "Have Trevor run by my place and pick up one of my novels, will ya? Give me something to do while I'm babysitting."

"I'll ask him," Jake said.

The sheriff yanked off his Stetson and waved it at Jake. "Hold on here just a blamed minute. He works for me, and I've got an investigation to conduct."

Darien raised his brows at his uncle.

The sheriff's brown eyes darkened and narrowed. "Well, hell, if it only takes a minute, I guess I can spare him."

Jake added, "Tom's asking to see you, Darien, and he wants to take a peek at Larissa to see for himself that she's all right, but Doc says he has to stay put for the time being."

"All right. Come on, Uncle Sheridan. We'll fill you in on all we know, though it's not much." Darien ushered everyone out of the room.

Larissa looked small, pale, the spitting image of Lelandi, except for the hideous black hair, now that the contacts, glasses, earrings, and hat were gone. His heart lurched when her eyelids fluttered open, and she caught him gawking at her. He refused to get caught up in the bewitching enchantments of his dead mate's twin.

She closed her eyes and released his gaze.

Crap, she was as much a lure as her sister. Best to keep distance between himself and the temptress.

He caught Silva's smug smile, his body heated to boiling, and he turned on his heel and stalked out of the room.

Boots tromped down the hospital hall, then everything grew quiet. The medicine took hold, the tranquility drawing her into another world, and Lelandi's heart lightened at the scene before her.

Mist filled her vision, and he *came to her.*

Naked. His bronzed body glistening in the brilliant light of the full moon. Proud, determined, his mission— to ravish her—again.

So what took him so long?

Tall with broad shoulders, his chest magnificently muscled, moving with the grace and ease of a wolf, he stalked toward her. Whereas most of her kind were shorter and the ones in power, squatter, more bull-like, this man was Adonis reborn.

She still couldn't see his face, doused in shadows, teasing her, making her strain to see his features. Her eyes shifted to his chest. Lower. To his erection. He was ready for her. Always ready, his sex jutting upward surrounded by sable curls.

She breathed in deeply, trying to smell his unique scent, wishing she could locate him in the real world upon waking, but her keen wolf senses couldn't pick up his manly scent—not in a dream.

Reclining on the grass on her side, she watched him as he strode toward her, every hard muscle rippling with his gait. Yet, just the vision of him five months ago had been enough to bring her into her first wolf heat, way long overdue. How could a fantasy lover have brought that about?

She wanted to call out his name like a lover would her mate, but she couldn't fathom what it was. The warm summer breeze stirred the Douglas firs, casting dancing moonlight across his body. His lips turned up slightly, bemused. His mouth, his sturdy jawline, his shoulder-length sable hair ruffled by the breeze. Show me more! She wanted to see his eyes, his nose, the rest of his face—but as much as she strained to see them, she couldn't—the rest of his features remained hidden in the black void.

He towered over her, took in a deep breath, and tried to smell her. She saw the intake of his breath, knew

*what he was attempting to do. A queer feeling of unease
washed over her. She squashed the unwelcome worry.
He was not real. Just the most consummate lover a
dream could conjure up.*

*He lay down beside her, and she ran her finger over
his brow, finding it furrowed. For the first time since
their union, he seemed contemplative, unrushed, as if he
wanted more than the sex they shared.*

*Leaning over, he nuzzled her lips with his mouth,
licking them, smiling. Positioning himself closer, he
rested his head on his hand and appeared to study her.
She opened her mouth to speak, but the words would
never come. He touched her hair, ran his fingers
through the strands, held them to his nose and took a
deep breath.*

Could he smell her scent when she couldn't sense his?

*He traced her arm, down to her hip, his heated touch
stirring a fire across her sensitive skin. She drew close,
pressing her breasts against his chest, took his face in
her hands, and moved her lips against his in a searing
kiss. She swore she heard him growl this time, but then
he glanced over his shoulder, as if something in the
woods had distracted him. Danger?*

*He shook his head and gave her a lusty smile.
Knowingly, she returned the expression, her nipples
already taut from touching his lightly furred chest, her
short curly hairs damp with need, her core aching for
his penetration.*

*In a heartbeat, he moved her onto her back, pushed
her legs apart with his knee, and thrust his rigid shaft
deep inside her. His mouth on hers, he conquered her,
and she gave into the rush of heat, the burning desire he*

stirred within her, the flickering flames consuming her as she climbed toward the ice-white moon.

Their bodies slick, they slid against each other, panting, thrusting, deepening the bond until she felt the mind-shattering release, the orgasm crashing through her like a heated summer storm.

Muffled voices farther down the hall invaded Lelandi's private, scattered thoughts.

Her dream lover slipped away into the shadows, vanishing, the moon winked out, and the sun took its place, peeking through the blinds. She wished she were back in the woods with her fantasy lover, no cares in the world but of being pleasured by him and pleasuring him in return. Groaning, Lelandi tried to run her hands through her tangled hair, her skin sweaty from her romp with him.

But something held her down—*him*?

Chapter 6

LELANDI OPENED HER EYES AND BRILLIANT WHITE LIGHTS
flooded her vision. Where was the ceiling fan in her bedroom? She closed her eyes and took a deep breath, trying
to orient herself. The odor of antiseptics filled the air.
Her eyes popped open. White sheets, railings caging her
in on an elevated narrow bed. What the...

She tried to reach up, to rub her temple as her thoughts
spun out of control, but she couldn't. Leather restraints
wrapped around her wrists pinned her to the bed—not
the man of her dreams.

Her sister. Oh, God, and her parents, too, were dead.

Tears filled her eyes and her heart lodged like a
lump of stone in her throat. She sobbed with a strangled
whimper and a teary haze blurred her vision. Yanking
at the restraints, she fought the mounting frustration, her
body heating by degrees.

Closing her eyes, she licked her dry lips. What she
wouldn't give for an icy pink lemonade. Summer heat
had returned with a vengeance, and she felt like she'd
been burned to a crisp under the broiling sun like she had
at the beach in South Padre Island a few years back.

A rustling noise caught her attention—Silva searching
through Lelandi's purse.

Silva smiled, her ruby lips glistening with fresh gloss,
a coating of brown eye shadow emphasizing the darkness
of her coffee-colored eyes. "No driver's license. How'd

you get to Silver Town? No rental cars unaccounted for. Deputy Sheriff Trevor checked the cars parked around town, and none belong to a Larissa Catterton."

It finally dawned on Lelandi. Her sister had switched first names with her. What a mess. "Catterton?"

Silva *tsk*ed. "So that wasn't Lelandi's last name."

No, and Lelandi wasn't her first name either, although no one had listened to her the times she'd corrected them before.

"So what *is* your real last name?" Silva poured a cup of ice water for her, then set it on the table.

With her wrists secured, Lelandi couldn't reach the water. "Lelandi." She wasn't about to reveal her real last name. "I'm... I'm burning up."

Silva's eyes widened, and she hurried over to the bed. Her long, icy fingers touched Lelandi's forehead, instantly sending a chill streaking down her heated nerves. "You're burning up."

"I already said that," Lelandi whispered, annoyed.

"Okay, okay, I'll get some help."

"Can you unfasten my *chains,*" Lelandi said sarcastically, "help me to sit up, and give me some ice water to drink?"

Silva shifted her worried gaze to the wristbands confining her. "I'll get the doc."

"Doctor Weber," Lelandi said, firmly.

"Uhm, you're at the hospital in Silver Town, sugar. I'm sure Doctor Weber wouldn't want to come all the way here from wherever you know him for one little ol' patient."

Lelandi yanked at the leather wrist bracelets to no avail.

If it had been a regular hospital, they probably would have used Velcro restraints, and those she could have tugged loose. She pulled at the restraints again, rattling the bed railings, but her movements were dulled and of no use, making her skin heat even more.

Satisfied Lelandi wasn't getting loose, Silva left the room. Within minutes, her worried voice echoed down the hall while she spoke to someone about the fever. But before she or the doctor returned, a woman wearing blue scrubs walked into the room.

"I'm Nurse Grey." The woman's face was matronly, with kindly gray eyes and lips that were pale, but slightly turned up. "Looks like you've been rather cantankerous."

"Not me," Lelandi mumbled.

The nurse chuckled, the sound good-hearted, while she read Lelandi's chart. "Busy girl. Heard some wild rumors. You're looking into your sister's death and already stirred up a heap of trouble."

Lelandi had made a royal mess of it, but whoever had killed her sister was bound to slip up. When he did, she'd make him suffer for what he'd done. She closed her burning eyes.

"Seems a lot of trouble for a little red *lupus garou* to get into first time in Silver Town."

Although the woman seemed nice enough, Lelandi didn't trust her. Lelandi was probably giving their pack leader prime grade heartburn, and she wasn't going away. Some would be wary, some outright rude, and some, sweet like Sam, Silva, and this Nurse Grey, but only on the surface. Deep down, pack mates stuck up for pack mates, and she was an outsider investigating *them*.

Tom was another story. He definitely indicated he had the hots for her, but she wasn't biting.

"If you'll behave, I'll remove the restraints." After Nurse Grey took her temperature, she frowned. "Hundred and three." She changed her antibiotics and removed the restraints.

Lelandi let out a low growl, and the woman smiled. Yeah, wolves didn't like confinement, and she was ready to bite anyone who'd helped restrain her, including Ritka and the doctor.

"Doc wants you to drink fluids, but slowly. You might feel nauseous from the surgery and pain medication."

"Nurse Grey," Silva said, walking into the room. "I thought you were off today and tomorrow."

The nurse shrugged. "I thought so, too. Seems we had some trouble during the night."

Lelandi hid a smile, then sipped cold water from a straw, shivered, and slumped back under her covers. If she didn't get more energy soon, she'd scream.

"She sure isn't like Lelandi." Silva studied her as if she could see her insides, too.

Nurse Grey refilled Lelandi's water cup. "Looks the same, except for the hair."

"Can you imagine Lelandi taking on Ritka and her gang?"

The nurse smiled. "Guess I ought to go to the Silver Town Tavern more often. Sam said when he saw her walk into the joint, he knew it would shake Darien out of the pit of despair he's been wallowing in."

"Yeah, but in a good way, or bad?" Silva raised her brows to punctuate her statement. "You should have seen the way he kissed her."

Nurse Grey glanced at Lelandi. "Already?"

"Hell, he wanted to kiss her in the tavern, but he was trying to keep up appearances." Silva pushed her hair back over her shoulders and placed her hands on her hips. "She started talking about *lupus garou,* and he had to stop her. But the kiss lasted longer than necessary and made her pass right out. I'm sure when the other eligible bitches hear about it, they'll be fuming."

Nurse Grey's eyes sparkled with intrigue.

"So, is she going to be all right?"

"When are we not? She'll be fine. However, the fever makes it more of a setback. I notice on the chart, Doc says he'll release her tomorrow. Might be too soon."

"She should be in jail for popping Ritka in the eye," a dark-haired man said as he strode into the room, his eyes black, his police khaki uniform perfectly pressed, a jacket slung over his shoulder. His Stetson shaded his eyes, giving him an even darker-tempered appearance.

Silva smiled at him. Well, more than smiled at him, nearly melted in his presence.

Truly smitten. Lelandi wondered if the same love bug had bitten him or if it was only a one-way street. He didn't show the same kind of moonstruck attraction when he looked at Silva.

"Why, Trevor, you done with that mess on the highway?" Silva asked, her voice sweet as spun sugar.

"Sheriff chewed my butt for not taking care of *her* mess." He jerked a thumb in Lelandi's direction. "Said shootings take priority over mud slides. Hell, they needed someone to reroute traffic. Four accidents out there. Six injuries."

"Silva stuck up for you when she didn't need to." Lelandi glowered back at the deputy. Silva's mouth dropped open. "Seems you owe her thanks. No one else bothered to defend your actions."

Trevor shoved his hands in his pockets and continued to glare at Lelandi. "Who was the man who shot you?"

She closed her eyes. *Question the bastard!* How would she know who he was?

"He shot you in the chest twice—"

"Three times," she said, her breathing still ragged, "but who's counting?"

"You're one of us, well, kinda, and you can see as well as we can in the dark, so who was he?"

Silva *tsk*ed. "Can't you question her later, when she's not so bad off?"

Trevor's face reddened. "That's another thing," he said, his voice elevating. "Who the hell shot him dead, and why didn't anyone question him first?"

Silva cleared her throat. "Trevor, we've given the sheriff our statements. Someone shot him from a distance. We never saw who it was, and after he did the deed, he never came down to see if Sam was all right. Unless he did, but just blended with the men who came to investigate the shots fired. The word is Darien might be so mad at whoever the shooter was for not just wounding the gunman, the guy's not telling."

"Yeah, anyone would be afraid Darien would be pissed, especially the way he's been acting lately."

"Did anyone tell you that you'll be guarding us at my place?" Silva asked, her tone sweet and innocent.

Trevor scowled at her. "Babysitting?"

"Never know. Trouble seems to follow her. You could be in the thick of it this time."

Nurse Grey shook her head. "You can't mean the young lady will be going to your town house, Silva. She needs to remain here."

"I think Doc's worried the hospital isn't secure enough for her."

"Jail cell will do the job." Trevor shoved his hat back and crossed his arms over his broad chest.

"Ah, Trevor." Silva furrowed her brow at him.

"Hell, I saw how she beat up Ritka."

Lelandi smiled. The woman couldn't have been more outraged when paramedics wheeled Lelandi into the hospital. Luckily, the doctor ordered two men to watch over her, making sure Ritka didn't finish what the gunman had begun.

"Hell, look at the way she's smiling about it. No remorse or anything. Criminal behavior if I ever saw it."

"They started it," Silva argued. "Three against one, and every one of them is bigger than her."

"Ritka said this one started it to prove she's after Darien, like her sister had been."

"Ha! Darien did the chasing. Hell, Lelandi didn't stand a chance."

Trevor's face grew crimson again. "I've got work to do, straightening out this mess. Then I guess I've got *babysitting* duty later."

Lelandi swore he looked hopeful something bad would happen so he'd get in on the real action this time and be able to prove to his boss how important he was.

He stalked out.

"I've got to check on Tom, but if she needs anything, just holler," Nurse Grey said, then left.

"Guess it's just you and me, kid." Silva sat in the vinyl chair against the wall. "You look like you can barely stay awake. Why don't you get some sleep?"

"My sister didn't chase Darien?" Lelandi squeaked, hating that her voice was so out of control like the rest of her.

"Hardly. Darien doesn't like women who chase him. He likes to do the pursuing." Silva leaned back in the chair and rolled her sun-streaked chestnut hair between two fingers.

She really was a striking woman and Lelandi wondered why Darien didn't seem attracted to her.

Silva smiled. "So if you're interested in getting his attention, don't go hunting him down."

"Wouldn't think of it." Lelandi wanted to roll onto her stomach, the way she normally slept, but she couldn't with the IV in place. Plus, she had a sneaking suspicion her wounds would give her fits if she tried.

"On the other hand, if you want him to leave you alone…"

Lelandi stopped struggling with her thin white cotton blanket and looked over at Silva.

"Act *really* interested in him."

"*Not* happening." This time Lelandi's words came out loud and clear, to both her surprise and Silva's amusement.

"Uh-huh, well your choice."

"Listen." Lelandi's voice did the raspy, hoarse bit again. "I'm here for one thing only. Finding out who killed my sister and why, and terminating him. I'm not interested in some alpha gray pack leader who just buried his mate who happened to be my triplet. End of story."

"Triplet? Ohmigod, don't tell me there's another one of you. The news will put Darien in an early grave for sure."

"My brother, and if he were here, he'd search for our sister's killer."

"Oh, he must be a rogue, an alpha male, and must have left your pack. So, where is he now?"

Lelandi's eyes misted and she shrugged, wishing to hell her brother or even her uncle, who was seven years older than them, would help her.

Silva chewed on her bottom lip. "What if the dead gunman killed your sister?"

"He didn't."

"You sound so certain. How do you know?"

Darien walked into the room, making both Silva and Lelandi gasp. How long had he been listening in on their private conversation?

"How do you know he wasn't the one who killed Lelandi, assuming she didn't commit suicide?" he asked, his voice harsh and accusatory.

"She told me."

Darien's jaw tightened. "Don't tell me. You had secret *triplet* communication."

"If you mean she sent me a letter, yeah, she did." Lelandi swore he looked sicker than she felt, which had to be pretty hard to do the way she was feeling.

"You okay, boss?" Silva asked.

An alpha male did not faint. But his face had turned paler than her sheets, and she figured he was on the verge.

He gripped the doorframe for a minute, then growled, "Where's the letter?"

She wanted to fold her arms to prove she wasn't afraid of his alpha wolf posturing, but she thought better of it when she remembered the IV. Instead, she closed her eyes and listened to the hammering of his heart against his ribs.

"Tell me, damn it! Where's the letter?"

His voice grew closer, his breathing hard. She might have been afraid of him if it wasn't for the medicine making her loopy. Opening her eyes, she tried glaring at him when he gripped her bed railing, glowering at her as if he wished to kill her himself, but she wasn't sure she was sharing her meanest look with him the way her eyelids kept drooping. She hadn't an ounce of energy to spare.

"She's in a bad way, Darien. Let her rest and you can question her later."

"Now, damn it. I want some answers now."

As a wolf, she could imagine his teeth would be dangerous, but as a human, they were beautiful, straight, white, clenched, and…

She yawned and closed her eyes.

"Damn it, speak!"

A small laugh sounded. It wasn't from her, but when she opened her eyes, both Silva and Darien were staring at her. She realized that it *was* from her, after all.

Chapter 7

GOD, SHE WAS EXASPERATING, AND BEAUTIFUL. BEAUTIFULLY exasperating. But Silva was right, the woman was barely out of surgery, pumped full of dope, and scarcely able to keep her eyes open. Yet she could manage a pitiful laugh at Darien's expense.

Darien gripped the bar tighter on her bed, then released it and stalked out of the room. Seeing his uncle questioning some others, he motioned to speak to him.

"Yeah, Darien, what's up?"

"Search Larissa's room. She must have been staying at Hastings Bed and Breakfast since she was headed in that direction when the gunman shot her. If she got a letter from Lelandi, bring it to me."

Pack laws ruled, no search warrants needed.

"And, pack up her things. She's staying at my place when she leaves the hospital. But until then... hell, I'll go with you."

"Not falling for another one of them, are you?" Uncle Sheridan's voice reflected stormy censure as they walked outside the hospital.

Darien rebuffed his comment with humor. "Not this time. Hell, I don't care for women who chase after me."

Uncle Sheridan shook his head. "Good thing she doesn't know any better." He cocked a dark brow, but his expression was still scornful.

Darien *wasn't* getting involved with the woman!

When they arrived at the Queen Anne Victorian bed and breakfast, Mrs. Bertha Hastings hurried to greet them, wearing one of her more colorful floral dresses. Didn't matter the time of year, she always dressed in flowery patterns. Told everyone who would listen she was probably a garden fairy in another life. Even now her lobby and check-in counter were filled with bouquets of flowers, ivies trailing down plant stands, and small ficus trees cuddled next to the big windows, leaning toward the sun, making it appear she'd brought the great outdoors inside.

"Is the young lady going to be all right?" Mrs. Hastings handed them a key to room five.

She shook her head before Darien could respond. "I know, I should have told you right away when she arrived. At first, I didn't recognize she was Lelandi's sister. But I caught her without the glasses and hat, and then I could see the obvious resemblance, despite the rest of the disguise. Oh, and her voice of course. Same sweet tone. How's she doing?"

Darien cleared his throat. "After a couple of days, she should be fine."

"Good. Tell her I'm saving her room for her."

He was going to tell her Larissa was leaving here for good, as soon as he found her pack and they came for her. But Uncle Sheridan beat him to it.

"She'll be going home to her pack as soon as she's well enough."

Mrs. Hastings's mouth dropped slightly. She hurried to pluck dead flowers from a vase of mums. "I'm sorry to hear it. I'd hoped…" She quickly glanced at Darien, but didn't say anything further.

That he would take Larissa as his mate? He shook his head. "Did anyone come here looking for her?"

"Deputy Trevor already asked. Some guy accosted her behind the house. I had my phone ready to call for backup when he grabbed her arm, but she swung her arm down and around, freeing herself. Just as quickly, she kicked up her knee like she was going to hurt him *you know where*. Looked like kung fu or something. Anyway, before he began to sing soprano, he jumped back, and that was the end of the confrontation. He stalked off toward Mervin's barbershop, and she headed for the tavern to see you. At least I presumed that's why she asked where you'd be on a Friday night."

Uncle Sheridan gave a derisive snort, his expression mirroring his response. "Chasing after you like you said, Darien." He pulled out his notepad. "Can you describe what the guy looked like?"

"Maybe five-foot-eight or so, lanky. He was wearing jeans, hiking books, a copper-colored coat. His hood was up, hiding his face." She shrugged. "Couldn't see much more."

"Copper coat? That should be easy to spot." Darien hoped they might finally have a lead.

"I haven't seen the guy again since the incident out back. And I don't recall having seen him before." She sighed.

"You figure Larissa knew him?" Darien asked.

"Yeah. I was repotting some flowers in the shed out back and heard her squeal. I peeked out the window and saw him draw close to her, and then heard them exchanging angry words. So I assumed they knew each other."

"A red from her pack."

"That's what I figured. You know, this girl's as sweet as her sister, but a mite more…" Mrs. Hastings smiled. "Spirited. More of a tigress at heart. Be careful of this one. She may look like her sister, but she's not the same. Danger seems to follow her."

If *that* wasn't the understatement of the day. "Did Trevor search her room?"

"No. He talked to one of the twin girls staying here, but that was all. I asked if he wanted to search Lelandi's sister's room, but he said he had more important things to do, and he'd return later. He hasn't come back and that was a couple of hours ago."

Uncle Sheridan swore under his breath. Darien was going to tell his uncle to find out what Trevor's problem was, but the stormy look on his uncle's face told him he didn't have to.

"If you remember anything more, let us know."

"Sure thing." She poured water into a pitcher. "She's not leaving right away, is she?"

"Not until she's well enough to travel."

"Good." She gave him a sugary smile and went back to watering her plants.

Darien and his uncle headed down the hall.

"So what do you think?" Uncle Sheridan asked.

"Pack member for sure giving her a hard time for entering another pack's area without permission and getting herself into trouble. Maybe boyfriend. Doubt it's the brother she mentioned because if he was and suspected Lelandi had been murdered, he would have come instead of Larissa."

"Unless he *is* her brother and doesn't believe Lelandi was murdered."

Darien shook his head. "She indicated she didn't know where he was." The way she seemed so tearful, he believed her. "I bet the patch of fur we found in the woods was this guy's. He's probably hanging around near the hospital, somewhere out of sight."

Darien stuck the key in the door lock, but a window slid open inside. "Someone's inside." He unlocked the door, but something blocked it, and his blood instantly heated. "Around back."

They raced through the hallway and Mrs. Hastings scrambled out of the way, spilling the pitcher of water. Darien and his uncle dashed into the kitchen and banged the back door open. No sign of any intruder, but footprints had been left in the manicured lawn shaded by firs that edged the forest. They dashed to the back side of Larissa's room. The window was now locked and curtains pulled closed so they couldn't see a thing.

Uncle Sheridan grabbed a flowerpot and broke the glass with a loud crash, sending dirt, golden mums, and bits of clay pottery flying.

Mrs. Hastings would have a fit.

They cleared away enough of the glass, climbed through the window, and found the place neat as if the maid had just cleaned up, except for the dresser shoved against the door blocking it, and the mess his uncle had made.

Darien shook his head, figuring the intruder had come for the same piece of evidence he was looking for. He and Sheridan searched the lace-covered canopy bed, underneath it, the dressers, and bedside tables, the closet and the small bathroom and found nothing. Not a toothbrush, comb, bag, article of clothing, or anything else.

Then a slight elevation of the mattress on the right side of the bed caught Darien's eye. He strode over to the bed and yanked up the coverlet. The mattress rode high in one small spot. Shoving his hand between the mattress and box spring, he felt the grip of a pistol. His heart pounded harder. Pulling the 9mm out, he checked the safety, then removed the bullets and studied them.

"Silver," Uncle Sheridan growled as he examined them more closely. "That's grounds for throwing her in jail. Possessing a firearm with intent to kill a *lupus garou*. Hell, Darien, she's a loose cannon."

Darien tucked the gun in his belt and shoved the bullets in his pocket. "She's not a threat any longer."

Uncle Sheridan groused under his breath some more.

After moving the dresser out of the door's path, they returned to the lobby to see Mrs. Hastings, her face ashen. She scooted a mop around on the wood floor, soaking up the water she'd spilled when he and his uncle nearly ran her over.

Darien handed her the key. "Someone was in the room and had blocked the door. We had to break the window. Just charge it to my account."

Mrs. Hastings took the key and moved around the counter. "The poor little thing really isn't safe." She glanced at the gun tucked in Darien's belt, and her eyes widened. "She was packing?"

"Was there anything else you can recall about her?" he asked, not wanting to get into it with his uncle over the gun again.

Mrs. Hastings pointed to the stairs winding up to a loft. "You might check up there. One of my teenaged guests told me a woman was reading a letter and crying.

When I investigated, it was Lelandi's sister. She must have wiped away her tears, and I didn't see any letter."

Uncle Sheridan hurried up the stairs to the loft.

"Do you remember anything else? Nothing was in her room to indicate she'd ever been there," Darien said.

"Emma cleaned up the rooms after the guests left for the day. She didn't mention anything." Mrs. Hastings looked at the gun again.

Uncle Sheridan stomped down the stairs and rejoined them. "Nothing."

As Darien suspected. The woman was as much a mystery as her sister. "Come on, Uncle Sheridan. Let's talk to the little lady again."

Tension filling every pore, Darien hovered over Larissa's hospital bed while Uncle Sheridan stood nearby, his arms folded. Sorely vexed with Trevor, Uncle Sheridan still couldn't locate him.

With her face cloaked in sleep, Larissa looked like a sweet, innocent angel. Yet in that petite body, the heart of a warrior beat.

When she groggily opened her eyes, Darien tried to keep a grip on his temper, but his voice verged on a low, menacing growl. "Where... is... the... damned... letter?"

His shock of white hair ruffled, Doc walked into Lelandi's hospital room. "I ordered bed rest, not constant interrogation of the young lady."

Darien gave him a disgruntled look. As much as he hated to admit it, he knew the doctor was right—but when it came to sorting out this situation with Lelandi and her sister, he needed answers and now!

If Lelandi had possessed the strength to smile, she would have. The white-haired man looked like a taller, older version of her cherished uncle. Too bad he'd left the pack when she was little and become a rogue, too much of an alpha to put up with the leader, but not strong enough to take over. Yet, Doc looked like he could stand his ground, and had a compassionate side that made him lovable like her uncle.

His eyes were the same color—dark amber. He had a manly chin and large hands. The same cheerful expression. Except when he confronted Darien. The doctor stared him down. Who would win the confrontation this time?

"You're the boss, but if you want to be the doctor, too, have at it. Otherwise, let the woman rest."

"I need some answers," Darien growled.

"Get them in the morning." Doc stood firm, his hands on his hips.

Darien motioned for Silva to leave.

Silva cast him an annoyed look, walked over to the bed, and patted Lelandi's hand. "I'll see you in the morning, sugar. Don't let the big bad wolves scare ya none."

Lelandi tried to manage a smile, but her body seemed beyond her control.

"Talk to you tomorrow, Uncle Sheridan," Darien said, dismissing him, too.

"Get with you if I have any late-breaking news." The sheriff inclined his head and gave the doctor a peeved look, then headed out of the room.

Darien took the seat where Silva had been sitting.

"Your brother's sleeping soundly. Finally got Sam to shut up. Think from the way he talks he'd been fighting World War III single-handedly. But she's been injured the worst of the bunch and needs to rest."

Darien glowered at her. "I hear you, Doc. But I have to know what we're up against."

Lelandi was sure she smiled that time, and Darien caught the look. She couldn't help it. Who'd ever think a gray could make the leader back down?

Darien crossed his arms and this time he gave her an evil smile back.

The doctor took a deep breath. "Peter's got guard duty. Trevor will follow him."

"Fine. Close the door on your way out, will you?"

The doctor nodded and retired from the room.

Darien glared at Lelandi, his brown eyes filled with fury.

She closed her eyes, unable to keep them open any longer. They burned, along with her skin, and the fever created an earth-shattering pounding in her head, like the time she went to a human rock concert—too much noise for a *lupus garou*'s sensitive hearing.

An hour later, she woke to rustling. Darien was searching through her purse. Lipstick, hairbrush, wallet loaded with cash, no credit cards, no driver's license, no name. She could have told him that.

He caught her eye, dumped her purse on the table and frowned, but he didn't question her. Man of his word. Good trait for a pack leader.

She must have drifted off to sleep again, because his low voice woke her when he spoke to the deputy in the hall. The smell of strong coffee reached her, then everything faded.

Until someone screamed, something crashed on the floor, and a slew of curses followed.

Lelandi's eyes popped open. *Holy crap!* Shapeshifting in her delirious state, the IV jerked out and dangling over the floor, the blasted hospital gown in between her front legs, Lelandi lay on her side in her wolf form. She hoped whoever cleaned bedsheets were *lupus garous,* because if not, humans would wonder why a patient shed red fur.

Darien and Trevor rushed into the room, instantly looked at the mess Ritka made on the floor, and then at Lelandi, drowsy red wolf extraordinaire.

"Odin's wounds, she's a royal," Darien said under his breath.

"Hell, Darien, if the word gets out, she'll have a whole mess of suitors. But if she's going to shapeshift without warning, she should be at the vet's," Trevor said.

Silva poked her head in.

"Get in and shut the door," Darien barked.

She scurried in, closed the door, and smiled at Lelandi. "My, my. She's a royal. Knocked that dye job right out. Told you so, boss."

"Shapeshift back," Darien commanded Lelandi.

Right. Just as soon as she had the strength. She yawned, stretched her legs, closed her eyes, and fell back to sleep.

When she managed to open her eyes again, she was in her human form, dressed in the hideous hospital gown, an IV stuck in her arm. Darien was sitting in the chair, his eyes glued to her as if he was waiting for the dawn to break, or maybe to ensure she didn't shapeshift back.

He'd grill her about the letter again, although she wondered why he hadn't found it concealed in her jacket yet. Unless she'd lost it. A deep-seated sadness slipped through her.

She shut the sight of Darien out and slept, but the squeaking of the door woke her when Nurse Grey entered the room to check her vital signs. The woman held her finger to her smiling lips and pointed to Darien, dead to the world, sitting upright in the chair. The nurse left her alone again, and Lelandi watched the gray. Proud, angry, his stern face almost saintly. In a heartbeat, she wanted to know what being his mate would be like, to feel his impassioned kiss against her mouth again, and so much more. Her heart sank when she realized how futile that notion was.

In sleep, the woman of Darien's dreams stood naked in a birch grove, watching him, her green eyes reflecting sadness, her hair stirred by the autumn breeze, dangling past her creamy hips.

Lelandi, his redheaded goddess.

He stalked toward her, her face lighting with desire. She twirled a red curl around her finger, tantalizing him all the more, although even without any encouragement, he was ready to take his fill of her.

Lelandi, he wanted to call out. But he had no control over the speaking part of the dream. He couldn't hear the birds in the trees or the breeze whistling through the leaves. He couldn't smell the pine needles or spruce or whether they were due for a shower, although the thunderous clouds building in the night sky indicated they would get a burst of rain soon. All he could do was feast his eyes on the vision before him, touch her, feel her soft as silk skin beneath his, the texture of her satiny hair, her heart beating beneath his... but he couldn't hear it, as if more than half his wolf senses had lost touch with reality.

She melted in his arms, her head resting against his chest, her arms clinging to him as if she never wanted to let go. He sensed she needed more, too, as if the dream was the most fragile connection, the tentative bond they shared never enough. How could he still find her here in his fantasy world, when in the real one she was gone? Forever, gone. He stroked her hair, kissed her head, wished he could smell the sweet fragrance cloaking her, smell her aroused state. Her nipples rubbed against his chest, kissable, tight, rose-colored nubs.

Lelandi, he mouthed against her cheek. Her gaze turned up, focusing on him. Her eyes had grown so big and green—greener than... than Lelandi's eyes? He combed his fingers through her hair, the strands shimmering in the moonlight. Redder than Lelandi's?

No... no, she was Lelandi. She responded to the name. She was the one he'd mated, the one he loved. He'd prove it to her once again, even if she was no more than his fantasy lover. He bent down and kissed her mouth, gently at first—but it wasn't enough. Touching her like this was never enough. He wanted to bury himself deep inside her, wanted to claim her, wanted to be part of her forever.

His tongue swept across her lips, and she parted them, inviting him in. He took advantage, deepened the kiss, pressed his mouth harder against her soft, velvet lips, tangoed his tongue with hers. His hands held her shoulders as he felt her falling away, so caught up in the kiss. His mouth smiled against hers, loving how she melted under his simple kisses. Thumbs caressing her shoulders, he let himself go, every molecule absorbing the feel of her, the heat coursing through his veins, the sweet softness of her calling to him.

Lelandi. But how could she be this real and no longer part of his life?

She moaned, encouraging him, her body slipping down to the sweet bed of grass beneath their feet. He took control, her eyes and mouth willing him to continue. God, she was so beautiful.

Pressing her legs apart, he quickly entered her before his fantasy lover vanished. Her fingers swept over his backside, pressuring him to delve deeper. His mouth tackled hers again, and he weighed her breasts, lifting, caressing the hardened nipples, loving the way she responded so promptly to his touch.

"How could I have lost you...," he whispered against her lips. "When all I ever wanted was to keep you safe."

It was him, really him. Lelandi loved the way he made her feel—loved, special, his. She opened her lips to speak, but when she couldn't say anything, he tongued her mouth again, his erection spearing her deeper and deeper. She arched her pelvis, wanting to reach the moon and back.

Why couldn't she see his face clearly? As if the dark side of the moon cloaked it in blackness. Why couldn't she hear his name when he knew hers so well? As if he *controlled the dream—the alpha male in charge. Why couldn't she have him in the real world when the night faded and the day renewed?*

"Ahh," she moaned, her body shuddering with climax as he filled her with his seed, and she wanted it to be real. She wanted to find him and be with him forever, not just for fleeting moments in her dream world.

Then a horrible pain radiated through her chest, and she tried to ignore it, tried to concentrate on her lover's lips, the only part of his face she could see. They were parted, grim, as if he recognized the pain she felt.

Lelandi, his lips mouthed.

She tried closing her eyes and pretending the pain wasn't shrieking across every nerve ending, her head ready to explode.

Lelandi, he said again, more vehemently, and his hard body began to fade away.

She couldn't lose him. Not now when she needed his comforting touch. But he was fading... fading...

"No!" she cried out.

Chapter 8

DARIEN HOVERED OVER LELANDI, REACHING FOR THE NURSE'S call button, his other hand on hers. No, she wouldn't take any more pain medication and become a zombie again, despite how much the pain filtered through every nerve ending with acute clarity.

Nurse Grey walked into the room and looked from Lelandi to Darien with a questioning gaze.

"She's hurting pretty badly," Darien said.

"No." Lelandi shook her head. "I can manage."

"No sense in putting up with it." Nurse Grey reached for the IV line. "Might as well be comfortable."

"No." Lelandi narrowed her eyes, giving the nurse and Darien a dagger of a look and tried to pull away from the IV. "I don't want any more."

Both Darien and Nurse Grey gave small smiles.

She wanted to jerk her hand out of his, and in fact she thought she'd tried, but he kept her hand hostage.

He looked down at her with such concern, a hint of confusion, even a touch of desire, she wasn't sure what had come over him. Gone seemed to be the need to make her confess about who she was and everything about her.

She swore his hand tightened on hers even though she felt her body slipping away, the pain medication zipping through her veins. Fine. Damn it. She'd find her fantasy lover. Somewhere. *Forget... the... real... worl...*

❖ ❖ ❖

Frustration filling every pore, Darien wanted his mate back. How could her sweet body torment him in his dreams still? Even now as he checked on Jake waiting to speak to him about the silver mine in the hall outside Larissa's room, he felt distracted, ill at ease, like a part of his soul had been ripped away. She had been a drug he couldn't get his fill of, and though six eligible females existed in his pack, only one would do—the petite woman of his dreams—and now she was dead.

Lelandi.

Jake studied him, then frowned. "Another bad night?"

Darien gave him a look like he'd better not go there.

Jake shook his head. "I'll get on with the business at the silver mine." He muttered under his breath as he stalked off, "Better there than here. Got to find another mate, brother, and give up the ghost. She's gone. You have to own up to it sometime."

Gone.

Would finding another mate stop the dreams?

He snorted. Even when he'd been with Lelandi, the dreams had continued. The fantasy, so much better than the real thing.

He glanced at Deputy Peter Jorgenson sitting on a chair, pulling guard duty. "Need a break?"

"Thanks, boss. Trevor just relieved me. I'll be here for another two hours."

Time to go home and try to get some much needed sleep. But if Darien could find Lelandi in the woods, even if it was only in his dreams… he'd forgo sleep for an eternity.

❖ ❖ ❖

The next morning, Lelandi sat up in bed, her head partially cleared, no restraints, although the medication still dulled her senses. Otherwise, she would have sensed the brooding man sitting in the room. Jake's eyes opened wider when it registered she was awake. Darien must have given up and gone home.

Jake stroked his whiskered chin for a minute. Finally he spoke, his voice condemning. "He doesn't want you. He sees you as *her*."

Nobody had to tell her Darien saw her as Larissa. Swallowing hard, Lelandi hoped at least her vocal cords had returned to normal after the snake had strangled them. She still didn't feel she had any energy, but at least she felt no pain. Her throat dry, she noticed her water cup was empty. The water pitcher was too far away to reach, but she wasn't asking grumpy to get it for her. The other solution was to hit the nurse call button. If Ritka was manning the desk, she might dump the water on Lelandi, or ignore her completely. Besides, Lelandi was used to fending for herself.

"He's already been through the wringer enough over your sister without having to go through the same thing with you. Damn it, woman, he needs to heal."

Like she didn't? Jake was talking about *her* sister! She'd loved her just as much as Darien had. Why else did they think she was here? To avenge her sister's death, damn it!

Lelandi twisted her mouth, her throat feeling drier by the second, probably because of the medication she was taking. Indecision caught hold. Should she try to go back to sleep, or get the water herself?

"He should have mated Trevor's sister. Hell, none of this would have happened if he had."

She ground her teeth. Trevor's sister? No wonder the guy didn't like her. But she would not give in to Jake's challenging her. Jake knew she wanted some water, but he made it clear he wasn't about to help her. Fine, she didn't need a gray's help anyway.

"I told him to leave her alone. That she wasn't right for him. He doesn't need you messing with his head, too."

Lelandi glowered at Jake. She had no intention of "messing" with Darien's head. Leaning over, she reached for the water pitcher. A cold draft sent shivers down her back where her gown opened up. Her head filled with fog, and she paused, nausea filling her belly, dizziness washing over her. *Slow. Take it nice and slow.*

The chair scooted back across the industrial-strength carpeting covering the floor and footsteps hurried in the direction of the hall.

She closed her eyes to shut out the dizziness when Jake said, "Get Ritka. The woman passed out."

What woman?

Lelandi opened her eyes, her thoughts still fuzzy. She had to get off this blasted medicine that made her feel so out of control.

Jake stalked back into the room. "Lie still. Go back to sleep."

Ignoring him, she tried for the water again. As soon as she leaned over the bed railing, her stomach and head started dog paddling, and she felt herself quickly going under.

"Damn it, woman." Jake laid his hand on her

shoulder and pushed her back, his touch gentle, his stern face anxious.

Nurse Grey stalked into the room. "What's the matter?"

"She needs those restraints back on."

Lelandi glowered at him. "Water." She limply lifted her hand and pointed to the container.

"She passed out twice and was about to do the same again."

"Trying to get the water herself?" Nurse Grey asked, her tone annoyed while she took Lelandi's temperature.

He shrugged. "She didn't ask."

"And you weren't going to offer. Take a seat, and roll up your sleeve."

"What… ?"

"Come on, tough guy. The little lady needs more of your blood. That's why she's passing out."

"Hell, I already gave her a river's worth."

The nurse *tsk*ed. "A big alpha male like you can give a little more."

Lelandi wished she were feeling more with it, able to respond, as she dearly would love to laugh out loud at the look on Jake's face. More than disgruntled. Every bit of blood she'd get from him was spitting fire.

Good. Maybe it would give her some energy.

After getting some sleep and feeling somewhat better, Darien walked into Larissa's room, saw his brother giving her blood again, and came to a dead stop. "What the hell's going on?"

Jake scowled at him. "You could have given her blood when you were here last. This is the second go around for me."

Larissa's face was still ghostly pale. "Feeling any better?" He sure as hell hoped so or he'd never get the truth out of her.

She nodded, but she seemed to be nearly as out of it as the night before. He guessed he shouldn't have insisted she got more pain medicine when she'd objected so strenuously. Still, hearing her groaning in the middle of the night...

"I gave her some more pain medication about an hour ago. It seems to be kicking in," Nurse Grey warned.

"Can I ask you a question?" he asked Larissa in the most sweet-mannered way he could manage.

Jake raised a brow.

Larissa headed off Darien's question. "Room broken into."

Her voice was clearer, not as raspy, but she sounded weary. "So Uncle Sheridan came by already and talked to you about it."

"An hour ago," Jake said as Nurse Grey released him.

Now *he* looked a little peaked.

"Come on, Jake. You can lie down in room five until you feel more yourself." Nurse Grey helped him up.

"Good thing we can manufacture blood more quickly than humans." Jake gave Darien another dirty look. "Next time, it's your turn."

"Wrong blood type." The nurse held Jake's arm as they walked out of the room.

"Good excuse," Jake said. "Hey, we're triplets. He's got the same blood..." His voice trailed off down the hall.

Darien pulled the chair closer to the bed. "The guy who broke into your place must have stolen your bag. Did Uncle Sheridan tell you that?"

She took slow, shallow breaths. "Gun."

"I found your gun. What had you planned to do? Shoot someone you thought killed your sister? You can't take matters into your own hands, damn it."

She stared at the ceiling for a minute as if trying to remember what had happened. Her eyes drifted to the bed, then she closed them.

"What's your family's name? Where are your parents?"

She stared straight through him. "Lelandi. Parents..." She swallowed hard. "Killed, accident."

"I'm sorry to hear it." But he hadn't even known his mate had a family, and he still wasn't sure Larissa had been telling the truth so he was having a tough time feeling any sympathy. "What did the letter say?"

"*Lupus* blackmailing her."

Darien's heart nearly stopped. "What, who—"

She studied the blanket, her fingers twisting the thin fabric.

"Yours or mine?"

Larissa looked up at him, her eyes revealing confusion.

"Do you think it was one of my grays or one of your reds?"

She didn't answer, which made him suspicious. "Why would anyone blackmail her?" Darien considered Lelandi's nightmares, her reluctance to discuss her past with him. It fit. When he opened his mouth to question Larissa, she had shut her eyes again. "Larissa?"

She didn't respond and appeared to be sleeping. He growled under his breath, swore he would not tell anyone to give her any more pain medication if she needed it, and took his seat again.

Two painfully long hours later, Larissa opened her eyes, and immediately Darien launched in with his questioning, determined to get the truth out of her this time. "What about the man who accosted you outside of Hastings?"

"Gunman?"

Being evasive on purpose? Or confused again? "No, the hooded man in the copper coat."

Instantly, her already pale face turned whiter.

"Larissa?"

She scowled. "No one."

He clenched his fists. "If he's from your pack and he followed you here, angered you'd be investigating this, it might be something."

Closing her eyes, she shook her head.

"Fine, when we catch the bastard, we'll find out all we want to know." He paused, waiting for her to give in. When she didn't, he started in on her again. "He broke into your room, got physical with you—"

"I… I don't think he broke into my room."

"How do you know?"

She didn't respond.

"Got physical with you then." Darien barely curbed his rage. Why did she protect the bastard?

"Little angry."

Darien paced across the floor. *He* was a little angry? *I'm* a little angry. Who the hell is he? And where is that damned letter? In your bag? Did you even have a bag?"

Deputy Peter knocked on the door and poked his face in. "A deputy sheriff's here who picked up a red *lupus garou* matching the little lady's description, hitchhiking. He's from Green Valley. Want to talk to him?" Peter's expression said there was lots more, but he didn't want to say in front of the patient.

Darien cast Larissa a smug smile. "Yeah, I sure do."

Silva sneaked a peek in the room, waving a bag from Chipper's Donuts like a white flag, the aroma of glazed icing, chocolate, and pastries filling the air. Silva smiled at Lelandi. "I brought some chocolate iced donuts. Sounds like we need some cheering-up food in here."

"Ask her who the guy was who accosted her behind Hastings before she came chasing after me at the tavern." He smiled at Larissa when her face reddened, then stalked toward the door. "Where's this witness at, Peter?"

"Doc's office. He said you could question him there."

"Good. Now maybe we'll get some answers." Darien left the room and headed down the hall.

"You know, sugar, you sure have him wrapped around your little finger. I've never seen him so out of control when he's around you. I'd say he can't decide whether to strangle you or kiss you." Silva set a donut on Lelandi's tray. "Coffee?"

Definitely he wanted to strangle her. And the feeling was mutual. "Milk?" Lelandi asked.

"Sure, darlin'. Be right back." Silva walked outside the room. "Want some donuts, Trevor?"

"What's she done to rile Darien this time?" Trevor grumbled.

Jeez, couldn't the guy ever say something nice to Silva?

"You know him when he hasn't had enough sleep. He's always a bear."

When *wasn't* he a bear?

Silva waved at Lelandi. "Off to get your milk."

Lelandi took a deep breath and allowed herself a self-satisfied smile. Darien could question the deputy sheriff from Green Valley all he wanted, but she didn't tell him a thing about herself that he could trace back to the pack.

She lifted her donut off the tray when Ritka walked in, her bruised and swollen eye back to normal—*too bad*.

"You're supposed to be eating the breakfast Doc ordered for you." She jerked the donut out of Lelandi's hand and dumped it in the trash.

Stunned into inaction, Lelandi's mouth gaped, and she stared at the wastepaper basket.

Ritka took her temperature. "Ninety-nine, point nine. Heard you had a break-in at your room last night. No suitcase. Just a gun—with silver bullets. But the most interesting news? That deputy sheriff who picked you up and gave you a ride here? He took your picture on his cell phone and scanned it through his database. Seems one pissed-off pack leader is looking for you and has offered a reward for your immediate return. A big reward." Ritka sneered at her. "Guess you won't be staying here long."

Lelandi's heart skipped several beats. If that bastard Crassus got hold of her, she'd have to kill him because he wasn't beating on her again. *Ever.*

Ritka got into her face. "What do you think about that?" She straightened and plastered a faux sympathetic expression on her face. "You look a little pale. Don't want to go back? Too bad. Now you can't have Darien, bitch."

Silva walked into the room with a glass of milk, her face scowling. "Finished with nursing business, Ritka?"

"You're a visitor, so stuff it. I can have your butt kicked out of here just like that." Ritka snapped her fingers.

"Larissa, you okay, honey? You don't look too well." Silva hurried over to the bed.

Tears rolled down Lelandi's cheeks. She couldn't help it. Probably was the pain medication. Maybe it was the fact she didn't have the strength to fight or flee. This was so not like her!

"What did you say to upset Larissa?" Silva accused Ritka, her voice angry.

"Lelandi," she sobbed. At least they could get her name right!

"You're just a dumb barmaid who reads literary books to try to make yourself feel smarter. Probably don't understand most of what you read. But you're a—"

Lelandi yanked the IV out of her arm and gritted her teeth against the pain. The medication had to go. It was making her say things she was sure she shouldn't. It was making her lethargic, dopey, and now weepy. It was keeping her in bed when she had to run. But most of all she wanted her damned chocolate donut back.

"What the hell do you think you're doing?" Ritka screamed, grabbing Lelandi's arm.

Pain stabbed through Lelandi's arm and chest. She swung her free arm and poked her fist into Ritka's other eye, then everything faded to black.

Darien walked into Doc's office and found Deputy Sheriff Smith, a tall, lean, uniformed man, sitting on the leather love seat, reshaping the brim of his

Stetson. He quickly rose and crossed the floor to shake Darien's hand.

He motioned for the deputy to take a seat, although Darien remained standing. "Tell me what you know."

Smith explained how he'd run a trace on her, worried she might be in trouble. Being that she was a pretty red loner *lupus garou,* he was afraid someone might grab her. "Before I knew it, here comes this frantic request for any information on the missing girl. The pack leader said his name was Leidolf."

Darien should have been pleased to hear that Leidolf was her pack leader and wanted her returned at once. So why the hell did Darien want to dismiss it as a case of mistaken identity?

"Did Deputy Peter Jorgenson tell you anything about what's going on here with Larissa?"

Smith bowed his head once. "I understand one of her own people, or one of yours, might have shot the woman. The assistant mayor of Green Valley, Chester McKinley, was here at the time of the shootings and being that he is also a licensed P.I. and concerned for the lady's welfare, he asked I keep this just between you and me. By the way, the name the leader gave for her was Lelandi."

Darien's stomach clenched into knots, and he looked at the floor as the feelings of desolation swamped him again. "He doesn't know she's dead."

"Apparently not. But I didn't find a similar request for a girl who looked identical to her. Probably misplaced."

"Where's he from?"

"Portland, Oregon."

In astonishment, Darien raised his brows. Why in the world had the two women come all the way to Colorado?

"Surprised me, too. I got the impression she was a local girl. I was trying to find out where she was from and started mentioning some of the wildflowers native to Colorado. She offered me the names of others she'd seen. I asked if she was from down South, but she said, 'No, Denver.' So when I got the notice some guy in Oregon is claiming she's missing from his pack, I was pretty darned surprised. What do you want me to do?"

"Sit on it. I need to find out what's going on before she goes home." Darien couldn't believe he said it. But something didn't ring true about this Leidolf character. And Darien wasn't letting her out of his sight until he found the shooter. "If you hear anything more, let me know."

"Sure will." The deputy gave him a sly smile. "I wouldn't let her go either, if I were in your shoes."

Darien let the comment slide, figuring the deputy didn't know the situation well enough to understand. As soon as Smith left, Darien called Peter in. "I know how difficult it is to locate packs or anything about them as secretive as we need to be, but I've got a lead. See if you can find a Leidolf out of Portland, Oregon. I want to know everything about him and his pack."

"Yes, sir, will do."

Intent on learning what Doc needed to speak to him about, Darien headed to the lounge where three of his cousins were talking to the doctor. As soon as his cousins spied him, everyone stopped speaking.

"Every time I walk into a room it gets awfully damned quiet. Someone planning a hostile takeover?" Darien only half-joked. If enough of his members got fed up with his leadership, one of the bolder males might just feel the need to end his role.

Before anyone could respond, a petite blonde wearing a black business skirt and jacket leaned over the check-in counter and raised her voice. "Listen, Angelina, I've given you my résumé and I just want to talk to the doctor about a job."

Angelina gave a snort. "Doc's not the one you have to convince. Darien Silver's the most important one on the hospital board, and he's calling the shots."

Now what? Darien sure as hell didn't need to deal with this right now.

"Come into my office, Darien. You might want to sit down when I tell you the latest," Doc said.

"Wait!" The blonde ran after Darien and Doc and stopped in front of them.

Holding out her hand, she gave them a broad smile. *Totally faked.* Human, pretty, with the biggest and clearest blue eyes Darien had ever seen.

"Hi. You might not know me, but Doctor Oliver set my broken leg when I was ten after a whitewater rafting accident and after that, I always wanted to be a nurse. I earned a nursing degree in Denver, and here I am."

Hoping to nip this in the bud from the outset, Darien didn't shake her hand. She quickly dropped hers to her side, her smile fading. "I'm not new at this. I trained well before I returned home." Her voice had taken on a tinge of annoyance. "My parents still live here. Dad's a carpenter. Mom has a home business and sells pottery crafts. I've never wanted to work anywhere else, but the lady at the front desk won't give my résumé to the doctor." The blonde shoved her résumé at Darien. "I'm Carol Wood, by the way."

Darien didn't take the résumé. "Check with the school. They can use a nurse. Just tell them I sent you."

The perky woman's face fell to the floor. "But…"

"The staff's full here. We don't need anyone else."

She folded her arms. "I've heard there's been a lot of trouble. Gunshot victims. More people moving in. You'll need more staff. At least, try me."

"Apply at the school. If someone quits here…" Darien shrugged. "You might get lucky."

She glanced at Doc, but he confirmed Darien's decision. "Mr. Silver is right. We don't need any more nurses for the time being." He motioned for Darien to follow him.

"See the school principal, Miss Wood." Darien headed with the doctor down the hall.

The woman's blood pulsed at a quickened pace, and she wasn't happy with his decision. He highly suspected that wasn't the last he'd hear of it either.

Doc led Darien into his office and shut the door.

The lingering aroma of chocolate donuts filled the air and a paper plate with remnants of chocolate glaze sat in the middle of his otherwise neat oak desk, everything in its place as usual, the heavyweight brass caduceus sitting on a stack of medical notes he'd transcribe later.

"Carol Wood sent me letters before she finished nursing school. I didn't mention it to you before because so many of the students drop out before they finish their programs. She's persistent, if nothing else."

"We can't have a human working in the hospital. Not when our people heal so fast."

Doc sat down at his desk. "What about assigning her to human cases only?"

"Too much of a nightmare to keep up with. What if she checked on a *lupus garou* patient like Larissa because the rest of the staff was busy? Can you imagine what she'd think if she saw the injuries, then Larissa leaves the hospital so soon after? If Larissa had been human, she would have died from the massive injuries she'd sustained." Darien shook his head and looked out the window at the majestic mountains. "Having one of their kind on the hospital staff isn't feasible." He took a deep breath and switched topics. "What did you want to talk to me about?"

"Because of her injuries, I ran tests to see if she was pregnant. She wasn't. Then I examined her to see if she was a virgin."

Knowing damn well why he was checking, Darien scowled at him. He wasn't mating with the red.

"She *is* a virgin. Which means she doesn't have a mate."

Although he fought feeling anything about the situation one way or another, Darien felt relieved. He told himself it was because he didn't want to have to deal with her irate mate if he came looking for her.

Doc leaned back in his leather chair. "The other news is someone tried to strangle Larissa after she'd been shot."

Darien felt he'd been kick-dropped off a cliff. "Why the hell didn't you tell me this before?"

"She needs rest more than anything—not a lot of questioning. I've already asked her if she saw who did it. But she was probably unconscious or nearly so and didn't remember anything. She said a snake strangled her, then slithered away when she heard voices. Yours and Jake's."

"A snake? We don't have anacondas or boa constrictors here."

"Her barely conscious imagination. He left bruises on her throat. Since she was wearing a turtleneck, you wouldn't have seen the marks. She was so battered from her fall, you might not have noticed now that she's wearing a hospital gown. Either he thought he had finished her or he heard you and Jake approaching and vanished."

"Hell, Doc, I need the area we found her in combed for evidence. I thought only Jake and I had been there with her. If we can find other footprints, size of shoe, scent, anything…"

"I asked your uncle to investigate, but not to tell you until I had a chance to discuss this with you."

Darien would not have this insubordination! No one withheld information from him that was this important! He opened his mouth to say so when Ritka shrieked from the direction of Larissa's hospital room.

Chapter 9

SILVA AND RITKA FOUGHT WITH EACH OTHER NEXT TO Lelandi's bed, as she tried to ignore the yelling. Jake leaned against the doorframe, shaking his head.

Until Darien and the doctor stalked into the room and Darien shouted, "Enough! What the hell happened?" He appeared somewhat rattled, his face slightly drained of color, and he studied Lelandi a little too closely. Her neck actually.

She took a deep, settling breath. *Good, peace and quiet now that the boss man has arrived.*

"She hit me!" Ritka screamed.

Yeah, and if they hadn't restrained me, I'd do it again!

"We can see," Darien said calmly. "I want to know why."

Lelandi fought to find the words, but the IV was hooked up to her arm again, and she figured heavier duty drugs were pouring into her veins because she could barely concentrate on what was being said, let alone keep her eyes open.

"She ripped out the IV and when I tried to stop her, the bitch hit me."

"You grabbed her sore arm and yanked her back so hard, pain filled her face. That's why she hit you," Silva scolded. "Haven't you ever heard of a good bedside manner?"

"Yeah," Lelandi said, slurring her word.

Without taking his eyes off Lelandi, Darien said to Ritka, "What did you say to her?"

Ritka shrugged. "Nothing of consequence."

"I just bet." Darien glowered at her like she was next on the head-chopping block. "Why isn't she any better, Doc?"

"Low-grade fever. She needs to stay until tonight at least. I'll see then how she's doing." The doctor motioned for Ritka to leave.

She glared at Lelandi, then stomped out of the room.

"Did Larissa say anything to you, Jake?" Darien asked.

"Not a word."

"Talked... 'bout... you... an'... me." Lelandi tried to scowl at Jake.

Darien shifted his attention to his brother, whose ears immediately tinged crimson. "You and I'll speak later. Did she say anything to you, Silva?"

"Nope. And whatever Ritka said to her happened before I arrived. She looks pretty glassy-eyed, Darien. Don't think she's really with it."

"What did she say to you?" Darien reached his hand out to touch Lelandi's, but then he seemed to think better of it and shoved his hands in his pocket.

"About... green... dep'ty."

Darien's eyes rounded. "She told you about the deputy sheriff from Green Valley?"

She managed a slow nod.

"Shit." He looked back at her neck and shook his head. "A snake, huh?"

Lelandi closed her eyes and hoped she'd be able to keep her mouth shut until they took her off the pain medication. Otherwise, she'd have to make up wild stories to mix in with whatever else she said.

Then she remembered her damned donut and lifted her finger at the wastepaper basket. "Donut," she mumbled.

After she fell asleep, Darien motioned to Jake to come with him. "I want to know what the hell you said to Larissa."

Jake shook his head. "She's a wildcat. Where Lelandi was too much of an angel, this one has the devil in her."

They walked into Doc's empty office to talk.

Jake shut the door. "But I really don't think she should go to our home."

"It's the safest place for her for the time being. But that's not what I want to talk about. What did you say to her?"

Looking defiant, Jake shoved his hands in his pockets. "I told her you've already been through hell with her sister. You don't need to have to deal with her, too. As for taking her to the house, you know how the rumors will fly."

"I'm not interested in having her for a mate, but it's my business, not yours. I'll deal with her as I see fit. Understand?"

"Yeah," Jake said grudgingly. "So what's the deal with this deputy sheriff from Green Valley and snakes?"

Darien explained everything, and how their uncle was investigating the crime scene where they'd found Larissa. "Did you see or smell anything when we were with her?"

Jake shook his head. "I was concentrating on alerting the rest of our pack that we'd found the lady, and then we learned Sam had been shot."

"Could the guy who strangled her be the same one who shot the gunman? Distance-wise, do you think he could have made it up there in time?"

"We don't know when he left her."

Darien frowned in thought. "Probably when we were drawing close. He heard our voices."

"Then there must be two of them."

"Great." Darien ran his hands through his hair. "Now that I recall, I distinctively smelled the odor of decomposing leaves, but no smell of any *lupus garou* in human form, just that god-awful perfume Larissa was wearing. Do you think the perpetrator was wearing human's hunter spray to disguise his scent?"

"I'll have Uncle Sheridan check out the location and see if rotting leaves were in the vicinity. Now that you mention it, I smelled it also. But remember the red I got a whiff of?"

"He was in wolf form and couldn't have strangled her."

"True. What about this Leidolf? Are you sure we shouldn't contact him?"

"We don't know who he is really. Peter is looking into it. What I want to know is did she have a bag and if so, was it stolen?"

Jake stared out the window at the mountain view where clouds perched on top in a mist, coating the peaks like whipped topping. "Trevor questioned Mrs. Hastings who said her grandkids were visiting when Larissa checked in, so she was distracted and didn't see if Larissa had a bag or not. She paid in cash and—"

"What name did she register under?"

"Melanie Weber."

His eyes narrowed, Darien thought about the name. "The name sounds familiar." He rubbed his chin as he thought back to her earlier comments. "She kept asking to see a Doctor Weber. He's got to be real." Darien glanced at Doc's medical degrees and other certificates displayed across the wall, updated periodically over the decades to make it appear Doc wasn't as old as he was. "I want you to find anybody by that name in the state who's a practicing physician."

"But Leidolf says she's from Portland."

"Deputy Smith said he was sure she was from Colorado. Another thing, Larissa said she received a letter from Lelandi before she died. It wasn't in her purse. If it was in her bag, it's gone. Apparently, a *lupus* was blackmailing Lelandi."

Jake swore under his breath. "One of ours?"

If it led to her death, whoever had been black-mailing Darien's mate was a dead *lupus garou*. "The letter didn't say."

"Larissa told you this when she was out of it?"

"She seemed pretty lucid, but she might not have been. Hell, I don't know."

"Where else could the letter be?" Jake asked.

"Maybe she burned it in the fireplace, or hid it somewhere else at the B&B. Mrs. Hastings mentioned Larissa was holding a letter in her lap in the loft and a teenaged guest said Larissa had been crying. It must have been the letter."

The answer struck them at once. "Her clothes," they said simultaneously.

They hastened back to her room where Larissa was still sound asleep, and Darien jerked open the metal locker. Empty.

"I'll find out what happened to them," Jake said.

Apparently eavesdropping from the hallway, Silva walked into the room. "I took them home to wash."

"Silva," Darien said, annoyed.

She smiled. "Sorry, bad habit of mine. Used to overhearing conversations in the bar. Guess because my life is dull at times."

"Her clothes?"

"They were bloody so I took them home to wash. Cleaned her jeans. With the bullet holes in it, the shirt was a total loss. She'll need a new peach lace bra to match her panties, if anyone's interested." Silva paused for effect.

Darien could have wrung her neck, although she got the result she wanted. The image of Larissa's lace bra and the creamy mounds they had confined came to mind. He knew damn well what she'd looked like beneath the turtleneck, and he didn't want to be reminded.

"I cleaned the lining of her leather jacket, too, but it'll need some patchwork. Oh, and I washed your shirt, too."

"The letter?" he asked, too angrily.

Smiling, Silva pulled an envelope from her pocket. "I had to soak up the blood, so the letter's a little hard to read in spots. Found it in a hidden pocket inside her leather jacket. It crinkled when I was mopping up the blood on the lining, otherwise I probably would have missed it."

"Why didn't you mention it before?" He stretched his hand out for the envelope.

She withheld it. "I was waiting for you to be in a better mood. Appeared that wasn't going to happen anytime soon."

Darien seized the letter from her.

"You might want to sit down when you read it."

"Larissa already told me what it said." He yanked the letter out of the envelope, barely aware Jake stood breathing down his neck to get a glimpse of it.

"Then you already know your mate had a living husband."

Darien jerked his head up and stared at Silva, not believing her words.

Silva folded her arms and looked smug.

Hell, he knew it. His worse nightmare realized. *Lupus garous* didn't divorce. They mated for a lifetime and only mated again if they lost their lifemate, *if* they found someone else they couldn't live without. That meant a female was a virgin when first mated unless she was widowed, or in rare cases had been with a human. Lelandi hadn't been a virgin. Too hung up on her to learn anything he didn't want to know, he hadn't questioned her.

He sat down hard on the chair next to Larissa's bed, hating that Silva knew how horrible the news hit him. So was it a red blackmailing Lelandi for mating a gray when she was already mated to a red? Or a gray who'd learned the truth, blackmailing her so that he wouldn't tell Darien? But why kill her?

Staring at the letter, he couldn't make himself open it. Now he wondered if the man who had accosted Larissa had been Lelandi's mate.

Her nightmares were now becoming his own.

Jake stood next to the chair, waiting.

  Pack leaders had to keep their packs together. No matter what, Darien had to get through whatever life dealt him. Clenching his teeth, he opened the letter and began to read.

Dear Lelandi,

  He glanced up at Jake.
  "So the letter's from her," Jake said, jerking his thumb at Larissa. "It's not from her sister."

If you're reading this, I'm dead. Might as well say it like it is. You know me, that's the way I always could be with you. No one else. Just you, sis.

  "Hell, no, it can't be from her," Darien said, waving his hand at the hospital bed. "Not if the letter is supposed to be from the dead twin."
  "Then Lelandi was Larissa and Larissa was Lelandi? I'll never get it straight."
  Darien felt a colossal pool of tension collecting in his temple. The more he found out about his mate, the more he realized she wasn't who he thought she was. "Seems that way."
  "That's why she kept saying she was Lelandi when we called her Larissa. I thought her confusion was a direct result of her wounds, and then later from the medication."
  So what else had his mate lied about? Having a family, a pack, a husband, her name. Part of him wanted to know, but part of him wanted the secrets kept buried. What difference did it make to know all the sordid details now?

I could never be what you thought I should, the good daughter, the perfect wife, but you always forgave me as a sister. You tried to steer me right a million times, but I finally had to find my own way. Who would have ever thought little ol' me would end up with two husbands living at the same time, eh? Sorry, L. Just like the rest of our family, we don't exactly go along with pack rules. In our blood, I guess.

If I could do it all over again, I wouldn't have been born. Honest.

I wanted to be just like you. Hope you don't mind too terribly. Didn't try to cause you any trouble. Don't ever get hooked up with the wrong wolf, and then find the right one.

But if Darien was the right one, why was she so unhappy? None of it made any sense.

One of the lupus found out. He's been blackmailing me. Been getting death threats, too. If Darien learns about my other mate, he'll be wishing I'd died the first time around.

The fear she'd be found out—that's what made her so inconsolable.

I've made a real mess of things. Like I usually do with my life.

Give Mom and Papa my love. I know they're white-haired by now over all of my shenanigans. Love you, sis. Find the happiness I was never meant to have. Larissa

He looked at—*Lelandi,* still sleeping soundly, wondering how the hell Larissa had sent her the letter after she had died.

"Maybe we ought to let him have some private time?" Silva said to Jake.

"You need anything, Darien?" Jake asked.

He shook his head, feeling like his whole body had sifted through a grinder. Leaning back in the chair, he closed his eyes. He'd wanted his mate to tell him what upset her so.

Now he almost wished he didn't know.

Later that afternoon, Jake poked his head in the room while Lelandi slept soundly and said to Darien, "We've got problems with one of the leather tanning machines, and I really need help on this one."

Darien figured he didn't, but wanted to get his mind off his troubles. As it turned out, it took more than an hour to fix it and Darien was thankful for the diversion.

Returning to the hospital, Jake opened the back door. "I can't believe anyone could screw up the leather tanning machine that badly."

"At least no one was injured," Darien said, "like the last time."

Ritka sleeping at the nurse's station caught his attention. She could be a real bitch, but she always worked hard, never slacking off.

"What the hell."

Jake gave her arm a rough shake. "She's out cold."

Darien's stomach clenched, and he glanced down the

hall. A janitor was passed out next to a bucket of mop water, and Deputy Peter lay sprawled on the floor next to his chair in front of Lelandi's room.

"Shit." Darien bolted down the hall and slammed Lelandi's door open, the force banging it against the wall. Lelandi was gasping for air, a black plastic bag covering her face, suffocating her.

"Odin's teeth!" In a couple of bounds, he was beside her bed, digging his fingers into the bag, trying to rip it open, his heart thundering.

Before Lelandi was fully conscious, she felt she was suffocating, the room pitch black, yet with her wolf vision, she should see clearly. She tried to move her hands, but her wrists were bound again. She could barely breathe as something pressed against her face. Something clinging and black. No oxygen. Blacking out. Where were her guards? Inside room? Outside…

Holes began to appear in the plastic as someone frantically tore at it and finally ripped it away. She gasped for air. Darien's anxious face and the blinding lights of the hospital room appeared before her, while he continued to tear at the bag.

Filling her lungs, she tried to reach out to him. He paused while ripping the tape off around her neck, and took her hand and squeezed tight. "Jesus, Lelandi." He didn't say anything more, just held onto her hand and gazed into her eyes.

Jake rushed into the room. "What the hell." He grabbed her wrist. "Her pulse is frantic."

"Find out who all was at the hospital, who had access to the coffeepot in the common area, whose fingerprints are on it. I want to know how many were drugged and if everyone's all right." Darien finished removing the tape and bag from her neck and head.

Still holding her wrist, Jake remained beside her. "Pulse is more normal."

Darien seized the leather strap tying her right wrist, and Jake grasped the other and yanked it off.

"I want her home with us until we get somewhere with this investigation."

Lelandi breathed deeply, unable to comprehend what had happened.

"Did you see who did this to you?" Darien brushed a strand of hair from her cheek, holding her hand again with a firm but tender touch.

The nightmare she was living was getting worse. "I must have been sleeping. I was pretty groggy. What happened?"

"It appears somebody laced the coffee that the staff and visitors drink with heavy-duty sleep medicine."

Even Sam was sound asleep in the chair next to the wall.

"Just to get to me?"

Darien ran his hand over hers. "Looks that way."

"Doc said she could be released?" Jake asked.

"Yeah. Check on the others, will you?"

"Sure thing." Jake rushed out of the room.

"Why didn't you tell me you were Lelandi?"

She frowned. "I told… you. No one would listen."

"Tell me who she was mated to."

Lelandi looked away.

He wasn't used to being disobeyed and her actions thoroughly compounded his irritation concerning what her sister had done. But it wasn't Lelandi's fault, and he attempted to curb his temper. "I have to know who's got it in for you. Maybe knowing who she was mated to doesn't matter at this point, but I can't help but wonder if he had contracted someone to shoot you. Was that who accosted you behind Hastings?"

"No."

"Lelandi—"

"It wasn't!"

Taking a deep breath, he nodded. Her eyes held his hostage, and he couldn't believe how much he yearned to have her, like he'd wanted her sister. He looked down at his sweaty hands. She made him feel like a pup vying for a female's attention the first time around. She wasn't even in a wolf's heat, yet he desired her like he had no business wanting her.

He took another deep breath and looked at her. "Until I find some answers, you're staying with my brothers and me."

Her lips parted, but she promptly closed them.

He expected her to object, or say something. But she seemed so withdrawn, he wondered if the attempted murderer had drugged her also. "All right?"

She nodded.

"Silva cleaned your jacket and jeans, but I'm afraid your shirt and…" He glanced down at her breasts covered in the thin hospital gown, her nipples pressed against the fabric. He raised his brows. "She picked up a couple of items for you to wear."

She gave a tentative nod.

"Did one of the nurses give you more medicine?"

"I… I don't remember."

Before Darien responded, Silva pushed a wheelchair into the room. "Jake's really uptight about something, but he wouldn't say what. He told me to hurry this down here. What's going on?" She glanced at Sam. "Boy, I've never seen him sleep on guard duty before." She lifted the ripped-up black plastic sack off the table next to the bed. "What's this?"

Lelandi shuddered.

"A death mask," Darien said. "Get her dressed. She's going to my place, ASAP."

Darien shook Sam's arm and woke him. Blurry-eyed, he glowered at Darien.

"Come on. Let's get some caffeine into you."

"What… what the bloody hell happened?" Sam growled, rubbing his head, his eyes squinting. "I feel like I've pulled an all-nighter and have a *lupus*-sized hangover."

"You've been drugged." Darien helped Sam out of the room and slammed the door behind him.

"Who did this?" Sam bellowed. "I'll kill 'em."

"What in the world happened?" Silva carefully helped Lelandi to the edge of the bed.

"Someone put something in the coffee and knocked everyone out. Guy tried to suffocate me."

"Ohmigod, it's a good thing I don't drink coffee. I ran home to get another book to read, thinking you'd be here a while longer. But when I returned, I found Jake trying to wake Ritka and a janitor. Jake yelled at me to get a wheelchair for you and wouldn't say what was wrong. Was the person who tried to hurt you a guy or a woman?"

"I… I don't know."

"Darien's got to catch the bastard."

Although Lelandi was healing well, considering she'd been shot the night before last, she was sore and weak. Silva took her arm and helped her down from the bed, but Lelandi's head began to swirl into darkness, and Silva pushed her back onto the mattress.

Silva's hands trembled. "Sit. Uhm, I'll get Nurse Grey to help. You're less stable on your feet than I thought."

She hurried out of the room, but Lelandi didn't need half of the people at the hospital dressing her. She meant to climb off the bed, steady herself for a minute, then get dressed. But as soon as her feet touched the floor, her mind and stomach began floating out to sea and the table started to tilt. Except the table wasn't tilting, and she grabbed for it when she started to black out, pulling it crashing down on top of her.

Where the edge of the table landed, dull pain hit her thighs. So much for dressing herself. New bruises for sure, but at least she didn't hit her tender wounds. If she wasn't so groggy she would have screamed bloody murder for her ineptness.

Darien and Jake rushed into the room, their expressions horrified. *Crap.*

"Odin's knees," Darien said, and Jake echoed his sentiment.

He and his brother hurried to pull the table off her.

"We should leave her in the bed, restrained." Jake offered her a wry smile.

Lelandi managed a low, feeble growl.

Jake raised a brow and Darien had the gall to smile, although she didn't know what he thought was so damned funny. If his arm wasn't so far away from her teeth, she'd bite him.

"Oh no... oh no," Silva said, hurrying into the room. "I shouldn't have left you alone for a second. Nurse Grey's coming in a minute. She was trying to revive Doc, who's passed out in his office."

"Is he all right?" Darien lifted Lelandi off the floor, but one of his hands slipped inside the gown opening at the back. His heated fingers pressing against her naked skin sent her temperature soaring, and the look he gave her made her sure it unsettled him as much as it did her. He set her on the bed and adjusted her hospital gown to draw the skimpy fabric lower, past her knees. "Leave, Jake."

"What?"

"We're getting her dressed and out of here."

"I'm staying at your place." Silva pulled clothes out of a pink bag from Lacy Garments & Accessories. "She'll need me to help her dress and shower. So, plan on a slumber party, boys."

Jake shook his head and closed the door.

"You know, Silva, you can be a real pain in the ass." Darien slipped on Lelandi's sock, his back to her while Silva pulled off her gown.

"You love me anyway, boss." Silva winked at Lelandi. "I couldn't find a pretty lace bra to match your panties. This crummy place isn't very style conscious, though Lacy Garments & Accessories has some nice see-through nighties. If we wore such a thing. But I thought this white lace bra was pretty and cut a little lower so it wouldn't touch your wounds and irritate them." She drew the bra up to cover her.

Darien paused before he put on her other sock, and she wondered if he wanted to look to see how low-cut the bra was. It was low. Nearly exposed her nipples, *and* it was a push-up.

"Looks nice, sugar, although you really didn't need anything pushed up."

Darien's heart beat harder, and she could smell his sex again.

Silva was pushing the poor gray over the edge. "I bought you this nice, loose, button-down shirt so that it would be easy to dress."

Darien growled low. Or moaned. Lelandi's hearing wasn't what it should be either because of the medication.

"Help me get her jeans on, boss, and she'll be ready to go. She doesn't need to put her boots on. We have to wheel her out to your SUV, and I'll follow behind in my car."

Darien focused on the shirt, and then his gaze shifted to Silva, who shrugged. "Ready to help with the jeans?"

His eyes strayed to Lelandi's new panties, and she wished she could see what made them seem so appealing to him. He was having a time helping her into her jeans, although she imagined he'd be a whiz at taking them off. Why she was even thinking such a thing, she hadn't a clue.

The jacket was last, and it was heavy and cumbersome because she felt so weak. Once she sat in the wheelchair, Darien pushed her out of the room where Jake waited beyond the door.

Walking beside Darien, Jake said, "Everyone's

slowly waking from the drugged coffee—Doc, Ritka, the new janitor, parents of a patient, Peter, Sam, and Uncle Sheridan. But, man, was Uncle Sheridan hotter than a summer heat wave. Even in his half-groggy condition, he's ordering Trevor about, taping off the break room. He warned us the attempted killer probably didn't leave any fingerprints behind. Sam's throwing a beer and pizza party at our place later."

"What?"

"You missed the leader's meeting because you were investigating the shootings. Figured now that you're taking the lady to your house, you'll want to have the meeting. And," Jake said, "since his barmaid will be there, she can serve, like always."

Silva gave him a disgruntled look, although the annoyance appeared faked. Lelandi figured she loved being the center of attention in a room full of men. Or at least tried to be. Or was it that she secretly had a yearning for Sam?

Jake shoved his Stetson on his head and pushed the side door to the hospital open. "He said you've got to earn your keep somehow."

"Like I don't work lots of overtime so the guys can drink longer? Ahem, is Trevor going to be working guard duty?" Her voice sounded suspiciously hopeful.

Lelandi wanted to kick the deputy next time she saw him act disinterested in Silva when she wanted so much to please him. Why did women chase after men who showed them no affection in return?

"What are we going to do about the sleeping arrangements?" Jake asked.

Silva looked back at Darien. "Yeah, boss, who gets to sleep with whom?"

Lelandi held her breath, waiting for Darien's word, feeling a mixture of hope he wanted her, and at the same time wishing he'd want to steer clear of her. She had a mission to accomplish. She didn't *need* any more of his kisses. And she sure as hell didn't *want* them.

Her tongue traced her lips, just thinking of the way he'd kissed her, and she closed her eyes and moaned. Could any other man make her feel like that? And if he could, she wanted to find him next. Forget about looking for her damned rogue brother.

She opened her eyes and found everyone watching her.

Darien's brows lifted slightly. "Lelandi sleeps alone."

She let out her breath, and he cast her a smile.

"I don't want anyone bumping into her wounds in the middle of the night. Unless one of my brothers wants to give up his bed to you, Silva…" Darien tilted his head to the side as if to ask if she had any objections, yet finality censored his words.

Silva frowned back at him. Obviously, she wasn't interested in his brothers.

"Not my bed. I stayed up most of last night and gave enough blood, I'm ready for a good night's sleep," Jake said.

"You've got guard duty from four to six in the morning, Jake." Darien wheeled the chair outside to the SUV.

"I can handle it." Jake said to Silva, "Guess you can sleep in whoever's bed isn't occupied during guard duty." He opened the passenger door for Darien. "What about Tom? He's doing pretty well, but you don't plan on having him serving on guard duty, do you?"

"He's champing at the bit to pull it. Think he's in love."

Jake frowned. "Tell him he'd better find a new girl."

Silva chuckled. "Yeah, this one for darned sure's already taken."

Lelandi stifled a growl. Once she found out who the blackmailer and killer were, and heck, found her gun and took care of them, she was out of here.

She caught a glimpse of her cousin Ural watching from across the street at some old movie theater, the sign faded like most everything else in Silver Town. Her heart nearly stopped. He wore his hood up, hiding his face, but everyone was sure to be looking for him, and that coat was like an orange prison jumpsuit on an escaped convict.

Damn him for hanging around. If the grays caught him, they'd crucify him, figuring he had something to do with her sister's death and the shootings. Plus, Mrs. Hastings had seen him manhandle her, and Darien was pretty hot about that. They wouldn't use kid gloves on him either, not like they did with her when they were trying to find out the truth. All because he wanted her home before the pack leader found out where she was, or maybe he wanted her to run away with him. She wasn't really sure what he had in mind.

Quickly, she looked away so no one saw what had caught her attention, but Silva saw, and Jake, too. Then Darien.

Chapter 10

JAKE CURSED AND TOOK OFF RUNNING AFTER LELANDI'S cousin.

Her heart hammering, Lelandi tried to climb out of the wheelchair, pain filling her chest. "Leave him alone!" she screamed.

"Calm down before you hurt yourself further," Darien ordered, and lifted her flailing body out of the wheelchair and into the backseat of his SUV. "Get in, Silva, and make her stay put."

"But I was going to follow behind and—"

"Get in!" he snapped, trying to keep Lelandi still. "Hell, drive the vehicle. I'll keep the hellion in her seat."

Lelandi struggled to get free when someone opened the other passenger door to the backseat of the vehicle and grabbed her arm.

She cried out. "Tom," she croaked.

The poor guy's head still bandaged, he gave her a toothy grin, but it looked like his struggle to calm her pained him, and she ceased fighting him. What did it matter anyway? She wasn't going anywhere, and Jake was sure to catch her cousin since he was longer-legged and had a lot more strength in his movement than the shorter red.

Darien leaned over her and locked her seat belt in place. The strap pressed against her injuries, and she gasped.

"Sorry, Lelandi." Darien's eyes turned to midnight as he motioned to Silva. "Drive."

Pressing her back into the seat, Lelandi slipped her hand between the seat belt and her chest, trying to avoid contact with the shoulder strap. Darien began to move it aside for her when Jake cornered Ural next to a fast-food pizza place. She willed her racing heart to slow, but her body wouldn't obey.

Darien shouted, "Pull into the pizzeria's parking lot!"

"No," Lelandi screamed and tried to tear off the seat belt.

"Quit it, Lelandi. We won't kill the guy."

Yet his icy look told another story. Darien attempted to brace her against the seat, his big hands pinning her shoulders back. She bit into the leather jacket covering his arm, but it protected him.

Pinning her left arm down, Tom chuckled.

Silva slammed on the brakes in the parking lot. "He got away."

Looking like the devil was after him—and for now he was—Ural dove down a side street, and Jake took chase again. Lelandi was impressed. She didn't think Ural could outmaneuver the gray in a footrace in their human form. But he *was* a wiry little guy. If he could turn into the wolf, he'd do even better.

"Drive us home," Darien said to Silva, pulling his cell phone out. He punched in a number and moved a tress of hair away from Lelandi's cheek. She scowled and turned her head away. "Uncle Sheridan, get your men to the pizzeria, south on Silver Maple Street, suspect wearing a hooded copper coat. Jake's on foot chasing him. Yep, same guy who accosted Lelandi behind Hastings B&B. No, Larissa was my mate. The guy in the copper coat is small, most likely a red. Gotcha." He looked at Lelandi, his expression one of deep satisfaction.

Despite what a jerk her cousin could be, she didn't want the grays to harm him. She gave Darien her meanest glower and would give him more hell as soon as she could.

Darien had every intention of putting Lelandi to bed when he got her home. But after what had happened with the guy in the copper jacket, he didn't trust her to stay put without a guard. And he didn't trust that the guy wouldn't come for her again.

He planned on securing her in the guest bedroom, but he was awfully tempted to put her in his bedroom suite to cut down on the amount of guards posted. Hell, as light a sleeper as he was, she'd never be able to slip away if she had a notion to. He didn't care how his people would view his actions either—they'd adjust, but he did care how Lelandi felt about it. To that end, he wasn't sure.

Although she sure as hell kissed him back when he kissed her. Which meant? She was probably half out of her head after being injured so badly. Or *was* that the reason she had clamored for his kisses? Then passed out. Yeah, it had to be the blood loss screwing up her brain.

But another thought took hold. The woman from his dreams *was* Lelandi. He stared at her. She refused to look at him. A sickening feeling instantly swept through him. Hell, he'd mated the wrong woman.

When they pulled into the circular drive of his wooded estate two miles from town, Darien had every intention of showing Lelandi she was his soul mate, but her injuries… he'd kill the bastard who tried to murder her.

"Tom, you have guard duty from twelve to two. Get some rest before then."

"I've been sleeping most of the day, Darien. I'm fine."

Darien lifted Lelandi out of the SUV, the fight out of her now. Soft and pliable, she looked damned kissable again, but when she groaned, he squashed that notion. "Watch her in the living room until Trevor gets here to guard her."

"Yeah, sure, Darien."

Darien had the greatest urge to carry her straight up to his bedroom, lay her in his bed, and ravage her. And he would, once she was healed, and he convinced her she was the one meant for him. Did she have the same dreams he did? If so, why hadn't she recognized him? Or had she, but she didn't want him now because he'd taken her sister as his mate? *Hell.*

With that damning thought, he carried her to the living room, the craving to have her growing with every step he took. Already he was as hard as granite and the friction from his jeans was making the situation worse. Her eyes widened and he was certain she could smell how turned on he was by touching her.

Clenching his teeth, he set her down on the longest velour sofa, nearly six feet in length. "Silva, can you get a spare pillow and blanket from the linen closet in my bathroom?"

"Got it." Silva hurried off.

"Tom, you can get her some ice water. Doc said the fever's abated, but she still needs to drink plenty of fluids."

"Yeah, I'll get it." Tom headed for the kitchen.

Lelandi wouldn't look at Darien, but held her chest lightly.

"Are you hurting?"

She nodded.

He touched her cheek and although she was still cool to the touch, the feel of her soft skin beneath his fingertips burned him. Hating how much the siren ensnared him, and he couldn't do anything about it, yet, he pulled away. "I'm sorry for being too rough earlier."

"My fault." Tears glistened in her eyes.

He felt like he'd shrunk to half his size. "Lelandi."

She quickly looked away. "I'm sorry for what my sister did. It must hurt to learn she'd…" Her voice broke and a wave of commiseration washed over him. Her lower lip quivered. "I'm sorry. I loved my sister and I wish she hadn't been mated to him. That she'd found you first and loved you like you both deserved. She would have been happy and… and no one would have hurt her."

He took Lelandi's hand and rubbed his thumb over her fingers, her skin silky soft, her hand small like her sister's. "It wasn't your fault, and I assume she had good reason for doing what she did, in her own way. Besides, it was partly my responsibility." He crouched in front of her and rested his hands on her knees. "Silva was right. I wouldn't let Larissa be. I pursued her and she repeatedly said no, but not why. I figured she was playing hard to get, maybe reluctant because she feared the grays wouldn't accept her like I did. I thought she was the one for me. When we mated, I discovered she wasn't a virgin. That she had a living mate never crossed my mind. I guess I was too proud to consider such a thing. Why didn't you tell me we've been together in our dreams?"

Her eyes widened.

He knew it.

She shuttered her eyes. "I... I don't know what you're talking about."

"What I'm talking about is this." He pulled her from the couch and with one arm wrapped around her so she couldn't step back, he kissed her mouth with a gentle sweep of his lips. Her eyes fluttered closed, her heartbeat quickened, and she fell under his trance. She wasn't as immune to him as she let on. The tension in her body melted, and he pressed further, his mouth caressing hers, his fingers touching her cheeks, the heat of her body setting his on fire. God in heaven, she was his soul mate.

She parted her lips slightly to take a breath, but the invitation was too great. He explored her mouth with his tongue, and her hand clutched his shirt, her eyes searching his. "You are she," he whispered thickly.

He pressed his heavy groin against her mound, showing her how much he wanted her. How much he always wanted her. "Lelandi," he said hoarsely with need, then bent his head down to touch her forehead with his.

Confusion reigned in her gem-quality eyes. "You are she," he repeated, kissing her cheek.

She winced and bit her lip.

He cursed silently. "Are you in pain?"

She seemed torn between telling him the truth and living with the discomfort to avoid being medicated. He helped her sit back down, then saw Tom standing with the glass of water, having witnessed the whole affair. A slight smile curved Tom's lips, and he raised his brows a hair.

"Silva's got Lelandi's pain pills. Get them for her, and check on Silva to see if she got lost," Darien said.

Lelandi smiled a little, but the same soulful expression Larissa had filled Lelandi's eyes, too. He wondered what had happened to the sisters to make them hurt so.

He helped her out of her leather jacket and stared at the shirt Silva had bought for her. *Vixen. Matchmaker deluxe.* In the soft glow of the overhead light, the scrap of lace pushing up Larissa's breasts showed through the blouse.

When Tom came downstairs with the medicine, Silva, the blanket and pillow, he meant to tell Tom to bring him one of his flannel shirts for Lelandi.

The doorbell rang thwarting him, and Sam barged in, his arms loaded down with pizza boxes. "Got tons of pizzas and beer, if anyone wants to give me a hand."

Darien covered Larissa with the blanket. "Sit with her, Silva."

"Sure thing."

But when he and Tom brought in an armload of drinks, he noticed Silva had helped Larissa remove her jeans, now folded on the arm of the couch. He silently groaned, imagining seeing the rest of her nearly naked underneath the blanket.

When Darien disappeared into the kitchen with his brother and Sam, Silva pulled a chair closer to the couch and asked Lelandi, "How do you do it? Man, oh man, I thought Darien would take you right there on the couch. I sneaked back up the stairs before Darien noticed me. Tom's gawking in surprise was audience enough." Silva grinned. "Darien's pants get so tight in the crotch when he's around you, he's probably strangled. But I can't get Trevor to feel anything for me."

Lelandi knew damn well Darien was projecting her sister on her, and she felt Silva's pain. Yet, she couldn't help wanting his heated touches. Nothing was worse than a *lupus garou* wanting another who didn't share the same feelings. Yet, she knew from past experience and from her other wolf mates that Silva would have to learn this on her own. No one could tell her what Lelandi and most, she was sure, could already see. Trevor was a bastard, knowing that Silva wanted him and giving her the cold shoulder, taking pride in having her salivating over him when he had no intention of showing her any affection in return.

As far as Darien was concerned, Lelandi wasn't Larissa and never could be. He'd have to find another mate. Not someone who looked like her.

Taking a deep breath, Lelandi advised, "Find someone else, Silva." She truly meant it, although she had to be a little more devious in her plan.

Silva's eyes widened.

"I don't mean for real. Convince someone to help you make him jealous, but be sure you make it clear from the beginning that you're only trying to get Trevor's attention."

Silva's whole face lit up. "I know just the guy."

"Make sure he knows why you're doing it. You don't want to give some poor guy hope when you don't really mean it."

Nodding vigorously, Silva loosened some of the curls piled on top of her head.

"So, who are you targeting?"

Silva grinned. "Sam. He's perfect. Ten years older than me, but he can really put on the charm when he wants. And he's used to my flirtations."

"I can see you turn on a lot of wolves."

"Yeah." Silva fingered her loose curls. "I kind of have a teasing personality. Guess I should tone it down."

"Not necessarily. Just channel it." To the right guy.

The fact Silva wanted Sam's help made Lelandi wonder if there wasn't some underlying interest in him that Silva couldn't recognize because she was so infatuated with Trevor. Plus if Sam *was* interested in her, the way she mooned over Trevor would be a dead turnoff. But if Silva gave Sam half a chance…

If Lelandi could, she would help show Trevor a thing or two before she had to leave. And maybe if she could win Silva over, she might be willing to share more pack secrets that could lead to Lelandi's discovering who murdered Larissa.

"What did you want to do about the little lady?" Sam asked in the kitchen, as Darien welcomed his men to the leader's pack meeting.

Sam was talking low, but Lelandi could still hear him, although the medicine was making her groggy again while she reclined on the couch.

"She needs to be taken up to the guest bedroom," Darien said. "She needs to sleep and get her strength back."

"Tom's got a slew of problems to discuss. Is he feeling all right to present the issues?" Sam asked.

Ice clunked into a container.

"Yeah. He'll be fine."

"Heard Jake lost that guy in the copper coat near the bank."

Lelandi breathed a sigh of relief. Her cousin was the runt of the litter—a beta. No true family loyalty. But if he took her home to Bruin, the leader would undoubtedly force her to mate his brother, Crassus, the bastard. One Wildhaven wouldn't be enough.

"I was Larissa's friend," Silva said to Lelandi, her voice whisper soft. "The only female friend she had. Although Nurse Grey was always nice to her. But I don't think Larissa trusted her or anyone else. Larissa wasn't an alpha, but she was sweet, had an innocence about her. She didn't lead Darien on, but I could tell she wanted to know what it would be like with someone who wanted her so badly and really cared for her. Darien seems hard, but he's still grieving for her. But… she told me some things."

Silva paused when the chatter in the kitchen died down. Her lips curved up slightly. "Let's move to the guest bedroom, sugar. Darien won't want us to hear boring pack business."

Jake slammed the front door and stalked into the living room, casting a glance in Lelandi's direction. He looked pissed. *Guess because he hadn't caught Ural.*

Lelandi's lips rose slightly despite willing them to remain still. He shook his head at her. Hearing Darien's voice in the kitchen, he headed that way.

"Well?" The sound of Darien's voice indicated he already knew his brother's answer.

"The guy got away. But Uncle Sheridan and a bunch of our men are searching for him. We'll get him." Jake sounded more like he was telling Lelandi the news—a warning.

"Trevor arrived. Take Lelandi up to the guest room, and he can guard her. Afterward, we'll start the meeting," Darien said.

"Will do."

Jake stalked back into the living room. When he lifted Lelandi off the couch, she noticed no one spoke in the kitchen. She was dying to hear what Silva had to say about her sister and bet Darien was, too.

Jake carried her upstairs and she admired a score of photographs on the walls, featuring clusters of mountain wildflowers. Beautiful, colorful, vivid—lavender columbine peeking out from the base of an alpine grove, pink, showy milkweed like starbursts, purple thistle, and golden mountain dandelions. "Who's the photographer?"

Jake's dark face brightened some. "Me."

"Oh." She thought maybe Darien had taken them. Despite feeling she shouldn't care, she wanted to know more about the gray, who had taken her sister for his mate.

"Darien doesn't have any real hobbies," Jake explained as if he read her thoughts. "Too busy keeping the town going, running two businesses, taking care of the pack. That's a lot of responsibility for one *lupus garou*."

"He has a whole pack to assist him."

Jake gave her a smug smile and carried her into a room. Vases of roses and wildflowers cluttered an antique dresser and one of the bedside tables, scenting the air with the most delightful summertime floral fragrance despite being autumn. He glanced at the flowers and shook his head, then laid her in a king-sized, canopied bed of white eyelet. *Fit for a princess.*

Silva hurried into the room with Lelandi's medicine, jeans, and the extra pillow. "Nurse Grey, Bertha Hastings, Tom, and a few others sent the flowers. Four secret admirers also." She pulled a card off a vase of wildflowers and handed it to her. "From me."

To one hell of a fighter! Go get 'em, girl! Next margarita's on me! Your friend, Silva.

Lelandi managed a groggy, heartfelt smile. "Thanks, Silva. I can't tell you how much I appreciate all you've done for me."

Jake headed for the door. "Holler if you need any of us."

"Will do." Silva handed Lelandi another card as Jake shut the door. "This one's anonymous. Your secret admirers probably hope Darien decides he doesn't want you and you'll be interested in one of them."

He didn't really want her. He wanted her sister.

Her heart in her throat, Lelandi read the card out loud. "You sure shook up the town, little lady. You'll make a first-class mate. From someone who would like a chance at being more than a friend."

Silva handed her another. "The anonymous guys probably called the flower orders in. I'll find out from Rosie who sent them."

"After I discover what happened to my sister and take care of the bastard, I'm leaving to find my brother." Lelandi glanced down at the card.

"I've been keeping myself for the best. Wanna tango, baby? Loving you."

She gave a short laugh. "I could never tango."

"I'm more of a rock and roll kind of girl." Silva

placed her hands on her hips. "I haven't a clue who any of these guys could be." She waved at a dozen red roses. "I'll let this guy give you his card in person."

"Who?"

"Tom. These burgundy and gold mums are from Bertha Hastings. She says,

'You kept your room as neat as a pin, until Darien and Sheriff Sheridan broke in and made a mess of it. To cheer you, here's a pot of flowers they didn't manage to break. Get well, young lady. Your room will be ready once you've recovered. Free of charge. Bertha Hastings.'

She's a sweet old lady. Really was worried about you." Frowning, Silva touched her finger to her lips. "Hmm, one vase of flowers is conspicuously absent."

"From whom?"

Silva wiggled her brows. "Darien. He probably didn't want to order any without raising any more speculation about you and him. Rosie would have told the world."

Lelandi took a tired breath and put her hand on her waist. "Jake didn't send me any either."

Silva laughed out loud. "He's too cheap. Woe to the girl who ever tries to win his heart."

"He could give her a framed photo of wildflowers. They're really lovely."

"Don't tell him you think so. That's why they're hidden on the staircase and not displayed in the living room for all to see. He loves doing it, but he doesn't like for anyone to know."

Except for Lelandi. She smiled at the contradiction.

"Hmm, the vase of carnations are from a couple of girls who are staying at Hastings Bed and Breakfast.

Caitlin and Minx. They said they worried about you when you were in the loft and hoped you were okay. I heard they're sixteen and want to join the pack."

Lelandi sighed. "How sweet of them to send me flowers." She wondered which of the twins had found her crying over her sister's letter that night. But she couldn't help feeling touched that they cared enough to send her the carnations.

"Another anonymous guy. You sure made a stir." Silva handed the card to Lelandi, then ruffled through another vase of flowers. "I don't see who this one is from."

"Stay around and get to know me, why don't you, honey? I'll be seeing you. A fun-loving lupus garou,*"*

Lelandi read out loud. "I'm surprised these guys showed any interest."

"It's the alpha in you. Turns them on." Silva bent down to retrieve a card off the floor. "Here it is." Her brow furrowed and she cast Lelandi a condemning look. "I thought you said your parents were dead."

Chapter 11

EXPECTING TREVOR TO CATCH EVERYTHING SILVA AND Lelandi secretly discussed while he was listening at the guest bedroom door, Darien sat in his favorite leather chair in the living room and motioned to Tom to get on with the abbreviated meeting.

"Uncle Sheridan called and said he's reconstructing the crime scene over the coffee-drugging incident at the hospital. And Doc Oliver hasn't fully recovered from the coffee," Tom said. "One of the lab technicians discovered it was that date rape drug, GHB."

"Crap. Any fingerprints?"

"Tons. Problem is everyone uses the coffeepot."

"All right. What have you got for me?" Darien asked as Sam served up the pizza.

"Carol Wood wants to work as a nurse at the hospital, but I heard you told her no. She asked if I'd try to sway you."

"I still say no. If she doesn't like working as a school nurse, she can move to another town."

Jake lifted a slice of pizza from his plate. "She'll be trouble. I'll bet my paycheck on it."

"Other news, Tom?"

"The town is gearing up for the fall festival. Uncle Sheridan is pretty mad that he has to be here again during the activities. That was one of the real reasons he took a vacation," Tom said.

"He can concentrate on the shootings."

"Yeah, but he says his men will be so busy with the influx of tourists…"

Darien motioned to Mason. "I need you to coordinate a thirty-man call-up police force for backup."

Mason raised a can of beer in agreement. "Will do, Darien. I know you didn't want to have the fall fair again, but it brought in around seventy-five thousand dollars to small business owners when revenues are way off this time of year. Good for the bank, too." He grabbed another slice of pizza. "Until we have our first good snowfall and the ski slopes open… we need to do something. The Silver Town Train Ride through the mines hasn't brought in much in the line of profits this summer either."

Darien didn't like the sudden swell in the human population. Too many things could go wrong. But he did believe in his peoples' say in matters that affected their well-being also. Not all pack leaders would agree.

Tom cleared his throat and flipped over another page from his notepad. "A family of five wants to join the pack."

Darien took a swig of beer. "Why are so many wanting to move into the town?"

Tom shrugged. "What do you want to do?"

"Has Uncle Sheridan checked them out?"

"They came in during the evening of the shootings. I figured that might change their minds, but they still want to be considered for inclusion in the pack."

"What's the breakdown of the family unit?"

"Father, mother, brother of the head of household, and sixteen-year-old twin daughters."

Jake gave a small smile. "As long as it's not any more cantankerous young males?"

"Yeah. Have Uncle Sheridan find out what they expect to work at here, their former job skills, training, any past records of problems, why they want to join our pack in particular. Where are they staying in the meantime?"

"Hastings B&B. Bertha knows the drill. She's taking notes and having them watched when she can't. What do you want to do about the Woodcroft boys?" Tom asked.

"I thought Uncle Sheridan was taking care of it."

"He deferred the decision to you about setting the punishment."

"Have the boys paint the school walls. Carpenter Myers can oversee the job to ensure they do it right. Mason, I want you to arrange that."

"Will do."

Tom waited further word, but Darien shook his head. "Should be enough. Did Uncle Sheridan explain to the boys that their parents didn't pay taxes to support the school? That only the humans pay them and the silver mine subsidizes the rest?"

"Some have grumbled that they want their kids to go to the school instead of homeschool them," Tom said.

"No. Just like with a human nurse working at the hospital, a testy *lupus garou* teen trying to prove something to one of the humans could get out of hand. We school our own. Several families are happy to teach the kids of other families who are too busy working."

Tom made a note. "We've got another gray wanting to learn all he can about the operation of our town."

Darien finished his beer. "Why all the interest? We've had three in the last month."

"Word's getting around we're a model town," Jake said. "How many leaders do we know who can boast running their own towns since their inception without human interference? Even though we try to maintain our shabby look to discourage too much interest, some alpha pack leaders want to build something like we have."

"All right, same as with the ones who want to join the pack, Tom. I want the guy watched. Do a background check on him. Report anything suspicious to either Uncle Sheridan or me. With this situation with Lelandi and her sister, we can't be too cautious. Any other business?"

Jake raised a finger. "Rosie delivered twelve vases of flowers for Lelandi, but she told me secret admirers sent four of them."

Darien snorted. "Hell, what next? Have the anonymous buyers traced."

"And then?" Jake asked.

"I'll talk to them."

Tom chuckled, but quickly coughed to cover his response when Darien gave him a sharp look.

Trevor hurried into the living room, his face hard. "I thought her parents were supposed to be dead."

Darien stared at him. "What? Who?"

"Silva said Lelandi got flowers from them."

Lelandi stared at the card signed: *Love, Mom and Dad,* typical order called in and signed at the flower shop. "It has to be a sick joke." Her eyes filled with tears, and she looked up at Silva, but disbelief filled her face. "Bruin's deputies told me my parents had died in a car accident. He put me under guard, but I escaped shortly afterward. They murdered my parents because Larissa ran away. I kept wanting my parents to move, but they wouldn't budge. I knew our pack leader would take revenge."

Silva pulled a chair over to the bed and took a seat. "What if your parents' deaths were faked? What if this Bruin character wanted you to look for your sister, then he'd know what became of her? Maybe he had you followed? The guy wearing the hooded copper coat, maybe?"

Bruin? Oh hell, she'd let the pack leader's name slip. "He put me under armed guard. He said he'd have me mated to his brother after he declared… my sister was dead."

"Her husband? Bruin's brother?"

Why did she have to mention his name? *Great, just great.* "What do you know about my sister?" Lelandi asked, before she gave away her whole frigging past.

She had to get off this pain medicine for good. Although she was surprised after Ritka had said that the Green Valley deputy knew who she was, Darien never mentioned it to her. Maybe it was a hoax.

"I'd never tell anyone else what Larissa told me in private. But I thought you should know. She was really worried someone would find her. I assumed it was her red pack or her family. That they wouldn't approve that she'd taken a gray mate, although she said she was a loner and had no living family." Silva glanced at the card in Lelandi's hand. "I never in a million years dreamed she might have been mated and the guy was still alive. Do you think he's the one who put a contract out on her?"

"But someone was blackmailing her before this. That makes me think it was someone else who knew she was mated, and she didn't want him to tell Darien."

"Yeah, that's a pretty low blow for a pack leader. So," Silva said, her eyes round, "was the other guy she was mated to high up in the chain?"

Lelandi ignored the question. "He's abusive, drinks too much. I... I wanted my family to leave—to find my brother. To settle somewhere new. But... they wouldn't."

Silva patted her hand. "Ties too strong to the pack?"

Lelandi didn't say anything. They had no ties to the pack—usurpers. Just a connection to the land. But revealing too much wasn't a good idea. As if she hadn't already.

When she didn't respond, Silva took up the slack. "Darien said he's returning you to your pack. But I figure the way he kissed you means he's changed his mind. You don't want to return to them, do you?"

Lelandi's face heated. "They killed my parents! I'm not returning. The pack leader will force me to mate his brother. I won't go back."

"You can't run off on your own on some wild *lupus garou* chase looking for your brother either. What if you never find him? You could be found out, hurt, killed. What about this guy in the copper coat? Is he a family member, or one of the pack?"

Lelandi shook her head.

Silva took a breath, then abruptly changed the subject. "I tried to get Larissa to tell me what was bothering her. I thought maybe it was the pregnancy. Hormonal imbalance kind of thing. "

Her sister had been pregnant? Lelandi stifled a cry and tears pricked her eyes.

Silva's eyes widened. "I... I thought you knew. Oh, sweetie, I'm so sorry. I'll get you a box of tissues." She hurried into the attached bathroom and opened a cabinet.

Lelandi couldn't believe her sister had been pregnant when she couldn't get that way with Crassus. Had she been taking birth control measures behind his back? No wonder Darien was so devastated. Not only had she died, but his offspring had as well. Oh, god, the travesty of it.

Silva returned to the bedroom and put the box of tissues on the bedside table. "Something about Darien and your sister's relationship was all wrong. Do you believe in soul mates among *lupus garous*?"

"No." Lelandi dabbed her eyes with a tissue. No. She didn't believe in such a thing even if a hunk of a *lupus garou* had invaded her dreams for the last several months. Alpha pack leaders often decided who could mate. But she'd never heard of their kind finding their own soul mate. Silva studied her so intensely, Lelandi finally opened up as she pulled the covers to her chin. "I've had really vivid dreams, and I sure wish the guy *was* real."

Silva's eyes widened. "Omigosh, you've been dream mated with... with..." She looked down at the floor, then gave an almost imperceptible smile.

"What?"

Silva's gaze shifted to Lelandi. "Dream mating. That's what Julia Wildthorn, the romance writer, calls it. When soul mates can't locate each other in the real world, if one has the ability he or she can reach out to the other, offer the bond that unites them. If the other accepts, they're dream mated."

"I don't understand how she can make all that stuff up. She says the *lupus garous* talk like humans in their wolf forms, stand upright even, and worse? Their clothes vanish when they shapeshift into the wolf's form and reappear on their human form without any effort."

"She can't reveal our true nature," Silva huffed. "Besides, I love how her *lupus garous* find meaningful, heartfelt relationships. We deserve something like that. Your sister said Darien told her he dreamed of her—that's why he pursued her. Except she didn't live up to his expectations in real life. Rumors abound that Darien's grandfather, father, and a couple of his uncles were dream mated." Silva took a ragged breath. "What if that's the reason he went after her? Only she wasn't the right one. What if you were? What if your sister realized this, too?"

Her heart racing, Lelandi stared at the bedcover, her thoughts in turmoil. What if everything Silva said was true? But she never saw her dream lover's face. Never heard his voice. Couldn't smell his scent.

Silva stood and looked out the window. "What if she was so depressed because she didn't want Darien to learn you were the right woman, and she probably wouldn't want you to know either? On top of that, she was mated to the beast before she met Darien, and she couldn't let Darien know about that either? Damn, I could see why she was so depressed."

Her sister couldn't have done this to her. How could she? But to get away from Bruin and Crassus, Lelandi could understand why Larissa had left. She deserved to be loved.

Silva turned to Lelandi. "What did he look like? This guy in your dreams?"

"I…" She shook her head. She wasn't sure.

"Maybe Darien isn't the guy." The elusive smile was fixed once again to Silva's lips. "Another thing is…" She let her breath out. "I think Larissa had some affection for a gray working in the silver mine."

In disbelief, Lelandi stared at her. Her sister couldn't have been having an affair with someone else.

Silva dropped into the chair. "What if that had something to do with her depression? She'd found the real guy of her dreams, and she couldn't have him. Three living male *lupus garous* at once who pegged her for their own is just not done."

How could Larissa's life have gotten so screwed up? Lelandi closed her eyes, fighting tears. "The medicine's making me sleepy."

Silva didn't move for what seemed an eternity, and then she stood. "All right, honey. You get some sleep." She strode to the door and closed it behind her.

If Larissa had had a lover, who else had known? How could she have done this to Darien?

In the hall, Trevor talked to Silva in a hushed voice. "Darien can't believe in dream mating. Damned hogwash if you ask me. That's why he mated the red?"

"Sounds to me like it," Silva said. "But I think he got the wrong girl."

Then everything grew deathly quiet.

Lelandi's head was spinning out of control. The damned medicine? Or Larissa's unbelievable sordid tale of the double mates, and a lover to boot. But was Lelandi really Darien's dream mate? What if she wasn't and she fed into his delusions that she was? She'd be no better than her sister, and she couldn't do that to Darien. Not after all he'd been through.

The medicine slipped through her blood, and Lelandi fell into another world, always the forest, near the creek where the water flowed over rounded stone in a never-ending, steady stream, crystal clear, but silent.

"Lelandi," her dream lover whispered to her while she read his lips. Why couldn't she see more of him? Speak with him? Know him. She pressed her fingers to his mouth, and he kissed them.

No, no, she wanted to read his lips. "Say something," she implored, but he took one of her fingers and sucked.

Her skin heated with desire, but she shook her head, pulled her finger free, and tried again. Pressing his fingers to her lips this time, she said her family name, "Wildhaven."

But he didn't repeat the word.

"What... is... your... name?" she asked. Could he see her face when she couldn't see his?

He kissed her lips, licked them, pressed his tongue into the seam, but she was determined to learn who he was. She pushed at his chest. "No. Tell me. Who are you?"

He shook his head. Not understanding? Or not willing to tell her? Did he already have a mate?

Oh, this was so ridiculous. He was just a fantasy lover.

She turned away from him, wanting him to be real, not some made-up illusion. He ran his hand over her shoulder with a tender caress, tickling her. She closed her eyes. He melted her annoyance, stirring a flicker of flame deep inside her. He licked her shoulder, touching her bare hip, not pressuring, using the most sensuous of tactile explorations. Trying not to give in to the lust, she clenched her teeth, lifted his hand from her hip, and moved it to her mouth.

"No," she mouthed against his hand.

She wanted him to communicate to her. But instead of helping, he pulled away... and vanished.

"No!" She felt the soft bed in the guest bedroom beneath her, and saw Tom sitting in a chair watching her, his look startled. She sat up taller in bed and frowned at him. "Are you all right?"

Although she felt remiss in not saying something earlier, it was the first time she'd even thought about asking him about his injuries. Then again, she hadn't been herself with all of the medication she'd been on. For the first time since the incident, she felt clear-headed, without any chest pains, just some strange prickling where her healing properties were busily taking care of the injured areas. Maybe by morning, she'd look and feel as good as new. Then again, maybe not.

Tom smiled at her finally, and she imagined he'd been half-asleep, he was so slow to react. He touched his temple where the bandage was gone. "Just a scratch and it's nearly healed. Head wounds bleed a lot, so I had to get a little blood. Jake wouldn't give me any. Said he'd used all he could spare on you." He winked, the most devilish twinkle in his light brown eyes. "Pretends he doesn't like you, but his actions tell another story."

Pulling her covers higher, she gave a ladylike snort. "Right. Nurse Grey forced him to give blood the second time. Probably the same the first time around, too."

"He's all show."

She didn't believe it for a minute. "He didn't like my sister, did he?"

"He didn't like that Darien was upset about what to do concerning her. She was deeply troubled, but she wouldn't let anyone close enough to find out what was wrong. Jake doesn't like the silent suffering type. Get it out in the open and deal with it. That's his motto. I figured whatever nightmare she was living, she couldn't handle on her own, but she didn't feel confident enough in herself even to tell Darien. Considering how she was mated to a red, and someone was blackmailing her to keep quiet about it…" He shrugged. "She hadn't known Darien that long. Probably was afraid he'd want to kill her for what she'd done."

The thought sent a shiver sliding down Lelandi's spine. "Would he have?"

Tom raised his brows.

She wasn't sure how to respond to his reaction. What if Darien knew she had a lover? Would Tom tell his brother she asked? Her whole body warmed with mortification. Tom didn't seem to mind her being here, and now she'd blown it big-time. But the truth of the matter was, what her sister had done could push some *lupus garous* over the edge. Being that Darien was the leader of his pack and could get pretty angry—

"I should be asking if you're all right. You've been talking a lot in your sleep. Nightmares?" Tom asked, consoling.

"What... what did I say?"

Sheesh, Larissa never wanted to stay in the same bedroom with her because Lelandi walked and talked in her sleep when she was overly tired and stressed out. But she hadn't done that in a long time... that she knew of. Of course, after Larissa had moved in with Crassus, no one would have known of Lelandi's clandestine nighttime activities, although her father scolded her for finding him in the den late one night watching an X-rated movie. She wouldn't have known if he hadn't yelled at her and woken her up. From then on, she guessed he knew better and sent her back to her room without waking her, or else he made sure she didn't catch him watching the movies in the den anymore.

Tom shook his head. "You didn't say much that made sense."

Thank god. She looked at her hands clenched into fists and let go, smoothing the comforter to release the tension filling every muscle fiber, while she listened to the voices downstairs, some heated, some calmly speaking, but none of which she could make out clearly.

Tom eased out of the chair and handed her the card from his roses. "From me."

She read the card.

You saved my life and I owe you mine. Love, Tom.

"You're... you're welcome. But it was all my fault that the gunman came after me. If you hadn't been with me, he wouldn't have shot you. Heck, if you hadn't been there, you wouldn't have called for help, and no one would have known what had become of me. So you saved my life."

Tom leaned over and kissed her forehead. "Then it means you owe me." He glanced toward the door. Someone was coming. "Looks like my relief."

Despite saying he felt fine, he looked weary.

The door opened slowly and Darien stepped in, first looking at Tom, who gave him a lopsided grin, then at Lelandi. Surprise reflected in his expression to see her awake. "Feeling pain?" A frown collected across his brow.

"No. Just woke up."

Darien turned back to Tom. "Are you doing okay?"

"Yep, fine as can be. I'll join the ruckus downstairs, and then retire."

Darien listened to the noise drifting upstairs. "Tell them to keep it down."

"Yeah, will do."

Secrets? She was certain whatever the grays wanted to discuss was not to be shared with the rest of the grays in the pack, and certainly not with her unless Darien said so.

"See you in the morning, Tom." Darien waited for him to leave.

Tom gave Lelandi a nod and a smile. "'Night, Lelandi."

"Good night, and thanks for watching over me," she said, with a hint of sarcasm.

She knew damned well they were not only making sure Ural didn't get to her again, but she had a sneaking suspicion they didn't trust her to stay put either.

Tom's smile broadened, then he closed the door behind him.

Darien opened his mouth to speak, but paused when Tom hollered halfway down the stairs, "Keep it quiet down there!"

To her surprise, Darien crossed the floor and touched her forehead, then used the back of his hand to feel her cheek. "No fever." He seemed somewhat relieved, yet the wrinkle in his brow didn't fade.

"I'll be ready to run laps by tomorrow morning."

A trace of a smile formed. "Wouldn't surprise me." He remained in place, hovering over her, and she wondered what he wanted now. He glanced at her water cup, still full. His gaze returned to hers. "Need anything?"

"Nope, thank you."

"All right." He opened his mouth to speak, then closed it.

Whatever was bothering him was starting to bother her. He seemed glued to the patch of carpet next to the bed, and she assumed he wanted to interrogate her.

Glancing down at the comforter pulled up to her chin, he said, "Doc's orders, we have to change your bandages every four hours."

Lupus garous were not shy around others. So why did she feel nervous? Her skin grew a faint coating of goose bumps. Maybe because *he* was acting anxious. Silva had already changed her bandages twice earlier in the day, no big deal. Yet, it seemed a big deal when the male gray leader wanted to change them. Maybe it was because he was waiting for her to say it was all right, when Silva charged in like she'd been trained as a nurse before she began waitressing, knew what she was doing, and had no qualms about it. Or maybe because every time Darien got near Lelandi, she felt the sexual tension in the air between them sizzling like exposed live electric wires, smelled the scent of his sex, could nearly taste the craving he had for her.

"Doesn't need changing."

Folding his arms, he lifted a brow. "Doc said the wounds weep until everything's healed. If the bandage gets too wet, you could get chilled again. That's what Doc said. Change it every four hours to keep it dry and free of infection." He glanced at the clock on the bedside table to emphasize the time. "Been four hours." He looked back at her, waiting for her to agree.

"I'll take care of it." She pulled the comforter away so she could get out of bed and go to the bathroom where she could use the mirror to see what she was doing. Big mistake.

The flannel shirt Silva had helped her into earlier that night had ridden up to her navel, exposing her nakedness all the way to her toes. She was sure her skin had turned as red as her short curly hairs, especially when she saw him taking in his fill.

She jerked down the shirt, and his gaze shifted from her bare legs to her eyes. He shook his head tightly, but she noticed that he shifted in his stance then. A glance at his crotch gave her the reason. Hard as a rock.

"Why don't you let me help you?"

"I don't need your help."

He pulled the comforter up to her waist. "Might as well get this over."

He began to unbutton her shirt, *his* shirt, but it felt too much like he was getting her ready for sex, and she quickly brushed his hands away. "I can do it."

"Just trying to be helpful."

She frowned when he watched. This was worse than if he unbuttoned the shirt. Problem was, his touching her was making her way too hot. But his watching her had the same damned effect. "Can you do something else? Read a book or something?"

"Just pretend I'm the doctor."

Oh, god, yeah, playing doctor and patient. She gave him a dirty look while he attempted to hide a saucy smirk.

When she finished unbuttoning the shirt, she grumpily said, "It's done."

He rubbed his hands together like he was excited to get started, and she frowned at him.

"Getting my hands warmed up. They're cold." Gingerly, he peeled back her shirt, exposing her left breast and the bandaged wounds. "Tell me if anything is sore or hurts." His demeanor was professional, well, maybe a little anxious.

She cringed, afraid it would hurt as much as it had before.

He pulled off the tape around the pads, and considered the wounds with considerable scrutiny. "How does it feel?"

"Itching, burning some."

He nodded and dumped the used bandages in the wastepaper basket. He applied some salve on the bullet holes with such a light touch that it tickled. She couldn't help smiling, although she fought it. No way did she want to show she wasn't mad at him.

He caught her look and his mouth curved up. "Guess it's not hurting."

She pursed her lips. "Tickling."

"Be done in a minute." He situated the new pad over the wounds, brushing her already taut nipple with the edge of his hand, and taped the pad in place.

"It's getting cold," she said, tersely.

"Looks like you're healing well. After Jake pulls guard duty, I'll change it again."

She pulled the shirt closed and began buttoning it. "Maybe Silva will be up by then."

"She's a late sleeper. Used to staying up late at the bar. And Jake doesn't have an ounce of doctoring sense. Tom will probably be asleep still, but even if he isn't, he'd probably forget what he came in here to do. Doc said you might be getting edgy about not healing faster. He wanted you to know it's because of the severity of the injuries. If you'd been human, you'd be dead. And if by some miracle you'd lived, Doc said it would take several months to heal. He said you might be feeling all right by the end of the week."

She gave him a disparaging look. "I'll be up and about tomorrow."

Darien shook his head. "You're not anything like your sister. Need anything? Something to eat?"

"No, thank you." She closed her eyes, hoping he'd go away, but he took a seat in the recliner and leaned back, making it squeak.

She tried hearing what was being said downstairs, but the conversation was too low. She was too keyed up to sleep while Darien watched her. The image of his bandaging her, the way he looked at her, the feel of his hand against her nipple made her ache for his touch again. She ground her teeth, willing her mind to crush the thought so she could sleep.

Darien could tell from the way she licked her lips and swallowed hard, then ground her teeth, she wasn't sleeping. He squirmed to get comfortable, his erection springing to life again, just from visualizing her naked supple body under the covers. He hadn't expected to get an eyeful when she pulled her covers aside. The problem was he had to see for himself she was healing adequately. He didn't just want Silva's word for it. Not when he had to prove to Lelandi she was the one meant for him.

But being more than just a *lupus garou* with a raging hard-on, he was a pack leader that needed some damned answers if he was to take her for his mate.

"We found your bag." Darien's voice sounded harsher than he intended.

Lelandi's eyes popped open.

He motioned to the tapestry bag sitting by the dresser. "It looked like you planned to stay for a while. That guy in the copper coat had taken it. Had his scent all over it, inside and out."

Her eyes grew big.

"Which means the guy *had* broken into your room when Uncle Sheridan and I were trying to get in. What kind of a pack leader would allow two of his females to run off? First your sister, now you? At least now I know his name is Bruin. Or maybe that's your cover. Maybe his name is really Leidolf."

Her mouth gaped, but she quickly clamped it shut.

That got a response. Although he wasn't sure what her response meant. "And your parents are alive."

Darien wanted to send word to her pack concerning her whereabouts, and he wanted to set things straight with her sister's mate—the honorable thing to do. Plus, this time he was getting the father's permission to take the woman for his mate. But he still didn't know who her pack leader really was, and he couldn't be sure that her pack was innocent when it came to the harm done to either Lelandi or her sister.

He folded his arms and leaned back into the recliner. "Why don't you tell me the truth now?"

Chapter 12

HOW IN THE WORLD HAD DARIEN LEARNED HER BROTHER'S name? Lelandi was dying to ask, but she couldn't. Better to leave Darien confused about who her pack leader was. Did he know where Leidolf was living now? Maybe Silva would, if Lelandi could ask casually without arousing suspicion. *Right.*

Ignoring Darien, Lelandi pretended to sleep. More than ever, she had to avenge her sister's murder and leave. The longer she stayed, the higher the risk Bruin would locate her. Probably Darien would want to contact the leader and tell him what happened to her sister and Lelandi. *Sense of honor.* Then Bruin would force her to return home.

After a couple of hours, Darien left the room and thank god, for a change, he didn't post a guard inside. She climbed out of bed and paced. She had to discover if her parents were alive. But how was she going to do anything when he had her guarded always?

Footsteps raced up the stairs. "Are you staying with her for a couple of hours?" Trevor asked.

"Yeah. Darien went with Jake and Tom to question the hospital staff," Sam said.

She slipped back into bed and pulled the covers to her chin.

Sam walked into the room, smiled at her, and shut the door. "Still awake?"

"Going to sleep." At least she hoped so. After all the time she'd spent lying on her back, the urge to run in her wolf form made her restless and irritable. She wanted to stretch her legs and take a run on the wild side, soon.

Darien finally went to bed, but was too angry to sleep. Unable to learn anything about who drugged the coffee at the hospital, he racked his brain for alternative solutions. At nearly two in the morning, he had to get some sleep, but he couldn't stop thinking of Lelandi. The way her nipple had firmed when his hand had brushed it. The way she barely breathed when he was removing the soiled bandages. The way she smiled when the salve tickled her skin, but tried to hide that she wasn't scowling at him even for a second. He *could* have woken Silva to have her change the bandages, but he had to see for himself that Lelandi's wounds were healing properly.

He shoved his arm underneath his head, his body craving the change. He wanted to take a run in the woods, the urge growing as the moon's appearance neared. A jaunt through the forest, hunting alone or with a few members of his pack, racing each other, the wind ruffling their fur, enjoying nature at its best.

He closed his eyes. Unable to visualize anything but Lelandi's gaze challenging him in his mind's eye, he tossed his covers aside and grabbed his jeans. The woman tormented his every waking hour no matter how much he tried to ignore his cravings.

He stalked into the guest bedroom, not sure what he

had in mind, but when he saw the empty bed, he gave Jake a questioning glance. His brother motioned to the bathroom. The toilet flushed and the sink water ran for a few seconds, then shut off. When she appeared, she looked like the redheaded goddess of his dreams. The startled look on her face when she saw him standing in the bedroom, gaping at her, endeared him all the more.

Jake wore an amused expression and shrugged.

"Leave us, Jake," Darien said, without taking his eyes off her.

His brother cleared his throat and walked over to the door. "'Night all." He closed the door on his hasty retreat.

His shoulders straight, his bare chest muscles taut, Darien crossed the carpeted floor and joined Lelandi standing like a statue. She couldn't move from the spot, knowing he wanted her. She couldn't draw on the courage to shove him away, to stop the yearning she had for him.

He cupped her face and raised her lips to his. The flecks of gold in his dark brown eyes disappeared as they darkened to black. He leaned in, his eyes closed, and he pressed his lips against hers. Lightly, like the flutter of an eyelash against a cheek. She'd never expected such a gentle touch to shatter her composure, but it did. His whisper-soft touch sent a message straight from her brain coursing to every part of her body. Take me, it shouted.

The only men she'd ever allowed to kiss her were her family members, in a strictly family way. Yet she lusted for Darien like she never had for any man except for her fantasy lover. She wanted to strip off her clothes and ravish him. Every inch of her warmed, and if she'd been wearing panties, they'd be soaking wet now, guaranteed.

No, no, this is wrong. His tongue probed her mouth with a murmur of a touch. No, she couldn't let him in. If she did, she'd give herself to him completely. She couldn't, not after what her sister had meant to him.

She opened her mouth to tell him no, her hands gripping his arms to push him away, but she gave him the wrong signal. His tongue parted her lips further, penetrating her deeper. He pressed his body firmly against her, his erection hard against her waist, her back against the wall. His heart pounded with a thunderous beat as fast as hers, lulling her under his spell with a soothing rhythm, encouraging her to take part in the mating dance. She should have shoved him away, stopped this nonsense, made him realize she didn't want this. Not from him. Not from a gray. Her dead sister's mate.

So why the hell was she touching his tongue tentatively with her own? Bringing a smile to his smug lips? To his heavily lidded, lust-filled eyes? He hesitated for an instant, then delved deeper, intensifying the kiss, and she let him! Kissed him back even. Pressed her body harder against his erection, wanting to feel what she had done to him.

No, no, damn it! He was feeling Larissa in his grasp, and Lelandi served as her sister reincarnated. Nothing more.

Despite the streaks of pleasure rifling her body, his hands shifting from her arms to her breasts, feeling the change in her nipples as they begged for more, the way her core ached for his penetration, she knew he didn't feel the same for her. She was not Larissa. She was Lelandi and not his to be had.

With the utmost reluctance, she pushed him away.

He looked chagrined, his lips parting, his dark brows furrowing. Then he swore under his breath, shook his head, and guided her back to bed. Covering her with the comforter, he used a tender touch. He hesitated to leave, his eyes still clouded with desire, and then he turned and retired from the room. Left her unguarded. Well, sure there was a guard at the door, but…

Footsteps drew close. The door opened, and Jake gave her a smug smile while he buttoned his shirt. "I'm back. Thought I had the rest of the night off, but…" He shrugged. "Darien will be hell to live with in the morning."

She would be hell to live with in the morning if she couldn't quit thinking about what she wanted with her sister's mate and couldn't have it.

Darien couldn't believe how Lelandi stirred him up. How could he have given in to her so quickly, so completely? *She-devil.*

For an hour he tossed and turned, furious with himself for losing control. He should never have kissed her. But he couldn't get the kiss he'd shared with her out of his mind either. Everything inside him felt alive again with her touch, and he craved having her, no matter how many times he told himself he couldn't until she was ready.

He ran his hands through his hair, more frustrated than ever. Until two pairs of footsteps headed in the direction of his bedroom, and he lifted his head off the pillow. Slow footsteps, deliberate, not hurried. If anyone wished to disturb him at this hour, it would have to be an emergency, and yet the footfall indicated otherwise. Like an assassin's sneaky attempt at slipping in undetected. He reached for his bedside drawer, opened it, and pulled out the gun.

The footsteps stopped at his door. Forever it seemed, as whoever they were contemplated what to do. He considered telling them to get on with whatever they were there for so he could take care of them. Then a slight tap sounded at the door. Before he could respond, the doorknob twisted, and Jake slowly pushed the door open. Lelandi stood in the doorway in Darien's flannel shirt, her red hair dangling past her hips, her eyes fixed, staring straight through him.

"Sleepwalking, like Tom when he's overly tired. Tom said she was talking in her sleep earlier. I wondered where she was going," Jake's voice was hushed. "So I allowed her to leave the guest room."

Darien slipped the gun back in the drawer. Lelandi walked slowly to the bed. The side he always slept on. All the moisture in his mouth evaporated. She lifted the covers.

He looked back at Jake, who shrugged. "Doc said never to startle Tom when he's sleepwalking. Guess the same goes for Lelandi."

Darien slid over so Lelandi could climb into bed. He pulled the covers to her chin, and she closed her eyes.

"Guess you have guard duty the rest of the morning."

A coy smile fixed to Jake's lips, and he shut the door on his way out.

Lelandi didn't remember much except jumping on Crassus's back when he readied his fist for Larissa's face again. And the pain when Crassus hit Lelandi in the head, and more pain when he jerked her arm behind her back. But she hadn't saved her sister and now she was dead. Tears rolled down her cheeks.

But then he came as a wolf, distinguished, beautiful, his amber eyes studying her, his ears perked up. Her dream lover. Her silver knight. Her fantasy. Why could she see the whole of him as a wolf, but not as a human?

Changing from the wolf into his human form, he wrapped his arms around her, held her close, chased away the night terrors. Crassus's and Bruin's cruel, hard faces faded in the mist. The pain and suffering vanishing.

Her lover kissed her head, caressed her arm, her face, made her feel safe, protected, loved, but he didn't initiate anything deeper. He moved his lips lower, kissing her cheek and sweeping across to her mouth. She opened her lips to him, felt his body harden, pressing against hers, his tongue slipping inside her mouth, the feel of his heart pounding furiously against her chest, his hands stroking her hair, and she wanted him deep inside her, thrusting, claiming her. But he wouldn't make a move to take her.

"Sleep," he whispered against her mouth, his voice husky.

She moaned, separated her legs for him, and he slipped between them, his erection pressing at her mound. But still, he would not take her. His lips smiled against hers, but he slid out of her grasp and pulled her back against his chest.

"Sleep, vixen," he said, his voice hushed, his arms tightening around her in a bear hug of an embrace. And in the warmth of the cocoon he provided, the woodland world faded away.

Later that morning, Darien woke with his arms around Lelandi, her head on his chest, her breathing shallow, her silky red hair caressing his bare skin. God of thunder, how he wanted her, but not like this. Not when she didn't know what she'd gotten herself into. Hell, he'd have to let everyone know now she walked in her sleep, if Jake hadn't warned them already.

Not wanting her to wake and find herself in his room, in his bed, and most of all, in his tight embrace, he carried her back to the guest bedroom, and nodded to Peter who would watch over her until she woke. Peter's brows rose so slightly, if Darien hadn't been observing him closely, he would have missed the subtle change in his expression.

At least the deputy wouldn't tell the world which bed Lelandi had slept in last night, although before long, she'd be in his bed every night once he had his way. He kissed her cheek, then covered her with the eyelet comforter. Still not believing she was a sleepwalker like Tom, he headed down to the kitchen and greeted his brothers. "Morning, Jake, Tom."

His beard even scruffier this morning, Jake flipped sausages and bacon in the frying pan and casually said, "Morning, Darien. Trevor mentioned something about dream mating."

Tom glanced up from the toaster. "Morning, Darien. Good sleep last night?" He gave Jake a conspirator's look.

Darien grabbed the pot of coffee and poured himself a mug. "Slept well enough." He would not rise to his brother's inquisitive nature. "What does Trevor know about dream mating?"

"He overheard Silva talking to Lelandi. She told her you were convinced Lelandi was your dream mate."

Serving up a plate of toast, Tom's mouth curved up. "Hot damn. The trait is inherited. Why didn't you tell us?"

Jake snorted. "What next?"

Darien plucked toast from the plate. "Maybe."

"No maybe about it. Dad had the ability and so did Granddad and two of our uncles." Tom beamed. "Means Jake and I have a good chance at having the ability."

Jake set the platter of sausages and bacon on the kitchen table. "Don't believe in soul mates."

"Our distant cousin, Devlyn, found his soul mate," Tom reminded him, lifting his refilled mug. "And Bella's a red, too."

Darien would definitely have a word with Trevor. He'd never said a thing to Darien last night about "that" part of the conversation Silva and Lelandi had.

"What else did Trevor say?"

Jake gave Darien a small smile. Yeah, he knew Darien would give Trevor hell soon.

"Nothing else. In other news, that Chester McKinley wants a word with you when you can spare a moment."

Darien looked up from his eggs. "Who?"

"The assistant mayor of Green Valley, checking out our town so he can go back to his own and recommend changes."

"What does he need to speak to me about? You know I don't have time to micromanage every little thing that goes on in Silver Town."

Jake poured himself another cup of coffee. "He says he runs a first-rate private eye operation and thought you might like to hear his advice."

"About what, Jake? Quit beating around the bush."

"About Larissa and Lelandi."

Darien frowned. "What does he think he knows?"

"He wouldn't say." Jake took his seat and speared a slice of bacon. "Said he'd talk to you about it though."

Tom grabbed three pieces of toast. "Uncle Sheridan said the guy is legit. He checked with the mayor of Green Valley already."

Darien swore their youngest brother could eat triple what they ate and still not gain an ounce. "I've got Uncle Sheridan and both of you checking things out. I'd rather keep it in the family."

"Never know when another mind or two can help give us a lead," Jake said.

Darien ignored his brother's comment. All he needed was for the details of this mess to get out to other gray packs. "Anything else I need to know about?" Darien stabbed a sausage with his fork.

"Fall festival starts today. Are you going to open the ceremony like you did last year?"

Darien gave Jake a dark look.

Jake's lips curved upward slightly. "Everyone expects you to be there. But it's your call."

With everything else that had gone on, he'd forgotten about it, and he wasn't interested. But running the town brought responsibilities he couldn't ignore. "What time?"

"Ten o'clock."

"I've barely had time to supervise the factory since the shootings began. And I haven't had a chance to check in at the mine at all."

"Everything's running smoothly," Tom said. "Both Jake and I have been keeping an eye on things. Everyone's doing what needs to be done."

Thank god he had brothers who could be counted on.

His eyes sparkling with humor, Jake cleared his throat. "Do we need to inform everyone who serves guard duty about Lelandi's nighttime excursions?"

Tom's brows shot up. "What exactly *did* I miss last night?"

Darien swore Tom already knew, but wanted him to reveal more of the details. Which he wasn't about to do. He opened his mouth to speak, but Tom and Jake's attention switched to the entryway from the living room. Darien turned around and saw Lelandi, his long flannel shirt reaching thigh-high, her legs and feet bare, her hands locked as if in prayer.

His gaze shifted to her hair, the sensuous curls garnering his full attention. He was unable to tear his gaze away from the beauty of her silky tresses. Even more red than her sister's, less golden, more like the woman's in his dream. How could he have not realized she was the one? Because of the switched names and that Larissa had lied about the dreams, damn it.

"Ahem." Jake said, breaking the spell.

She looked sweet, innocent, edible, her lips parting to speak. "I smelled the food and thought if I ate something, I'd feel more energetic."

Tom hurried to escort her to his side of the table. Jake got her a plate and piled it high with eggs and sausages. Darien stared at her rumpled, shiny hair. No matter how much he didn't want to show his feelings for the woman, he couldn't block the emotions. Already he was hard as a rock, and he shifted uncomfortably under the table.

Lelandi sat in the seat Tom pulled out for her, and then he returned with a mug in hand, the coffeepot in the other. "Black?"

"Cream and sugar," she said, her voice so demure, Darien suspected something was brewing in that pretty head of hers, and he bet he wouldn't like it.

"I want to go to the fair."

Not expecting that, Darien sat back hard against his chair. "Absolutely not."

She furrowed her brow at him. "I feel one-hundred percent better, and I want to get out. I told you I'd be ready to run laps today."

Tom grinned and saluted her with his coffee cup.

"Not after all that's happened to you," Darien said.

"That guy in the copper coat is still running loose," Jake reminded them. "Mason thought he saw him running near here as a wolf last night."

Darien frowned. "The answer is no. You'll stay here and continue to recuperate."

Sam called out from the foyer. "Everyone decent?"

Even Darien managed a small smile at the comment, although he was trying to maintain his hard line with Lelandi.

Sam stalked into the kitchen and cast Lelandi a broad smile. "You're looking good." He handed Darien a stack of mail. "Is Silva around?"

"Upstairs sleeping in my bed," Jake said. Sam looked a little bothered. Jake added, "We're playing musical beds. I had last guard duty. She slept in my bed while I was pulling duty."

"Oh. I need her for the big opening ceremony. Free sodas for the first fifty customers."

"First bedroom on the right," Jake said. "We woke her and made her move six times last night. *I* don't want to disturb her again, so be my guest."

Sam hesitated.

Lelandi stood. "I'll get her."

"Sam can. Eat and get your strength back." Darien lifted one of the envelopes off the table and frowned.

Lelandi plopped back down on the chair. "For what? So I can stay here and watch soaps all day? You won't even let me go to the fair."

"She could help Silva and me hand out the free sodas," Sam offered. "We'd watch over her."

"Sure, that would be fun." Lelandi cut up her sausage. "I can serve drinks in between Silva and Sam. You wouldn't have to post a guard for me for a few hours."

"Where will you be set up?" Darien asked Sam, then lifted the envelope to his nose and breathed in deeply. His heart nearly exploded when he smelled Larissa's scent on it.

"The tavern. I can make sure only the front door is accessible. Lelandi can stay behind the bar with me."

Looking for a return address, Darien flipped the envelope over. None. He glanced up at Jake, who was watching Darien with concern. "All right. I want a guard on the place just in case."

"Mitchell will do it," Jake said.

Lelandi's face brightened and Darien hoped to hell he wasn't putting her in any more danger. But seeing her expression, he figured she'd feel better and heal faster if she got out of confinement for a while. He considered the envelope again, typewritten, so no clue there. But the postmark indicated it had been mailed from Wildhaven.

"Anything wrong, Darien?" Jake asked.

"Tom, get me a map of Colorado."

"Sure thing." Tom cast a questioning glance at Jake, missing out on what was going on.

"If you hear screaming and things being tossed about, you'll know Silva wasn't happy I woke her." Sam grinned and then headed out of the kitchen.

"Where's Peter? He should have come down with you when you joined us," Darien said to Lelandi, his voice dark.

Lelandi shrugged and waved for Jake to get her some more coffee.

As much as Jake had acted annoyed with her, Darien was surprised to see his lips lift slightly, while he refilled her coffee mug. For being such a petite little thing, she sure had everyone wrapped around her will.

"Poor deputy was bone tired," Lelandi said.

Jake gave her the coffee and headed for the doorway. "I'll take care of it."

Lelandi frowned at him. "Don't be too rough on Peter. You're overworking him."

But Jake just stormed out of the kitchen.

"I'll talk to that McKinley fellow and tell him you're too busy to see him, Darien," Tom said, returning with the map, but waited while Darien looked up the cities listed in the index. "What's wrong?"

Darien looked up at Lelandi. "I got a letter post-marked Wildhaven. I wondered where it was and who might have sent the correspondence."

"Wildhaven? Never heard of it," Tom said.

But Lelandi looked peeked. She glanced at the enve-lope and dropped her fork on the table.

Darien seized his knife, slipped it underneath the envelope flap, and ripped.

Jake rejoined them. "I've spoken with Peter." His gaze switched to the envelope and the map spread over the table. "What's up?"

Pulling the letter out, Darien barely breathed. The paper was hers—a light rose color, her scent, her hand-writing. "Larissa," he said under his breath.

Dearest Darien,

If you're reading this, I'm no longer of this world, and I regret I've brought you so much sorrow. I beg your forgiveness for lying about my family, about saying I had dream mated with you. I wasn't your soul mate, but I wanted to care for you like you desired me, a love I didn't have in my first mating. I wished with all my heart to be who you thought I was. When I found the right man, it was too late for me to take back what I'd done to you. Now, all that matters is that you know the truth. My sister came into her first wolf's heat after she was dream mated. Since you think it was me, I believe you'd truly seen my sister. Ask her, Darien. Don't lose your true soul mate for what I've done. My sister will seek you out to avenge my death, and I plead with you with all my heart, if you ever loved me, you will protect her. She doesn't think she needs your protection or anyone else's, but she'll be in grave danger as soon as I'm dead.

Whatever you do, do not turn her away. She had nothing to do with what happened between you and me, but I have harmed her greatly with what I have done. If nothing else, I pray you will protect her for my failings. I craved to be her, free, unattached, until you took me in. But now she'll pay for my crime if you don't help her.

Love me in death as you did in life by taking care of my blood, my sister, Lelandi.

Your mate, Larissa.

Chapter 13

DARIEN STARED AT LARISSA'S LETTER IN DISBELIEF, HIS whole body numb. He reread the note, trying to fathom the hidden meaning of her message.

He rose from his chair and walked out of the dining room. How could he have been so blind? The woman he'd mated had loved another? Who? He'd kill him.

Darien didn't remember walking into his office, or sitting at his desk. He stared at the letter, and then clenching it, he hollered, "Jake!"

Jake entered the office, a look of confusion crossing his face.

"Get Lelandi in here, now."

Jake's brows raised, he quickly nodded, then closed the door.

Tom entered a minute later, his eyes wide. "What's wrong, Darien? Jake says you're ready to kill someone. Want me to sit in on the little talk?"

"No."

"But—"

"No!"

His neck muscles tightening, Tom gave a brief nod. "You're the boss."

Jake ushered Lelandi into the room. She looked pale and her eyes quickly shifted from Darien to the floor.

Darien motioned to the love seat in his office, then gave his brothers a look that meant one thing. *Get out and stay out!* Although he had no doubt they would loiter beyond his office door in case things got out of hand.

They both glanced at Lelandi as she took a seat, looking like they wanted to rescue her, then finally obliged by leaving the room and shutting the door.

Folding his arms across his chest, Darien tried to settle the fury in his blood before he spoke. "Tell me about Wildhaven, Bruin, your parents, the whole deal."

She clenched her teeth and glowered at him. "Wildhaven's my family's name."

"It's the name of a town."

"It's my family's name," she reiterated, indignant.

"Then you're a pack leader's daughter? The Wildhavens settled the area? And both you and Larissa disobeyed him? Terrific. Then tell me about your family. All of it."

Lelandi pulled the shirt lower, which drew his gaze to her bare legs. Instantly, he wanted to take her, confirm that she was indeed the one of his dreams, his soul mate. But her soft voice penetrated his lust-filled thoughts. She looked at the letter in his hands, then tilted her chin up.

"My father was a pack leader when I was a child but his people had died in flooding and mudslides that wiped out his town. A few, who were not relatives, took off to join other packs. Father was devastated, living like a mountain man for ten years with my mother, brother, sister, and me, until he felt the call of the pack and joined my mother's reds. She was the pack leader's daughter, and had fallen in love with my father at first sight. She tried to heal his inner self after the tragedy had struck his pack while we lived amongst her reds. But when her father died, a new and ruthless leader took over. Most of her pack fled, and Bruin's flourished. Father had been injured in the mudslide, a spinal injury, the kind that can permanently damage a *lupus garou*. And so he was confined to a wheelchair. He couldn't fight for the pack, but he stubbornly refused leaving the land that was his ancestors'."

"Being a born leader is hard to give up," Darien said, the fury quieting in his blood. But he couldn't believe how her father would have cared more about the land than his own family.

"He challenged the leader, yet couldn't lead. The natural disaster in his town hadn't been his fault, yet until he died, he blamed himself. The pack leader's brother wanted either my sister or me for a mate. We were descendents of the first leader lines of Wildhaven, and since our pack leader, Bruin, was already mated, his brother took Larissa for his own. Bruin figured it would get my father in line if he gave up one of his daughters. My father assumed my sister was the best choice because she was a lot more… even-tempered than me. He feared if Crassus bullied me, I'd attempt to kill him. And I tried, once."

Darien opened his mouth to speak, but she shook her head. "It was a foolhardy venture. Do you and your brothers have a… well, a connection?"

Darien frowned. "I'm not sure what you're asking."

"I could sense when Larissa's emotions were out of control. When she was angry, or hurt, when she was terrified. We shared the ability to detect extreme emotions in the other. Every time Crassus beat her, if she was within a fifty-mile radius of where I was, I knew. Can you imagine knowing someone is beating your sibling half to death, and you can do nothing to stop him?"

Thor almighty, and he'd considered sending her back to her pack? He'd kill the bastard first. "Lelandi—"

"Four times, I allowed it. I told my father, but he could only speak to Bruin, who denied his brother's cruelty. The fifth time I felt my sister's pain, her emotions running from sheer terror to hating the bastard, I couldn't allow it to go on any longer. But I wasn't prepared to face him. I barged into their home and found my sister's face bruised and battered. Sobbing, she looked up at me, her eyes filled with pain and horror. Horror because I'd be next to suffer the brute's beatings. Jumping onto the bastard's back when he took another swing at her, I yanked at his long hair and reached around and gouged his face. I tried to strangle him. But I don't remember what happened afterward. A few days later, I woke to find myself at home in bed with a concussion, a broken arm, and collarbone."

She lifted her eyes to Darien, but they weren't filled with tears as he'd expected. Hatred burned brightly in the jade gems. And he couldn't blame her. His blood craved revenge. No *lupus garou* would ever touch a woman like that in his pack and get away with it. She looked so vulnerable he wanted to pull her into his arms, and for a minute, he hesitated. If he attempted to console her, he feared she'd quit talking. And he needed to hear her whole story.

Hell, he couldn't bear to look at her and not do something. He rose from his chair, and she looked ready to bolt. With a couple of lengthy strides, he crossed the floor and took her hand, then sat down beside her.

He wanted to embrace her hard, give her his strength because she looked so peaked, but her back remained rigid. He sat beside her on the leather love seat, opting to hold her hand instead.

"Tell me all of it, Lelandi."

"She shouldn't have suffered such cruelty at the hands of the beast. Crassus told me if my sister died, he'd take me for his own. I didn't perceive the threat lightly. But my father didn't believe Crassus would kill Larissa to have me." She pulled away from Darien, her eyes sad as her gaze dropped to the floor. "For a couple of weeks, my sister seemed to tolerate the forced marriage. I think Bruin had told him to lay off because I was a witness, and he'd pummeled me so badly also. Like a sickness he couldn't control, Crassus beat her again a week later, and she told me she had to find herself."

Darien swore softly under his breath. He had meant to tell her pack where she was as a goodwill gesture, but now he had every intention of crushing the brute who'd made the women suffer.

"When I asked what she meant, she said, 'You know, get a hobby or something.' She meant to run away. I didn't realize that until she'd been gone several weeks. Crassus hid the fact she'd run away, probably figuring he'd find her before anybody knew she had left him for good."

"He won't hurt you again, Lelandi. I promise. But if Bruin was your pack leader and Crassus was Larissa's mate, who's Leidolf?"

Lelandi's eyes widened. "My brother. How did you learn about him?"

"Deputy Sheriff Smith from Green Valley said your leader was looking for you."

"Leidolf's a pack leader? Where?"

"Portland, Oregon."

"Did you tell him I'm here?"

Darien shook his head. "No. I didn't know who the hell he was."

"Oh."

"Do you want me to tell him?"

She hesitated. "He'll want me to join his pack."

Darien leaned back into the love seat. "You're not going anywhere."

She took a deep breath and toyed with the hem of the shirt, her fingers skimming her bare skin. "You might as well hear everything I've got to say about my pack. Bruin kept his pack in line and didn't tolerate any rebellion. I feared he'd seek revenge against the rest of us when Larissa ran away. Then my father and mother died in a fiery car accident."

"Murder."

She gave a little *hmpf*. "No doubt."

"But you received flowers from your parents."

"Someone's sick joke. Bruin kept me under guard, stating he would declare Larissa dead and have me mated to his brother. I received the letters from Larissa, one for me, and the other for you, and escaped the night before I was to be mated with Crassus, dropping the letter for you at the post office on my way out of Wildhaven."

Darien threw Larissa's letter to him onto the coffee table. Lelandi's eyes lit on it. "Why the charade? Why did she claim to be you?"

"She was mated; I was not. She probably thought if she took my identity, no one would find out who she was, but if they did, they would discover Lelandi wasn't mated. But she fell in love. You were obviously good to her when Crassus wasn't. She wanted what others had, what our parents had had."

He grunted. "She wasn't in love with me. No bond existed between us. Now she's dragged you into this mess."

"Knowing my sister, she probably thought you'd want me like you wanted her. Then you could take care of me, and I'd be good for you." Lelandi shrugged. "That's what I figure anyway. She was more of a dreamer than me. I tend to be totally realistic."

"Uh-huh. So you're saying you and your sister didn't cook this whole scheme up so you could be my newest mate." After all that her sister had pulled, he didn't know what to really think.

Lelandi stood up from the couch so suddenly she wavered a minute, but then her eyes glowed with fury and her face flushed. "You may think all women are after you, Darien Silver, you… you arrogant bastard. But I have no desire to mate with you or any other gray."

She turned and stormed toward the door. Yanking it open, she gasped to see his brothers in the doorway, then shoved past them.

"Watch her, Tom." Darien motioned for Jake to come in, grabbed the letter, and walked back to his desk.

Sitting in his chair, Darien still couldn't believe his mate had been the daughter of leaders on both her mother's and father's sides of the family, a rare and highly prized quality in a mate. Which made him wonder why one of the pack members hadn't already claimed Lelandi. He also considered the despicable possibility that the sisters' parents had been murdered.

One thing he knew, Lelandi wouldn't be safe until he figured out who killed his mate. And Lelandi was his whether she believed she was his soul mate now or not. Plus, he would deal with this Crassus sooner or later. The bastard would come for Lelandi, if he assumed she'd be his mate. The red was a walking dead man. His pack leader brother, too, if he interfered.

Darien let out his breath in exasperation. "Did you check into the factory's accounts, Jake?"

"Yep, like you suspected. Larissa was siphoning off money."

"To pay a blackmailer."

"Most likely."

"How much?"

Jake pulled out a notepad and flipped to a page. "Nine-hundred and fifty-two dollars the first month. Tried to make it look like a strange amount to fit in with some of the purchases for supplies in the tanning processes. A thousand, sixty-five the next month. Went up to eleven-hundred and some change. Each month it went up, until her death, and then the withdrawals stopped. Hosstene said your name was on the checks so she never considered anything was wrong with them."

Darien shook his head.

"Can I see the letter?"

After passing it to his brother, he watched as Jake read it slowly.

"Do you think it's just a matchmaking venture?" Jake asked.

"What with the attempts on Lelandi's life? Nope. Then we have the stalker in the copper-hooded jacket to consider. The blackmailer won't want to get caught.

Find out if anyone had been getting some extra monthly pocket money. And if anyone's been throwing around more money than usual, or has let anything slip."

"What about this business with Larissa's former mate?"

"He's a dead man."

Jake nodded. "The red pack won't like it that you took his mate, then want to fight him for Lelandi."

"Then they shouldn't have allowed the bastard to beat on their women."

Jake set the letter on the desk. "Larissa says there's someone else—"

A rapid knock sounded on the door.

"Come in," Darien said.

Tom shoved the door open, his eyes excited. He grinned.

"Why aren't you watching—"

"Uncle Sheridan caught that copper-hooded guy skulking around the leather goods factory again. He sure didn't get far."

Darien nearly knocked his chair through the wall he got up so fast.

Tom quickly added, "You can't talk to him."

"Why the hell not?"

"He's a real fighter and the boys got so riled when they tried to subdue him, they knocked him unconscious. Doc said it would be several hours before anyone could question him now."

"Can't anyone do anything right? Who's watching Lelandi?"

"Sam's watching her."

"Whatever anyone does, don't let her know we caught the guy."

Tom's face fell. "Mason told both Sam and me in front of her."

"Shit." Darien stormed out of the office, expecting to find a hysterical Lelandi like she'd been in the car when they'd first gone after the man. Instead, he found her quietly sitting on the couch, staring at the coffee table. Which worried him more than when she was misbehaving.

Darien crouched in front of Lelandi, trying to use his most persuasive tone of voice. "Who is he?"

She looked up at him, eyes glaring. "He's my mate."

Swearing under his breath, Darien rose to his full height. "Doc examined you and found you're a virgin, so try another story."

Sam and Darien's brothers chuckled, but Lelandi's cheeks grew sunburn red. "Who the hell gave him permission to examine me?"

"Doc doesn't need permission."

"You arrogant bastard! You thought I wanted you and so you made sure I was available?" she screamed at him.

Everyone was deathly quiet. How could one little woman change the whole scenario around so that he was defending himself now?

"Like hell I did," he growled.

"Well, sorry if I don't believe you." She rose from the couch, shoved him out of the way, and headed for the stairs.

"Where do you think you're going?"

"To get dressed!"

Darien stalked after her. "You'll tell me who the guy is who accosted you."

"Ask him, if he comes out of the coma your men put him into!" She stomped up the stairs.

Blowing out his breath, he stomped up the stairs after her and followed her into the guest bedroom. Lelandi stiffened her back, whipped around, and glared at Darien.

For a moment, it was a standoff, Darien standing in the doorway, face red with barely repressed anger, and Lelandi's feelings just as hot. Then he closed the door and a trickle of fear ran through her veins.

He had the look of a feral wolf—angered, cornered, only she was the one he was backing into a corner when he stalked across the carpeted floor in her direction.

His eyes darkened, his gaze intent, determined.

"I won't tell you who he is no matter how much you try to intimidate me."

His grim lips almost seemed to smile, but they didn't exactly either. She wouldn't give in to him though. The powerful gray pack leader had a lot to learn about a stubborn red female.

"Back off," she growled as soon as he invaded her personal space.

He grabbed her shoulders, watched her expression intently. Did she look as terrified as she felt? Or did she put on a good enough show to hide the way her insides shook?

She knew what he wanted, what she assumed he'd craved the first time he saw her, to touch her, to kiss her, to love her—but not her, damn it. Rather, her sister.

"You don't want me." She meant to speak firmly, angrily, but the words came out breathlessly, almost desperate.

"You're not mated, Lelandi." His thumbs kneaded her shoulders in a sensuous caress, his fingers still gripping her. He leaned over and nuzzled her cheek with his smooth face. "Larissa was mated, wrongly, but still mated, and she was not the one I dreamed of loving under the pale light of the moon, naked in the woods."

The feel of his heated skin against hers set her blood on fire, but the realization he made love to her sister, calling her by the same name...

"Don't fight me," he whispered against her ear, his breath warm, his tongue tickling the sensitive lobe. "Tell me about your dreams."

Chapter 14

LELANDI MEANT TO SHOVE DARIEN AWAY, BUT SHE TOUCHED his waist tentatively instead, wanting to rip off his shirt and run her fingers over his bare chest, his face, to caress every inch of him while he touched her—just like the man had done with her in her fantasy world. She wanted to be sure he really *wasn't* the man in her dreams.

Yet liquid heat pooled between her legs and fire filled her belly. No *lupus garou* had ever smiled so sexy-like; none had ever set her blood afire like he did.

"It's…" She meant to tell him it wasn't right. He didn't really want her, just wanted to recapture the love he'd lost with her sister.

But he covered her mouth with his and stopped her objections. Kissed her—like she was the last woman on earth and he'd been deprived for years—greedily, hungrily, unabashedly.

Her heartbeat quickened. Now that she was no longer in pain or on medication that dulled her senses, she recognized the feel of him, the firmness, strength, the subtle way he touched her, claimed her, only it was so much more real. The beating of his heart sounded in her ears, the heat of his body burned at her soul, she tasted the sweetness of his lips, smelled the musky scent of him. He was her lover, his face no longer hidden in the shadows of her dreams, but genuine, his expression filled with hope and sexual craving.

Touching his tongue to the seam of her mouth, then penetrating, exploring, teasing her tongue with his, he pressed his advantage. And she let him, cherished the feel, but couldn't give in to the lust. His fingers roamed over her arms, tracing the skin, sending trails of tiny caressing sensations up and down, while her fingers remained cemented to his waist. She was afraid to touch him further, afraid to lead him on when she knew what they were doing was wrong and no good would come of it. Bruin and Crassus, her brother even, would not permit the union between the gray and her.

He maneuvered her away from the wall toward the bed. Not good, yet she didn't want to stop him. Her reluctance to encourage him didn't seem to faze him. He kissed her jaw, then swept his tantalizing mouth down her neck, licking a trail to the hollow of her throat.

She melted. Not being able to stand, she collapsed on her butt on the bed. "We shouldn't…"

He pushed her knees apart making her feel vulnerable, exposed to his desires. He moved between her legs and reached for the first button on her shirt, but she seized his wrists.

"I want to make sure you're healed, Lelandi."

"I am," she said, still holding tight, having to stop this madness.

He smiled and the look was pure devil. "For what I want to do."

She frowned. "I meant, I was healed. That's all. You don't have to look."

"Doctor's orders." The devilish gleam intensified in his darkened eyes.

"Liar!"

"Why didn't this Bruin select a mate for you earlier?" He pulled his hands free and finished unbuttoning the shirt, then slipped it off her shoulders.

His gaze focused on her nudity, an appreciative gleam in his eyes, and her skin flushed. "I told you. He thought my temper was too volatile."

"Try again." Darien pushed her back against the mattress. Straddling her leg with his, he leaned against her, his arousal hard against her thigh as his finger outlined the tip of her breast, then the other.

Her body tingled, her nubs peaking to the barest of his touches, and a moan welled up from deep within her throat. She couldn't fight the attraction she had for him even if she wanted to.

"Tell me the truth. You'd never come into a wolf's heat, had you? Not until we mated in our dreams. Not until you became mine. Come to me, Lelandi, like you do in my dreams." Darien kissed her forehead and waited, watching to see her reaction.

She studied his heavily lidded eyes, the look of lust filling them. "It was only a dream," she insisted. "But Larissa knew I'd had the dreams of… of a man who was Adonis reborn."

"Adonis?" He gave her a wicked smile.

She pursed her lips. "He's extremely handsome."

"He looks like me." He unbuttoned his shirt, leaving it hanging open.

She looked at his chest, and yes, the corded muscles, the smattering of dark hair stretching down to his waistband, the bronze skin that took her breath away whenever she spied him in the woods of her dreams…

She wanted to reach out to touch him, to feel his skin sizzling beneath her fingertips.

"Why didn't you tell me we've been dream mated?" Her gaze shifted to his eyes. "I never saw his face."

He frowned, cupped her face, and thought for a moment. "Ah. Because I'm the one who has the gift. But you pick up on some of it because you're my soul mate." He pressed her hands firmly against his chest. "Do you remember the beating of my heart? The way I feel? The way my mouth feels against yours? Lelandi, you were always the one. The first time I came to you, someone had called your name and in your dream state you had mouthed your name, trying to make sense of it, unable to wake fully. You said your name against my mouth again. But I could never learn your last name."

He was the one. So why was she still reluctant to give herself to him? Her sister. She couldn't break free of the notion her sister had meant something to him.

He pulled Lelandi from the bed into his embrace and held her tight. "What I'd had with Larissa didn't feel right, but she'd told me she didn't have any family. And she used the name I knew you by. I assumed the dreams I shared with you were fantasy and making love with you in the flesh wasn't supposed to be as erotic."

Her sister had lied. She'd duped him and… and he hadn't meant anything to her as Lelandi had feared.

She touched his chest with trembling fingers, wanting what he offered, the sexual connection she'd shared with him upon sleeping, but afraid, too, of the consequences. "There's… there's no going back."

"As if I'd give you up for anything in the world, Lelandi. You're the one I've searched for every night, longing to be reunited with you. The one who haunts my dreams until we're together again. It's you."

Right or wrong, she pressed her lips against his, giving herself willingly to him and was immediately transported to the dream. Except it was no longer a dream. This time he captivated all of her senses. His sexual pheromones filled her nostrils like an aphrodisiac, his essence overwhelming her senses.

"There's no going back," she repeated, her voice soft, worried.

She'd defy her pack and her family's wishes. But she wouldn't be like Larissa. Her mating would be final, like it was for other *lupus garous*. No other would come between them.

He stroked her hair with loving caresses. "You couldn't come into a wolf's heat until I reached out to you. You are mine."

Like a feral wolf who caught his prey and claimed her, he kissed her greedily, possessively. No more gentleness, waiting to make sure she agreed. And she loved it. His hands tangled in her long hair, and he grabbed handfuls, his smoldering gaze raking over her nakedness. But she couldn't take her eyes off his face, the chiseled features, the predatory look, the face she'd so wanted to see, but couldn't in her dreams.

Releasing her hair, he slid his hands down her shoulders to her breasts, his palms massaging them. His thumbs caressed her nipples, teasing them to beg for more. His tongue plunged into her mouth, melting any denial she might have that he was the one. Tremulous shivers of pleasure sizzled across her bare skin. His rigid erection pressed against her waist, urgent, hungry to batter down her virginal barrier.

She maneuvered around him so that his back was to the bed, then using his shirt to hold him hostage, she pushed him onto the mattress. His mouth curved up and his eyes sparkled with dark delight. She pressed his legs apart and moved in between them. This time she was in charge, uninhibited like in her dreams.

Intending to work up nice and slow and torture him, she already craved flopping on her back and letting him take her. So much for her wanting to be in charge. She reached down to unfasten his belt, and he folded his arms behind his head and watched her struggle. But she couldn't unhook the belt no matter how much she tried. Finally, he chuckled low, quickly stripped, then pulled her on top of him, bare skin to bare skin.

He was gorgeous—every buff, corded muscle tensed in anticipation. The smattering of dark hair covering his chest trailed down toward the curly hairs between his legs, and she considered the way his erection was already ramrod stiff, thick and readied, poking her in the belly. This was the way she remembered him in the pale light of the moon, the look and feel of his hard muscles, the touch of his soft skin, the way his nipples pebbled with her mouth and tongue grazing them. He swept his hands down her arms, sending a rush of tingling straight to her core, a thousand times more pleasurable than in the dreams.

She ran her fingers over the muscles in his chest, and his arousal jumped. She smiled and looked up at his face, his eyes glazed over, his lips curving up slightly. She shifted, straddling him, her knees bent, spreading them outward, wanting to capture the pike poking between her legs. Hot and wet and way past ready.

He groaned and rolled her onto her back, then leaned against her. She loved it when he took charge. He was like her dream lover, but the feelings were richer, his touch more arousing, every sense on high alert as she smelled his sexual desire, heard his heart pumping pell mell, and felt his aroused breath against her cheek. Pure eroticism stoked every nerve ending.

Clutching handfuls of his shoulder-length hair, she arched her pelvis against him, seeking gratification, her body screaming with unfulfilled need. Responding to her, he rubbed his heavy groin against her folds and elicited a soft; deep-throated moan from her.

But he refused to enter her yet. Instead, he smiled and flicked his tongue against her sensitive nipple, his gaze focused back on hers. She bucked against him, wanting him to enter her, to make her his mate, to complete the bond that would last forever. But he wouldn't hurry no matter how much she desired him to, and instead, swept his fingers down her waist, then lifted his body off her slightly, touching the erotic zone at the apex of her thighs. He stroked her hard and fast, and she could barely take the delicious pleasure of his touch. Slipping his fingers lower, he inserted them deeply inside her.

Hoarsely, he said, "You're wet for me."

She bit his shoulder with a mock nip, and he thrust his head back and laughed. Of course she was wet. As soon as he'd advanced toward her in the bedroom with that hungry, feral look in his eyes, the moisture had gathered between her legs.

He thrust his fingers deep inside her, simulating what he would do with his engorged erection, soon, she hoped as he wrung out every emotion, pumping up her craving, just a thread short of completion. Then her internal muscles convulsed with orgasm and a wave of heat surged through her. His fingers stilled inside her, he gave her a satisfied smile.

Oh heavens, she'd come with just his fingers inside her. Sweet passion spiraled through her and with a soft moan, she called out his name, loving that she could now say it, no longer silenced like in the dream.

Darien's expression filled with deep satisfaction, and she loved seeing how much he enjoyed giving her pleasure. But they weren't done, not until they'd truly mated.

"Finally," he whispered in her ear, "you know me. And now, it's my turn." His eyes held a roguish gleam. And she was ready.

God of thunder, Lelandi was beautiful. Darien wanted to laugh when she took charge, then quickly ceded, melting to his strokes. And now he had her where he desired her, the vixen.

For the first time, he wanted to go slow and control the outcome, not wishing to hurt her when he broke through her barrier. He spread her thighs wide and entered her carefully, stretching her to accept his engorged erection.

"You... are... huge."

He smiled, but slowed his penetration. "Are you all right?"

"Yes, but I was supposed to be in charge."

He chuckled, his voice drenched in lust. "You were taking too long," he rasped, then paused to take her nipple between his teeth, scraping gently.

Her inner muscles clenched him tightly, but he gently pushed forward. For a moment he paused, then he watched her face, flushed with arousal, and with a sudden thrust, he breached the maidenhead. She opened her eyes and he worried he'd hurt her.

"Are you all right?" he asked again, caressing her cheek with his thumb.

Her muscles clenched again, and she nodded. "I've… I've never felt anything like this… not even in the dreams."

He gave a wolfish grin and brushed her hair away from her cheek. "I don't doubt it. Not when you were a virgin."

With slow, deep thrusts, he plunged into her over and over again, loving every inch of his dream mate in the flesh. She was his, now and forever.

Lelandi couldn't catch her breath as Darien pushed her toward the peak. Julia Wildthorn was right. Sex with a *lupus garou* who was your soul mate was nothing short of miraculous.

Darien's heated gaze swept over her again, his body desiring her with an urgency she felt, too, and she wanted to heighten the pleasure as her body shouted to reach climax again. But he pinned her shoulders down, claiming her, possessing her, making her his for as long as they both lived. She loved what being *lupus garou* meant—the intensity of the lovemaking, the unbreakable bond between them, stronger even than the familial one, the craving so great, it couldn't be denied.

"Thor almighty," Darien groaned, filling her womb with his hot seed, spasms of orgasm rocking her body, washing through her like a rogue tidal wave. For a moment, he lay heavily against her, his and her breathing hard, their hearts pumping at breakneck speed. "Life will never be the same," he said, huskily, trying to lift his weight from her, but she held on tight. "I'll crush you." His eyes smiled.

"You feel so good against me, I don't want you to ever let go."

He kissed her cheek and let out a tired breath. "It's about time you knew where you belonged."

She bit him on the shoulder, hard this time. He laughed and moved off her, then pulled her on top of him and caressed her waist with a gentle sweeping touch. She cherished the way he could be so loving.

But then he was back to business. "What did you talk about with Silva last night?"

"Didn't Trevor tell you everything?" Lelandi asked, feeling peeved.

They were supposed to cuddle for a while, luxuriate in the feel of one another, the bond they'd just created. She realized tangling with a pack leader meant business was a heartbeat away.

Darien could see convincing Lelandi that as soul mates there would be no secrets between them, he would have to wear her down on that issue, too. But as much as he wanted to hold her tight and enjoy her heated little body, he had to protect her from harm. That meant knowing all he could about Lelandi and her sister. "I'd rather hear it from you."

"I don't remember. Must have been the medicine."

Darien *humpf*ed under his breath. "Guess you're as good a liar as your sister."

Lelandi gave him a half smile and licked Darien's nipple.

He'd expected her to come out fighting. He was quickly learning she was like her sister—totally unpredictable. It sure as hell kept him on the edge of his seat.

"He's going to miss the opening ceremony," Jake said downstairs in the living room, loudly enough for Darien and Lelandi to hear.

"Considering the importance of what he's doing, don't you think this takes priority over the fair?" Tom asked.

"Hopefully, he won't be so grouchy anymore," Jake added.

Tom laughed.

Glancing up at the canopy over the bed, Darien rolled his eyes.

Lelandi kissed his cheek. "I'm sure Sam's waiting for me to go with him to serve drinks."

"I'd rather keep you here with me for the rest of the day."

"Was it… was it better for you than in the dreams?"

He twisted a curl of her hair around his finger. "You have to ask? I can't begin to describe how it made me feel, like a joining of our souls, the consummation of a lifelong search, the dream I've been trying to make real for months."

She sighed heavily. "The same for me. Only I thought you'd be less—big."

He chuckled. "The real thing feels more…"

"Real."

"See you at the opening ceremony," Tom hollered, and slammed the front door.

Darien groaned. "Got to go. But we're leaving the festivities early so we can return here. Sure you don't want to stay here until I return?"

"Nope, you've promised to let me out of confinement, and I'm going to the fair."

"I want to keep you safe, Lelandi."

"I'll be safe, and thinking about the festivities *after* the ceremony."

Darien rose from the bed and looked down at Lelandi's nakedness. "You're beautiful. Absolutely god sent."

"You're not half-bad yourself."

"Adonis, remember?" he said grinning.

"I hear them stirring, Sam," Jake said. "But if they don't hurry, you can take Silva to the tavern, and I'll bring Lelandi later. Unless Darien has decided to skip the opening ceremony."

Darien shook his head and dressed while Lelandi watched. Her eyes held his hostage and he growled. "Come back early, vixen." Then he gave her body another long look of approval, groaned, and shut the door on his departure.

The smoldering gaze in Darien's eyes made her want to tackle him and return him to bed, forget about the fair or her freedom for a few hours.

Silva soon joined her, her face unreadable, although Lelandi thought something was wrong. Then Silva said, "Darien must have woken on the wrong side of the bed again. First, he ordered Jake to take Peter to task for sleeping on guard duty. Then Darien told me I had to give you a more decent shirt than what I bought you to wear." She shrugged. "I don't see anything wrong with what you were wearing." She gave a sly smile. "But I guess he doesn't want the rest of the guys to see. I really can't believe he's letting you out of the house to work with us."

"I think he's feeling better now. I guess he trusts Sam to keep a good eye on me."

"He will." The look Silva gave and the way she said the words was a warning. *Don't plan on slipping away.*

Lelandi pulled a cashmere sweater out of her bag. "He found my suitcase."

Silva stared at the bag. "Who had it?" She walked over to it and smelled it. "The guy in the copper coat."

"It smells like several grays." Lelandi finished dressing. "Even Sheriff Sheridan's paws have been on it."

"They should be. He's the sheriff. Ready to go, sugar? Sam's waiting downstairs. Doc Mitchell, our local veterinarian, will be the guard on duty."

"Veterinarian?"

"Yep, horse doctor during the Civil War. He's been a practicing vet forever. Does a super job when we're in our wolf forms. And he's one of the best shooters we've got."

"Like, good enough to have killed the gunman from a distance?"

"Among the grays quite a few are like that."

Great.

"What the hell's holding you up, Silva?" Sam shouted from the bottom of the stairs. "We've got to get a move on."

"Yes, sirree, boss." Silva led Lelandi down the stairs. "Didn't want to leave our star guest behind."

Sam motioned to a gray-bearded man, his eyes black and beady, but sharp as a wary wolf's, taking in every inch of her, his mouth expressionless.

"Doc Mitchell," Sam explained. "He's riding shotgun."

The vet patted the gun in the holster at his hip. Wearing a leather vest and denims, cowboy boots, and a weather-beaten Stetson, he just needed chaps and a horse—though the distinctive odor of horse clung to him—and he'd be right at home in the part of a grizzly old gunslinger.

He tipped his hat in greeting.

"Nice to meet you, Doctor Mitchell," Lelandi said.

"Mitchell—no need to be formal, miss." He motioned to the black Suburban parked in front of Darien's house.

Lelandi smelled snow in the air and wished she'd managed to steal away with some of her warmer clothes.

Silva sat next to Lelandi in the backseat, then her mouth curved up in a wide smile. "Ohmigod, Darien and you…" She squeezed Lelandi's hands and didn't say anything more.

Sam pulled out of the driveway and headed back to town while Mitchell watched out the front windshield and mirrors for signs of trouble.

Silva said with a smirk, "Unofficially, I'd say you're a bona fide official member of our pack."

Sam glanced over the seat while Mitchell looked in the rearview mirror. "Why?" Mitchell asked. "Did Darien say something to you?"

"Nope," Silva said. "It goes a little deeper."

Mitchell glanced over the seat at Lelandi. She was sure her face was crimson as hot as it felt.

"Whoa, I take it the boss will officially announce this soon?" He shook his head and watched the road again. "Going to be some pissed-off bitches. Although we knew where this was headed."

Yeah, and Lelandi was ready to deal with every one of them to keep her dream lover at her beck and call.

When they drove into town, Lelandi stared at the transformation. Colorful banners hung from every covered porch, and arts and crafts and food booths crowded all the wooden walkways down the main street. Even the shabby building across from the tavern was decorated in silver and red banners, proclaiming it to be the first hotel in Silver Town, haunted since its inception. Souvenirs of Indian arrowheads and other old western artifacts were on display. The aroma of sausages and turkey legs grilling filled the air, and Victorian music wafted in the chilly breeze. But the costumes of the townspeople garnered Lelandi's attention most. Dressed in Victorian era clothing, they wore sunshiny smiles and seemed to be enjoying themselves.

Lelandi took a deep breath. "I remember wearing the cage when I was a young girl. I can't imagine dressing like that again." And the awful corsets, too.

"Sure. It's part of our heritage, our history. Even before we started the fair, we had a Victorian Era Day to celebrate the beginning of our town. A train ride winds up through the mountains, too, and anyone dressed in period costume gets on half price. Looks like a lot of the tourists came prepared this year. Hosstene, Darien's accountant at the factory," Silva said, pointing at a stall, "is renting costumes for the day for those who don't have one and want to fit in." Silva patted Lelandi's arm. "But, you don't need to rent one. I've got just the dress for you."

"Good, because I wouldn't pay any money to that woman," Lelandi said, recalling their confrontation in the tavern's restroom.

Mitchell snorted. "There's already a welcoming crowd waiting for their free drinks at the tavern. Give anything away free and it's a madhouse. Waste of money, I say."

"Like when you spay and neuter cats and dogs for free once a month to avoid unwanted pets, right, Mitchell?" Sam asked, humor coating his words. "Got a ton of business last year by offering a few free sodas. Before we knew it, everyone was ordering the harder stuff and we made a bundle." He turned to Lelandi. "Just a warning, this is the one day of the year that humans are allowed to enter. Otherwise, it's a private club."

"But you let me in that one day."

Sam smiled. "Private as in only *lupus garous* are allowed. I didn't know you were Larissa's sister at first, but I recognized you were one of us."

His brow furrowed, Deputy Trevor waved at them from the tavern as they pulled into a parking space.

"What's *he* doing here?" Mitchell grumbled.

"Darien's orders to ensure we get the little lady into the tavern safe and sound," Sam said.

The crowd parted to make way for Sam to unlock the door, but he relocked it after he, Silva, Lelandi, and Mitchell entered the establishment.

A shudder ran down Lelandi's entire body, remembering her apprehension when she'd first visited the tavern, and what transpired after she left.

Silva squeezed her hand and led her to a room off the bar. "Here's where we store our costumes. We celebrate Blow Me Timber Pirate Day, Viking Day for those of us who were from the Norselands, and Celtic Day for the Scots-Irish among us. German

Fest is filled with German foods, song, and drink. We never advertise the events, but the word is spreading and we're getting more tourists every year. The guys will change in another room."

Shelves filled the large room and two doors led into a walk-in closet where costumes hung on poles. Silva pulled out a drawer in a chest at one end of the closet. "Time to return to an earlier era when men wore the pants in the family."

Lelandi shook her head. "They think they still do." She slipped out of her sweater and unfastened her bra. She'd never thought she'd wear a corset again after she'd ditched hers in the Victorian Age.

Lelandi fingered the gowns and pulled out a brilliant blue satin one.

Silva dangled a pair of garters. "Remember these?"

"Nobody will know what I wear under the gown."

Silva smiled. "Darien will."

"I bet he doesn't dress up for these occasions."

"Ha!" Silva said. "He's the one who insisted on it. *And* he was the one who started Pirate's Day. I swear he was an ancient Viking, but he isn't old enough. Here are your drawers."

"Crotchless. Those were the days." Lelandi laughed.

Silva slipped a sleeveless, knee-length cotton chemise over Lelandi's head. She lifted a robin's egg blue satin corset, heavily boned with whalebone out of the drawer.

Lelandi folded her arms. "Not the corset."

"Got to have something to hold you up. You know what they say about women who don't wear their corsets."

"They're loose women, but…"

Silva laced up the ties, but not too tightly. Then she pulled the crinoline cage out and opened it up. "Better than the five or six petticoats we used to wear to give our skirts shape." She slipped a camisole over Lelandi's head.

"I remember how long it took us to dress."

Silva fitted a simple petticoat over the frame. "And how we needed help getting into all this. For most, it didn't matter, but for us, trying to shed our clothes when the moon first made its appearance…" She shook her head. "What a chore. I ripped more petticoats trying to ditch them." She layered an intricately embroidered petticoat over the plain one. "Now for the finale." She helped Lelandi on with the gown.

The neckline dipped low, the mere strap of a sleeve rested off the shoulders, and Lelandi felt more exposed than usual. "Do you have anything that's cut a little higher?"

"Nope," Silva said with a knowing smirk. "Besides, for serving in the tavern, it seems appropriate."

"Ha! They're Victorian ballroom gowns." Lelandi fingered a peach one. "Not what the serving wenches would have worn."

Silva pulled the peach gown out. "High-classed tavern in the New World."

Lelandi helped Silva dress and they pinned their hair up, then fastened hats covered in feathers to each other's hair. "We'll skip the gloves," Silva said. "I tried them last year, but spilled a tray of customers' drinks, and Sam said enough with the authenticity of the period."

Behind the counter, Sam was pouring drinks, wearing a swallowtail coat and black satin knee breeches tight over high boots.

"Wow, Sam, you sure look dashing." He gave Lelandi a broad smile. Doc Mitchell was wearing a dinner coat without tails and a satin vest. He tipped his head in greeting. Lelandi smiled back at him. "You, too, Doc. I feel like I've definitely traveled back in time." Especially since the place still seemed part of the Victorian Age.

"Ladies." Sam kissed each of their hands in succession. "You look divine. But if Darien knew how striking Lelandi looked in that blue gown, he'd send her home."

"Here's hoping no one will spill the beans." Silva motioned to the glasses stacked underneath the bar. "Bring them out and I'll fill them."

Sam motioned to Mitchell to open the door. The crowd surged forward and within minutes, the place was filled with humans and *lupus garous*. Laughter and conversation quickly filled the silence.

Dressed in a tweed suit, Joe Kelly, the miner who'd paid for her bottled water the first time she'd been here, walked up to the bar with a smile. This time he was clean, not a speck of grime on his baby-round face. His gaze focused on her low-cut bodice, which sent a prickle of anxiety sparking across her skin. No matter how many times she'd tried to pull the bodice higher when she crouched to get glasses from beneath the bar, the darned thing wouldn't budge. And Sam had caught her in the act every time.

"Can I have a beer?" Joe asked.

"Sure." Lelandi filled a glass.

"You look a lot like your sister."

Triplets often did, she wanted to say. "You were her friend?"

His eyes darkened and his mouth curved down.

He didn't like being thought of as Larissa's friend? Maybe he'd stalked her and she'd turned him down. Maybe he'd hired the killer or did the job himself.

He lifted his gaze slowly. "Will you… leave with me? I… I don't want you to get hurt, too."

She assumed he'd cared for Larissa. A gut instinct. "Do you know what happened to my sister?"

Sam moved closer to Lelandi. He didn't look at her, just continued pouring drinks, but he had no reason to close in on her, except to hear what was being said. For her protection? Or was there more at stake?

Joe slid Lelandi a piece of paper. She considered stuffing it in her bodice, but when Trevor showed interest in the note, she opened it. Joe bowed his head and took his beer back to his table.

The paper was blank. Trevor seized it and Joe gave her a satisfied smile. The deputy shot Joe a blistering look. Joe lifted a shoulder.

Trevor asked Lelandi, "What did he say to you?"

"Why don't you ask Sam? He's been eavesdropping."

Sam gave her a reserved smile.

Trevor's expression darkened. "Because I'm asking *you*."

Having dealt with his kind before in her pack, she shrugged off his attempt at intimidation. Given a little power, it would go straight to their heads.

"He wanted a beer. I gave him one. He worried for my safety. Considering what happened the last time I left this tavern, his concern probably is justified. Oh, and he said I look like my sister. No real revelation there." She raised a brow, waiting for Trevor's response.

He glanced at Sam who nodded, confirming she'd

spoken the truth. The deputy crumpled the note and tossed it on the bar, then walked off. Before Lelandi could grab the note, Sam did. Why? Did he think there was some secret communiqué written on the paper in invisible ink?

Sam shoved the note in his pocket. She hoped if Joe had written anything to her in secret, he wouldn't get in trouble for it. Unless he had a hand in her sister's death. As much as she thought he was okay, she couldn't rule out anyone yet.

The stocky bitch who'd pulled Lelandi's hair in the restroom the night she was shot sidled up to the bar. Silva was carrying a tray of drinks to a table, Sam was filling more glasses, and Lelandi set more drinks on another tray, trying to ignore Angelina.

"Got you tending bar, I see. Earning your keep?" Angelina snarled. "Three bullets weren't enough to keep you away, were they? What will it take?"

Chapter 15

LELANDI WANTED TO SHUT ANGELINA'S MOUTH FOR HER AS she leaned haughtily against the bar. In mixed company, *lupus garous* were careful about what they revealed. But this woman was too angry to care.

"Three bullet wounds?" a blonde human female asked, her blue eyes round. She wore jeans, snow boots, and a tight-fitting ski sweater that showed off her ample breasts while she sat on a heavy-duty parka—not into the Victorian-era festivities it appeared. "She's not the one everyone is talking about, is she? The one people said looked like death had claimed her?"

"Superficial wounds." Lelandi gave the *lupus garou* bitch a warning look.

"You should have died." Angelina grabbed a glass of Coke off the counter, and took a seat with Ritka and Hosstene. Guess Hosstene had found someone else to man her costume rental booth for the day.

"Angelina's a pain in the ass." Silva left the empty tray on the counter and grabbed another full one. "It's rumored she fears tackling you again." She carried the tray to a table.

"My name's Carol Wood." The blonde stuck her hand out.

Lelandi's parents had taught her not to make friends with humans. Close human involvement could cause a world of trouble—period. In all these years, she had heeded their advice and was thankful for it. The woman reminded her of a reporter, eager for a headline that would propel her into an overnight news sensation. Lelandi wiped off her hands on a dish towel and shook the woman's hand.

"I love your costume. I didn't realize people were dressing up. Next year, I'll get something. But an early snow's coming so I was dressed for that."

The weatherman had said nothing about an early snow, although Lelandi and her kind could smell it coming. She wondered how this woman knew.

Carol took a seat at the bar. "Chablis, please. So you're… Larissa, right? The sister of Darien's deceased wife?"

"Yes, but I'm Lelandi. My sister was Larissa."

Lelandi moved away from the woman, but caught the eye of a dark-haired guy sipping a soda, watching every move she made. He wasn't wearing a costume either, just a sweater and turtleneck and a pair of denims. But it was the intrigued way he observed her that gave her pause. She took a deep breath and breathed in his scent. A gray. And he'd been listening to her conversation with Carol.

His expression remained serious, and he finally set his glass down and leaned against the bar closer to her. Joe raised up out of his chair, but one of his companions seized his arm and shook his head. His face scowling, Joe retook his seat.

"Nothing is as it seems, miss. Just watch your step." The man's voice was friendly, but dark.

Trevor came up behind him and growled low, "Move along."

The man's lips rose in a coy way, then he bowed his head to Lelandi, and took his glass and headed to one of the tables.

"Who is that?" Lelandi asked Sam in a hushed voice.

He glanced at the table where the gray sat. "Chester McKinley. He's checking out our town so he can make recommendations to his mayor of Green Valley. Why? Was he bothering you?"

"No."

Chester still observed her with a cool, appraising expression. As much as she tried to ignore him, even when she went back to filling another tray of drinks for Silva, Lelandi noticed he was still studying her.

Trevor had moved to a position near the restrooms and watched the tavern's patrons. Mitchell stood near the front door doing the same thing as if he and Trevor were bouncers who usually served on duty. At any rate, she felt safe.

"So is this your regular job?" Carol moved a barstool closer to where Lelandi worked.

What *was* she doing here? She was supposed to find her sister's murderer. Now she'd joined with her sister's widowed mate and the word would soon spread throughout the pack. She'd intended to find her brother next. But at least Bruin was out of the picture. Or she assumed he was. She knew he'd retaliate against her and her parents when Larissa ran off. But she didn't think he'd try to take Darien on for mating her.

"I guess you were paying your condolences. I'm so sorry about your sister. I had one who suffered from severe depression. Hers was an organic thing. She finally slit her wrists and well, no more depression." Carol offered a weak smile, but tears filled her eyes. She stared at her empty wineglass, then frowned. "Sorry. That didn't sound very nice the way I said it. I loved my sister, but my parents doted on her, trying to 'fix' her, trying to placate her. Me, I was upbeat no matter the hardships that came my way so my parents acted like I never needed a support system whenever anything horrible happened in *my* life. My sister had nothing to complain about. Always ticked me off that she was so jealous of everyone when she had everything. But… I guess I'm still angry with her for ending her own life." Carol handed Lelandi her empty glass. "Another Chablis?"

"I'm sorry about your sister." Lelandi poured another glass of wine.

"We were really close when we were little. Then…" Carol hurriedly wiped tears away. "So… what do you normally do when you're not filling in?"

"Taking care of my father."

That left a bitterness in Lelandi's mouth. She hadn't really considered what she would do beyond looking for her sister's murderer and finding her brother. If her mother hadn't worked and needed Lelandi home to take care of their father, she would have worked as a… well, maybe a psychologist. Everyone used her as a sounding board for their troubles. Maybe she would be good at that. Yet, becoming Darien's mate left her unsure of her next move.

"Oh. Is your father sick?"

Lelandi looked away. "He's dead."

She wondered who could be so cruel to send her flowers, saying they were from her parents. Yet a crumb of hope nagged at her. What if they were truly safe? But how?

"Oh. I'm sorry. What are you going to do now that you have no father to look after?"

"I'll figure it out later," Lelandi said, not willing to reveal anything else about herself, particularly to a human. "So, what do you do?"

"Ohmigosh, let me tell you." Carol leaned forward and whispered, "Can you keep a secret?"

Right, as if this woman had anything to tell her that would be worth her time. "Sure," Lelandi said, doing her faux bartending psychology work and leaned over the counter. "What?"

"I'm psychic, sometimes. It comes and goes," Carol said, her voice still hushed, then she straightened and grinned.

Lelandi stared at the woman. She didn't believe in that stuff. Just like she figured the haunted hotel across the street was part of a big hoax, and soul mates didn't exist. Except after making love with Darien, she was reevaluating her stance on that.

"I don't know why I mentioned it to you, but you seemed the sort that wouldn't tell the world. And, well, maybe because we both lost a sister to severe depression. Means we have a connection, sort of. Plus," Carol said, shrugged, and added, "you're probably not planning on sticking around. Kind of like telling a stranger on an airline flight about your wildest sexual fantasies, and you'll never see that person again."

Lelandi's mouth dropped open. "You've done that?"

Carol laughed. "No, but I've wanted to."

"So what does being psychic mean for you?"

What if the woman could envision humans turning into wolves under the full moon or something else that could really cause problems if anyone believed her?

"I've seen… things. Have since I was a little girl. Really strange things. But you don't want to hear about that. Most importantly, I'm a trained nurse—trained in surgery. But the only opening here is for the school nurse. I want to work at the hospital, except that woman…" She waved her half-full wineglass at Ritka's table. "… the shorter, fat one, Angelina, she wouldn't give my résumé to the doctor." Carol shook her head. "Darien Silver is on the hospital board and apparently *he* has the final say about hiring staff. Said I could work at the school. Sure enough, they said they'd hire me. That the old school nurse, and believe me she looked ancient, was ready to retire. But I'm trained in surgery. Why would I want to work with kids with runny noses? Waste of my training."

"The hospital's staff must be full," Lelandi said, understanding why Darien wouldn't hire her.

"Can I see your wounds?" Carol pointed to Lelandi's stomach.

Lelandi gave her a faked smile. "Sorry. If I begin exposing body parts, the guys will think they're in a strip joint."

Carol laughed out loud and slapped the bar. "Strip joint. That's funny. Here? A strip joint? This place is as backward as they come. I don't even know why I left Denver after I got my training."

"Why did you?"

"My parents. I'm the only daughter they have left, and I wanted to be here for them." Carol finished her drink. "Let me tell you, I'm not easily dissuaded." She handed her glass to Lelandi. "Another Chablis?"

"Forgive my asking, but do you usually drink this much?"

Carol gave her a lopsided grin. "I missed the fair last year. What are celebrations for if you can't have some fun? Fill 'er up."

Lelandi poured the wine into the glass and deposited the woman's cash into the register. The tavern was so packed, Silva was getting way behind on service. Hoping she wouldn't drop a tray of drinks, Lelandi grabbed the next one and meant to carry it to a table full of gray males. Maybe because Darien and his brothers weren't around or because the five men had a little too much to drink, they were making fools of themselves, trying to get her attention—grinning, wolf whistles, a few comments she couldn't make over the din of noise in the place. Before she reached the table, Ritka shoved an empty chair into Lelandi's path.

The back of the chair knocked the tray into Lelandi's chest, giving her heart a jump start and a dull thud radiated outward. Before she lost the drinks, Chester McKinley leapt from his chair and seized the tray. He set it on the men's table, while Ritka gave Lelandi an evil smirk. Lelandi grabbed the chair, her knuckles straining with tension, but fought the urge to knock Ritka's teeth down her throat. Yet, the male grays waited to see how she handled the situation. Alpha females didn't back down, although she had to curb her natural *lupus garou* instincts because of the humans in the establishment.

"Are you all right?" Chester seized Lelandi's arm and moved her away from the impending fight, as she warred with her natural instincts. "Did she hurt your injuries?"

"Thanks, no, I'm all healed." Maybe a new bruise though. Lelandi cast Ritka a warning look that she'd deal with her later. "Thanks for helping out."

"I admire a woman with spunk. Your courage reminds me of my sister, around the same age as you. She's gotten herself into predicaments that have forced me to rescue her a few times."

Deep inside she wished her brother had been more like Chester and stuck around to help her family. "What did you mean about me watching myself?"

"Darien's too close to this situation concerning your sister. I've been there before. He needs an outsider. Someone who isn't as easily influenced by family or long-time friendships."

"Someone like you?"

"I've been a P.I. for a number of years. The cases I've worked I'm not emotionally involved in. That's all I'm saying."

"What do you know about this case?" Lelandi hoped he could give her something to go on.

"Nothing. Darien's people watch me day and night. I'd need his permission to investigate."

Lelandi folded her arms. "You've got *my* permission."

Chester smiled. "You're really cute, you know?" He shook his head. "Darien has to approve."

"All right then. What do you suspect?"

"Plenty. But I need Darien's approval. Right now, his brother tells me Darien's too busy to speak with me."

Lelandi frowned. "I'm investigating my sister's death even if he doesn't like it."

Chester let out his breath. "Better let the grays handle this. They may not get to the bottom of this as quickly as I might, but you don't need to get yourself shot up again."

She hadn't intended to. But then she realized she needed to find her gun. Where could Darien have secured it? His office? His bedroom? "How long are you staying?"

"I'd planned on being here for just a couple of days and report back to my mayor about Silver Town. But when I saw you shot to hell, I decided to stick around longer. Maybe you'll need me. And maybe you can change Darien's mind in the meantime. In any event, you stay—"

Trevor stormed toward them, gave Chester the evil eye, then continued on past.

Chester raised his brows, his gaze following the deputy out of the tavern. He squeezed Lelandi's hand. "Get me a beer, will you? I have a feeling I'll be tossed out of here shortly for being an outsider talking to you. Although I imagine any of the guys in this place who attempt to speak with you would torque him off."

Trusting her wolf instincts, she felt Chester McKinley might be able to solve the mystery of the killings. What was wrong with Darien to brush his offer of help aside? As soon as she saw Darien, she would try to convince him to capitulate.

Her spirits lifted as she imagined that they might discover the murderer sooner with Chester looking into it. She returned to the bar and got him a beer. Before she could take it to his table, Silva seized it.

"Don't need any more 'incident's.' As soon as Trevor tells Darien that Chester McKinley was molesting you, there'll be hell to pay." Silva gave Lelandi a broad smile.

"You sure know how to do it, sugar. I haven't managed to do anything with Sam to make Trevor jealous."

"Maybe your heart isn't in it?"

"No… no. Sam was totally agreeable. Said he'd do anything for a good cause, and I do want to give it a try. But…"

"You don't want to make Trevor jealous. You're afraid it may backfire."

"I guess you're right. Trevor's got a hot temper. I guess I'm afraid he might take it out on Sam."

"I wouldn't worry about it." Lelandi brought out some more glasses. She figured Trevor wouldn't react because he wouldn't care what Silva did, truth be told.

Silva took the beer to Chester's table and handed it to him. He smiled and thanked her. Returning to the bar, Silva grabbed another tray of drinks. "Chester seems a likable sort. Hope Darien's not too hard on him."

"He wasn't molesting me, by the way."

"As an outsider, he was getting *way* too friendly." Silva took off with the tray of drinks.

"Another refill?" Carol asked Lelandi, lifting her empty wine glass. Her eyes glassy, she appeared as though she'd had enough, a drink or two ago.

Lelandi handed her a bottle of ice water. "Your head will thank me in the morning." She hoisted another tray of drinks and headed for a table of humans when Ritka shoved Angelina's shoulder.

That was all the cue Angelina needed, and she rose from her seat and rushed to get in Lelandi's face this time.

"Getting all the guys hot and bothered now, eh? Not enough that you've got Darien panting for you? Even

some damned outsider can't keep his hands off you.
You're just like your sister."

If she hadn't been holding a tray, Lelandi would have
slapped the bitch in the face, but the place got awfully
quiet. Instantly, Lelandi saw the reason. Darien, flanked
by his two brothers, was on the warpath. God, he was
gorgeous. Dressed in a coat with long tails and a gold
paisley brocade vest, he outshone everyone else in the
tavern. But his brown eyes turned even darker when he
saw her, his measuring gaze taking in every inch of her
bodice—way too exposed.

Now, if nothing else would, the cut of her gown
would force him to return her promptly to his secure lair.
Fine. She'd search his house for clues concerning her
sister's murder while everyone was enjoying the fair.
And locate her gun. She wanted to read her sister's letter
to him also. If she'd thought of it earlier, she could have
stayed home and done so already.

Jake targeted Chester, who was promptly asked to
leave. Darien motioned to Ritka and the other woman
and mouthed the word, "Out."

Tom yanked Angelina out the door before she could
utter a word. Darien took the tray of drinks from Lelandi,
delivered them to the wrong table, then led her behind
the bar.

Carol rested her chin on her hands. "How
romantic. Why can't I find a hero like you to rescue
me? All I need is a job as a nurse at the hospital." She
waved her arm toward the door and nearly fell off
the barstool. "Maybe I could replace that nurse who
rammed a chair into Lelandi when she was trying to
serve drinks."

His brow furrowed, Darien looked from Carol to Lelandi. "Did she hurt you?"

"Ritka? No."

He didn't look like he believed her. "What did Chester McKinley say to you?"

"He wants to aid in the investigation. I said he could."

Darien's dark expression lightened, and he even managed a small smile. "What did he say to that?"

"I'd have to talk you into agreeing."

"Damn right. And it isn't happening. From now until you want to return home, you're staying behind the bar. Got it?"

She frowned back at him and lowered her voice when she spoke so Carol wouldn't hear. "If he can help us locate Larissa's killer, then we should hire him. I know pack leaders don't like interference from *lupus garous* from other packs, but if he can aid us…" She gave Darien a look like she meant for him to agree or else.

He rubbed his hand over her bare arm, as though he was contemplating something. Taking her home? She thought so. But then his expression turned devious, his eyes darkening even more, a slight smile curving his lips. He took hold of her arm and led her into the room off the bar and closed the door. "Silva has the devil in her when she dresses you to entice me, but she doesn't need to make the effort."

"What do you think you're going to do?"

"This." He kissed Lelandi's lips, hungry, demanding, his hands on her bare shoulders, caressing, and just as needy. He broke the kiss, his breathing and hers labored. "I haven't told my people officially yet that you're mine." He growled under his breath. "Until I have done so, more than half those yahoos out there think you're still available."

Although she craved having him, she gave him her meanest glower, wanting the situation with Chester resolved. "I doubt it, Darien. But I still want Chester on the case."

He growled again and tackled her mouth. "You're too damned enticing for your own good." He rubbed his fingers over the satin fabric covering her breasts, let out his breath in exasperation, then reached lower to lift her skirt.

"What are you doing?" she squealed, holding her gown down, startled, but loving how much he wanted her, his wolfish possessiveness, his urgent craving. "I want Chester on the case."

For a minute, he stared at her, his expression stormy. "Lelandi, this is something I have to do as a leader, and I don't want investigators from outside our pack. As for you…" He took a ragged breath. "You are mine. I will remind you of this. I don't want any *lupus* hitting on you." He looked down at the cage around her legs. "I have never done this before when a woman was wearing this metal contraption. How do I remove it?"

She seized his hands. "We have to discuss Chester."

As focused as he was on wanting to ravish her, she realized after his hearing rumors that other *lupus* were "hitting" on her, he was giving into his more primitive wolf instincts. Compelled to show her he was hers and she was his, that no one else had any right to her, he seemed determined to satisfy this basic need.

She sighed. "We talk about Chester when we get home, or else."

He gave a sharp nod, although his eyes were so smoky with desire, she wasn't sure he was listening. But she meant what she said. Either they talked when they got home, or she took the case into her own hands.

He yanked off the lightweight steel crinoline, tossed it aside, then slipped her bodice down, exposing her breasts. Her body heating with the compulsion to mate, the frustration over his leader stubbornness melted. She cherished the sensation of his hands on her breasts, the way he massaged and lifted, bent his head over one and kissed the nipple, making it pucker and tingle. She slipped her fingers through his hair, felt a tinge of icy dampness. Snow.

He slid his hand down her waist and pulled the long skirt up again. He had a one-track mind. But her fingertips chased away the frown across his temple, and she kissed his mouth, stopping him momentarily.

A shudder shook him and he quickly pressed his hand between her legs, finding the opening in her crotchless drawers and gave her a lusty smile. "Hmm, Lelandi, you're hot and wet for me."

Always, whenever he observed her with that lascivious look in his eyes. He slipped his arms under her and laid her down on the wooden floor. "Just think, September 19th is Talk Like a Pirate Day. You'll be my sea wench and I'll plunder your treasures."

She slid her hand down to his trousers and rubbed the bulge already hard and readied for her. "I'll be the Pirate Captain, sir, not the treasure."

He laughed.

"You laugh, but I'm serious. I could be the Viking pirate Princess Sela or Princess Rusla."

His eyes sparkling, he kissed her again. "You've already stolen my heart, princess. Now I'll steal yours."

Lelandi tugged at his trousers. "Fine. Hurry, Darien."

His fingers parted her feminine core as his tongue touched hers. "Heaven on earth, love. That's what you are."

"It's not fair that my breasts are bare and my skirts are tugged up to my waist so you can have your fill of me while you're dressed to the teeth."

"Complaints, complaints, woman." He moved her hand from his waist to the crotch of his pants. "Release me and end my pain."

She unbuttoned his pants and reached inside and touched his rock-hard erection.

"It's all yours, madam."

"Then send me to the moon, sir. Make me climb the peak." She stroked his member, long, hard, faster, soliciting a groan from deep within his throat, his eyes glazed over with lust.

"Enough, you vixen."

He centered himself between her legs, then entered her, easing in at first, then thrusting hard.

His hand closed on her breast, massaging the mound as his mouth sought her free breast, his lips suckling at the nipple.

She arched against him, reveling in the feel of his hard thrusts, her pelvis meeting his with as much enthusiasm, her eyes closed so she could concentrate on the feel of his penetration, and of his tongue licking at her sensitive nipple. His heartbeat thundered in her ear, mixed with the sound of her own heart pounding. He gripped her bare shoulders as she slipped her hands underneath his waistcoat and yanked his shirttail out of his trousers. His eyes fluttered opened and he grinned, wicked, amative.

She traced his abs, the muscles flexing beneath her fingertips. Closing her eyes again, she breathed in the wild, spicy scent of him, of the piney woods and spruce, and felt suspended in time between now and the past, the centuries bridged.

"My princess," he mouthed against her lips, "my goddess."

His chest rubbed against hers, the satin fabric of his vest, teasing her nipples, and then the power of Niagara Falls washed over her in a rush of heated passion, carrying her over the edge, sweeping her toward… toward…

She moaned as a second wave stole her thoughts, his hot seed filling her womb. "Adonis," she gasped. "In the flesh," she breathed in his ear.

He nipped her chin and squeezed her breast with one final thrust. "My… dreams… have… come… true…, love." His head sank next to her face, his hand cupping her breast. "I have died and gone to Valhalla."

Her fingers caressing locks of his damp hair, she gave a contented sigh. "I never want to move from here."

He chuckled. "Next time we'll do it with fewer clothes. I would never have lasted with you in the earlier time. In truth, I'm glad the days of long gowns and the like are gone." He swirled his tongue around her nipple as if he was licking the ice cream on a sugar cone. "Though I like the cut of this gown on you." His gaze shot up to hers. "But not for everyone in town to see. Silva is absolutely the devil."

He rolled off her, adjusted his pants, and tucked his shirt back into his trousers. He helped her stand. Pulling her bodice up, he covered her nipples, his thumbs rubbing the sensitive nubs underneath the lace-trimmed satin. Focusing on them, he let out a low growl. "Wear a shirt over them until they settle down."

Lelandi laughed. "It's all your fault, Darien."

He kissed her lips, his tongue penetrating her mouth, his hands wrapped securely around her waist. "I love it when you call me by name, Lelandi, for all the times we made love together, and you didn't know who I was." He kissed her forehead and brushed his hand down her waist until his fingers reached the apex of her thighs. He cupped her mound through her skirts and rubbed and let out a husky breath. "Hurry home and I'll join you."

"Hmm," she moaned in response, then smiled and pressed her lips against his, nipping his lower one. "Don't make me wait long."

"I won't," he said with lustful promise and escorted her out of the storeroom.

Sam stopped filling a mug and looked from Darien to Lelandi and gave a knowing smile.

Some difference from the first time she'd been here, sitting at the table in the corner, an outsider in disguise.

Darien kissed her cheek and left her behind the counter. "No more serving drinks to the tables." He glanced at the table where the grays had been trying to get her attention. "I'll have to keep you under lock and key," he muttered under his breath.

"Right," she said. "As if that's ever happening."

Trevor walked back into the place, but Tom and Jake took seats at an empty table also.

"Killjoy," she said to Darien.

He gave her a smug look. "It's for your protection, Lelandi. I've got some business I have to take care of. Let Jake know when you want to return home."

The humans talked like nothing had gone on. But every gray in the house watched Darien, and when he left, Tom and Jake would observe them next.

Silva gave her a big smile. Lelandi tried to fill a glass, but it dropped from her grasp and Sam caught it.

"You can put out some chips." He gave her one of his wolfish grins.

Silva joined her behind the bar and *tsk*ed. "Boy, you sure have a stranglehold on that man. I keep trying to learn from your example, but I'm not sure what it is you're doing to garner his attention. Just when I think he's going to confine you at home, he takes you in the back room and ravishes you." She sighed. "Now half the grays in the tavern had their eyes on that door, just waiting to see what the two of you looked like when you came out."

Feeling sated, Lelandi poured chips into a bowl.

"Darien's chest was so puffed out, he looked like a peacock strutting out of there. And you, well," Silva glanced down at Lelandi's bodice and sighed heavily again. "A fresh bloom to your cheeks and lips, your hair tousled in the throes of passionate lovemaking, and you've even lost your hat. In the olden days, that would have been utterly scandalous." She laughed.

"For humans," Lelandi reminded her, speaking low so only Silva could hear, although she imagined Sam was eavesdropping as well. "Not *lupus garous*."

"Ah, but most of these yahoos didn't know you and Darien were mated yet. Besides, he's the pack leader.

Whatever happens in regards to him is important to them. When he's happy…" Silva shrugged. "Makes him easier to live with."

Lelandi glanced in the mirror on the back wall. Most of her hair hung to her shoulders in curls, no longer bound.

Silva gave her a hug. "I want to know all your secrets. Julia Wildthorn has nothing on you."

Lelandi smiled, brushed a curl of hair away from her cheek and returned to the counter. Conversation renewed and she could just bet the topic of conversation. Red wolf strikes again!

Silva ran her hand over Lelandi's arm. "Everyone's glad for the two of you. Darien's come out of his dark mood, except for the other deadly business. Soon you'll be carrying his babies and the pack will be well on it's way to mend."

"Triplets." Carol raised her nearly empty container of bottled water, eyes glittering, but her expression was deadly serious.

Lelandi stared at her, her heart nearly stopping. What had the woman overheard? Could she really see the future? More importantly, did she know about the *lupus garous*?

Chapter 16

WAS THE WINE TALKING OR DID CAROL WOOD REALLY SEE things that others couldn't? Lelandi wanted to question her further—alone, but Silva stuck close to her at the bar.

Lelandi gave a disgruntled sigh and handed her two bowls of chips. "Darien won't let me serve anything to the tables or I'd help you out more."

Silva gave her a smirk. "I'm used to the crowds. Think nothing of it."

As soon as Silva skirted around the bar, Lelandi leaned over the counter and asked Carol, "Do you... see this for real?"

"What?"

Lelandi pursed her lips. "Do you see that I have triplets?"

Carol waved her hand at the tavern. "Multiple births abound in Silver Town. Darien's a triplet. You're a triplet. So sure, you'll have triplets, too."

"How did you know I was a triplet?"

Carol looked cross-eyed, then her blue eyes straightened. "Don't you have a brother, too? I thought someone said you did." She shrugged and rested her elbow on the counter, then leaned her head against her hand. "I think."

Lelandi poured chips into another bowl.

"Your sister was pregnant with triplets. But you'll be feeding yours at your breasts, juggling one after another when the time is right."

Sam had moved closer and although he hadn't looked in their direction, Lelandi was certain he'd heard. "You're probably right, statistically speaking," she said, not wanting anyone to know if Carol truly had psychic powers. But could she know anything about the tragedy that had befallen her sister? She had to find out when the woman was sober, and without big ears listening in on their conversation.

Silva came behind the bar and cast a glance in Trevor's direction. He was looking their way, but Lelandi was certain he was watching her, not Silva. But Silva coyly smiled, then made her move on Sam. She kissed him on the cheek. Nothing too risqué or noteworthy, but Sam seized her arm, pulled her into a bear hug and started kissing her like they were in bed, getting ready for the big bang.

At first, Silva seemed taken aback, stiff, but when Sam kept working on her lips, Silva melted in the big guy's arms, giving him as much as she was getting.

Lelandi glanced around at the now quiet tavern, saw Trevor watching, but no scowl marred his expression. Everyone else was rabidly entranced. Some amused.

Jake shook his head and slugged down some beer.

Tom took his eyes off Silva and Sam and smiled at Lelandi. Her body warmed with chagrin.

"Man," Silva said, her voice low but because Lelandi was close enough she heard her words. "You never told me you knew how to melt a lady's core."

"Just needed the right woman to do the kiss justice." Sam patted her rump. "Now get back to work."

With a grin stretching across her face, she grabbed up another tray. "Hmm-hmm."

Belatedly, several of the guys in the tavern whooped and cheered.

Silva's face turned crimson.

"Wow," Carol said. "Now, I wouldn't mind a hunk like that kissing me either."

Then her head sank to the counter.

Lelandi shook her head and motioned to Jake, who hurried to the bar. "You want to go home now?"

"Carol Wood needs a ride home."

Jake waved at one of the grays at a table. "Take Ms. Wood to her place."

The guy looked pissed, but nodded and carried Carol out of the tavern.

Right after that, a husky human male walked up to the bar and handed Lelandi a note. "Guy outside asked me to give this to you."

Before she could take it, Jake pulled it out of the man's hand. "Thanks. I'll give it to her."

Jake stood his ground as the man looked from the note to Lelandi. Finally, he shrugged. "All right. Whatever." He gave Lelandi a sly smile, then sauntered over to one of the tables.

Jake opened the note, then shook his head. "Time to go."

"It's a note from…" She started to say, *Darien,* but then she realized Jake would have given it to her. *Ural.* She rounded the bar as if she planned to go with Jake, then snatched the note from his hand.

He could have taken it back, but instead gave her a superior smirk while he watched her read it. *Ural.* She'd recognize his scrawl anywhere. *I'm coming for you, Lelandi. Be ready.*

But he was in jail.

Jake motioned to Trevor, talked to him for a minute, then the deputy went to a table of grays. All six rose and headed outside.

"What if I wanted to stay longer?"

"I can tell you it isn't going to fly with Darien." Jake took her arm, and he and Tom led her to his SUV.

"How did Ural get out of jail?" she asked.

"Apparently he had help," Jake said, his voice dark.

When they saw Trevor and the other grays outside of the tavern, they shook their heads at Jake's questioning look. Maybe this time Ural had the sense to return home without her and leave well enough alone.

On the drive back to Darien's house, Jake wore a perpetual smile and Lelandi finally asked, "What's so funny?"

"*You,* for putting Silva up to kissing Sam at the bar. Won't work, you know. Trevor won't fall for it."

"That's the whole point, isn't it?"

He glanced at her, his brow perplexed.

"Trevor's not the right one for her."

Tom laughed. "We have a matchmaker in our midst. Sonja said she's getting too old to do it anymore. Now we have her replacement."

"Ha!" Jake responded. "Everyone was relieved when she quit matching bachelors up with their intended mates."

"The bachelors you mean were relieved," Lelandi guessed.

"Well, I for one am ready for a mate," Tom said. "Human girls don't have what it takes." He winked at Lelandi.

Having no plans to become Silver Town's new matchmaker, she rolled her eyes. "I'm taking up psychology."

Jake glanced at her. "You've okayed this with Darien?"

She folded her arms and stared out the windshield. If she wanted to become a psychologist, by god, she was going to do it.

Jake shook his head. "Let us know when you talk to Darien about this so Tom and I can be at the factory or mine for the day."

She *hmpf*ed. "I hope you weren't too hard on Chester McKinley."

"Trevor said he got intimate with you. I don't think I've seen Darien so mad. Not only that, but when we checked into it, we discovered he was one of the ones who sent a vase of wildflowers to you, anonymously."

Her mouth dropped slightly, then she recovered. "I'm not a member of this pack officially yet, and I damn well can do as I please. If I want to talk to Chester, it's my business. And for your information he wasn't intimate with me."

"We know you mated with Darien. It's the real deal," Tom said. "And that's as official as it gets."

Lelandi glowered at Tom over the back of the seat.

"Did you find out who the other anonymous guys were who sent flowers to her?" Jake asked Tom.

"They were much more discrete. Seems Chester McKinley wanted us to discover who he was easily enough. But I did find out that Joe Kelly was another."

"Hell, what's he up to?" Jake asked.

"Found out he bought Lelandi her first drink when she arrived at the tavern, too. Sam finally told me. Said it had slipped his mind because of the shooting incident."

Tom chuckled darkly. "Darien better let everyone know she's his soon or he's going to be rescuing her from every bachelor's clutches in the area."

Boy, that would really make her popular with the pack.

When they arrived at the house, Jake sequestered Lelandi back in the guest bedroom. She guessed since Darien hadn't officially declared they were mated, no one would put her in his room without his order. It really didn't matter where she was. She just wanted to be free to see her sister's letter to Darien and locate her blasted gun. But Jake stayed with her and so that was the end of that.

He finally brought her downstairs for dinner, but Darien was noticeably absent. And Tom and Jake were keeping a real close eye on her. Because of Ural?

A shiver trailed up her spine. Who was here now who would have freed Ural? Had to be someone from her pack. And no doubt, to get into the jail, several had arrived. Which meant Bruin and his thugs must have found her. All of a sudden, she didn't feel safe.

She asked again, "When's Darien coming home?"

"Soon," Jake said. He didn't try to humor her, although Tom had tried to lighten the mood.

Finally, Jake motioned to the stairs. "It's getting late."

"I want to wait up for Darien."

"He'll come to you when he's done with business."

Exasperated, she retired to bed. But soon, Jake left her alone. She listened for any sounds outside the door. A guard would be posted.

She closed her eyes and listened, waiting for someone to come into the room. Then she inhaled deeply. Darien

DESTINY OF THE WOLF 235

would come to her and wrap her in his heat. Then, nothing else would matter.

Something woke Lelandi from a deep sleep. She listened closely. Branches scratching at the window. She stared at the midnight blue comforter and wondered what happened to her forest green one. Realization hit her with a sick thud that she was in Darien's home and not in her family's, that her parents and sister had died, that Bruin might be here.

The scratching started up again and she glanced at the chair where someone sat during guard duty. No one still. Bathroom break?

A gentle rapping at the pane forced her heart to leap into her throat. She climbed out of bed, then peeled back one of the blue velvet window panels.

Standing on a ladder with his nose pressed against the glass, his hood up protecting him from the blowing snow, her cousin Ural scowled at her, motioned to the glass, and mouthed the words, "Open the damned window!"

"Ural," she said under her breath.

One of his eyes was swollen shut, his lower lip was covered in dry blood, and he had a gash across his brow. She cursed and unlocked the window, then shoved it up.

"Took you long enough," he growled, climbing inside. He shook off the snow from his coat and slipped his hood down.

"How did you know which room I was in? How'd you get out of jail?"

"Woke up and the door was open. Walked right out."

Her skin grew clammy and she wrung her hands. "T—this is a setup."

"Come away with me. I'll take you somewhere safe." He reached for her hair.

She stepped back. "Leave before they catch you."

"You can't mate with a gray. And when Bruin learns you're here he'll send a delegation for you. You won't stand a chance. We can go across country where he can't find us, start our own pack."

Fearing he'd fly into a rage, she wasn't about to tell him she'd mated Darien. "I'm staying here and finding out who murdered my sister."

"See what hanging around grays got your sister? Someday you'll thank me." He pulled out a hypodermic needle.

"Ural, no!" she cried out.

He lunged for her, sending the bedside lamp crashing to the floor. She could have managed him herself and would have as she held his wrist, keeping the needle from jabbing her. But the bedroom door slammed open, and Darien, his brothers, and Deputy Trevor poured into the room like a river run amuck.

Jake pulled her free and rushed her out of the room as she tried to remain there to ensure the guys didn't kill Ural.

"Let me go, Jake," she screamed, but before she could twist free, he lifted her off her feet and hurried her into another bedroom.

She figured it was Darien's room because she could smell his scent more heavily here, and she noted the pale blue comforter and seascapes hanging on the wall. Her sister's favorite color and wish to live by the sea.

Jake dumped her on the bed. When she tried to bolt from it, he blocked her. "Stay!"

"I don't want him killed."

"We're not barbarians."

But she knew better. Pack laws. A rogue *lupus garou* had infiltrated another's territory and tried to interfere with pack business. Even more than that. He tried to steal the pack leader's mate, which meant he could be terminated. Law of the wild prevailed. Might not have looked civilized to outsiders, but it had been their way for centuries, the way they had survived.

"I don't want him killed," she said again when Darien walked into the room, his face flushed.

"Are you okay?" he asked.

"Where are you taking him?"

"Back to jail."

She folded her arms. "You set him up."

"You wouldn't tell us who he was. Now we know who and what he wanted."

Darien motioned for Jake to leave. "Send Silva up in a few minutes."

Lelandi didn't like the look in Darien's eyes. Feral, dark, and intense, making her believe he was ready to lose control in response to Ural's actions. She rose from the bed and tried to brush past him, but he grabbed her arm and dragged her close. "This is your room from now on. Anyone tries to get to you in the other room, they'll get a surprise. I've got to talk to Ural, then speak with Uncle Sheridan about some other matters. Try to get some sleep. I'll wake you later." His mouth sealed the promise with a kiss, but she was too mad to take the bait.

And she hadn't even had a chance to make it clear she wanted Chester investigating her sister's death either. She looked as cross as she could. "If you hurt Ural, you might as well sleep in the other room—by yourself."

Darien laughed and gave her another quick kiss on the lips. "In your dreams, Lelandi." Then he stalked out of his room, and Silva walked in, shaking her head.

With Deputy Trevor, Uncle Sheridan, and Darien's brothers looking on, Darien sat in the jail interrogation room across the table from the red, and growled, "If you'd stuck Lelandi with that needle, you'd be a dead man. So who the hell are you, and what do you want with her?"

"Name's Ural. What would I want with the dead sister? I came for Larissa."

Darien glanced at his brothers. Both shook their heads.

"Why did you want to return Larissa home then?" Darien asked, drawing Ural into the trap.

"She belongs to the pack leader's brother. You can't have her, too."

"So Lelandi wasn't mated."

"No, she wasn't mated."

"Why not?"

Ural shrugged, but winced.

"How about guessing why not?" Darien said, his voice growing lower, more of a growl again.

The red's split lip curled up. "She's pretty headstrong."

"So you're saying Lelandi wouldn't accept a mate."

"Not Bruin's brother. Besides, Larissa would never have mated another when she was already mated to the leader's brother."

"I see. There's one problem with your story. Larissa gave me a letter stating she was mated to a red and hoped I'd forgive her for mating with me also."

Ural's jaw hung open.

"Furthermore," Darien said, "our local doctor examined Lelandi, the living sister. She'd never been touched. Got another story?"

Ural tapped his fingers on the table, then crossed his arms over his chest, leaned back in the chair, and gave Darien a conceited look.

"Time's up, Ural. Why did you come to take Lelandi back with you?"

"She doesn't belong to your kind. Neither did her sister. Hell, you had to have known the woman had already been mated." Ural leaned into the table and gave Darien a steely-eyed glower. "One of your people killed Larissa and now they'll succeed with Lelandi if I don't take her somewhere safe."

"The man who set up the murder could have been Larissa's prior mate."

"Nope. I saw the shooter."

"Like hell he did. This guy probably shot the gunman!" Uncle Sheridan roared and advanced on Ural, who looked like he was ready to have an early heart attack. "Hell, he probably is his pack's clean-up man and was ordered to come here and take care of this mess."

Ural cast a nervous glance at Uncle Sheridan,

breathing down his neck like a giant grizzly ready to make a quick meal of him. "I saw her," Ural spit out.

Not sure what to believe, Darien wondered if Ritka, Angelina, or Hosstene had managed to sneak by them and kill the gunman. They were the only women who might have hired a killer, since they hated Larissa and Lelandi both.

Uncle Sheridan gave a half smile. "A woman? Really."

Ural stuck his chin up, but wouldn't look at Uncle Sheridan. "A woman from your pack."

"You know her? To see her, you can identify her?" Darien asked, sitting on the edge of his chair. He wasn't sure he could trust Ural, but if the red had been a witness to the shooting—

"Yeah, I'd know her." Ural gave a satisfied smirk and wiggled his brows. "For a gray, she has one hell of a sweet ass."

Before Darien could stop him, Uncle Sheridan hit Ural in the head with his fist so hard, he knocked him out cold, and Ural fell to the floor in a ragged lump.

"Damn it, Uncle Sheridan!" Darien jumped to his feet and waved his hand at Ural. "What the hell did you do that for!"

"He had the nerve to talk lewd about one of our women. Son of a bitch."

Darien placed his fists on his hips and glowered at his uncle. "Trevor, get some water to splash on Ural. Tom, call Nurse Grey in, just in case Uncle Sheridan did some major damage to Ural with that iron fist of his. Jake, take a break."

The three hurried out of the room and Jake shut the door.

An intimidating figure even when he didn't mean to be, Uncle Sheridan stood taller and towered over Darien by four inches. But even so, Darien could have knocked his uncle out he was so mad. "We nearly had something to go on!" He ran his hands through his hair. "Why don't you… check out some more leads on the blackmailing scheme."

Uncle Sheridan had the nerve to look unremorseful and for a tense minute, he stood his ground. Then he bowed his head slightly. "As you wish. But I'm not sorry. Tell that son of a bitch if he says anything more about our women, I'll hit him harder." He stalked out of the room and slammed the door on his way out.

Jake peered in through the small window in the door and knocked.

"Come in." Darien crouched next to Ural and felt his pulse. Thank god, he had one.

"Do you think Ural's making it up?" Jake leaned over Ural with a cold pack and applied it to the side of his head.

"I thought so briefly. But if he wanted to make something up, why not say it was some guy he didn't know? I think he was up there, saw her, and knows who she is."

"Silva was the only woman there."

"Maybe. Maybe not. What about Ritka or one of her two girlfriends?"

Jake's eyes widened. "Ah. Yeah. Good candidates. Although I doubt with the way Ritka's eye was swollen, she could have seen well enough to shoot. But Hosstene and Angelina, that's another story."

"See if either of them have an alibi. And question everyone who might have smelled the women's scents."

"Will do."

Tom knocked on the door. Darien rose from his crouched position and waved at him to come in. Trevor followed him in, carrying a bucket of water.

"Nurse Grey's on her way." Tom shook his head. "Uncle Sheridan's in a real snit."

"He's been like that ever since he had to cut his vacation short." Trevor splashed some cold water on Ural's face.

The red didn't move.

Darien swore under his breath. "No one is to beat on him any further, understand? I want to know who shot the gunman."

"I'll question some folks like you asked," Jake said.

"I'll stay with him and see if he comes to," Tom offered.

Nurse Grey walked into the room and looked at Ural passed out on the floor, his shirt, face, and hair wet. "What happened now?"

Silva sat on the edge of Darien's bed and gave Lelandi a small smile. "Sugar, don't worry about the red they've got in jail. They won't kill him, although that was a pretty stupid thing he pulled. How was he going to ferret you away after he pumped you full of drugs?"

"He never was much to think things out ahead of time." Lelandi stretched on the bed, dressed in her jeans and sweater again. "If Darien or any of his men kill him, I won't be staying."

Silva's eyes grew huge. "Oh, honey, you can't mean that. You're mated to Darien now. You can't leave him."

Then she narrowed her eyes. "The red's related to you, isn't he?"

"Do you know what became of Chester McKinley after Darien made him leave?"

Silva tilted her head to the side. "Why?"

"I thought he could help us solve Larissa's murder."

"After the incident at the tavern, Darien sent him packing."

Damn Darien. *Fine.* She'd take matters into her own hands then.

"Will you be all right? I have a date with Sam tonight after we close the tavern."

"For show, right?" Lelandi hoped she was wrong and that Silva finally realized Sam was right for her.

Silva gave her a slip of a smile. "Sure, just for show until Trevor gets the point. I'll tell you how it goes. Can you sleep?"

"No."

Silva turned on the television and flipped through the channels. "Ah, here's one of Julia Wildthorn's romances made into a movie. Want to watch it?"

"Sure."

"See ya in the morning, sugar."

"Have a good time."

"Thanks, 'night."

Silva left the bedroom and greeted Darien on the stairs. "Lelandi is going to watch a movie."

Lelandi ground her teeth.

"Are you going back to work?"

"Yes, sirree, boss. Just as soon as I move some of my clothes from the washer to the dryer. Sam will be firing my butt if I keep using Lelandi as an excuse."

"Tell him Lelandi takes priority." Darien entered the bedroom.

Lelandi folded her arms and glowered at him. "What did you do with Ural?"

"He's staying in jail for a while. After what he pulled with you, that's the only place he's going." Darien gave Lelandi a hug, but she tensed. "What movie are you going to watch?"

"One of Julia Wildthorn's werewolf romance novels made for television, *By the Light of the Moon.*"

"Hmm." He nuzzled her cheek and rubbed her shoulders, and she began to dissolve under his insistent touch. "After I discuss business with my brothers and Uncle Sheridan, I'll show you what real *lupus garous* do in the name of love."

He kissed her lips, his hands massaging her breasts through her blouse and was really getting worked up when Jake shouted, "Uncle Sheridan's here. And Tom's just arrived."

Darien let out a husky growl. "Be back in a bit."

"I'll be ready and waiting." She gave him a sweet smile and leaned back against the pillows.

As soon as Darien shut the door, she flew into action. Somehow, she had to sneak into his office downstairs and see if she could find anything of importance there. But first, she searched through his bedside tables, and her heart did a flip when she spied Larissa's letter. She grabbed the letter and read through it, and nearly quit breathing.

I wished with all my heart to be who you thought I was. When I found the right man, it was too late for me to take back what I'd done to you.

Her sister had another lover? My god, no wonder Darien had been upset when he read the letter. But it confirmed what Silva had said about Larissa seeing some miner. Then the sickening thought swamped Lelandi. What if the triplets weren't Darien's?

Hospital records. She had to get into town and search for Larissa's records and know for sure. Maybe the doctor said something about her depression, or gave some other clue that might aid her investigation.

She opened the bedroom window, letting in a gust of snowy wind, and peered out. A rose trellis clung next to the brick wall. If it could hold her weight, she'd make it. She searched in Darien's closet and found a well worn leather jacket that smelled of him, and she took a deep breath and inhaled his sexy essence. He'd kill her for slipping away. But she was damned tired of being confined and kept in the dark. And if he was going to ignore her wishes to have Chester on the case…

She shoved on her boots and Darien's leather jacket, the size overwhelming her. After searching through his closet further, she couldn't locate any gloves.

Car keys.

Rummaging through Darien's chest of drawers, she found spare keys for his SUV and something metallic hidden under a pile of socks. Shoving them aside, she gasped. Her gun! And the bullets. She reloaded it and made sure the safety was on, then tucked it in one of the big pockets of his jacket.

Looking out the window, she considered the drop from the second story. As long as nothing dangerous was hidden in the snowdrift beneath the window, she should be fine. She climbed onto the windowsill, then swung around, grasping the wooden trellis. The flimsy redwood gave way with a snap, her heart flew into her throat, and she fell on her butt in the pile of snow. She was having a very bad feeling about this.

The powdered snow cushioned her fall, and she let out her breath in relief. Once she was able to plow her way out of the snow pile, she rushed to reach his SUV. The door locks were frozen and it took longer than she liked to get the driver's door open. After climbing in, she slammed the door, hoping Darien and his family hadn't heard.

She planned to return before Darien even missed her, although she'd have to come in the front door, but at least she'd learn what she could about her sister.

As soon as she drove out of the drive and hit the road, she realized how bad the visibility and treacherous the conditions had become. Darien's country home provided more privacy for *lupus garou* gatherings, but right now the two-mile stretch of country road seemed more like fifty. But she was free and she couldn't stop now.

The wipers swiped across the windshield at full speed, but the snow piled up so fast, she couldn't see a thing and wondered if she was even on the road any longer. Sheesh, that was an awful thought.

The SUV began to slide. Turn the tires into the slide? No, away from the slide. Hell, who could remember? The next thing she knew, the SUV sailed into the woods. She held her breath before the vehicle lunged into a steep embankment, taking a nosedive into something solid. The impact threw her hard against the steering wheel. Pain radiated through her chest. Bang! Something exploded. A blanket of white filled her vision.

For a moment, she sat dazed. *I'm in heaven.* Except for the pain in her chest and her throbbing head that jolted her back to reality. The air bag deflated like a parachute that had lost all its wind, but the scene in front of her was still cloaked in white. The snow blew through the windshield crumbling in a spider web of glass crystals, courtesy of the force of the air bag.

Snow swirled around inside the SUV, and a cold wetness dribbled down her forehead. Reaching up, she felt a gash on her forehead. Blood painted her fingertips red. *Great. Just great.* How was she to do her sleuthing? Not to mention Darien would *really* want to murder her now for turning his SUV on its nose in a pile of snow or rock, or whatever it had managed to slam into.

"Well, there's bound to be hell to pay anyway," she muttered under her breath, and jerked her seat belt free, then struggled to open the door. Wedged tight, the frame had crumpled with the impact. *Super.* She eased herself over the console and tried the passenger door. Same result. Growling under her breath, she leaned back in the seat and kicked through the remaining broken glass.

After crawling out of the SUV's window, she slid over the hood, still warm, the snow quickly melting into a frozen glaze, which left her jeans wet. The cold wind whirling around her, turned the denim fabric into ice. Blowing snow blinded her. But she was probably closer to town than to Darien's house at this rate anyway. No sense in trying to hike back. Although survivalists said, "Stay with the vehicle." But town couldn't be very far. And she had a mission to accomplish. She was certain the doc would have written about her sister's frame of mind during the pregnancy, maybe some clue about what was going on. And after reading her sister's letter about the affair she'd been having, Lelandi couldn't block the feeling something more was wrong.

A little snow and cold wouldn't stop her now.

Darien shook his head at Uncle Sheridan, while Tom and Jake looked on in the living room. "We're not making an example of Ural. If he has accomplices intent on coming for Lelandi, they'll come. We'll deal with them then. For now, he's fine where he is. What I want to discuss is who was blackmailing Larissa, how she died, and who hired the gunman to kill Lelandi. But first, any word on Ural, Tom?"

"Still out cold. Nurse Grey had us move him to the hospital. He's confined and Trevor's pulling guard duty. Charlotte said she'd let us know when he came around."

Looking unruffled, Uncle Sheridan set his pad of paper on the coffee table. "Here's what I've learned so far. We've run ballistics tests on all guns purportedly taken out in the woods the day the shooter killed the gunman. No matches. Which means either the test rules out it was one of our men, one of them had a second gun and gave us the wrong one to test, or the shooter was one of our men, except none of us knew he was out there."

"Or," Silva said, walking into the living room, carrying a load of laundry, "… it was a woman."

Darien wondered how Silva had learned of the news so fast. But she always knew the gossip well before anyone else did. His brothers and Uncle

Sheridan gave him shakes of their heads or shrugged a shoulder, indicating they hadn't told her. *Trevor.* "Only woman out there was you. And you were with Sam the whole time."

Uncle Sheridan snorted. "As if any of our women could shoot that far or accurately."

Silva's back stiffened. "I did."

Hell, what now? Darien motioned to a chair. "Have a seat, Silva. Tell us what you know."

She plunked down next to Tom. "I didn't say anything before because I knew you'd be mad that I'd killed him. I did it by accident. I swear it. We were sure the gunman was stalking us. So Sam told me to take his gun and go up on the ridge. If the bastard came after me, I was to shoot him. But he went after Sam and although Sam tried to tackle him first, the guy got a shot off, hitting him in the arm instead. I meant to hit the guy's gun arm, but he bolted when Sam dove for him, and I struck the gunman in the head. I swear I didn't mean to. When Lelandi said she figured the shooter killed the guy to tie up loose ends, I got scared. Sam didn't want to say anything either because you'd given orders that we were to stick together. He assumed you'd learn who the guy was who hired the gunman without involving me. But it seems you already know the shooter's a woman so…" She shrugged.

"Sam knows better." Darien blew out his breath. "Did you have Sam's gun checked, Uncle Sheridan?"

He looked peeved. "Hell no. The lunatic shot Sam. I thought he and Silva had stayed together. At least that's what they led us to believe. I would never have guessed she killed the gunman."

"Run a ballistics test on Sam's gun. I want to know right away. And Silva, next time, tell the truth."

"Yes, boss. I'm so sorry. I well, I couldn't let you think some shooter was out there still gunning for her."

More likely she figured she was about to be found out when Ural came to. "Damn it, Silva," Darien said. "You knew how important this is."

"I'm sorry, boss."

"When you were up on the ridge, did you sense anybody else up there? Smell anyone, hear anyone?"

"I didn't smell or see anyone either. But I was pretty worried about the gunman and Sam so I might have blocked everything else out. Once I shot the guy, I hurried down to check on Sam and see if the guy was alive."

Uncle Sheridan said, "You made a fine mess of it. And although you're probably not involved in this, it sure can make tongues wag."

"I only meant to wound him. All right? I'm… I'm late getting back to the tavern. Can I go?" Silva asked Darien.

He bowed his head, but he still couldn't believe Silva was the one who'd killed the gunman.

Looking dejected, Silva hurried to the front door. From the foyer, she yelled, "Have you guys seen how bad the storm is getting?"

Darien and the others joined her and considered the whiteout conditions. "You'd better stay the night. Call Sam and tell him I said so."

She sighed. "All right. I'll be in the den watching a show. If anyone needs me to fix something to eat later, just holler." Silva headed for the den.

Itching to return to Lelandi and smooth things out with her, Darien and the others retook their seats in the living room and he asked, "Anything else?"

Uncle Sheridan flipped through his pad of notes again. "Mason reviewed bank accounts to see if anyone had received large amounts of money before Larissa's death. No one had. Which could mean that whoever was blackmailing her kept bank accounts somewhere else. So that was inconclusive. Jake found out some more stuff though."

Jake took a sip of his beer. "Since we couldn't find money in a local account, Trevor and Peter questioned folks to see if anyone bragged about receiving lots of money. Mrs. Hastings's aunt died in a neighboring town. She received a substantial inheritance and put in the outdoor sauna and enclosed the deck to expand the bed and breakfast."

"She's above reproach," Darien said.

"We thought so, too, but we had to double check every story."

Tom walked back into the room with a Coke. "Then there's Ritka."

Darien sat up taller. She'd certainly hated both Larissa and Lelandi, and she definitely could be suspect.

"She bragged she won at the tables in Las Vegas. Angelina and Hosstene vouched for her, but you know how thick they are."

"Did the amount she won match up with how much was stolen?"

"Her winnings amounted to about a fourth of what the blackmailer had received."

Deep in thought, Darien rubbed his chin. "What if the three women were in on it together?"

"We had the same idea. If Angelina and Hosstene got any extra money, they hid it somewhere, aren't spending it, and aren't telling," Jake said.

Darien mulled that one over. "Anyone else have any suspicious money dealings?"

"Nope." Uncle Sheridan flipped to the next page of his notepad. "Concerning the family who wanted to join our pack, they'd heard you were a fair pack leader. As far as training, the man is a lumberman by trade. His brother is a male nurse. The mother makes jewelry and is a renowned artist in her trade. The girls are in school. One wants to be a lawyer someday. The other hasn't decided. Both girls want to help out when the ski lifts are running."

"And the reason they left their former pack?"

"The leader, who was highly respected, died. Another took over and they couldn't live with his rule."

"We could really use the brother who's a male nurse. If we learn the family is troublesome in the future, we can release them from the pack. But for now, they can stay," Darien said. "What about the smell of rotten leaves at the site where we discovered Lelandi in the woods?"

Uncle Sheridan nodded. "It's kind of a hollow and lots of leaves have collected there. Wet and shaded, it's the perfect environment for making compost."

But Darien figured whoever the attempted murderer was had to be wearing one of those hunter sprays that either made his scent invisible to others—even to bloodhounds, which could pick up the more subtle scents more so than any other animal including *lupus garous*—or he was wearing that humus type spray to blend in with the smell of the forest.

Jake cleared his throat. "Carol Wood keeps asking to speak to you about adding another nurse position."

"Tell her it's not possible."

"She'll have a fit when she learns we added another when we said no to hiring her," Jake said.

"Tell her he was hired some weeks ago but just got here, if she asks. The woman will have to learn that when I say no, I mean no. What about the other two vases of flowers sent anonymously to Lelandi?"

"Still haven't discovered the identity of the buyers. But the flowers her parents supposedly sent?" Tom said. "Ural bought and paid for them."

Darien swore under his breath. "Doesn't he know how upsetting that is for her? Giving her false hope that her parents are alive?"

"That's another thing," Uncle Sheridan said. "Chester McKinley informed me he located them."

"What? Where are her parents supposed to be?"

Uncle Sheridan's face darkened. "He wouldn't say. If you want to hire him as a P.I., he'll share his information."

"Damn him anyway." Darien lifted his beer mug. "All right, schedule a meeting for a couple of hours from now. Anything else?"

"Nothing else. I'll check Sam's gun."

"Think you can make it out in this weather?"

"No snowstorm has ever kept me homebound. Call you later." Uncle Sheridan grabbed his jacket, shoved his hat on, and left.

"I'll see you both when Chester gets here," Darien said to his brothers.

Intending to show Lelandi how lame Julia Wildthorn's romance stories were compared to the real thing, Darien headed up the stairs. He couldn't help how annoyed he was with Silva and Sam over the shooter incident though.

How many man hours had his men spent on the case, wasted now that they knew Silva was the shooter?

A man and woman were getting it on with all the moaning and groaning he heard on the television in the bedroom. He hoped Lelandi's movie had gotten her in the mood for some real *lupus garou* sex and that she wasn't still miffed with him over Ural. He gave Peter a nod, then opened the door to the bedroom and closed it.

She wasn't in bed, no sound came from the bathroom, and the window was wide open. A willful breeze blew in snow all over the carpet. His blood running cold, Darien raced over to the window and peered out. Two of the rungs on the rose trellis were broken and the imprint of a body had impacted with the snowdrift.

"Peter! Jake! Tom! Lelandi's gone!" He didn't see any sign of a struggle, but it didn't matter. If her past history was any indication of her current situation, she could be in real danger.

Peter flung the bedroom door open.

Jake yelled, "I'll call Uncle Sheridan."

"Tell him to notify Trevor since he's taking care of the prisoner if she has a mind to try and free him." Darien ran down the stairs with Peter on his heels.

"If she does try?"

"Trevor can throw her in a jail cell until I get there, damn it!"

Tom offered, "I'll call reinforcements to search the town for her."

"The woman is an absolute menace to herself!"

Darien swore he'd tie her to the bed, and there she'd remain until he eliminated Larissa's killer.

Chapter 17

NORMALLY, LELANDI COULD SEE IN THE DARK, BUT THE blowing snow was blinding her. She trudged in the direction in which she smelled smoke from a chimney. More than half of the time, she stumbled knee deep in snowdrifts, and although she tried to keep her bare hands in her pockets, she constantly had to brace herself to keep from taking a nosedive. She was certain she'd been at it for over an hour, and she wasn't sure if she was getting any closer to finding the town. Autumn definitely was her time of year. Winter was for the Arctic wolves and polar bears. *Sheesh.*

A blood-curdling scream pierced the frigid air. A girl's.

Lelandi's insides froze. "Hello?" she shouted.

The scream had seemed ethereal, everywhere and nowhere at the same time. She stood still and listened. The wind howled through the spruce, haunting her, but she was certain the scream came from a girl.

"Hello!" Lelandi called out.

"Here!" a girl screamed. "Oh god, help us!"

Tears sprang to Lelandi's eyes, and she ploughed through the thick, wet snow, hoping she'd reach the girl and whoever else was in trouble in time. "What's happened?"

"It wasn't my fault!" a boy said. "How did I know the storm was going to worsen?"

"Oh, our parents are going to kill us," the girl said tearfully.

They didn't sound very young, probably teenaged. Lelandi opened her mouth to speak, but another boy said, "If you hadn't talked us into this…"

Jeez, how many were there?

"Hello!" Lelandi hollered again, sure she was getting closer to the sounds of their voices.

"She's coming!" a different girl said.

"A *woman*. Just great. Like she could help us," the first boy said.

"Listen, Cody, anybody would be welcome. Even Darien. Although he's going to be pissed. Maybe the woman's got a cell phone," the other boy said.

Darien. They were probably *lupus garou* teens. *A cell phone.* Wish she'd had one, but hers was still back at her house in Wildhaven, and she hadn't had time to grab it when she made her escape. Although she wasn't sure where she was. Or where the teens were. So calling for help might not have brought anyone to their location anyway.

"Hello!" all of the kids shouted.

Sounded like four of them, their voices muffled in the snow and wind. But she was sure she was nearing their location.

A branch snapped several feet away, and she whipped around, but saw nothing in the white bleakness except trees laden with snow, their heavy branches dipping toward the drifts, making them look like weary old men.

A deer might have made the sound. Her wolf instincts remained on high alert.

"Hello!" the kids shouted again, but Lelandi didn't budge. A shiver shook her but it wasn't only the cold that created it.

She moved cautiously forward, listening for any other sound that might indicate someone was tracking or hunting her. The wind howled and the blowing snow blurred visibility down to a couple of feet, but even so she watched and strained to see or hear anything else.

"I think she's not coming," one of the girls said, her voice frightened.

"Over here!" a boy shouted.

I'm coming. I'm coming. But if someone was following her, Lelandi didn't want him to know where she was. She wrapped her frigid fingers around the pistol grip, and the knowledge she had it, helped.

Then something raced in her direction. A *lupus garou* in wolf form? It charged at her and she aimed her gun. But as soon as it emerged from the blanket of white, she exhaled a tentative sigh. A buck. As soon as he saw her, he dodged off and disappeared into the woods.

A second passed before she realized something must have startled it in her direction.

"She's lost," one of the girls said.

Lelandi moved more quickly now, although she couldn't shake loose of the feeling a predator had spooked the deer. But if she could reach the kids in time, if someone was stalking her, he would have too many witnesses, and he would most likely stay clear of them.

"I think I hear her!" Cody shouted.

"Hello! What's happened?" Lelandi shouted back, keeping her gun at the ready.

If worse came to worse, the kids could turn wolf *if* they were *lupus garou* now that the moon was out again. As long as the teens had an adult chaperone it would be acceptable. Their wolf coats would protect them from the cold, they could run faster, and find their way to town more easily.

"We're here!" one of the girls shouted. "She's getting closer!"

Nearly there, her legs weary from the trek and her body trembling with cold, Lelandi waded through the last of the drifting snow.

"We're here!" the four teens responded again.

"But don't come much closer or you'll be down here with us," the boy named Cody warned.

Lelandi froze in place. "Is anyone hurt?"

"I think Caitlin might have fractured her leg," the other girl said, her voice breaking.

Lelandi tucked the gun inside the jacket pocket, then got down on her hands and knees and tried reaching out for solid ground, hoping to god that no one would sneak up behind her and shove her off the cliff. Her hands were so chilled, she couldn't feel anything.

"The snow was banked up against the trees, and then the whole side of the mountain gave way," Cody said. "Anthony's sprained his wrist. But Minx and I are okay."

If they were *lupus garous,* it wouldn't help the injured kids to shapeshift. Not if one of them had a sprained wrist and the other a broken leg.

"I'm coming to you, but I'm not sure where the drop-off is yet."

"You're getting close," Anthony said.

"We lost two of our sleds down the mountainside, but there are another two up there somewhere," Cody said.

Winded, Lelandi took another deep breath; the frigid air burning her lungs. "We can use one to take Caitlin out of here."

"It's awfully steep and I'm not sure either my brother or Caitlin can climb," Cody said. "I can't either without a rope."

"But we can't leave anybody behind!" Minx sounded on the verge of hysteria.

Lelandi drew closer and felt the land give way. Her heart thundered as snow cascaded down the cliff and the girls screamed.

"Back up!" Cody shouted.

As if she wasn't already! Scrambling backward, she moved away from the edge. "Everyone okay?"

"Yeah!" the teens shouted.

The two sleds were wedged up against a tree, both wooden, both had long ropes attached. "We're not leaving anyone behind. I've found the sleds."

For a minute, she surveyed the forest, looking to see if anyone watched her, took a deep breath, and tried to smell anyone. Nothing, but the fresh, frigid air.

Fighting the numbness in her fingers, she managed to slip one of the sled's ropes around a sturdy oak near the edge of the drop-off and tied a knot. "Okay, I'll slide the sled over the edge. Let me know if it reaches you."

"The rope's too short by about ten feet," Cody shouted.

Lelandi dragged the sled back up and again studied the forest. Still nothing.

For several painfully excruciating minutes, her frozen fingers worked on untying the rope from the other sled, then she fastened it to the rope from the first.

"Are you still there?" Anthony hollered.

"Combining ropes from the two sleds," she said. "Okay, here the sled comes again."

"It's long enough!" Minx shouted after a few minutes.

"But you couldn't pull any of us up," Cody said. "You're just a woman."

She rolled her eyes. Male teen *lupus garou* for sure. "First, everyone take off their belts and anything else that you might be able to use as ties, scarves, whatever. Then tie Caitlin onto the sled. Can you make secure knots?"

"Boy Scouts," Anthony and Cody yelled.

Unless the *lupus garou* had their own Boy Scout troop, she feared they *were* human kids. Which could be bad news for Caitlin's injuries and the frostbite they may have suffered.

"Once she's secure, I'll need you, Cody, to use the rope. I've tied it securely to the tree. Once you're here, we can ease Caitlin up together."

"Okay, I'm coming."

Her body shivering endlessly, Lelandi waited, her hands shoved in her pockets, her right hand gripping the gun just in case. When Cody's rainbow-colored jester hat crested the top, she got on her belly, reached down, and helped him climb the last few feet. She took a deep breath, then smelling his scent, she was relieved in part. At least the boys were *lupus garou*.

"Man, that was awesome."

"Let's get Caitlin out. Then you climb down and tie Anthony on the sled. With his bad hand, he won't be able to climb or tie secure knots."

"That'll leave Minx by herself."

"I'll survive," Minx shouted. "Just get my sister out!"

Lelandi and Cody pulled while she prayed the teens had tied Caitlin securely to the sled. Every few inches Caitlin groaned or cried out, but they finally got her to the top, and Lelandi and Cody hurried to untie her. *Lupus garou,* too, thank god. She recognized her as one of the twins staying at the Hastings Bed and Breakfast, the one who'd come to check on her in the loft when she'd been crying over Larissa's letter.

With care, they transferred the girl to the bigger sled, too cumbersome to lift up the mountain with a body tied to it. "Now, take these belts and scarves back down and tie Anthony securely."

While Cody climbed down and he and Minx secured Anthony to the sled, Lelandi rubbed Caitlin's arms. Her lips were as blue as her hand-knit beanie. "Hold on, honey. We'll get you help soon."

Tears filled her eyes. "I'm… I'm pregnant."

In stunned silence, Lelandi stared at her. No one mated an underage *lupus garou* without facing severe consequences. "One of the boys?" She motioned to the cliff, dreading Caitlin's response.

Caitlin shook her head.

"Who?"

She wouldn't say.

"How far along are you?"

"Five months."

"Are… are you feeling any pains in your abdomen?"

"Just my leg."

Thank god. "All right, honey. We'll get you to the doctor as soon as we can. He knows about this, right?"

Fat tears rolled down Caitlin's cheeks. "No," she whispered.

Lelandi frowned. "Do your parents know?"

Caitlin closed her blurry eyes.

"Caitlin, they have to be told."

She sobbed. "They know."

Lelandi imagined they were pretty upset with her. Shamed. Was that the reason they'd left their pack and moved here? She had a sneaking suspicion Darien didn't know.

"Ready!" Cody said. "I'm coming up."

Lelandi squeezed Caitlin's hand. "I'll be back after we get Anthony up." She returned to the edge to watch for Cody.

When he finally reached the top, he was huffing and puffing, trying to catch his breath. He didn't say anything about it being awesome this time, but when Lelandi gave him a worried look, he grinned. "Let's bring my brother up so we can fetch Minx."

Because of Anthony's heavier weight, the rope cut into Lelandi's hands, and she gritted her teeth against the pain of the burning cuts.

"Hey, brother! Next time eat fewer eggs and sausages for breakfast and only one ham sandwich for lunch instead of three, okay?"

Anthony laughed. "Good thing you ate so much. You've probably burned it all off by now."

"Two hours ago, I'm sure."

When they got Anthony to the top, they hurried to untie him.

Lelandi peered over the edge. "We have a choice, Minx. Either you can climb up using the rope, or we can tie you to the sled."

Anthony looked at Lelandi's bloodied hands. "You can't do any more. Let me." He handed her his ski gloves.

"You can help with your good hand. But I'll use Caitlin's gloves."

"I don't know which way to come up," Minx said, her voice desperate.

"I'll tie her to the sled," Cody said. "I don't think she can make that climb. It's pretty icy and the hand and foot holds are a long reach for someone who's smaller."

Before Lelandi could say a word, he disappeared over the edge.

Anthony gave a worried chuckle. "He's the adventuresome one. Always gets me into trouble."

"I heard that!" Cody shouted. This time it took him longer to secure her. But then he tugged on the rope. "I'm coming up. Hope the rope isn't fraying."

Lelandi leaned over the edge and watched Cody's jester hat shaking, the bells jingling on the four tassels.

Cody collapsed next to them and Anthony, sounding frustrated that he hadn't helped more, urged, "Come on, let's get Minx."

"Let me catch my breath, will you?" Cody gave him an annoyed look. "Okay, let's do it."

With all three of them pulling, and because of her slight weight, they had Minx up in half the time it took to bring up Anthony. "She must not eat nearly as much as you, Anthony, thank Odin," Cody said, hurrying to untie her. "We were headed for a cabin not far from here. Do you know where it is?"

Lelandi shook her head. "No, I'm new here."

Cody stared at her for a minute, then took a whiff of the cold air. "Oh, oh, you're the red who got the town all shot up. The one Darien wants."

Caitlin moaned and Lelandi hurried over to her. "You'll tell Darien, won't you, since you're going to be his mate?"

"No, I won't tell him, but he needs to know."

"We were going sledding, but the truck got stuck in the ditch. The boys still wanted to sled, but the snow got too bad." Minx wrapped her arms around Lelandi and gave her a big hug. "Thanks so much for rescuing us."

Lelandi shuddered to think the kids could have been stuck on the rocky ledge for hours if she hadn't found them.

"Let's get to the cabin," Cody said. "Who needs a ride?"

"Let's take the other sled, but we'll pull Caitlin for now. If anyone else gets worn out, we'll use the other sled." Lelandi tried to give Caitlin's gloves back to her, but she shook her head.

"I'll keep my hands in my pockets. You'll need the gloves to make it through the snowdrifts." Caitlin bit her lip as if another shard of pain sliced through her leg.

Lelandi nodded and brushed snowflakes off the girl's cheeks.

"Let's get moving. Standing here, we'll be frozen statues before long," Anthony said.

"What were you doing out here?" Minx asked Lelandi.

Lelandi wrapped her arms around herself, attempting to get warm. "Trying to get to town. I had an accident."

"Oh, that's why you have a gash on your head. Do you know the way?"

"Before I heard your voices, I smelled chimney smoke from that direction." Lelandi motioned into the stark, white bleakness.

"There's the cottage!" Cody pointed in a different direction, and stumbled toward the blurred outline of a log cabin that seemed to appear out of nowhere like a lake mirage on a desert island.

Part of the roof was gone, and the icy wind whipped through the dilapidated building with a vengeance. Lelandi had hoped it would have been a safe haven, walls and a roof to keep the wind and snow out, a place to build a fire. No such luck.

"We can't stay here." Minx rubbed her arms. "It's too cold and our dad will skin us alive when he learns we're missing. We've got to get Caitlin to the doctor."

Caitlin shook her head. "We're going to get grounded for sure."

"Hope Darien doesn't make us do anything like he already did," Cody said.

"What did he make you do?" Lelandi peered into the snow, trying to get her bearings, smelling the air.

"Paint the school, because we wrote on the walls. Nothing bad. Just that our parents shouldn't have to pay school taxes when we can't go to them."

"Were they paying school taxes?" Lelandi tied Caitlin more securely to the sled.

"No. It was all Cody's fault. He's *always* getting us into a mess."

Cody grinned, not in the least remorseful.

Minx asked Lelandi, "Will you get in trouble for the car wreck?"

Lelandi offered her a small smile. *Most likely.*

"She's the pack leader's chosen mate. Dad said. She won't get in trouble," Anthony said.

"Oh yes she will. Dad said someone was supposed to guard her at all times because somebody tried to kill her." Cody banged his gloved hands together, shaking off some of the snow. "She shouldn't be out here by herself so that means Darien's going to be pissed."

"So why are you out here alone?" Minx asked. "You weren't running away, were you?"

"Oh, she couldn't do that. She belongs to Darien and the pack now," Cody said, matter-of-factly. "Dad said."

"I was taking a drive into town, but I hadn't realized the snow was so bad. And Cody's right. I'm Darien's mate and I'm not going anywhere." Except to the hospital, if she could make it.

"I suggested we could turn wolf," Cody said.

Minx frowned at him. "Our parents would kill us if an adult wasn't chaperoning us."

Cody pulled his gloved hand out of his parka pocket and waved at Lelandi. "We have a chaperone."

"Minx and Cody, go ahead and shapeshift. With his good hand, Anthony can pull the sled carrying our clothes. As a wolf, Cody can pull Caitlin. Minx will stay with the rest of you while I scout ahead. Stick close together so we don't lose anyone. If you sense anything that will help us find the town, just holler or howl."

Lelandi didn't think any of them could trek for miles in this snow as humans. If the situation became too dire, she'd have Anthony and Caitlin shapeshift, and they'd huddle together until the storm let up.

Lelandi helped bury Caitlin under Minx's and her own coat, while Minx and Cody quickly shapeshifted. Then she helped tie Cody's coat over Anthony's shoulders to give him some extra warmth. Afterward, she tied Cody to Caitlin's sled, while Anthony gathered the rope for the sled carrying their clothes.

Lelandi stripped off her clothes, tossing them on the other garments. Man, was it cold. Her face and body began to shift, but it wasn't until the fur began to cover her body before she quit shivering.

Everyone watched her, waiting for her to make the first move. She considered Caitlin and Anthony, who appeared bundled up enough. She listened, smelled the air, then headed south. At least Caitlin and Anthony were dressed in ski bibs, snow boots, parkas, hats and gloves—much more prepared than Lelandi had been.

"Are you sure we're going the right way?" Caitlin asked for the hundredth time.

Lelandi was quite a distance from the teens when she spied the glint of amber eyes watching her from deeper in the woods. *Crap.*

As a red female, she'd never be able to fight a male gray and as big as he was, he was male. Her only hope was getting back to the kids because she was certain he wouldn't want witnesses, or to have to kill them, too. *She* was the target.

He growled low and the hair on her back rose. Tail straight, she whipped around and raced back to the sleds, prepared to fight the gray if she had to.

"What's wrong?" Anthony asked, as soon as she drew close enough.

"What's the matter?" Caitlin asked, unable to see from the sled.

A cow mooed in the distance. Their salvation. *She hoped.*

Anthony waved his arm. "It's got to be Doc Mitchell's ranch. He's the vet. He can set Caitlin's leg until we get into town."

Great. Doc Mitchell would not let Lelandi out of his sight once he saw her, just like when he guarded her in the tavern during the fair. She stuck close to the sled, but made them stop as soon as she spied the house's snowy silhouette. Hating to shapeshift in the blizzard again, she didn't have much choice. As quickly as she could, she changed and then hurried to dress.

"Doc Mitchell will get you warmed up and notify your parents. I've got to go back to the SUV and wait for Darien."

"But it's way too cold out here," Caitlin said. "And you might get lost."

Anthony frowned at her. "You should come with us and get warm, too. Doc Mitchell will call Darien for you also."

Lelandi gave them each a hug. "I'll be fine. Hurry to the house. And, Caitlin, honey, your parents need to talk to Darien."

She nodded, although she didn't seem happy. "Keep my gloves, all right?"

"Thanks. I'll return them first chance I get. Take care. I'll see you later."

When they wouldn't leave her, Lelandi motioned for them to go. "Hurry."

"If you're not going to come with us, take Cody's coat. It's warmer than yours."

She looked at Cody and he bowed his head in acknowledgement.

"All right, thanks." Cody's white parka would blend in better with the snow and it would be much warmer. Lelandi threw Darien's jacket on the sled and yanked on Cody's coat, figuring Darien would be pissed about this, too. If Cody realized he was wearing the pack leader's leather jacket, he was sure to tell all his friends, and he'd be the hit of the day.

The teens disappeared in the snow in the direction of the house, and Lelandi headed for the freshly plowed road. The wind hadn't let up any when she saw a sign declaring it was Silver Town and another posting the speed limit.

But it wasn't long before she sensed the wolf following her, hidden in the woods. Running wasn't an option. He'd chase her down and kill her. She turned and stood her ground, although she knew she didn't stand a chance. But there wasn't anything else she could do. And wolf to wolf was a better end than human to wolf. She yanked off Caitlin's gloves and shoved them in Cody's coat pocket.

The wolf's fur bristled, his ears erect, staring her down, angry. She wished she could smell him, know who he was, before he attacked, before the end. His lips curled back, showcasing his killer canines, and he snarled. She fumbled with the buttons on the coat. He was waiting, allowing her the chance to change, a contest between wolves. *Some contest.* Bastard.

Suddenly, his tail straightened out, parallel to the ground, signaling danger. She felt the road tremble with an approaching pickup headed toward town, its headlights a warning. Her heart racing, she threw on the gloves and ran, waving at the truck to stop, hoping he'd see her in the white coat in the blinding snow. Despite being thankful her rescue was imminent, if it was one of Darien's men, she was sunk.

That's when she heard the wolf growl and knew the bastard risked killing her in front of a witness, closing in on her fast. The pickup sped up and veered off to the side of her, its brakes squealing, the tires spitting snow. She dodged away from the truck and fell into a snowbank.

The wolf yelped and darted out of the truck's path in the opposite direction.

"Hey, little lady, get in! Hell, that was close. Looks like you had an accident. I'll take you to the hospital."

She took a deep breath. *Human.* She managed a frozen smile and murmured a thanks.

"I've never seen a wolf attack a human in these parts. I'll have to contact the police and let them know. Might be rabid."

She stared out the window, keeping an eye out for him, wishing she knew who the *lupus garou* was who had attacked her.

The grizzled old man kept talking, but all she could think of was the teens telling Doc Mitchell she'd been with them, he'd alert Darien, and they'd know her last whereabouts soon. Which meant she hadn't much time.

Chapter 18

DARIEN PLOWED THROUGH ANOTHER SNOWDRIFT, GLAD Tom's four-wheel drive monster truck could handle just about any road conditions, but he still wasn't letting either of his brothers drive, figuring if he had a wreck it would be his fault, no one else to blame.

"We've been driving for an hour in this mess and have barely made any headway," Jake said. "How was Lelandi acting before you came down to talk to us?"

"Pissed off about Ural. She probably headed to the jail to make sure we didn't kill him." He could barely see the road, or whether they were driving on it, the shoulder, or in the ditch. The only thing he could make out were the trees on either side of the road. Darien squinted, but it wasn't helping.

"Wait, Darien! I think I see something," Tom shouted from the backseat.

"Where?"

"To the right… looks like the tail end of a green pickup."

Darien stopped the truck and they got out. "It's the Woodcroft boys' truck. I recognize the crunched right side where Cody backed into their mailbox by accident when he was learning to drive last year." Now, stuck in the ditch, half-buried in snow and ice. He rubbed the snow off the driver's side window. No sign of anyone. "Call their dad. See if they made it home, Tom."

Tom pulled out his cell phone while Jake and Darien scouted around the truck for tracks. "If they hiked out of here on foot, the blowing snow covered their tracks already," Jake said, rubbing his gloved hands together. "Hope they were dressed warm."

"Hi, Anthony, this is Tom. Are your boys at home?" he yelled into the phone above the blowing wind.

Darien pointed to a couple of trees nearby. "Branches are broken. They walked this way, marking a trail at least. That abandoned cabin is located half a mile west of here. They'd know about it. Maybe they went there seeking shelter."

Jake made a disgruntled noise. "Hell, the whole thing might have blown down in this storm. But it's worth checking if their dad says they're not home."

They looked at Tom, whose face puckered into a frown. "I'll let Darien know. We found their truck and it looks like we've discovered the direction they're headed." He paused. "A mile south of Darien's place and the truck's stuck in the ditch and buried in snow." Tom looked at Darien. "Yeah, Lelandi's still missing. All right. Let you know if we find anyone." He pocketed his phone. "Anthony, Sr. said they went sledding and were late in arriving home. Peter called him to help in the search for Lelandi, so he's heading out, but his wife will be home waiting on news of the boys. Not only that, but the sixteen-year-old twin girls that joined our pack were with the boys."

"Hell," Darien said. "Grab some flashlights. They might be able to see them. We'll check that abandoned cabin. Call Uncle Sheridan and tell him we've got some missing teens out here now, too. He'll need to report the girls are with the boys, have abandoned the vehicle, and are on foot somewhere in the woods. And call Bertha Hastings and tell her to start the alert roster calls to account for everyone else."

With heartfelt thanks, Lelandi climbed out of the Good Samaritan's truck and headed for the hospital entrance. Glad to have made it, she felt a sliver of relief, knowing she still might get caught before she discovered anything.

What of the receptionist? Lelandi hadn't thought about how she could get past her if that blasted Angelina was on duty. With trepidation at being discovered, Lelandi opened the hospital door and let in a blast of cold, but the heated air inside welcomed her like a hot blanket.

A woman she didn't recognize manned the front desk and was talking to a human mother. The woman's son was coughing nonstop. While the receptionist was busy, Lelandi slinked on past in her wet clothes down the hallway.

The smell of antiseptics brought a flashback of her stay at the hospital. She shivered, not wanting to think about it. Doc was talking to someone in one of the exam rooms and when she passed it, she saw Ritka adding something to a patient's IV in the next room.

Ohmigod. Deputy Trevor was peering into a hospital room, his back to her.

Two more hospital rooms to get by and she'd reach Doc's office at the end of the hall. She hurried past the

deputy and into Doc's office, then shut the door behind
her. Her hands shaking, she took a steadying breath.
Immaculately neat, everything was in its place. A brass
caduceus sat on a stack of papers in the center of the
mahogany desk, and she removed Caitlin's gloves,
shoved them in her pocket, then flipped through the
papers. Current patient notes, nothing old enough to
relate to Larissa's case.

Certificates decorated the walls, and a portrait of a
white-haired, elegant-looking woman and a distinguished-
looking Doc was hanging on one of the walls opposite his
desk over a file cabinet.

Trying the top drawer, she slid it open. Files of current
patients. Files of more patients filled the second drawer
also. No Wildhaven here though. No, it would be under
Darien's name, Silver.

And there it was. *Lelandi Silver, DECEASED*.
Lelandi's skin prickled. She slipped the file out of the
drawer and opened it, her heart fluttering at a quickened pace.

9/6 Lelandi cut her wrists as a plea for help.

Her sister had attempted suicide? Hating how much
her sister had to have suffered, Lelandi sat down hard
on the doc's chair.

*She must have known she couldn't die in that
manner. I've tried speaking with her, but she
won't tell me what's going on. Nurse Grey spoke
with her at some length, but couldn't determine
the cause of depression. Probably brought on in*

*part by fluctuating hormones from the pregnancy.
Suspect underlying reason, but can't say without
further information.*

Lelandi's eyes pricked with tears, and she wiped
away a couple rolling down her cheeks. How could she
not have been here for her sister?

*9/8 Released Lelandi from the hospital. She
seemed more upbeat and I had Doctor Craighton
visit her from Green Valley. He'll be seeing her
once a week for a month to work with her through
her psychological issues.*

*9/12 Lelandi seemed somewhat less distraught.
Silva has made friends with her as well. I'm hoping
that she'll adjust to life here with the pack sooner
than later as the pregnancy progresses.*

*10/6 Darien spoke to me about Lelandi's
crying spells. They're much more pronounced
than for a normal pregnancy. The only thing
I can attribute it to is the possibility that the
babies aren't Darien's. I don't want to speculate
further about that.*

Lelandi reread the entry. Did Darien know? What
about the rest of the pack? Silva. Maybe Larissa had told
her. Or as bad as the news was, maybe not. No wonder
Larissa was so distressed.

*10/20 Lelandi had to be hospitalized for dehydra-
tion. Darien says she's not eating properly. Too ill
with morning sickness.*

10/24 Autopsy revealed cause of death: broken neck from strangulation. Deemed a suicide, considering suicide note found in patient's handwriting, past history of severe depression, and previous suicide attempt.

10/26 Autopsy of fetuses indicate the DNA does not match Darien's.

Tears streaked down Lelandi's cheeks, and she quickly brushed them away. How could her sister have done this to Darien? To the family? She'd shamed them all. It was bad enough that she'd mated another wolf when she was already mated, although Lelandi could forgive Larissa's transgressions considering how cruel Crassus was. But how could Larissa have conceived someone else's babies?

And who was the villain who seduced her sister? Silva said Larissa was seeing a miner. The only one she knew was Joe Kelly. If not him, would he know her sister's lover?

She couldn't believe how bad the situation with her sister was turning out.

"Doctor," Ritka said from down the hall, jarring Lelandi from her morbid thoughts. "Mrs. Waverly wants more medication, but she's had enough morphine to put a cow under."

"Mrs. Waverly's bone cancer has spread to many of her vital organs. She doesn't have long to live. She's entitled to whatever pain medication helps ease her suffering. Anything else?"

"Just Willy Wilkerson. His lungs sound like they're full of fluid. Might be pneumonia. And Ural seems to be regaining consciousness."

Ural was here? Unconscious! Lelandi ground her teeth. That's why Deputy Trevor was here. *Damn Darien and his men.*

The doctor and Ritka walked past the office and Lelandi didn't stir.

Once they'd reached an exam room, Doc Oliver said, "Mrs. Wilkerson. We'll have Willy on medication and better in no time."

Lelandi refiled her sister's health records and made for the door. Whether Trevor liked it or not, she was going to see her cousin and find out what they'd done to him.

The door eased open and Lelandi's heart nearly quit. But it wasn't Doc.

Joe Kelly hurried inside and shut the door. Snow covered his coat, hair and whiskers, and his eyes had a madman's look. "Searching for Larissa's file?" He pulled a gun out and motioned for Lelandi to back up against the wall.

A sickening feeling rippled through her. Her gaze shifted from the gun to his grim face. "You were the father of her triplets, weren't you?"

"We thought Darien knew. But he either pretended not to, or was too arrogant to believe someone else had captured his mate's heart. All that crap about dream mating."

Hoping for a distraction, Lelandi backed toward the desk where she could reach the caduceus paperweight. Then she recalled her gun. Hell, she could have used it on the wolf stalking her. Slipping her hand into her pocket, she realized with a sinking heart she'd exchanged jackets with Cody. Oh, god, an underage *lupus garou* had her gun filled with silver bullets. Darien would kill her if this lunatic didn't beat him to it.

Joe waved his gun at her and spoke in a hushed voice. "Silver bullets, Lelandi. So don't try me. She was my one true mate. She told me everything about that abusive red mate of hers, how she couldn't stand Darien's touch, but went along with the mating so he'd protect her against Crassus. Not to mention that Darien insisted she was his because he'd seen her in the damned dreams. When I saw you, I figured you were the one he dreamed of."

"What… what are you going to do?"

"Clean up loose ends."

Which meant? He'd kill Doc because he'd known about the pregnancy. She lunged for the heavy brass paperweight, but Joe grabbed her arm, and they fell to the floor with a thud. "Shit, woman. I'm not going to kill you. I have to get rid of the medical records."

She didn't believe him for an instant. She and Doc knew about her sister's babies. Why wouldn't Joe kill them both? Hell, he had silver bullets in his gun. Why would he even be armed if he didn't intend to murder someone?

She tried to squirm loose, but Joe kept her effectively pinned down.

"Listen, I'll get the records for you and you can leave," she coaxed.

"Nice try, Lelandi. What would prevent you from telling Darien everything you know? Even if you tried to keep your promise, he could force you to tell him the truth. I've made arrangements with your cousin Ural to take you away from here, and I want to stay with the pack. So you'll have to leave," he whispered against her ear.

And Doc? She wanted to ask him what he intended to do to Doc, but she had a pretty good idea. She feared Joe would be desperate enough to do anything to cover up his deeds.

"Okay, I'll go quietly with you. Let's get the files." She hoped she could come up with a plan before anyone got hurt.

"What the hell are you doing here?" Ritka hollered down the hall at someone. "Visiting hours are from ten to five, and as far as I know you don't have any relatives in the hospital."

"I need to see the doctor. It's an emergency."

Carol Wood?

"Oh, no you don't. Darien already said you can't have a job here."

"It's urgent and has nothing to do with working."

Joe pulled Lelandi off the floor and motioned for her to brace the wall. Then he began shuffling through the files.

"You can't go down there to see him! He's with a patient right now!" Ritka's footfalls pounded after Carol Wood's.

Then a thud sounded against the doctor's door. Carol swore, but the door banged open, and she fell into Doc's office, landing on her hands and knees.

Lelandi and Joe froze.

For a heartbeat, both Ritka and Carol stared at Joe and Lelandi, then Ritka shouted, "Deputy Trevor! Break-in in progress!"

Joe whipped the gun around and fired two shots at Ritka, the gunfire exploding in Lelandi's ears. She leapt at Joe and seized the weapon as Ritka crumpled to the floor. He thrust Lelandi aside. Carol screamed and scrambled to her feet, but Doc Oliver appeared in the entryway, blocking her escape. Joe fired at Doc. Clutching his chest, his eyes round, he collapsed. Carol dashed out of the office, and Lelandi dove for the brass weight.

With a lightning reaction, Joe struck the butt of his gun against her head and sent her sprawling. Flashes of pain streaked through her skull. Momentarily, she saw nothing but blackness, heard nothing, felt nothing. But then files crashed to the floor while Joe ransacked the file cabinet, until he found Larissa's. He shoved it inside his jacket, went to the window, and jerked it open.

A mixture of snow and ice blew into the office, chilling her. She blinked her eyes, trying to clear her head.

Where the hell was Deputy Trevor? And what if Doc Mitchell arrived with Caitlin and became embroiled in this mess. And the other teens, too. She could see Cody and Anthony trying to rescue her.

Doc Oliver groaned. His face was sickly pale. Lelandi crawled over to him. Ritka was out cold, and Carol had vanished. Lelandi ripped open Doc's shirt and meant to dig out the bullet with her fingers, but Joe grabbed her hair and yanked her back. Pain shot through her scalp. "Time to go."

"No!" she screamed, wanting to save Doc, and clawed at Joe's fingers to free herself.

Joe seized her arm and wrenched her to the window.

"You hadn't done anything wrong before this. Why now?" Lelandi struggled to break free of his iron grip, trying to control her tears. She couldn't fall apart now.

Carol peeked through the doorway with a cell phone to her ear.

"Get the bullets out of the nurse and Doc! They'll kill them. Don't wait for help!" Lelandi shouted, hoping the bastard wouldn't shoot her, too.

Joe shoved Lelandi through the window, and she fell into a blanket of snow. Before she could move, he climbed after her, then aimed through the window at Carol. Her heart in her throat, Lelandi scrambled to her feet and jerked his gun arm upward. The gun went off with a bang, and the bullet struck the ceiling. Bits of plaster and paint snowed down on the desk. Carol screamed and ducked down the hallway.

"Damn it, woman. I ought to kill you."

Lelandi believed he would anyway. "Why shoot Ritka and the doc?" she sobbed. She hoped Carol could save their lives.

"Doc knew about your sister's pregnancy. Larissa was certain of it. He'd have told Darien, and by pack law Darien would terminate me." He yanked her toward a pickup.

Lights flashing and sirens wailing, several vehicles surrounded the hospital.

"Shit." Joe took off running, pulling Lelandi into the woods.

Hell, not again. "You can't outrun all of Darien's pack," Lelandi said as Joe nearly pulled her arm out of the socket, tugging her over the rough terrain.

She stumbled knee deep in a snowdrift, and he yanked her up. She growled. He gave her a slight smile, then they scrambled down a steep incline, half-sliding, half-falling until they reached the bottom of the ravine.

He pulled her across a brook, the icy water freezing her to the core again. The snow was still falling so heavily and the wind blowing it so hard, she could barely see.

"Where are you taking me?"

Joe dragged her up the mountain on the other side. "Climb," he hollered at her.

She balked.

He pointed the gun at her temple. "Darien can't save you here. If I put a bullet in that pretty head of yours, they wouldn't arrive in time to get it out. So climb. It's your only hope."

Clenching her teeth, her hands numb from the frigid water and her wet clothes sticking to her like icy Saran Wrap, she struggled to make the climb.

"Keep going straight up," he ordered.

She looked up, but couldn't see where he had in mind to take her. They couldn't climb mountains all day. Unless… She glanced back at him. He was to the right of her, resting while she did.

"Go!"

Unless a cave was up here. She began climbing again. Maybe a secret hideaway where he'd taken Larissa? Lelandi wanted to empty her lunch and kill the bastard for shooting Doc and Ritka.

Men shouted on the ridge from the direction of town. Darien and his men were coming for her. Her heart lifted, but Joe's expression turned darker. "Move!"

She tried to make it appear she was too weak to climb quickly, although as frozen as she was, it wasn't all pretense. He drew closer and struck her in the shoulder. She gasped and nearly fell. Her heart pounding furiously, she clung to the rugged rock face, her fingers so numb she couldn't feel the jagged edges, wishing she could have put Caitlin's gloves on.

"Move, damn you! Quit stalling. Larissa wasn't half as capable as you, and she made it up this ridge twice as fast as you're going."

"I'm half-frozen," Lelandi snapped back.

She moved at the same pace as before, hoping she wouldn't fall to her death on the icy mountain, until she saw the ledge he pointed to. He yanked her up the last few feet and pulled her into the cave. Hopefully, someone in Darien's party knew about it.

"Was this a silver mine?" She tugged Caitlin's gloves out of the pocket and shoved her icy fingers into them.

"Until it played out seventy years ago. Then it shut down." He grabbed a lantern and lighted it, despite not needing it. But even the flicker of flame radiated a tiny glow of heat she welcomed. Inside the cave, it was slightly warmer than the blowing snow outside, and he handed her a hardhat. "Put it on."

He was going to shoot her in the head with a silver bullet, but now he wanted to protect her from falling rocks? That was the least of her worries though as they traveled deeper into the bowels of the cave. The walls drew closer, the passageway narrower, the ceiling shorter and Lelandi began to feel hemmed in. "Does this open up pretty soon?"

He shook his head.

"They came this way!" Darien shouted.

Lelandi's spirits soared when she heard Darien's voice. But it was so far away, she imagined they hadn't even begun the climb up the mountain.

"Where are you taking me?" she asked Joe, raising her voice, hoping her words would carry through the cave and back down the ridge.

"Shut up!" Joe yanked her deeper, and she gave a hopeful smile, thinking Darien might have heard Joe's yelling if her words hadn't carried that far.

Water glistened off the granite walls and dripped on her hat, and she jerked her head to look up. The place smelled like wet earth and the air turned colder. She shivered.

"Forty-four degrees down here no matter what the temperature is outside," he said.

Still, it was warmer than the raging blizzard outside. But her wet clothes made it feel colder.

The ceiling sank so low, they had to crawl. The rough stone tore at the gloves, and her jeans were no protection for her knees, bruising with every inch she traversed. The place reminded her of the time she got lost in a cave of tunnels, playing hide-and-seek with her brother and sister, then fell into a small hole she couldn't get out of. Boy, were their parents mad. But since then, she cringed whenever she had to go into small places, even as a wolf.

Joe forced Lelandi to go first, and her breathing grew more labored. She attempted to steady her breathing, calm her racing heart, ignore the tightness in her chest. But nothing was working. Time seemed to slow and the fear of dying in the tomb-like tunnel escalated.

She paused for the third time, trying to get her anxiety under control, hating that she couldn't manage it.

"Don't tell me you're claustrophobic," he snarled.

"Well, I am, damn it. Larissa wasn't. She could hide in the smallest caves back home, curl up in one and wait my brother and me out when we were playing hide-and-seek, but I can't do that."

"Why?"

As if she'd tell the bastard.

When she didn't answer him, he laughed. "Doesn't matter. Just suck it up. Now move!" He shoved at her butt and she kicked back with her foot, connecting with some part of him… probably his head as it was so hard.

He yelped. "Damn it, Lelandi, you're asking for trouble."

Rocks tumbled together from up above, but the cave was so narrow at this point, she couldn't look back to see what had happened. The sound of falling rock sent chills racing across her skin. Buried alive in a rock tomb came to mind.

"I have a little surprise waiting for them."

What was this maniac planning? As she reached the opening into a large cave, the mountain shook and rumbled.

"What have you done?" Her heart nearly stopped. Darien? His men? What if… what if anyone was badly hurt or killed in the rock slide?

She scrambled into the cave and Joe followed her out of the tunnel, her boot's imprint on his forehead.

"I made some assurances that if anyone tried to come in here when Larissa and I were having our special time, they couldn't tell anyone, and if they did manage to survive, they wouldn't be able to locate us."

He was crazier than she suspected. "But you've locked us in a tomb."

"Don't be ridiculous. Two more tunnels lead out of here that are never used."

Another rumble of rocks shook her. She looked back at the tunnel they'd come from. Joe seized her arm, but she jerked free, her teeth clenched, tears filling her eyes. She'd found her soul mate only to lose him? "If you killed Darien, you might as well shoot me and get it over with."

"And if I haven't? Would be a shame if he found you dead, too."

He was right, the bastard. If Darien found her dead, he might not get over the grief. A clear plastic bag drew her attention, a pile of furs folded inside.

"I brought them here for Larissa and me, except she died before we had the chance to use them. I tried to convince her to come away with me, but she was afraid Darien would come after us. He still thought the triplets were his. He would have killed me and taken her back if he'd had to tear the world apart looking for her."

He grabbed Lelandi's arm again and yanked her toward another tunnel. "This one's shorter, not as narrow. After we make it down the mountain, we'll backtrack to town, pick up my truck, and be on our way."

"You don't need me. Darien won't care what happens to you if you leave me behind."

"Darien took Larissa from me. Now you'll be her. Just like everyone thought in the beginning anyway."

"But he'll look for me, just like he would have searched for Larissa. He'll never quit coming after us."

"If I'd risked it last time, maybe Larissa would still be alive."

As much as she didn't like the idea, Joe might be right. If Larissa had left with this man, whoever wanted her dead might not have bothered to kill her.

"You said you were taking me to Ural. That he knew where my parents were. Were you telling the truth?"

Chapter 19

BLOCKED FROM HIS BROTHERS AND THIRTY OF HIS MEN. MORE stones rained down from the initial explosion that rocked the mountain. Darien choked on the dust and rubbed his eyes so he could see the mess he was in. The rocks barricaded the tunnel entrance and no one had made it inside but him.

"Everyone all right out there?" he yelled, hoping to hell no one had been caught in the slide.

Jake hollered, "We're fine. You?"

Highly pissed. "Fine here."

He listened, trying to hear any sounds indicating where Joe Kelly and Lelandi were. Nothing. At least Darien could still go after them.

Sam shouted from the other side of the blockage, "We could move the rocks, but it will take hours, boss. Mason and I used to come in another way. Less hard on the knees."

"Show the men," Darien growled. He'd kill that son of a bitch as soon as he got his hands on him. If he'd done anything to Lelandi…

Jake hollered, "We'll meet you around the other side, but damn it, Darien, don't get yourself shot in the meantime. Those bullets are silver."

Darien had no intention of waiting for his men to reach him while Lelandi was in Joe's clutches. "How long will it take?"

"When I was younger, about half an hour. Maybe longer now," Sam said. "The way's easier once you're inside, no low crawling, but to reach the cave, the climbing's much harder."

"See you in half an hour."

"Wait for us, Darien, damn it," Jake said again.

Darien was sure everyone knew he wouldn't. He raced through the sections of the tunnel that he could, but soon came to an area where he had to crawl. The slight scent of Larissa and Lelandi remained in the tunnel. He ground his teeth when he smelled Lelandi's fear. Joe was letting off a panicky scent also. *Good.* Darien hoped he was sweating fear. Damned cowardly male *lupus garou* who had to use a weapon to fortify himself. The notion Larissa had been here with Joe curdled Darien's stomach though.

Down on hands and knees, he traversed the narrow, low ceiling tunnel, and he envisioned Lelandi's skin being torn up by the rough-edged rocks. Damn that Joe. How could Larissa have managed? He would have seen any injuries she'd incurred. Unless they'd usually come in another way. *Sure.* Sam said the other tunnel was easier to maneuver. But this time since Joe was trying to outrun Darien and his men, he had used the cave closest to town.

When Darien finally reached the cave, he climbed out, but saw no sign of them. Except for fur blankets packed in a plastic case. His stomach and fists tightened. Two more tunnels opened out of the cave, and he hurried to one, walked in a couple of feet, but could find none of Lelandi's or Joe's scent. He raced across the cave to the other tunnel. But the sound of footfalls from two individuals approached him, making him stop dead. What the hell was Joe up to?

"How would I know the damned cave-in would trigger one over here? Or maybe someone set off the cave-in a couple of weeks ago," Joe growled.

"What about the other tunnel? What if we're trapped?" Lelandi sounded desperate, her voice shaking.

Darien wanted to dive into the tunnel, snap Joe's worthless neck, and hug Lelandi in his secure embrace to prove she was safe and loved and the likes of Joe would never harm her again.

"Shut up! Don't get hysterical on me. The other tunnel's fine. It's a little trickier getting out through that one, but we'll manage. You have to watch for the pits. Drop something in them, and you never hear it hit bottom. Lost my hardhat down the first one once. Must have stood there twenty minutes or more waiting for it to hit rock bottom, or water, or something. Nothing. Just went on forever."

Don't worry, Lelandi. You won't be traversing any damned pits with this maniac. Darien stripped off his jacket, then shirt and ditched his boots, careful not to make a sound.

Lelandi and Joe's footsteps echoed off the tunnel wall as they drew closer. "He'll… he'll come after you. You know he will. If you just leave me behind—"

"Shut up! I told you you're going to replace my Larissa."

"I can't be like her."

"You look just like her. That'll be enough for now. You'll grow on me."

You'll never have the opportunity, Joe. Darien peeled out of his jeans and stretched his arms above his head, physically and mentally preparing for the change. His face elongated into a silver snout, his teeth growing into killing weapons. His body became furred in a silver pelt and his claws extended, readied for a fight. Dropping to his pads, he waited, preparing himself for the leap that would separate Joe from his mate, his teeth itching to sink into his blood, to kill the man who would endanger his mate's life.

"Damn it to hell! This one's blocked, too!" Jake said on the outside of the cave at the tunnel entrance. "Is there another way, Sam?"

"One other tunnel. But that way's too treacherous without climbing ropes."

"I'll get some," Mason said.

"I'll go with you," Deputy Peter added.

"How long will it take to get to that tunnel, Sam?" Jake asked.

"About forty minutes straight up. When I was younger."

"Let's get going."

Joe gave a sickly laugh, the sound echoing off the walls. "We'll get through the tunnel way before they do."

"But they said we needed climbing ropes," Lelandi warned.

"I've got some. You wouldn't think I'd be unprepared, would you? Now come on, quit dawdling. Wouldn't want them to reach the tunnel entrance before we've made our getaway."

You'll never even reach the tunnel entrance, Joe. Rest assured.

Joe shoved Lelandi out of the tunnel into the main cave. At once her eyes lighted on Darien, and for a minute, she looked like she was trying to figure out which wolf he might be. He bowed his head in greeting. She took a deep breath and her eyes widened. *Yes, Lelandi, your silver knight in wolf pelt.*

As soon as Joe stepped into the cavern, Darien leapt. No waiting for the miner's recognition that he was face-to-face with the pack leader. No long-winded staring down scenes to show who was the boss. The gun loaded with silver bullets precluded that. He couldn't risk Joe getting a shot off and possibly hitting either Lelandi or himself and leaving her in even more danger.

Joe's gun hand went up and he fired at the ceiling, a smattering of pebbles and dust raining down. He fell back with Darien's pounce, hitting his back and head against the unforgiving rock with an *oof.* Darien's teeth sank into Joe's jugular. The man never had a chance to utter more than a gurgled cry, his amber eyes wide.

Lelandi collapsed to her knees, and Darien released his grip on Joe, then swung around and nuzzled Lelandi's arm. She wrapped her arms around his neck and sobbed. Hell, he needed to be in his human form to comfort her best. He quickly shapeshifted and pulled her up. Her clothes were damp, and she was trembling hard from the cold.

"I… I was so afraid he'd killed you, your brothers, or some of the rest of your people in the rockslide."

Darien crushed her to him, warming her body, rubbing her arms, kissing her cheeks and her lips. "We're all right. Everyone's all right." The left side of her temple was swollen and red and a gash cut through to her eyebrow, the blood dried now along its seam. "That son of a bitch," Darien said, smoothing away her hair from the injuries.

She didn't say a word, maybe in shock. He held her close to his body and tried to warm her, although the chilly cave was beginning to get to him. Then he noticed the glass in her hair. "Hell, Lelandi, did Joe hit you with a glass?"

She looked like she was going to be sick. "With his pistol." She paused, her eyes focusing down. "I… I had an accident before that."

"You wrecked the SUV?"

She nodded, her eyes glassy with fresh tears. He let out his breath and hugged her tight again. "All I care about is what happens to you. We didn't see the vehicle anywhere in town and we'd trekked through the woods to locate the teens that you'd found. I never thought you might have been in a wreck. Why didn't you stay at Doc Mitchell's place?" He threw up his hands in resignation. "Forget it. You were too busy trying to get yourself killed."

"I'm sorry about the SUV. It's probably buried in snow off the road somewhere."

"Odin's teeth, Lelandi, I don't care about the damned vehicle. You… your safety, that's all that matters to me." He pulled her close and she sighed against his bare chest. "It'll be a while before my men can get us out."

"But Joe said there were climbing ropes for us to use."

"I wouldn't trust anything he said. Will you wait here?"

She wiped the tears from her cheeks and looked so forlorn, he gave her another hard embrace. "I want to get rid of his body."

"In one of the bottomless pits?"

"Yeah, he can join his hardhat."

"I'll… I'll go with you. I don't want to be left behind."

He squeezed her hard, then released her. "Let's get this over with." He yanked Joe's lifeless body off the floor and tossed him over his shoulder, then took Lelandi's hand. "Are you all right?"

"Now that you're here, yes. How are Doc and Ritka?"

Lelandi didn't look all right. She was pale and shivering uncontrollably. Darien tightened his hold on her hand. He didn't want to tell her the news, not while they were still stuck in the cave, and after all that had happened to her.

"They're dead," she said under her breath, her voice tearful.

So much for not telling her. "Even if Joe hadn't taken you hostage, he'd signed his death warrant for killing Doc and Ritka."

"Carol couldn't get the bullets out in time?" Lelandi asked, her voice barely above a whisper.

"Doc was old. He couldn't withstand the silver in his heart. By the time Carol had put on gloves, found the proper tools, and removed the bullet from Doc, then dug the two bullets from Ritka, she didn't stand a chance either."

Lelandi's body sagged and Darien released her hand and wrapped his arm around her waist. "Lelandi, honey, we'll be all right."

"He died because of me," she sobbed.

"No, he died because Joe killed him. Because Joe had mated with Larissa. Because the babies were his and not mine. And because Doc knew it. Ritka was just a bystander. None of this has to do with you." He kissed her cheek. "Do you want to wait for me here while I get rid of Joe's carcass?" The sooner he could get rid of the bastard, the quicker he could take care of Lelandi.

She shook her head and stood straighter. "Doc was like an uncle I dearly loved."

He moved her farther into the tunnel. "Doc was a good man. His mate preceded him in death a decade ago, and he had no offspring, but he treated us all like his sons and daughters."

Lelandi looked up at Darien, tears clouding her eyes. Darien smiled at her. "Even me. Didn't matter that I was no longer just another pup but now pack leader. He was like a revered advisor when it came to anyone who was injured or sick in the pack."

"I'll miss him," she said quietly.

"We all will." Darien pulled her to an abrupt stop. "The first of the pits. Wonder if this is the bottomless one Joe mentioned. I'd hate for it not to be."

"Only one way to find out," she said, with a bitter edge to her voice.

Darien lifted Joe off his shoulder. "This is as much of a burial as you deserve, Joe, you bastard." He tossed him into the pit, then he took Lelandi's hand and walked her back to the cave.

She sniffled and wiped away another cascade of tears. "Don't you want to see if he hits bottom?"

"No. I want to warm you up."

She glanced at his hard, nude body, and he smiled back at her. Her eyes met his. "Your people will be here soon."

He shook his head slowly back and forth. "Not as long as it takes to return to town and back again with the ropes. By the time they reach us, we'll even have time for a quick nap."

She clung to him and nuzzled her cheek against his shoulder. "I... I *am* cold."

"I love you, Lelandi." He swept her up in his arms and held her hard against his chest; the heat of her body mixed with his, helping to warm them both.

When they reached the encased furs, he set her down, then ripped open the plastic covering and spread the faux polar bear skins out. No scent of Larissa or Joe on the skins, thank god. Lelandi took a deep breath and started to pull off her pullover sweater. Darien quickly worked on her belt. She looked so contrite, he was certain she felt sorry for having slipped away from him at the house, endangering herself and upsetting everyone. But she had rescued the kids from the cliff and the word of her good deeds was already spreading throughout the pack.

"I'm sorry for what my sister did to you, Darien."

"Don't be. It's all in the past." His mouth tasted her cold lips. "Just be glad we found each other."

He finished helping her undress, her body trembling from the frigid air. Then he quickly sandwiched her in between the soft furs and himself.

The furs felt comforting, dry, and warm against Lelandi's back, the contrast of Darien's lean hardness resting on top of her. He rubbed her arms, then her shoulders, and with a devilish smirk plastered on his face, his hands shifted to her breasts, heating her up. She still envisioned him in his wolf form, self-assured, feral, beautiful, her protector. She should have known he'd be the one to come for her.

She dragged her fingers through his satiny hair and his teeth grazed her neck, sending a thrill through her. She swept her hands down his back, the muscles tensed with need. "I love you, Darien," she mouthed against his ear.

His eyes glazed over, he growled low. "Never ever leave me like that again."

She stiffened, her hands stilled on his waist. "I won't quit trying to find out who killed my sister."

"Lelandi…" He groaned and circled a nipple with his tongue, then kissed the tip. He lifted his gaze to her eyes. "I can't ever lose you. Promise you'll let me handle this."

She pressed her lips tightly together. It didn't matter that she was the female alpha leader in the pack now, as much as it mattered that she took part in avenging her sister's death. And she would, one way or another.

"Damn it, Lelandi, I won't have you getting yourself into dangerous situations like this while you're searching for your sister's killer."

She raked her nails down his back and caressed his buttocks, squeezing and releasing. He gave out a husky moan and instantly capitulated. "All right. Ask me when you want to investigate something or someone, and I'll make sure you're properly guarded."

Smiling inwardly, she loved him all the more.

The wet tip of his erection poked against her mound, and he gave her a lusty grin.

At first she rubbed against him, his eyes darkening, and he reached up to caress her breasts. "Hmm, Darien, you could hire out as a masseuse."

"Only one body I'd be interested in massaging," he said, his voice ragged. "Are you going to torture me much longer?"

Before she could respond, he pressed his fingers between her legs, parted her folds, and sank his fingers deep. His wet fingers rubbed her sensitized

nub with exquisite strokes pushing her to the edge
while his tongue danced across her nipples, teasing
them into submission.

Every move Darien made heated her further.

He swept his lips over her closed eyes, down her
cheek to the corner of her mouth, then brushed across
her mouth in a warm, tantalizing caress. His heartbeat
pounded in sync with hers, and his warm breath fanned
her cheek.

"Lelandi, my love." His smoldering eyes took his
fill and his lips curved up in a feral way while he
continued to ply his strong strokes, and she forgot what
she'd intended to do to him, her body enraptured by
his touch. If she didn't slow him down... no, keep...
keep going.

Oh, oh, heavens. She felt her body elevated, her spirit
soaring, elation and... and a gush of warmth flooded
her, her system filled with white hot completion. The
orgasm rocked her body, sending pleasurable ripples of
heated passion through her, and she moaned in ecstasy.

His sizzling gaze pierced her, and he didn't wait
for her next move. Slipping into her swollen folds, he
plunged his thick cock deep, lifting her hips so he could
drive into her inner core as if seeing her body come, he
was pushed nearer the edge. His eyes heavily lidded and
his face flushed with pleasure, he stretched her, thrusting
hard and deep and fast.

Never while she'd made love to him in their dream
state had she enjoyed sex this much. "Oh, oh, faster,
harder." She dug into his buttocks. "Don't... stop...
now," she growled, not believing she could come again
so soon after.

He chuckled and drove harder, his hands planted beside her head, and gave a final thrust, a warm bath heating her deep inside. Sinking on top of her, their bodies slippery and hot and satiated, he let out a gratified growl. "Thank... Odin... you... were... all right."

"Just all right," she whispered against his cheek.

"This side of heaven." He rolled off her and pulled her on top of him, his arms wrapped securely around her while he tugged the fur that had slipped off them back in place. "Don't ever leave me again like you did."

"Hmm." She cuddled against his hard, sweaty chest. "Thank you for rescuing me. Some rescue, by the way."

He growled, nipped her shoulder, and forced her head down on his chest. "Don't forget that whatever happens, I love you, Lelandi, and would never let any harm come to you."

She snuggled against his chest and licked his nipple, making him groan. "Better not, or I'll give you a hard time."

He grinned. "You already do, honey. A *really* hard time. Rest. We'll be out of here soon, but we have a long, difficult trek ahead of us."

Hearing footfalls a couple of hours later coming from the tunnel of pits and the shorter one that was supposed to be more navigable, Darien opened a sleepy eye and hugged Lelandi tighter against his chest, her breathing shallow, her eyes closed in slumber.

"Hell, Darien." Jake entered the cave with ten men

from the shorter tunnel, and Tom and another twenty men came from the other. "I thought you were dead."

Glad everyone was okay, Darien gave him a small smile. "Thought so, eh?"

"Nah, not me," Tom said. "I knew you'd be all right. Jake's the worrier in the bunch. Kept hurrying the guys to move those boulders and loose rubble, afraid we wouldn't reach you through the other tunnel in time. It was taking so long for Mason and Peter to get back with the ropes. So…" Tom looked around at the cave, spied blood on the floor and took a deep whiff of the air. "Where's Joe?"

"Still making his peace with the devil in the center of the earth," Darien said.

Tom snickered. "Pit burial, eh? Perfectly appropriate."

Jake motioned to Lelandi. "She all right?"

"Yeah, she'll be fine. Give us a moment and we'll get dressed."

Mason dropped a bundle next to Darien's clothes. "Some gloves, snow shoes, and a heavy-duty parka for the little lady, more her size. The blizzard's whipping up pretty hard out there." He gave Jake a stern look. "Which is why it took us so long to get back to the mountain. It had nothing to do with my age."

Tom laughed and slapped Jake on the shoulder as the men hurried out through the short tunnel. "See, what'd I tell you? Here we are slaving away to protect Darien's ass, and he's cozied up with his mate in a love nest of furs."

"Yep, pack leader thinking." Jake headed out with Tom.

"I still can't believe you moved those boulders to clear the passageway," Sam said, inside the tunnel.

"I didn't want Lelandi to have to take the hard way out. Blizzard's going to be difficult enough to get through," Jake remarked.

"Good thing we have those ropes," Tom said.

Jake chuckled. "Yeah, so we can all get lost together."

Wanting to get Lelandi home safely, Darien kissed her ear to wake her. "Honey, time to get dressed."

"Hmm, maybe everyone should stay here in the cave until the storm blows over," Lelandi murmured.

"Not enough furs to keep everyone warm."

"We could all turn wolf."

"I'd rather be in the privacy of my bed with you. Come on, sleepyhead. Time to get up and get dressed."

"It's so warm here, and so…" She shivered. "So cold out there." She pointed one finger outside the furs.

He kissed her finger. "I'll help you dress faster." Darien slipped out from under the covers, threw his clothes on, then slid his cold hands under the furs to Lelandi's feet.

"Oh heavens, Darien. Your fingers are like ice."

"By the way, Cody gave me back my favorite leather jacket. He warned me it had a gun in the pocket and figured you took it with you to protect yourself." He tilted his chin down and gave her an exasperated look.

"He offered me his parka so I'd stay warmer."

"And for that," Darien said, helping her into her clothes, "I was grateful. But sheesh, Lelandi…"

"I didn't remember the gun was in your jacket pocket until Joe pulled his on me."

"Thank Odin for that. I could imagine you shooting each other and neither of you making it."

He bundled her up to her neck in the winter parka, although he wished it was a bright color and not white where he could lose her in the blinding snow.

"We could return as wolves," she said.

"The climb is too steep on this side of the mountain. Better suited to a mountain goat... or humans with climbing gear."

After what she'd already been through, that didn't bode well.

Chapter 20

THE GUYS ALL GAVE LELANDI SURREPTITIOUS SMILES WHEN she walked into the tunnel with Darien. Yeah, here they'd been busting their butts, trying to save their pack leader and his mate, and what do they find?

But heck, if any of them had been stuck in a cave with their mate, they would have done the same!

The wind whipped snow in through the opening where there had been none when Joe forced her through the tunnel before. If the snow wasn't blowing so hard, she would be elated to see the sight of the mountains, but all she could see was a white blanket, disguising everything in its path.

Many of the men had started down the mountain, some waiting at various points along the trail, some down at the bottom wearing their wolf coats. If the climb hadn't been so steep, she would have welcomed shapeshifting.

Jake handed Darien a rope already attached to Sam and Mason and several others who were partway down the steep incline.

"It's gotten really icy," Mason warned.

Darien tied the rope around Lelandi's waist and kissed her lips hard. "Take it easy. The guys down below will stop your tumble if you slip. I'll hold you from up above. Just concentrate on getting good toe and finger holds, and you'll be down at the bottom before you know it."

"Thanks, Darien." She glanced at Jake and Tom. "And to all of you who came to my rescue."

Jake took the rope that Darien had tied to himself. "All in a day's work. Think nothing of it."

Tom grinned. "Hey, we were rescuing Darien, too, but he'll never admit it."

Darien chuckled, his icy breath mixing with the blowing snow. "I didn't think you'd arrive in time."

He crouched down on the ledge and helped ease Lelandi over it. Her stomach iced with fear. Climbing up, no problem. But this side was much steeper, and the hand and foot holds were so far apart, much better suited to the grays' long reach, that she had to slide down partway to reach the next toe or finger hold. Every time she did, Darien held tight to the cliff face to ensure she didn't pull him and the others off the mountain. Sam and the others below waited until she caught hold of something.

"How's it going?" Tom shouted from several feet above Jake.

"Slow," Jake said.

"She's getting tired." Darien's voice showed concern.

She wished he hadn't said that because although every muscle ached with fatigue, she didn't want it advertised to every gray out here. What would they think about her ability to be the female leader?

"Wait up, boss." Sam began to climb back up. "She can't reach a foothold."

She wanted desperately to jump down to the bottom of the cliff, wishing the snow would cushion her fall.

"Try to grasp onto anything, Lelandi. Sam will help you."

Everyone waited while Sam climbed below Lelandi, the wind-driven snow buffeting her, threatening to pull her from her tentative grip on the jagged rocks. But she couldn't make a move down or to either side. She wondered if Larissa could have come this way. How could she have managed? But maybe the snow and ice made the difference.

"Put your right foot in my hand, and I'll guide you to a shelf," Sam coaxed.

"I'll pull the rest of you off the mountain." Lelandi's voice wavered, although she was trying to keep it together for Darien.

A pack leader's bitch was strong. Not a panicked weakling. But her arms and legs were growing wearier by the second, and her fingers and toes were already dead from the cold. If she could have had viable foot and hand holds all the way down, she'd be at the base of the mountain by now.

"Lelandi, concentrate on what Sam's saying. As petite as you are, you weigh nothing. The rest of us are fine."

She reached out her foot, not believing she could stretch that far, and touched Sam's hand.

"Good. Now put your weight on my hand and lean to your right. I'll move you to the ledge. It'll be slow going. Easy does it. One inch at a time."

Sam crept across the rock face while helping her. "Okay, here you go." She grasped a rock and pulled herself to the ledge. "There's enough room for two, Darien."

Darien was down in seconds, standing on the ledge with Lelandi, holding her body against the rock face, warming her. Jake and Tom moved farther down. The rest who were tied to the rope waited.

"You can make it." Darien kissed Lelandi's cheek, heating her icy skin.

"I… I wish I were a lot taller."

"I wouldn't wish you any other way." He squeezed her hand. "Let's get you down from here. The longer we're in this cold, the harder it will be."

"I'm sorry I'm holding everyone up so much. They'd all be warm in their beds by now if I wasn't so slow."

"Lelandi, believe me when I say everyone here wants nothing more than to bring you back safely. You're one of us. Don't worry."

"Okay… I'm ready." But she wasn't. She figured that however long she had to climb was going to be as difficult as the many feet she'd already traversed. She was wrong.

Darien eased her down over the ledge, and she found her first good foothold she'd managed to find in the last half hour. Sam waited before he moved back down. Probably a good thing because if she got stuck like the last time, he'd have to waste more energy climbing back up to her. Poor bartender. She hoped Silva would give him a really good backrub when he made it back to town.

She reached for another rock, but couldn't grasp it, and made a slight jump for it, like she'd done so many times before. But the rock was icy and she lost her grip and slid.

"Hold on!" Darien shouted, and everyone braced themselves as Lelandi fell below Sam, the wind twisting her until she was dangling upside down.

She was nearly eye level with Mason, and she offered him a frozen smile. "I just found a faster way to get down."

He grinned at her and began to climb up, tugging at her until he was able to get her feet below her body and one planted on a sturdy rock jutting out. He looked up at Darien and Sam. "She's secure. One hell of a trooper, Darien."

Man, the pack would be laughing about this for eons. Yet no one looked like they thought she was ready for a clown suit. Instead, everyone looked like they worried she'd never make it. But damn it, she would make it. Even if she had to go down headfirst to get there. At least she'd made some more progress!

Sam made his way past her and then men on either side of her roped together with their own lines, reached for her to move her down another few inches, and then another few, while Darien and his group hung on tight to the cliff every time she slipped.

"I'm at the bottom!" Mason shouted. "You're almost here!"

Thank god. Lelandi was frozen to the bone, and she didn't think she'd thaw out until summer.

Sam shouted next, "I've got you!"

But although he reached for her, two other men brought her down to the base of the mountain, and she sank in the deep snow.

Darien was beside her in the next instant and untied the rope from her waist. "Can you shapeshift, Lelandi?"

Peter shouted from somewhere deep in the white bleakness, "Got a sled, boss! We'll tow her in."

"I can shapeshift," Lelandi objected, not wanting to show how inept she was, yet when she tried to take a step, her legs were shaky and to her mortification, she stumbled.

Darien grabbed her arm and pulled her tight. "Everyone down from the mountain?"

"All down," Tom confirmed.

"Let's see that everyone gets in safely."

Peter and his sled came into sight, pulled by a dozen wolves. Lelandi smelled their *lupus garou* scent and gave a tired smile. Several of the men deposited their clothes on the sled and shapeshifted, then spread out on the way to Darien's place.

"Little lady okay?" Mitchell asked from somewhere in the mist of snow.

"Yeah, Doc, cold, but we'll have her home and warmed up in no time."

"You shouldn't have slipped away like you did after leaving the kids off at my ranch," Mitchell said, his gruff voice scolding. "The kids were upset when they heard the same maniac who took you hostage murdered Doc and Ritka."

"Are they going to be all right?" She hated how guilty her voice sounded.

"Yeah, they'll heal in no time."

"Caitlin… is she…"

"She's fine. But I need to talk to her parents."

Apparently, Darien was still in the dark about Caitlin's pregnancy.

"I take it Joe is no longer a problem," Mitchell said.

"Pit burial," Tom piped up from some feet behind, sounding proud as he yanked off his gloves.

"Better than what he deserved," Jake grumbled.

Peter said, "Several of our men wanted to know if they could pull guard duty. Despite the weather, six reds drove into town."

All at once, Lelandi felt sick to her stomach. It had to be Bruin and his brother Crassus looking to return Larissa and her home. Darien rubbed her back.

"One of them said he was Larissa's mate. The other was named Bruin, the guy's brother and pack leader at Wildhaven. He says Lelandi now belongs to Crassus, and he wants both women returned to the pack at once. So our guys want to know if you need them for guard duty."

"Yeah, I do."

Darien shielded Lelandi from the blowing wind while she removed her clothes and shapeshifted. Stretching her arms above her head, she welcomed the painless change. Her face elongated into a nice-sized feminine snout, the red furred mask reaching the length of her nose, and the underside of her chin and chest—an elegant white. She stretched her legs out, her tail straight and proud. Her eyes looked more amber than green when she was in her wolf's pelt, and she took a deep breath.

Darien smiled at her wolf form. "You're beautiful, you know."

She nudged his leg and he hurried to strip and change. Once he had, she stuck close to him, but kept examining the other wolves. Trying to learn who they all were? Eventually she'd know the whole pack, but unless she could smell them, she wouldn't be able to recognize who they were unless she'd seen them change.

He rubbed her muzzle with his face as they trotted to his house, a couple miles away. Even so, she seemed wary, the way she pulled her ears back, her body snug against his so she'd keep her bearing as they moved, but she kept looking around at the other wolves. He wished he could ask her what was wrong. Attempting a calming signal, he turned his head and licked the back of her head. She whipped her head around, and he nuzzled her face. Her narrowed eyes softened. Several of his pack watched her behavior, knowing something was wrong. He wished she'd told him what the matter was before they'd shapeshifted.

As soon as they arrived at Darien's house, Sam began making coffee and hot chocolate for the men, while Darien and Lelandi shapeshifted and dressed in the den, then he ushered her toward the stairs to take a hot shower. "What was the matter in the woods?"

"A gray attempted to attack me earlier."

"Hell, Lelandi. Why didn't you tell me? I take it you didn't get his scent."

"No."

"Can you describe him?"

"Gray and big. Really big."

Jake pulled a sweater over his head. "That describes more than half of our men."

"I know, Jake," she said, her voice irritated. "If I saw him in wolf form again, I'd probably know him." She let out her breath. "What about Bruin and his men?"

Trevor sauntered into the living room and gave her a disgruntled look. "They've been put up at Hastings Bed and Breakfast. They didn't like that they couldn't see you right away, Darien, especially since she's one of their pack. He's a pack leader so should be treated accordingly."

Darien's jaw tightened. "Any pack leader who allows his males to abuse the females has my condemnation, not respect."

"The sheriff is keeping them occupied. He's got another four guys down there, watching to make sure no one gets out of hand. Bruin's brother, Crassus, a subchief, demands the release of his mate from our custody."

"Did you tell him she had a proper burial?"

Trevor skirted Darien's comment. "He said Lelandi is his mate."

"Guy's a bold-faced liar," Tom said.

"Bruin said that it's a pack law, if a mate's life was ended and a sibling was available, if the male wished her to replace the dead mate it was up to him, the pack leader, and her father."

An ancient law. *Great.*

"Convenient since the pack leader's his brother," Darien said, his face tight, his eyes narrowed.

Trevor lifted a shoulder. "And her father is dead. He said he did the mating ritual with her *in absentia.* It's an ancient ritual. But it's valid."

She'd never heard anyone actually use it in contemporary times, but Darien wouldn't go along with it, so it was a moot case.

"Not as far as we're concerned." Darien gave Lelandi's hand a squeeze.

"Is this a fight we want to get involved in?" Trevor asked.

"Have to. You say the sibling has to be available?"

Trevor's lower lip dropped. "You're not thinking of—"

"One way to claim a mate permanently."

"She has to be agreeable." Trevor glanced at Lelandi.

"I'll have to convince her, then, won't I?" Darien moved Lelandi toward the stairs. "I'll start your shower."

Trevor's eyes couldn't have widened any further.

"Guess you didn't get the word. They're already

mated." Tom gave Trevor a slap on the back. "So, where were you while the rest of us were rescuing the lady?"

"Hell, I was with the sheriff, trying to sort this red pack business out. It would have been helpful to know that Darien took her as his mate."

"*He'll* have to tell the pack leader the news," Tom said. "He hasn't had time to tell the rest of our pack yet. But I'm sure after the cave incident, the word will quickly spread."

"What happened at the cave?"

Jake laughed. "You should have been with us. Much more interesting I'm sure than what you were up to."

Darien smiled and kissed Lelandi as he walked her up the stairs. "Guess I've been a little remiss in letting the pack know you're one of us."

"You don't have any regrets, do you? I mean, you're not afraid I can't deal with the fallout, are you?"

He pulled her into his bedroom and shut the door. "Like what? That you won't be loved by my people? You will be."

"Not by everyone."

"The women who wanted me as a mate?" He laughed and pulled off her sweater and dropped it on a chair.

"I'm sorry about Ritka. I never said so before because I was so upset about Doc. But I really am sorry. She didn't deserve to die either."

"I know, Lelandi." He took a deep breath and slipped her boots off. "This will cause us trouble."

"Bruin will want to fight you, don't you think?"

Darien gave her a brilliant smile. "No. Well, maybe. But the outcome won't be what he'd expect. No. I was thinking about the staffing at the hospital. With Ritka gone, Carol Wood will insist that she's hired on at the hospital. I've got a real problem with that."

"I don't have any nurse's training, but I'll do whatever I can to help."

He placed his hands on her face and tilted her head back. "I'll send human patients to other hospitals in nearby towns until we get it sorted out. Don't worry about it."

She frowned at him. "What happened to Ural? Why was he in the hospital?"

Darien sighed deeply. "I didn't authorize it, but Uncle Sheridan knocked him out when Ural made a crude comment about one of our female grays."

"What did he say?"

"She was the shooter."

"And the sheriff nearly killed him for it?"

Darien lifted her chin and looked into her eyes. "I didn't authorize it. Uncle Sheridan took it upon himself to knock Ural out."

"Before Ural revealed who the shooter was?"

Darien stared at her for a minute, then shook his head. "I know what you're implying, but Ural just pushed Uncle Sheridan's buttons."

But had Ural pushed Sheridan's buttons or did he have something to hide?

"So is Ural all right?"

"He's fine, back in jail with a swollen cheek, but Silva told us herself she was the shooter."

Lelandi couldn't believe it.

"Long story. I'll tell you later about it." He pressed her lips with a warm, hot kiss and her whole body liquefied.

"Hmm." She sighed deeply. He was trying to get her

mind off the problems the pack faced, but she couldn't quit worrying about it. "What about Nurse Grey?"

"She can handle a lot of the cases—mostly *lupus garou*. But she'll be shorthanded for anything major. Although we have Matthew now, too." He unfastened her belt.

"Doctor Weber!"

Darien lifted his head from kissing her throat and gave her a questioning glance.

"He's a *lupus garou* from my father's original pack. We have to bring him here."

"He's a red."

She gave Darien an annoyed look. "I'm a red."

"That's different." He kissed her lips, forcing her to kiss him back. She couldn't resist and probed his mouth with her tongue. "What I mean is he might not want to join a gray pack."

"He will. I know he will."

"I'll send the correspondence offering him a job." He sighed heavily. "I don't want you digging into this mess concerning your sister on your own anymore." She tried to pull away, but he held her firm. "I mean it."

She glowered at him. "What am I supposed to do?"

He raised his brows and gave her a wickedly provocative look.

"Oh, no, I'm just supposed to be your sexual playmate?"

"Works for me," he teased. He grabbed handfuls of her hair and touched his nose to the strands. "You smell like the great outdoors, wild and sexy."

"Hmm." She licked his lips. "You taste feral and sinful." With a fever that couldn't be quenched, she wanted him. She grasped his hand and tugged him toward the bathroom. "You were going to help me with my shower. Right?"

He wrapped his arm around her and pulled her back tight against his chest. Leaning over her, he rested his mouth next to her ear, and slid his fingers into her jeans, then touched her between the legs. "Hmm, nice and wet."

"It's all your fault." She wriggled against his fingers. Oh man, she'd never make it to the shower at this rate.

His cock had grown rock hard and was prodding her backside. "If I don't get you into the shower now…" He slipped the lace of the low-cut bra down, exposing her breasts. Turning her around, he leaned down, licked a nipple, and blew on it, sending shivers streaking across her skin. Instantly, the cool air made the nipple pucker. He smiled and licked the other with his tongue in a circle, then blew on it, too.

He tackled her jeans, his breathing heavy, his heartbeat accelerated.

Lelandi unbuttoned Darien's shirt and slid it down to his elbows, then held him hostage, his chest and shoulders bare. Strong and virile, he was a *lupus garou* in his prime, and all hers. Leaning down, she licked his nipple and gave him the same wisp of breath to tease him. His nipple pebbled, and he groaned low with need.

"Hmm, like that, do we?"

He nipped her chin with a playful bite. Lelandi laughed and licked his other nipple. He shivered and the craving for satisfaction swept her up in the feel of him, his satiny skin, tangy velvet against her tongue. He held Lelandi's arms tightly and nuzzled her neck with his mouth, and took another deep breath, no doubt smelling her musky scent of arousal. She tilted her head back, her crotch tingling because he touched her throat so exquisitely.

Whispering in his ear, "I love you," she licked inside, then nibbled the lobe.

Growling, he swept her off her feet and carried her into the bathroom. He set her down, reached into the shower, and turned on the water. "I want you, Lelandi. Now."

The feeling was mutual, and they shed the rest of their clothes. She reached for the peach body wash so she could run her fingers over every inch of him with the light sweet scent.

As soon as the water was hot, he lifted her into the tub and sprayed the silky water all over her body, then aimed the pulsating nozzle between her legs. She squealed and laughed.

He soaped her breasts and she flicked her nails over the soft soap coating his nipples. They quickly moved their hands lower, his sweeping erotically between her thighs, while she enjoyed scrubbing his erection and watched fascinated when it jumped in her hands.

He chuckled darkly and hurried to rinse them off. "You will be the death of me."

"Seems appropriate since you wring out my emotions, too," she said, kissing his throat.

But he didn't comment, except to give her a smoldering smile, then lifted her against the tile shower wall, wrapped her legs around him, and thrust deeply into her slippery sheath.

"Adonis," she moaned against his shower-kissed skin. He was *so* hot.

He smiled. "My redheaded goddess."

The pleasurable assault of his kisses on her lips, her cheeks, her throat, drove her toward the peak of pleasure while he buried himself inside her. Plunging deep and slow and hard, the tension in his face eased, he let out a tired groan, and a wash of heat filled her. His hot kisses teased her mouth to open for him, his tongue tangled with hers, and her body exploded into a million earth-shattering pieces of pleasure. She collapsed in his arms and wanted to cuddle with him in bed for all eternity. After drying and slipping into bed, they slept.

But their sleep was cut short when Jake hollered from downstairs, "Darien, Uncle Sheridan's here and so is Chester McKinley."

Chapter 21

NOT PLANNING ON BEING LEFT OUT OF ANY MORE BUSINESS concerning her sister, Lelandi nearly leapt out of Darien's arms and headed for her discarded clothes in the bedroom. "I'm sitting in on this, Darien." But she wondered what had changed his mind about talking to Chester.

"I guess I have no say in the matter." He yanked on his jeans, his expression lightly teasing.

"Nope. I'm not a beta wolf." Lelandi quickly buttoned her shirt.

Darien walked over and rested his hands on her shoulders, his lips pressing against hers. "You're an alpha for sure. For now, I'll allow it… as an alpha male." He rebuttoned her shirt.

"Better put on a sweater or I'll have to kick Chester McKinley's butt out of here, because no doubt he'd take a longer look at you than I'd care for."

She jerked on a pullover sweater and slipped into a pair of jeans. "Despite whatever anyone told you, he was a perfect gentleman."

"I'll be the judge of that." Darien zipped her jeans for her. He lifted her chin and gazed into her green eyes sparkling with fire. "I have no intention of keeping you out of the picture if you're going to look into this by yourself and put your life in more danger. I understand as an alpha you can't wait for others to do everything for you." He leaned his forehead against hers. "Together, we'll solve this."

She threw her arms around him and squeezed tight, her head pressed against his chest. "I love you, you big gray."

Cheered to see her feeling better, he tousled her hair, then led her downstairs to the living room.

Upon seeing Lelandi, Uncle Sheridan raised his brows in question.

"I'm staying for the meeting," Lelandi said.

"When women start ruling things, that'll be the end of life as we know it," Uncle Sheridan said.

"We'll improve it, I'm sure," Lelandi said.

Uncle Sheridan gave her a disparaging look.

Darien couched a smile and sat down with her on a sofa, then motioned for Chester McKinley to get on with the news.

"I know you don't want an outsider sticking his nose in your business, Darien, but I do this kind of work all the time and what I discover goes no farther than this room. If you want to reveal to your pack what we find, that's up to you. Nobody will hear it from me."

"Fair enough. So what's your plan?"

"Make a list of everyone who would benefit from Larissa's death and all who had grudges against her."

Darien rubbed Lelandi's hand. Although she seemed determined to be part of this, she shivered, and he thought she wasn't holding up well. But he couldn't blame her. "We've done this."

Uncle Sheridan handed the paper to Chester.

He perused the checklist and nodded. "Normally a blackmailer continues to milk the victim for all it's worth. So there wouldn't be any reason to kill the victim and get rid of an easy source of income."

"Unless the blackmailer feared getting caught. What if Larissa had recognized who the blackmailer was?" Lelandi asked.

"Bingo. Of course, it could be there was a killer and a blackmailer and neither had anything to do with the other, but I'm betting they're one and the same."

"Why?" Darien asked.

"Thirty years in the business."

"I'd like more solid evidence than that," Jake said.

"All right. So we have a shooter who kills the gunman so he can't talk. And—"

"Silva, the waitress at Silver Town Tavern, says she shot him, although she was only protecting Sam, our bartender, and didn't mean to kill the gunman," Darien said.

Glancing down at the checklist, Chester rubbed his beard. "Is she on the suspect list?"

Lelandi frowned. "Of course not. She was friends with my sister and has been my friend ever since I first arrived."

"Right. And oftentimes a perpetrator is the one you least suspect."

"She's *not* a suspect."

"The thing is, Lelandi, even you are a suspect," Chester said.

Lelandi's mouth dropped open, then she snapped it shut. Darien shook his head. "Watch what you say, Chester McKinley."

After a minute of silence, Lelandi said, "Of course, Chester. I see what you mean. I came here to chase after Darien, but I had to get rid of my sister first."

"Exactly. My point being that even Darien's brothers are suspect. Darien himself also, if you want to go that far. What about Sheriff Sheridan? He hasn't taken a vacation in ten years and then he suddenly ups and goes on one?"

"Wait a blamed minute," Uncle Sheridan said. "I earned that damned vacation."

"Not to mention Uncle Sheridan wanted to get out of town before the second annual fair arrived," Jake said.

Chester raised his hands in conciliation. "I'm saying we can't look at only the ones we suspect, but those who appear to be above suspicion. Keep an open mind. I have to in this business. But it's easier for me since I'm not connected to anyone in town."

"I'm not investigating Lelandi, my brothers, or Uncle Sheridan and if this is the kind of bull—"

Chester raised his brows. "You want solid proof." He dug around in his jeans pocket and pulled out a bullet and bullet casing. "I found the bullet casing up on the ridge."

"The shooter's," Tom said.

"I found the bullet several feet short of where the dead gunman's body had lain. Now, what if Silva's bullet fell short, but someone else fired at the same time? Did anyone hear separate shots fired?"

"Yes. The gunman shot Sam in the arm first," Darien said.

"But at least two more shots were fired. One that hit the gunman, fatally wounding him, and the other that missed its mark."

Uncle Sheridan put the bullet and casing into a plastic evidence bag. "I'll get these checked right away."

"You might want to ask Silva if she heard another shot fired or anyone moving around near her. Smelled anyone, sensed she wasn't alone."

"I've already asked her and she said no," Darien said. "What about Lelandi's parents?"

Lelandi's eyes widened.

"Sorry, I meant to mention that first. Her cousin Ural and I had a nice, long chat. He learned your parents were being targeted for termination so that your father couldn't object to your mating Crassus. Ural moved them to Oregon, somewhere safe, then staged the car accident. When he came back for you, he discovered your pack leader had already posted a guard. So Ural waited until you escaped. He followed you here, discovered your sister had died, and wanted to take you with him to see your parents."

"Jeez, why didn't he say so? Do you have any proof they're alive?" Lelandi asked, her face growing red.

Chester handed her a letter. "Your mother's handwriting, correct?"

Lelandi's eyes misted as she read the note. "It is." She choked up. "My mother says my father wants me to join them, and that they're with my brother and uncle."

"You'll stay with me." Darien tightened his hold on her hand. "They can live with our pack."

She shook her head. "Knowing my father, he wouldn't want to live with a gray pack, no offense."

"As long as *you* don't mind…" He watched her, waiting for her response.

"I want to see them. Do they know about Larissa? They must if Ural has talked to them." She sank into the cushions, looking drained and Darien wrapped his arm around her shoulder.

Sam hollered into the house from the front door. "Sorry for the interruption folks, but there's a Miss Carol Wood here to see Lelandi. Is she free to speak with her?"

Lelandi closed her eyes, then opened them, so not wanting to talk to the poor lady. First this business about her parents—she couldn't be more pleased they were safe, but she knew how badly they must feel that Larissa was dead. And Carol—she must be feeling horrible about losing both Doc and Ritka, despite their deaths not being her fault.

"I'm not hiring her at the hospital if she thinks she can win you over and try to get to me." Darien patted Lelandi's leg. His chin was down and his eyes were narrowed, conveying a guarded threat.

"You have nothing to worry about." Lelandi rose from the sofa and the men all stood.

Carol and Sam remained in the chilly foyer waiting for her, Sam's expression solemn, Carol's even grimmer. Her vivid blue eyes, wearing a wealth of worry, watched Lelandi, then she turned her attention back to the living room that was hidden from their view in the foyer. None of the men talked and Lelandi wondered if that was making Carol uncomfortable, or if it was the way Sam, as big as he was, continued to chaperone them.

Lelandi took a deep settling breath and reached for Carol's hand. She didn't want to make friends with a human. Keeping the *lupus garou* secret precluded that, but she had to know what this was about. "Let's go to the sunroom. Even though it's pretty cold out, someone probably started a nice fire. If it's not comfortable enough, we can find some other spot to sit."

"I... I didn't mean to disturb you after what happened, but we have to talk."

Lelandi led Carol through the living room where the men all stood up from the couches and chairs. "Ladies," Darien said, his expression hard.

As if he had to warn her not to get too friendly with a human. She gave him an annoyed look back. Carol noticed; her anxious expression didn't waver.

They walked to the back of the house and Lelandi opened the door to the sunroom. Two men she didn't know were talking inside, but as soon as they saw Lelandi and Carol they both made their excuses and left the room. Lelandi shut the door and motioned to a couch that faced the fireplace and a floor-to-ceiling window that showed the winter scene outside.

"Unusually early snow," Carol remarked.

But Lelandi knew Carol wasn't there for chitchat. She wasn't sure how to approach a human about human frailties. But she could be a good listener. So instead of saying anything, she sat in the chair close to the end of the pale green couch where Carol perched herself.

Carol spoke low. "I'm sick with worry for your safety."

Lelandi tried to hide her surprise, but she was afraid she'd failed.

"I... I felt terrible about Doctor Oliver and Nurse Ritka. I... I didn't save their lives." Carol quickly brushed away tears.

Lelandi reached over and took hold of her hand and squeezed. "You did everything you could for them. I know you did."

"Do you believe in fate? That our lives are predetermined? That nothing we do will change our fate? Do you?" Carol pulled her hand away from Lelandi's and pushed her fingers through her wind-tousled blonde curls. "I saw Joe Kelly shoot Doctor Oliver."

"Yes, of course you did."

"No… no. I saw it happen before it happened. Don't you see? I have these damned psychic abilities, and what do they do for me? Nothing. I couldn't save him, could I? I came to stop Doctor Oliver from confronting Joe. But instead I got him killed."

"No." Lelandi moved to the couch. She put her arm around Carol's shoulders and realized how much it was like when she comforted her sister after her mate beat her. Regret filled her with a sense of loss, knowing she could never comfort her sister again. But she wanted to help Carol get through her troubles now. "Joe intended to kill Doc. He told me so."

Carol pulled a tissue from her pocket and blew her nose. "You're not safe with them."

"With Darien and his brothers?" Lelandi had a very bad feeling about this.

Carol's eyes glistened with fresh tears. "You don't know what they are. But if you stay with them, they'll make you one of them."

Lelandi's heartbeat did double time, but she tried to keep the panic hidden. If a human learned the truth about the *lupus garous,* Bruin discretely terminated them. A car accident, drowning, whatever it took to make it appear the human had met his end accidentally. But she couldn't be sure Carol knew about the *lupus garous* either.

"What do you mean?" Lelandi asked as innocently as she could manage.

Carol studied her face for what seemed an eternity. Lelandi's hands grew sweaty.

"You're not one of them already, are you?" Carol looked down at the floor as if she was considering something, then her head rose quickly, and she looked at Lelandi's face again, her own filled with horror. She jumped up from the couch, then offered a fake smile, her body trembling slightly. "I've got to get home and feed my cat. I forgot to leave food out for him."

Lelandi had to stop her from leaving. She had to know the truth. Did Carol realize what they were? With the gentlest of touches, she reached out to Carol. "You're right, I'm in a lot of danger. I don't have anyone to talk to because Darien doesn't want me involved. But I am involved. Will you listen?"

Carol glanced back at the door like a rabbit looking for a quick escape from the little red wolf.

"Carol." Lelandi resumed her seat on the overstuffed chair next to the couch, trying to put some distance between them so the woman wouldn't feel so cornered. A secret for a secret? She had to know what Carol suspected. "Someone was blackmailing my sister."

Carol hesitated.

"Maybe you can help me find out who with your special abilities." She raised her brows. "I don't know if this person was the one who killed her or not, but…"

Carol sat down on the couch, leaned forward, and patted Lelandi's hand. "Do you have any suspects?"

Lelandi's heart filled with hope that Carol might be able to help her, but she shook her head. "No one that I have any evidence on. But Ritka and her girlfriends hated Larissa. With her out of the way, they had a chance to…" She almost said mate. She wasn't used to having a human confidant. Rubbing her arms, she let out her breath. "Darien would be available to marry again. Maybe one of them was the blackmailer. Maybe they thought he'd divorce her if… oh, I don't know."

"No," Carol said with certainty.

"No?"

"All three."

Lelandi closed her gaping mouth and stared at the petite woman.

"I'm just supposing here, but the three of them were Super-Glued together. If one did it, the others were bound to know. But the others would want a share, too. What would they blackmail her about?"

"She was already married."

"Oh. You're a prisoner here, aren't you?"

"Darien is determined to keep me safe, but I want to find out who was blackmailing my sister and who killed her."

"You're not one of them, are you?" Carol asked again, her expression hopeful.

"No, of course not. I'm not from here and—"

"I've seen things that no one should ever witness. Unnatural things."

Oh, god, no, no, Carol, don't say it.

Carol glanced back at the door, then turned to Lelandi. "They're part of some cult. When the moon appears, they strip off their clothes, then cover themselves in animal skins and run around in the woods howling."

Lelandi barely breathed. "You've seen Darien and the others do this?"

"Well, no, not for real."

"Are they like nightmares?"

"You can say that again. It's always dark and difficult to make out what's happening because the cool night air mixes with the sun-warmed earth, creating a screen of fog. Some of the men and women have sex in the wilderness like they're a bunch of wild animals. You know, the men mounting the women from behind."

"In animal skins?"

"Yeah." Carol looked at her curiously. "You wouldn't do that, would you?"

"Sounds a little kinky. Although I recall you saying you wished you could tell someone you'd never meet again about a sexual fantasy of yours."

"That's definitely not one of them." Carol shook her head a little too vigorously.

"I'm certain Darien and his family and friends aren't a part of a cult. He's too busy running the factory and silver mine."

"You're probably right. But some of the people living here are in it. You have to believe me."

"Are your psychic powers ever wrong?"

"Sometimes I have difficulty sorting out what everything means. I saw an injured girl and felt the pain in her leg, saw her washed in a blanket of white mist. I guessed later it was the girl you rescued in the woods during the blizzard before Joe kidnapped you. But I couldn't see where she was, who she was, what happened to her, who was with her. The visions are not all that clear most of the time."

"Like a nightmare? Where the dreams are mixed up and run together with the oddest images?"

"Maybe," Carol said, but she sounded like she didn't think so, that she figured Lelandi didn't believe her. "I... I felt bad when Joe took you hostage. I hadn't seen that happen. I don't know why I can see some things and not others."

"What do you see now? Anything in my future?"

"A man threatens to take you back home. He's a redhead, not as tall as Darien, but heavy-set. And he has a savage streak."

Lelandi's heart fluttered. "Crassus."

Carol stood and began to pace. "But there's someone else. A man. I can't see who, but I sense he holds a lot of anger, directed at your sister, then at you. You're not only the embodiment of Larissa, but you're trying to find her killer—him. He's frustrated because he hasn't been able to get to you. But he's someone Darien trusts."

Chill bumps erupted on Lelandi's arms. "You don't know who he is?"

"No."

"Do you know how he plans to kill me?"

"I don't know." Carol tried to smile. "I really admire you. No matter what, you stand up for yourself. I wish I could be more like that."

"I think you are, Carol."

"Yeah, and I still don't have a job at the hospital. But you never give in. If I see anything else, I'll... I'll let you know."

Lelandi stood and took Carol's hand, but Carol gave her a warm hug back. "Somehow we've been thrown together... maybe because our sisters both died and were so depressed. I don't know. But I... I have to help you if I can."

"Thank you, Carol. Maybe with your abilities, you can." But how in the hell could Lelandi help Carol? If

anyone learned she might be seeing *lupus garous* mating
in the woods on moon-filled nights, the powers-that-be
would eliminate her.

"I've got to get home," Carol said. "I really did forget
to feed Puss this morning. He'll be roaring by the time
I return."

"I'll walk you to the front door. If you learn anything
more…"

"I'll call you."

Lelandi shook her head.

Carol ran her hand over her arm. "I'll drop by.
They'll be listening in on your phone conversations,
won't they?"

Lelandi snorted. "Probably. They think everyone's
suspect."

"Rightly so. First, that guy shot you, then Joe took
you hostage, then… why were you in the blizzard with
the girl who'd been injured?"

Lelandi smiled. "Searching for evidence about my
sister. I escaped the house." Her smile faded. "But it
won't happen again."

"I can see why not. You could have died out there."
Carol opened the door to the sunroom, and they headed
to the living room.

The men stood. Darien's face looked dark and
his brothers and the others—Chester, Sam, Uncle
Sheridan—all looked as concerned. Had one of them
listened in on Carol's conversation with Lelandi through
a vent or some damned thing?

"Can I have a word with you, Miss Wood?" Darien
motioned to the sunroom.

Carol looked like she was ready to have heart failure.

Lelandi's whole body chilled with fear, and she felt sick to her stomach.

Jake said to Lelandi, "I need to talk to you. Do you mind?"

Torn, she didn't know what to do. She wanted to protect Carol from her mate when she should have been totally loyal to him and to the pack, to all *lupus garous,* first and foremost. Darien gave her a look like she better do what was expected of her.

That's when Lelandi snapped.

"Sure, but I want to see what Darien has to say to Carol first." She gave the men all her sweetest smile, faked to high heaven.

"Fine." Darien didn't sound like it was fine with him.

The three of them walked into the sunroom. Carol looked pale and as uncomfortable as if Darien and his family had just pronounced she was a witch and at any moment the inquisition would burn her at the stake. Lelandi didn't feel much better.

None of the men looked happy with either Lelandi or Carol. But Lelandi didn't care. If Carol hadn't wanted to help her, the woman wouldn't be in this untenable situation now.

Darien waited for them to sit and then gave his full attention to Carol as if Lelandi wasn't there. "I'm concerned about Lelandi's health," he said smoothly.

Carol glanced at Lelandi, her look one of disbelief. Lelandi was sure she appeared as astonished. What the hell was he up to?

"We're afraid someone plans to kill her, and that's why she's constantly under guard. She wants to learn who blackmailed her sister and murdered her. But I can't let her run around town on her own. You know what's happened to her already. In that light and because you're unhappy with your job prospect as a nurse at the school, I'm offering you a job as Lelandi's personal nurse. If anything should happen to her, your medical knowledge could save her life. Your salary would be commensurate with what you would earn at the hospital, but you would only need keep Lelandi company when she wishes it."

"But I have a cat and…"

"Jake will see to the cat's care. Doc Mitchell will board him until you're ready to return home."

Lelandi felt cornered into making a decision. But she was certain if she didn't agree, Carol's life would hang in the balance. "Until you can catch the bastard who murdered my sister, I think it's a perfect solution, Darien. Of course, if you agree to it, Carol."

Carol didn't appear comfortable with agreeing to the conditions of her new employment. "Would I be free to go and—"

"No." Darien's face remained stern, determined. He would have his way, one way or another.

"If I don't?"

He shrugged. "You're free to go. It's up to you. I would hope that you'd consider my terms favorably for Lelandi's sake though. If you don't stay here around the clock, however, there's no sense in you being here. Who knows when the killer will strike again?"

"Can I go home and get some clothes?"

"Tom will take you."

"All right." Carol offered a smile, but the warmth didn't reach her eyes. "I'll do this for Lelandi. And hope to god I can make a difference if need be." She rose from the couch.

"Good." Darien motioned to the door and when he opened it, he said, "Tom, take Miss Wood to her place to get some clothes. Jake, you can take her cat to Doc Mitchell's for boarding until we get this situation cleared up with Lelandi."

Carol still looked like she thought they were going to burn her at the stake.

"I'll see you in a little bit," Lelandi promised. "I haven't baked anything in eons with my sister. Maybe we can whip up something."

"An apple pie?"

Darien looked somewhat mollified with Lelandi's response. "Run her by the grocery store and get whatever ingredients they need."

Carol's expression brightened and she had more of a spring to her step when she left the house with Darien's brothers. But as soon as the door shut, Darien gave Lelandi a look like she'd overstepped her bounds. He took her hand and led her up the stairs without saying a word and although everyone watched them, no one said anything either. She was in trouble now.

She had no good reason for getting on Darien's bad side either. If Carol knew they were *lupus garous,* she put them all at risk. Lelandi had no business covering for her.

When they reached the bedroom, Darien released her and shut the door. She felt small and unworthy under his steely gaze. She didn't say anything, not sure how to respond, and he finally blew out his breath. "What the hell was that all about?"

"She wanted to warn me I was in danger. We all know that. So what's the big deal?"

"Lelandi." Darien ran his hands up and down her arms. "She's dangerous. How long have you known she has psychic abilities?"

"I've only met her once before."

"And she told you then?"

Tears filled her eyes. "I... I don't want her killed."

He held her tight and kissed her forehead. "We have to do what's right for the pack. In days gone by, we could have someone institutionalized if they'd seen one of us turn wolf. But we can't do that anymore. If she does have visions that involve you and whoever this maniac is, I want her here. And I want to know about it immediately. We'll put her talent to good use and take it from there."

"And when she's not of any more use... ?"

"I'm sure we can work something out."

Lelandi didn't think he would. The pack took priority. *Lupus garou* took priority. One human woman was of little consequence.

"Do you believe she sees us as humans wearing animal skins, howling at the moon?"

"She says it's dark. And it would be for her. We can see at night. She wouldn't be able to."

"And there's a fog. Yet, she seems to see a hell of a lot despite it being nighttime while the cultists run around in a fog."

"What are you implying?" Lelandi asked.

"I'm implying that she sees us as wolves, not as humans wearing furs. She was testing your reaction, seeing how you responded to the news."

"Because she's afraid I'd think she was crazy?"

He kissed her cheek. "Or, because you're one of us, and she wanted to see if you'd betray this."

"Does she think I am?" Lelandi asked.

"What do you believe?"

"At first, I don't believe she thought I was. Then something made her reconsider. In the end, I felt she wasn't sure. Maybe she trusted me. Until you said she had to stay here."

"For your safety *and* hers. If anyone found out she might be able to identify whoever murdered Larissa, Carol would be a dead woman." Darien paused for a minute, letting the seriousness of the situation sink in.

"Oh, I hadn't thought of that."

"If any of the *lupus garous* of the pack discovered she might be able to tell the world about us, one of them might not wait for me to make a decision concerning her disposition."

"I understand fully."

He hugged her tightly, wanting to keep her safe from all the evils of the world, but already he was worrying about Carol and her abilities to see the *lupus garous* as they were, and what he would have to do if things got out of hand. He knew if he didn't handle the matter right, he'd end up driving a wedge between himself and his mate.

Chapter 22

AFTER SETTLING IN, LELANDI AND CAROL MADE TWO APPLE pies, while Tom and Jake took Darien aside to speak to him privately in his office. He figured there had been more trouble with their new live-in guest.

"Carol tried to sneak a gun into her bag, but I told her you and your men were the only ones who would be armed. She didn't like it, but finally gave in," Tom said.

"She's going to be a problem. But maybe she can use these abilities of hers to warn us before whoever murdered Larissa strikes at Lelandi again," Darien said.

A rapping at the door sounded.

"Yes?" Darien asked gruffly.

Lelandi opened the door, her face strained.

"Where's Carol?" Darien asked, already leaving the office. He was sure the woman would attempt to flee if given the opportunity. She didn't appear to be the fighting sort.

Lelandi grabbed his arm. "Darien, Silva's here helping her with the pies. But Carol had a... premonition. A group of men are coming to see you. They're angry, but they're not the real problem. Another group is planning on slipping into a bedroom to steal me away. She doesn't see what happens afterward, just that we've got trouble coming soon."

Darien's phone rang and Tom grabbed it off the desk. "Yeah?" He looked up at Darien, his expression darkened. "Uncle Sheridan says he couldn't keep the reds at Hastings B&B. They're on their way here."

When everyone glanced at Lelandi, she lifted a shoulder. "Carol sees things sometimes. I guess she really does have psychic abilities."

He was having a hard time believing it, but already adrenaline was coursing through his veins, getting him ready for a fight. "Tom, tell Uncle Sheridan I want him and both his deputies here." Darien took Lelandi's hand and kissed it, hoping not to show how anxious he was about her. "I want you and Silva in the bedroom."

"And Carol?"

Jake said, "She can't be allowed to see what happens when we have to fight. She'll be traumatized."

Everyone headed out of Darien's office.

Carol would be more than traumatized. Tension filled every muscle in Lelandi's body. She wasn't worried that the grays would beat the reds. Well, maybe a little. Bruin and his brothers could be pretty underhanded and brutal. But she was worried about Carol and Silva, too.

"Uncle Sheridan's getting his deputies and a few others to guard the place," Tom said. "Do you want me to watch Carol?"

"You'll be with Jake. Are you ready to play the alpha leader again?"

Jake gave him an evil smile.

"What about Carol?" Lelandi asked, her blood growing cold.

"Ask her. I'm sure she knows what's going to happen already." He led Lelandi toward the kitchen. "Have both Silva and Carol go with you to the bedroom. You'll watch something on television, pretend like nothing is out of the ordinary."

Uncle Sheridan barged into the house with Peter and Chester McKinley.

"Where's Trevor?" Darien asked, his tone annoyed.

"He's on his way."

"I want to help even though I'm not one of your pack, if you'll let me," Chester said.

Darien glanced out the front window. Several gray wolves were positioning themselves around the estate. "All right. You stay with Jake and Tom."

Darien amazed Lelandi at every turn. Normally, a pack leader wouldn't want interference from a wolf he didn't trust and know well when a serious crisis was at hand.

He kissed Lelandi's cheek. "Go, move the women upstairs."

"Hope the pies are done." She hurried off to the kitchen, praying Darien knew what he was doing concerning Carol and that no one would hurt her in the impending fracas.

"The reds arrived in the drive," Tom warned.

"Carol, Silva, how far along are the pies?" Lelandi asked, her pulse pounding.

Silva gave her a knowing look. "We brought them out to cool."

"Super. Why don't we go up to one of the bedrooms and watch some TV?" She motioned toward the living room.

"Sure, sugar. Sounds like a great idea."

Carol offered a wary smile. "Love to until the pies are ready to eat. We need to make sure we get some before the guys scarf them up."

"You're right about that." Lelandi waited for Silva and Carol to leave first. She tried to keep the panic from her voice, but she was sure both women noticed.

On the way to the stairs, they headed toward the men gathered in the living room.

Darien grabbed Jake's shoulder. "Are you sure you can handle this?"

Jake's face lit up with a sinister cast. "You bet, Darien. They won't know what hit them."

"All right. Uncle Sheridan?"

"All set. Go protect the little lady. You know they'll pull something sneaky to take her out of here."

"Chester?"

"I'm with you. Thanks for trusting in me."

"Sam?"

Sam patted Tom on the shoulder. "We'll take care of Jake in case anything gets out of hand."

"Where's Trevor?" Silva asked.

"Late. I'm sure he has a damned good excuse though," Darien said, his words sarcastic.

Lelandi thought Silva had given up on that worthless Trevor. What now? "Is Jake going to be all right?"

"Jake will be fine. Every time I have to leave town, he takes over." Darien looked at Peter. "Ready?"

"Yes, sir."

A knock sounded at the front door and Darien took Lelandi's hand and rushed her up the stairs with Silva and Carol following, and Peter bringing up the rear. "You were supposed to be upstairs already," Darien scolded.

But as soon as Darien and Lelandi reached the landing, he shoved her against the wall, and she smelled the reds' scents, too. "They're here," he whispered. "Must have slipped in before my guards were in place on the property."

Carol's eyes looked like they were going to pop out of her head. Silva and Lelandi breathed in deeply and listened, trying to sense where the reds were located.

Darien nodded to Peter and they both began stripping out of their clothes.

"Where do you want us to go?" Lelandi asked Darien, knowing he planned to shapeshift and soon couldn't tell her anything.

"Where do you need to go?" Darien deferred to Carol.

She looked too stunned to answer.

Lelandi shook her hand. "Carol. Where do you see that we need to be?"

"We're in a big blue bedroom with a sitting area."

"Darien's bedroom." Lelandi led Carol down the hall with Silva trailing behind.

"A security monitor is in the room. Hit the green switch for the living room. We should be able to hear the conversation," Silva said.

Carol glanced back at Darien—both he and Peter were now naked. Lelandi pulled her into the bedroom so she wouldn't see them shapeshift. No smell of the reds in here. They must have broken into Jake's or… or maybe the guest bedroom, thinking she was still staying there.

In their wolf pelts, Darien and Peter loped after them and Carol cried out.

"Good pet wolves," Lelandi said, patting Darien on the head.

Carol hadn't seen the men transform, but she did see their clothes lying on the floor in the hallway, and Darien and Peter had vanished. *She knew.*

Lelandi closed the door and Peter sat next to it, his ears perked up, listening.

Silva motioned to one of the two chairs. "I'll put something on. Like comedies?"

Carol nodded heartily, but her attention was glued to Lelandi who flipped on the monitor switch, then took a seat on the bed. Darien jumped up on the mattress and nuzzled her hand with his nose.

She scratched his head and smiled. "Want me to rub your belly, too?"

Peter and Silva glanced back at them.

A wolf that would bear his belly to another showed his complete trust in the other, but Darien pushed his nose into her crotch and sniffed. Smiling, Lelandi shoved his head away. Silva chuckled and turned on the television.

Peter observed Darien and Lelandi for a minute more, then when Darien laid his head on her lap, Peter concentrated on the door.

"I'm Bruin Stillwater," the red pack leader said to Jake downstairs.

Even hearing Bruin's dark voice sent chills streaking down Lelandi's spine. Carol watched the monitor with rapt attention. Silva turned the TV lower.

"I'm the pack leader of Wildhaven."

"Darien Silver of Silver Town. I understand you already know Larissa died," Jake said, his tone conciliatory with a hint of gruffness.

"One of your people murdered her, you mean," Bruin corrected.

"We don't have conclusive evidence either way. It's possible even a red murdered her for mating a gray when she was mated to your brother already. Which of these gentlemen is your brother, Crassus?"

"I'm Crassus."

Lelandi's skin crawled. Whispering, she said, "That's not his voice."

"Then he intends on coming for you," Silva said.

"Crassus," Carol whispered. "The one I saw in the vision."

Lelandi had figured the bastard would come for her. Afraid someone else would fail. And, too, she assumed he wanted to show her how she couldn't escape him. He'd find so much more satisfaction in returning her home if he did so himself.

"As I've already relayed to you through the sheriff, Lelandi belongs to the pack. Now that her sister is confirmed dead, Crassus will mate her. Has in fact—*in absentia*—as is our right."

"When was this done?" Jake asked.

"You question my honor?"

"I mated her as soon as she arrived here," Jake lied. "You see, we were dream mated. For months we'd made love in our dream states, and she came into her first wolf heat when we met. So you see, we're soul mates. And we won't be separated."

Lelandi glanced at Darien. He had told Jake about her wolf heat? If he'd been in his human form, she would have slugged him.

"You stole Crassus's mate from him. You will give Lelandi back or else…"

The sound of growling came from the hallway. Carol jumped from the chair she was sitting on. Lelandi and

Silva rose. "They can't open the door," Lelandi said under her breath. Then she belatedly realized they hadn't locked it and dashed for it.

The door slammed open, throwing her against the wall. She recognized the two reds right away. Carruthers and Connors, the black-haired twin cops from Wildhaven, the two *lupus garou* that had guarded her back home before she escaped, looking smug, their lips curled up slightly, their amber eyes revealed a small sense of delight in bringing her the news. "You're coming with us. Bruin says."

Then all hell broke loose. Darien lunged for Carruthers and Peter went for Connors. But three red wolves dashed into the room. Carol screamed. Silva grabbed for a lamp while Lelandi searched in Darien's sock drawer. He hadn't put her gun back here. Damn it. Why didn't he tell her where it was? Too late. She and Silva could shapeshift, but Lelandi wasn't any match for a male, gray or red. She was sure Silva wouldn't be either. She seized the other bedside table lamp.

"Get into the bathroom and stay there!" Lelandi shouted at Carol.

But Darien had one of the wolves by the throat, pinning Carol into a corner.

Then Crassus stalked into the room like he owned the place, his strawberry blond hair unbound, his dark eyes challenging her. For an instant, she felt an inkling of terror. He could snap her neck in two and end her life easily. But even worse, he could claim her for his own if he could kill Darien.

Lelandi moved in Carol's direction, her lamp readied, her eyes challenging him back. Cowering before the son of a bitch was not an option. But her heated blood ran cold now. He was bigger, stronger, and meaner than she could ever be. He wouldn't hesitate to take her.

Like most of the reds in his pack, he wasn't tall, but he was bulky, like a football player in his prime and was always itching for a fight. His older brother, Bruin, was the only one stronger, more deadly.

The sound of fighting was going on downstairs, and she hoped Jake and the rest would win against Bruin and his men. More than six reds had come into town.

As if he had no worries, Crassus folded his arms, and his lips rose in a gloating sneer. "Your father wouldn't give you to me. I suspected it had to do with your temper. Would have made our mating much more—challenging. Or it might have been because you hadn't come into a wolf's heat yet, and he was afraid you wouldn't be worth having." His eyes as cold as ash, he added, "But Larissa is dead and you will now be mine."

His words cut through her like an icy blade, but she tried to act nonchalant and waved a hand at Darien who was tackling another wolf. "Meet my mate. You're already too late, Crassus. Live with it."

He reached out to touch Lelandi's hair, but she slapped his hand away. He laughed from the gut, sinister, cruelly. But before she could react, he grabbed her by the throat and slammed her against the wall. A streak of pain slid down her spine, and she dropped the lamp. "You hoped Bruin would give you to another pack member—another subchief, even though your father insisted, but Bruin wouldn't. Not unless I told him I didn't want you. You can't have a gray. You're mated to me, albeit *in absentia.* But we'll get to the good part after we rid ourselves of the grays."

She struggled to twist free, his meaty hand tightening on her throat. Her vision darkened, she gasped for air, then Darien chomped down on Crassus's arm.

Darien's focus had to remain on the wolves in the room first, more deadly with their powerful bites, more of a threat than any of those in their human forms. But as soon as Crassus grabbed Lelandi's throat, Darien had to get rid of the wolf he was fighting, then he aimed for the bastard. No contest existed between a wolf and a human, and he'd hoped the beast would have changed so he could take care of him wolf to wolf.

As soon as Darien bit Crassus's arm, he screamed and released Lelandi. He ripped off his shirt, though his swarthy face exuded pain, and he struggled with the effort, his arm dripping with blood.

The twin cops who had entered the room initially, quickly turned wolf to deal with Peter now that the other reds were dead. Darien bit one of them while he waited for Crassus to change.

Lelandi was still clutching her throat, trying to draw air into her lungs when Carol cried out. She slid to the floor, her eyes dazed, her throat dripping with blood from a nasty gash. Lelandi skirted around the four wolves battling each other and reached Carol, her hand on her throat, stemming the blood. "Ohmigod, Carol. You'll be… all right." Some reassurance. It didn't matter that Carol's death would be the easiest solution now that she knew they were *lupus garous.* Lelandi desperately wanted her to live.

Silva was already on the phone. "Angelina, call Nurse Matthew right away and dispatch him to Darien's home. We have multiple injuries." She clicked off the phone and punched in numbers. "The new male nurse is on his way," she said to Lelandi. She paused. "Charlotte? It's Silva. Come right away to Darien's house. We've got casualties, but the fight's still ongoing."

Silva hung up the phone and climbed over the bed to get to Lelandi, while Crassus ditched his trousers and shapeshifted. "Is she going to live?"

Lelandi yanked a pillowcase off one of the pillows and applied pressure to the wound. She didn't think Carol was going to make it. The woman's heartbeat was fading, and she was bleeding too much. "I... I don't know what to do."

"I'll get some of that leftover bandaging Doc gave me to use on your wounds." Silva climbed back over the bed and raced into the bathroom.

Standing as a wolf, Crassus bared his teeth at Darien. Crassus looked so damned arrogant. Didn't he know he was no match for a gray alpha pack leader?

The two circled each other while Peter and the remaining red stopped to watch the fight between a leader and a subchief. Silva returned with the bandaging and she and Lelandi bound Carol's wound. Darien lunged at Crassus, but the wolf twisted away so hard to avoid Darien's snapping jaws, he fell on his butt, then quickly retreated.

"Hell, there's more of them!" someone shouted from downstairs.

Lelandi took her eyes off Darien and Crassus to look at Silva. She looked as worried as Lelandi felt.

"No, they're going after the reds."

Lelandi's mouth dropped slightly. What reds in their right mind would fight Bruin and his pack here? Then anger welled up to volcanic proportions deep inside her—not her emotions, but her brother's, the symbiotic reaction she had when her sister or brother's feelings ran high. Leidolf was here.

Darien took a chunk out of Crassus's ear, and he fell away in a panic, his ear bleeding. But Darien didn't wait for another run. He cornered the red, bottled him between the sofa and the wall and leapt in the air.

Crassus yelped before Darien planted his teeth into his neck. It was the last sound the bastard would ever make as Darien's canines snapped the wolf's neck in half, then released him.

"Where are you, Lelandi, Silva?" Nurse Grey cried out from downstairs as lamps and tables crashed downstairs.

"Upstairs, end of hall, Darien's room. Hurry!" Lelandi shouted.

Darien eyed the lone red wolf standing next to Peter, but he tucked tail and lay down on his stomach.

Nurse Grey and Matthew bolted upstairs with a medical kit. "Oh my, what's happened?"

"Can you take care of her?" Lelandi asked, holding Carol's hand.

"Yes, let me get in there and I'll see what I can do."

"I'll… I'll be right back." Lelandi dashed out of the room and down the hall.

"Lelandi!" Silva shouted. "No, wait!"

Darien chased Lelandi down the stairs, and she was sure if he could, he would force her back into the bedroom to keep her out of harm's way. But her brother was in the thick of it, and she couldn't let anyone in Darien's pack kill him, mistaking him for the enemy.

"No!" she yelled, trying to get beyond the grays to get closer to her brother, but one of the grays snapped at her, keeping her away from the reds battling each other. Her brother was fighting Bruin, and the grays were letting him? Then she saw another familiar red, her uncle, tearing into Bruin's youngest brother, Cindon—as mean-hearted as Crassus and Bruin. It was rumored their father was a real psycho and bullied them until they became just like him.

Her uncle turned his head in her direction briefly. He shielded bared teeth instantly, his look shifting from her to Darien standing next to her, his stance protective. Her heart lifted to see both her uncle and brother back together again. But then she cringed when Bruin knocked Leidolf on his hip.

Leidolf quickly recovered and dodged the heavier wolf's lunge. Bruin weighed at least forty pounds more than her brother, was shorter and stockier and thicker necked. But Leidolf had a regal way of moving, swiftly, silently, dangerously. He'd taken down a stag without a sound, killed a bear that had attacked her mother when they were living in the mountains, and now he seemed even more serious, determined, deadly.

Darien watched, as if he was ruler of all the land, and the tournament was for his and his courtiers' sport. Everyone's tongues panted from exertion and blood tinged a fair amount of the wolves' pelts. A couple sat down. The rest stiffly observed, wary of the fight, promising to take on the pack leader and his brother if the reds who fought them lost the game. Old Mr. Hastings, who had shouted that her brother and uncle had arrived, was the only one in human form.

Darien glanced up at Lelandi and licked her hand. She crouched down next to him, wrapped her arm around his neck, and gave him a hug. "Thanks for avenging my sister's tormenter." She spoke loud enough for Bruin to hear.

He jerked his head in her direction, and Leidolf slammed into him, knocking the pack leader off his pads. He crashed into a table and broke one of the legs. Leidolf growled low at Bruin, then savagely attacked his throat. Bruin bit back, but Leidolf held on for dear life, growling. After several seconds that felt like hours, Bruin sank to the floor, dead.

Uncle Hrothgar seemed to smile, then he tackled Bruin's last living brother, biting him in the face when Cindon turned his head to protect his throat. None could be left standing if they were to oust the red pack from their lands.

Two more of the grays sat down, the fight nearly ended.

Silva came down the stairs and gave Lelandi a somber nod. But Lelandi didn't know how to take the message. She wanted to check on Carol, but she had to see her uncle win against Bruin's brother.

Leidolf watched their uncle for a minute, then turned his attention on her. He was heaving with weariness, but anger still filled his soul. His gaze shifted to Darien. He knew. He understood she was his now, and she sensed he didn't like it. He didn't have to like it. He'd left them to fend for their own, and she'd found her soul mate.

Uncle Hrothgar pounced again at Cindon, this time snapping his neck in two like Darien had done to his brother, Crassus. For several minutes, no one did anything, the grays watching what the red wolves did next, and the reds eyeing Darien.

"My brother, Leidolf." Lelandi stood and motioned to the red wolf standing next to Bruin's dead body. "And Uncle Hrothgar." She motioned to the other.

Darien panted, then licked Lelandi's hand and ran up the stairs. Still, no one moved, waiting for Darien's word.

A few minutes later, he returned dressed in his jeans, while he yanked a shirt on, a trail of blood running down his chest. "Leidolf," he addressed Lelandi's brother first. Then he bowed his head slightly at Uncle Hrothgar. "Welcome to my pack."

The two considered Lelandi, then loped out through the front door.

Darien gave her a weary smile and kissed her cheek. "Change, and get this place cleaned up," he said to his pack. He looked around and frowned. "Where the hell is Trevor?"

Uncle Sheridan jerked on his clothes and gave a disgruntled growl. "I'll check into it and let you know." He took off for his truck.

Darien still couldn't believe Lelandi's brother and uncle had arrived so unexpectedly, but he suspected Ural must have sent word to them.

Tall for a red, a man walked back into the house, his chestnut hair tinged red, his eyes as jade as Lelandi's, narrowed, wary. Darien suspected his height had to do with his royal heritage and the fact he was directly related to the first *lupus garou*—a gray. His body erect, wiry, ready for confrontation, a proud and sturdy jaw, angry lips and brows deeply furrowed defined him. Again he looked at Lelandi like she belonged to him, and he wanted her back. Lelandi's uncle walked in afterward, somewhat older, same height, more cautious, a lot less cocky.

"She's mine," Darien growled, unable to welcome the intruder like he'd intended, unable to curb his feral possessiveness when it came to his mate.

Leidolf cocked his head slightly, his lips curving upward a hint.

Lelandi stood stock still, not saying a word, but her eyes were wide and expressive. She appeared worried that Darien and Leidolf would fight.

Darien took the aggressive red male's cue though, and bowed his head as Tom and Jake flanked him. "She is mine," he reiterated, not about to make any flowery speeches.

Leidolf kissed Lelandi on the cheek, and she appeared to be holding her breath, pale and unsure of herself.

"So it seems," Leidolf said, his voice a deep, threatening timbre. "I had planned to bring Lelandi home to my pack."

Lelandi let out her breath. "To Wildhaven? You'll lead them now?"

"No, in Oregon. Mother and Father have joined me there. Uncle Hrothgar will take on the pack in Wildhaven. Will you come with me?" He lightly took hold of her arm as if to persuade her to follow his lead.

"No, Leidolf." Her cheeks reddened and she jerked her arm out of his grasp. "You left us two years ago! We could have used your help! You think you can waltz in here and dictate to me because now you're a pack leader? *That* would be the day."

"Then, that's settled. Several prime-aged reds joined the pack and were looking for a mate and were very much interested when I said my sister was available, but..." Leidolf gave a shrug and cast Darien a seething look.

So, had Leidolf already promised his sister to a pack member? When a pack had a severe shortage of females as many do, bringing in eligible mates could improve a new leader's standing, not to mention it tied more of the clan's loyalty with the bond created. Darien folded his arms, trying to appear relaxed, but if Leidolf grabbed Lelandi's arm again...

"I'm not available. I'm mated. And this is where I'm staying."

Loving seeing Lelandi's ire unloaded on her brother after what he'd pulled, Darien agreed.

Leidolf shook his head. "I don't approve."

Darien ground his teeth. If Leidolf had any intention of taking Lelandi with him, Darien would shapeshift and change the red's mind.

"But what's been done, can't be undone under our laws. If your mate should ever expire and you want a home with us, you'll be welcome, Lelandi." Leidolf turned to Darien. "If you'll permit me, I'll take Ural off your hands. He'll return with me to my pack."

"Gladly," Darien said.

She kissed her brother on the cheek. "Be safe, my brother. I'd like to visit you and your pack soon." She squeezed his hand, released him, then wrapped her arm around Darien's waist. "With my mate."

The phone rang and Lelandi gave a little start. Tom grabbed the phone half-buried under the sofa. "Yes, Uncle

Sheridan? I'll tell Darien you haven't located Trevor yet. Darien wants Ural released into the red's care and they're leaving. Leidolf will meet you at the jail."

"Would you stay and share a meal with us at least, brother?" Lelandi asked.

"Some other time," he said, his eyes still challenging Darien.

Darien pulled Lelandi out of the red's path, glad her brother was leaving. Jake finally moved aside, his posture stiff, his gaze intent on Leidolf.

Leidolf smirked at Darien. "You're lucky you had brothers. Sisters can be so much trouble."

Darien could imagine.

Turning to Darien, Tom asked, "Should I go with Leidolf?"

"No need," Leidolf dismissed him with a wave of his hand, then stalked toward the front door.

Darien was glad Lelandi didn't have any airs.

Leidolf yanked open the door and turned to Darien. "Take care of her, better than you did our sister Larissa." His conveyed the deadly threat with a look of contempt.

Darien wouldn't be tested, but Lelandi jerked free from him and slugged Leidolf in the shoulder. "You're a real bastard. We had to fend for ourselves. You should have protected Larissa from Crassus's brutality. You! *And* you should have forced Mother and Father to move before the demon took Larissa as his mate."

Leidolf's darkened eyes softened. "If I had, Larissa would have been alive, granted. But you would have been mated to one of my reds, and not to the one you've given your heart to." He bowed his head and stalked out the door.

The phone rang in Tom's hand, and he lifted it to his ear. "Uncle Sheridan? Sure."

He handed the phone to Darien. "He's steaming."

"That son of a bitch knocked Trevor out and already freed Ural from the jail. Trevor's tied up like a calf, fuming, ready to kill a couple of reds. But he's all right. What do you want me to do?" Uncle Sheridan asked.

"Release him."

"Leidolf?"

"Trevor."

Leidolf and her uncle got into the Humvee and Ural waved out the window. "See ya later, Lelandi. Don't be a stranger," Ural shouted.

Darien pulled Lelandi into his embrace and hugged her hard. "Whenever you want to see your family, I'll take you."

"You're my family now. But I'd like to see my parents. Oh… oh, Carol."

Darien motioned to Jake. "See how she is."

Darien moved Lelandi back into the living room where the furniture had been righted and the table with the broken leg removed. Bruin's body and his brothers' and the rest of his men's had been taken from the house. "Where's the red who gave up the fight?" Darien asked Peter.

"He took off when Bruin died."

Jake ran down the stairs. "I'm taking Carol to the hospital. Anybody else need patching up, come along with me. Nurse Grey and Matthew will take care of the injuries."

"Is she… she…" Lelandi swallowed hard.

Jake scratched his stubbly chin. "You know how a little *lupus garou* genetics help with the healing process."

"She's… she's turned?" Lelandi asked.

Darien took a deep breath. "That solves one problem."

"Like hell it does," Jake said, scowling. "She's already bitching about wanting to be a nurse at the hospital… again."

And there would be more trouble inherent with a newly turned *lupus garou* in the pack—particularly a female. Which of the wolves had so savagely bitten her? A red, because she was easy prey, or a gray to get rid of the threat to their kind. "Who bit her?"

Jake snorted. "One of the reds. Seems red females are going to be overrunning the pack."

"*Hmpfh.* Guess you'll have to get used to it." Looking up at Darien, Lelandi tightened her grasp on his hand. "Now can she be on the hospital staff?"

Chapter 23

EARLY THE NEXT MORNING, LELANDI TOOK A DEEP BREATH AS she and Silva headed for Carol's hospital room, hoping Carol would be awake this time.

"Nobody's turned a human in the last one-hundred and thirty years in Silver Town," Silva said, her voice hushed. "I can't even imagine what she might be feeling."

"Angry maybe. Frustrated. Probably scared. I still can't believe the bite turned her instead of killing her since she lost so much blood."

"Carol's a fighter." Silva sounded proud of her.

"Good thing, too." Lelandi was grateful Carol had survived but worried about how she would accept all the changes.

Guarding Carol's hospital room, Trevor looked pissed.

Silva straightened and put on her hopeful-smiley look, and Lelandi wanted to slap her. Trevor didn't look at Silva once, but glowered at Lelandi.

"No visitors," Trevor snapped.

"Try and stop us," Lelandi said.

Silva turned her head to conceal a smile.

Immediately, Trevor rose to his six-foot height. "The sheriff said no visitors unless Darien approves."

"Considering the circumstances, he means no *human* visitors," Silva contradicted him.

"Or, maybe he's concerned for her safety, but *we're* not a threat," Lelandi said.

Trevor stood firm, his hand resting on the pistol at his hip.

Not wanting to delay seeing Carol and tired of this macho bull, Lelandi stiffened. "Move, deputy, or I'll call Darien. You don't want to explain to him why you won't let his mate see the patient."

His eyes flashed murder, but he shoved his hand at Silva, stopping her from entering. "You're not authorized."

"She's my bodyguard today, Trevor. Don't make this hard on yourself."

He didn't budge.

Palm up, Lelandi extended her hand to Silva. "Phone?"

Silva dug around in her suitcase-sized leather bag. Trevor still wouldn't move, but as soon as Silva found her phone, Trevor growled. "I'll report this to the sheriff."

"Do," Lelandi said with a lift of her chin. *Jerk.*

Grudgingly, he half-moved out of the doorway so that Lelandi had to brush past him to get into the room. She thought about shoving him out of the way, but rather enjoyed pushing his buttons in a more feminine way. Silva shut the door after them.

Carol watched them from the bed. Sitting up, her face was glum and she turned away. Her neck was bandaged and a light stain of red colored the cloth. Her skin was pale, her blonde curls tangled around her shoulders as if she'd had a bad night's sleep.

Her skin was icy; Lelandi hated being in unfamiliar settings. Dealing with a newly turned *lupus garou* made her particularly uncomfortable, no matter how hard she tried to shake loose of the feeling. But she couldn't leave the poor woman in isolation either. She wished

Silva would help her out, like she usually did in a tense situation, but Silva seemed as unsure as Lelandi as to what to do.

"Carol, we came by to… sit with you for a while," Lelandi said.

"He won't let my parents see me," Carol said softly, blinking away tears.

"Darien?" Lelandi pulled a chair close to the bed.

"Who else?"

"He… he's afraid you'll tell your parents what happened."

Carol gave a derisive laugh. "My parents would have me certified. Just as crazy as my sister. That would really go over well."

"Would you like to see your parents?"

Carol's dull blue eyes sparkled.

Silva wrung her hands.

"One of us will have to stay with you while they visit," Lelandi warned.

Carol quickly nodded.

Silva let out her breath. "Are you sure Darien will approve?"

"Only one way to find out." Lelandi called his cell phone, but there was no answer. Carol's jaw tightened. Lelandi smiled. "Always another way to get around the big boss." She punched in another number and was instantly rewarded.

"This is Tom."

"Lelandi here, visiting Carol at the hospital. She's pretty down. Can you authorize her parents' visit if I stay in the room while they're here?"

"Silva can stay, too," Carol hurriedly said.

Silva smiled and pulled up another chair.

"I'll check with Darien and get back with you." Tom sounded so concerned, she wondered what was up.

"Where is he? I tried calling, but there wasn't any answer."

"The silver mine. An accident occurred with one of the tourist cars on the train."

"Is anyone hurt?"

"I probably shouldn't be telling you this, Lelandi, not until Darien approves. But, Angelina and Hosstene were on the car that Darien said was rigged to break free. The car tumbled down several hundred feet, striking a number of trees before it impacted with a boulder."

Lelandi stared at Silva in disbelief. "Were… were they injured badly?"

"Hosstene was decapitated. Angelina is on her way to the hospital now."

"Why would they have been riding on the train? Only the tourists take that trip, right?"

"Meeting someone? We don't know."

"Murder."

"Seems that way. Darien suspects Angelina, Hosstene, and Ritka were three of the ones blackmailing your sister. He believes whoever rigged the accident is the fourth and wants to eliminate his partners in the crime."

Lelandi sat down hard on the vinyl chair next to the bed. "How bad is Angelina?"

"Several broken bones. Internal bleeding. Not sure of the severity of all her injuries until a doctor takes a look. Darien didn't want to tell you until he was more certain of the women's guilt. Let me speak to Doc Mitchell, will you?"

Lelandi's face warmed. "He's… well, he had to check out Mrs. Fennigan's dog who was having symptoms of a stroke."

Tom didn't say anything for a moment. She was in trouble now. "Who's watching you?" Tom's voice was deep with barely repressed anger, and he sounded like Darien, except he would have sworn.

"Silva."

"Damn it, Lelandi. The murderer is still out there and someone has to watch you at all times. Why the hell didn't Doc Mitchell call in someone else? Forget it. He would have. But you didn't wait. Who's watching Carol's room?"

"Deputy Trevor."

"Fine. Stay there until I can get someone else to the hospital to escort you straight home after your visit."

Not liking that she had to be constantly watched, Lelandi clenched her teeth. "Will do. What about Carol's parents?"

Tom grumbled, "Darien will go ballistic when he learns you've been running around without protection. I'll make arrangements for her parents' visit. But don't you leave there *until* I have a security detail for you."

"Yes, sir." She smiled and hung up the phone.

"I could hear Tom's voice all the way over here," Silva said.

Carol was frowning so hard, Lelandi took her hand and gave her a reassuring squeeze. "Tom will make the arrangements."

"You… you risked your life to be with me?"

"Nonsense," Lelandi said.

But Silva disagreed. "Yes, she did. We were all set on coming here when Doc Mitchell got the emergency call. Peter was supposed to meet us at the house, but when he didn't show on time, Lelandi insisted we get to the hospital. She worried about you and didn't want to wait any longer, assuming Trevor would be here in case anyone threatened her."

"You shouldn't have risked it," Carol scolded.

"How are you feeling?" Lelandi hated that everyone worried about her like she was a child who couldn't deal with adversity.

"My throat still hurts. Tom gave me blood and I'm feeling a little better, but…" She laid her head back against the pillow, her eyes soggy, dark circles coloring the skin.

"Do you… want to talk about it?"

Carol inhaled deeply. "It's driving me crazy. Like Silva, I heard everything Tom said over the phone, he was so angry. I heard him say Hosstene was dead. And Angelina's in a bad way. That Darien thinks they were in on the blackmail. That the car they were riding in was sabotaged. I can even hear your heart beating rapidly. The smell of antiseptics in the room is overwhelming and burning my eyes. Even when the lights were out last night, I could see as if it were daylight. Although it wasn't exactly like daylight. More like a dark day when the clouds are getting ready to dump rain."

"I'm sure it'll take getting used to." Lelandi wished she could give her better advice.

"Is this how it felt when you were turned?" Carol asked.

Silva shook her head. "We were born as *lupus garous*. In fact, you're in the presence of a royal." Her voice full of pride, she motioned to Lelandi with a bow of her head, and Lelandi rolled her eyes at her.

Carol's eyes grew big. "A royal?"

"What Silva means is I'm a direct descendent of the original *lupus garou*. We believe he was a Norseman, although no one knows exactly how he contracted the *lupus garou* condition."

"Some say a wolf bit him but instead of dying, his blood fought off the infection by mutating," Silva suggested.

"I didn't think Lelandi was a werewolf because she's so small compared to the rest of you."

"We're gray wolves." Silva sat taller. "Lelandi's a red."

"Are… are there Mexican werewolves, too? Other kinds?"

"Mexican wolves are really grays," Silva said. "In the Southwest they call them Mexican wolves. And in the Northeast, timber wolves are also grays."

"I don't know about other kinds of *lupus garous*." Lelandi motioned at the window. "Normally, we don't go searching for other packs unless someone's looking for a mate, and even then, many find rogues instead. But we don't write down the histories about our lines either. Too dangerous. All we know is what's passed down orally from generation to generation."

Carol touched the bandage on her neck. "What kind am I?"

"A red bit you. So now there are two of us in the pack." Lelandi smiled.

"The pack. I'm one of you now?" Carol seemed unsure as to whether this was good news or bad.

"Yes. As long as you wish. Some become loners, rogues. Most stay with a pack for protection."

"What about real wolves? Do they get you mixed up with them?"

Lelandi chuckled. "One time a female wolf in heat lifted her tail and was trying to entice my brother to mate with her. My sister and I couldn't stop laughing. Except the next day, a male loner wolf tried to mate me. Then it wasn't so funny. Leidolf went after him and that was the last we saw of him in our territory."

Carol laughed, then her expression turned contemplative. "I've read a lot about wolf behavior. How once they've chosen a mate, they'll copulate with them several times over and over again, then back up to them, sometimes even putting their leg over them to protect their mate."

"A defensive measure, sure." Lelandi smiled. "But *lupus garous* are a little more civilized."

"So reds were the first kind of werewolves?"

Silva laughed.

Lelandi looked at her, surprised at her reaction. "Yes, Carol, a red *was* the first *lupus garou*."

"A gray." Silva bit her lip, suppressing another giggle.

Carol's brows and lips raised. "The problem with oral history? I thought since Lelandi was a royal and a red, the first must have been a red."

"She's a royal because she has ties to the original, this is true. And she's had very few human influences afterward, but my ancestors say the first was a gray who mated with a petite redheaded Celt. One of her sons mated with another. And so on until eventually a line of reds was born."

Lelandi frowned. "Not true. The first was a red. One of his daughters mated a gargantuan of a berserker, a king of the Norsemen. That's where the first gray line began."

Carol grinned. "I can see living with a gray pack, but being a red, is going to cause me problems already."

Lelandi patted her hand and whispered conspiratorially, "The reds came first. That's all you have to remember. I'll fill you in on the rest later."

Silva gave her a devilish smirk. "I'll bet Darien's never heard that version before. Wonder what he'll think."

"He'll agree with me." Lelandi turned to Carol. "But I have a question for you that's been nagging at me. Darien said you must have seen what happens when we ditch our clothes and mate in the woods. That you didn't see humans wearing animal skins like you said."

Carol's cheeks blossomed with color, and she began playing with her thin blanket. "I... I did see you as werewolves. I was trying to find out if you were one of them. I... I wanted to protect you. I knew it was too late for me."

"Too late for you?"

Carol looked steadily into Lelandi's eyes. "When I had the vision, the scene was set in the woods at night, but I could see as if it was a cloudy day. Just like last night in the hospital room. Which could only mean one thing."

"When the scene you envisioned finally occurs, you would be one of us," Lelandi said.

"Wow," Silva said. "You *really* can see into the future?"

Sam burst into the room, slamming the door against the wall, his look feral. "Darien read the riot act to the pack. You are *not* to go anywhere unescorted," he directed at Lelandi.

Silva got up from her chair, sauntered over to Sam, and ran her hands over his sweater-covered chest. While Trevor was watching from the hall, she kissed Sam on the lips. "I missed you, too."

"You know, Silva, you'd think you were afraid of letting our relationship go too far, the way you get me worked up in public, and cool it when we're in private." His hands cupped her face like she was a precious porcelain doll, then he kissed her lips, gently at first, then building up the momentum until her hands pressed against his back, encouraging him to go further.

Lelandi smiled. Trevor looked disgusted and closed the door.

Sam broke the kiss, his breathing labored, and so was Silva's. "Next time, we'll get a room," he promised with a caddish wink.

"Who says I'd be your mate?" Silva's lips curved up a hint, her eyes sparkling.

He chuckled darkly, released her, and motioned to the door. "I'll be right outside while you visit Carol." He gave Lelandi a warning look, then stiffly walked out of the room and shut the door.

"As to your question, Silva, yes, I see glimpses of the future," Carol said, smiling. "You won't be getting a room."

Silva frowned. "Meaning?"

"You two were some of the... pack members I saw in the woods that night."

Lelandi laughed. "Good, that means Trevor's out of the picture."

"That one's dangerous," Carol warned.

"What do you mean?" Lelandi asked. "Do you see his complicity in all this?"

"Can't you hear the threat in his voice? I wouldn't trust him one iota." Carol sipped some water. "Has he ever been treated as a suspect?"

"No." But Carol's comment made Lelandi think of Chester's words. What if it was someone Darien trusted? Someone close to him. "I doubt Darien would suspect him of wrongdoing."

"Was he ever noticeably absent when you needed help?" Carol set the empty cup on the table.

Lelandi refilled it. "When Darien fought Bruin's brother. But my brother had tied him up at the jail cell to free my cousin, Ural. So Trevor was truly all tied up."

"What about when you were shot? Was he with any of the search parties? Also, what about the shooter who killed the gunman? Was Trevor's gun checked?"

"Trevor was taking care of mudslide victims on the highway. And… uhm, I was the shooter," Silva explained.

Carol gave her a puzzled look.

"Long story," Lelandi said. "Silva can tell you about it later. But Chester McKinley discovered another bullet and casing. He thought your bullet fell short, Silva."

Silva's jaw dropped. "You're kidding."

"He gave it to the sheriff to check out."

Carol frowned. "I don't remember reading about any mudslides on the highway in the *Silver Town Express*. The shooting was important and would make the headlines, but if anyone was injured in the mudslide, it would have been mentioned. What about when that maniac took you hostage? Was Trevor looking for you with the rest of the pack?" Carol asked.

"He was helping the sheriff watch my old pack at Hastings Bed and Breakfast," Lelandi said. Although he'd had perfectly good excuses every time, the feeling there was more to the story made her skin tingle.

"I don't know. I wouldn't trust him."

"Thanks for the warning, Carol. Believe me, I don't."

Silva didn't say anything for several seconds, then she abruptly stood. "Will you two be all right? I'll ask Nurse Grey when Carol can be released."

"Sure." Lelandi exchanged a look with Carol.

Silva gave one of her faked smiles, attempting to hide her anxiety and hurried out of the room. "Be right back, Sam." She closed the door, and her boots clicked down the hall.

"Something's wrong, don't you think?" Carol asked.

"Yeah. Like Silva suddenly became suspicious of something."

"Considering Trevor, right?"

Lelandi took a deep breath. "Since she's had such a crush on him, I think so. She constantly kept tabs on him, until she switched her affections to the one who really counted."

"Sam," Carol said, dreamily. "She couldn't do wrong by him. I have another question though."

Lelandi figured she'd never hear the end of them, although she couldn't blame her. She hadn't even given Carol the spiel concerning the semi-immortal part. And she figured Carol wasn't a virgin. But Lelandi had to warn Carol that she couldn't have casual sexual relations with a *lupus garou*. That if one acted interested in her—and with shortages in most packs she'd have lots of interest—if she responded in the same way toward a male, she could be mated and it would be a done deal, for life. But this wasn't the time or place to talk about it.

"The bullets that killed Doc Oliver and Ritka were silver, weren't they?" Carol asked.

"Yes."

"But how are werewolves able to work in the silver mine? I mean, they do, don't they? Wouldn't it kill them?"

"No. It's only deadly if it strikes the heart or brain and isn't removed immediately. Silver doesn't bother us otherwise."

"I'm sure you're going to get tired of all my questions."

"Carol, this is such a big change for you. Feel free to ask me anytime. Darien will want you to stay with a pack member until you adjust. The moon's out and whenever it is, the pull to shapeshift can be strong. But since you've been only recently changed and are still injured, you might not experience it for a while."

"Oh, I have to shapeshift then even if I don't—"

"We're here to see our daughter, Carol Wood," a woman said beyond the hospital room door, sounding brusque and noticeably upset.

Lelandi patted Carol's shoulder. "Will you be all right?"

Tears misting her eyes, Carol nodded. "Darien gave me a cover story."

He would. Although Lelandi trusted Carol not to tell her parents what she'd become, she had to stay with them in the room until they left. But she was dying to see what Silva was up to. And she wanted in the worst way to question Angelina.

Sam opened the door and allowed Carol's parents to enter. Their eyes widened when they saw Lelandi with Carol.

"Nurse Grey said you couldn't be seen at first, and we thought you were really bad off. She told us we can't visit for long." Carol's mother grasped her hand, her blonde hair as golden as her daughter's, her eyes as blue. Her father towered over them, but didn't say a word, his rail-thin body bent with weariness, his dark eyes worried.

"You'll be all right, dear?" her mother asked.

Carol managed a small, tearful smile. "I'm fine, Mom. I'll be out of here soon." She motioned to Lelandi. "This is Lelandi. I'm sorry I don't know your last name."

"Silver," Lelandi said.

Carol's mouth gaped. "You married Darien?"

Her mother and father looked as shocked.

"When things aren't so hectic, I'm sure he'll make the announcement." Lelandi hated that part of fitting in with human society. Their kind didn't do the wedding bit. Their mating meant more than any kind of ceremony could mean. They stayed with their spouse until one died. Or at least that's the way they normally lived their lives.

Finally finding her voice, Carol said, "Oh, sure, I knew it would happen sooner than later. I'm so very happy for you. This is my mother, Lori, and my father, Christopher Wood."

"My pleasure," Lelandi said.

"I don't understand. Aren't you the one who was shot a few days ago?" Mrs. Wood took a ragged breath. "Kidnappings, more shootings. And all of it revolves around you." Running her hand over Carol's hair, she said, "Nurse Grey told us a wild wolf bit Carol and it's been destroyed. But why's Deputy Sheriff Trevor

Osgood guarding her room? And Sam? What in the world is going on?"

Carol paled even further.

Lelandi realized living with a pack that didn't associate with humans had its advantages. "They're here because of me," she lied.

Mrs. Wood's eyes narrowed. "Then *you* shouldn't be here. If danger follows you wherever you go, I want you out of here. Now."

Mr. Wood cleared his throat. His wife looked sharply at him. "Honey, if Carol wants Mrs. Silver's company, then don't you think she should have her friendship? Mr. Silver *does* run the town, and Carol hasn't made any friends since she returned home."

Mrs. Wood looked like she could strangle him with her glare.

"Dad's right. Lelandi made friends with me as soon as I met her." Carol gave her a warm smile.

Lelandi wondered how Carol had ever gotten that notion, but she was glad to be her friend now.

"She's even convinced Darien I should work at the hospital. You know how much I've wanted to."

Great. Put me on the spot, why don't you, Carol?

"I couldn't have asked for a better friend," Carol said. "We're so much alike. I can't even say how much so."

Nurse Grey walked into the room. "I'm sorry, but I'll have to ask everyone to leave so I can change Miss Wood's bandages. She'll be released tomorrow afternoon."

"Then… then it's not as bad as we expected?" Mrs. Wood asked.

Nurse Grey checked Carol's vital signs. "She'll be fine, but she needs to rest."

"Come back and see me soon," Carol said to Lelandi, her expression mournful.

Lelandi gave her a cheerful smile. "I'll be back later. Behave yourself until then."

"As long as you take Trevor with you."

"I will." Lelandi left the room and snagged Sam's arm, then walked him down to Doc's office. "Tell Darien he needs to remove Trevor from guard duty for Carol."

Sam folded his arms. "He'll want to know a reason."

"Carol's a target, too. Darien knows the specifics as to why. She doesn't feel safe around Trevor. Give her some peace of mind, okay? See if maybe Tom or Jake will watch her in the meantime. I'd do it, if Darien would let me."

Sam gave a snort. "*You* are supposed to be guarded, not guarding others."

"Right. Or otherwise I'd kick Trevor's butt out of here."

Sam shook his head. "You'd try, too."

"Are you going to make an honest woman of Silva?"

A smile lit Sam's face, but he didn't answer. Instead, he grabbed Doc's phone and made a call. "Darien? Sam here."

Lelandi slipped into the hallway. As soon as she saw Peter guarding a room, she headed in his direction. "Who's in here?"

The deputy quickly stood. "Angelina Mavery."

Lelandi's heart skipped a beat, the idea sinking in that whoever had tried to kill Angelina would try again and now she had to have a guard posted, too. "Do you mind if I see her? I won't take long."

Chapter 24

IF PETER DIDN'T HURRY AND ALLOW LELANDI INTO Angelina's hospital room, any number of people—Darien, top of the list—would stop her. Peter looked down at his Stetson in his hands, and then his gaze rose again.

"Peter, please."

"Jake told me you stuck up for me when I fell asleep on guard duty, ma'am."

She wanted to tap her foot in impatience. Time was of the essence, and if Sam discovered she was not with him... "Yes, because you were pulling too many hours."

"Trevor was supposed to have relieved me halfway through the night, but he never showed up."

Ohmigod. "Did you tell Jake?"

"Yes, ma'am. I didn't want to get Trevor in trouble, but I couldn't have Darien firing me for not protecting you." Peter motioned with his head toward Angelina's door. "The way I look at it, you deserve some answers. If Angelina had anything to do with my own sister's death..." His eyes took on a menacing cast. "Go right in."

Lelandi hesitated, then reached up and kissed Peter's cheek. "Thanks. Darien will make you sheriff when his uncle wants to retire, if I have any say in it."

Peter's face turned crimson, but his lips turned up slightly. "Thank you, ma'am."

She slipped into the room and closed the door.

Angelina's face was bruised and bloodied, the skin around both eyes blackened—her gaze glowering at Lelandi. A bandage was secured across her forehead, a long, jagged line of blood tinting it red. Her neck was in a brace and her arm and leg were in a cast.

Lelandi started in on her. "You were blackmailing my sister, you bitch."

Angelina cast her a simpering smile. "Your sister was a whore. Three men! Three men she was fooling around with that we know of, and Darien should never have mated with her."

"Who else was in on this? You're not clever enough to mastermind it. And since your two compatriots are dead and the fourth undoubtedly wants you the same way—"

"Think what you will."

"Darien will discover you're involved. Then what?"

"He'll find his darling mate was depositing money in an account meant for her and her lover to make their getaway. Had nothing to do with me." She jutted her chin out, her brown eyes black, a couple of stripped leaves sticking out of her muddy-colored hair.

"You're saying Joe Kelly and Larissa pretended there was a blackmailing scheme?"

"They had the perfect motivation. Joe was stealing from the silver mine also." Angelina shrugged and winced.

"No. You, Ritka, Hosstene, and the mastermind blackmailed my sister. Except Joe shot Ritka before you could pin the blackmailing crime on him. Seems ironic. Then the fourth person wanted both you and Hosstene dead."

Angelina's eyes misted.

"Why would he or she want to kill you if you had

nothing to do with the blackmail scheme and murdering my sister? Can he get to the money that all of you hid?"

Angelina's mouth turned down even more.

"Now who should get out of town before you end up dead like your friends?" Lelandi asked, playing on Ritka's words telling Lelandi to leave town before she ended up like her sister. "I normally don't want to see people dead. But in your case, I'd make an exception."

"Go to hell," Angelina spat.

"Whoever your mastermind is *will* kill you. Seems a shame you'll die and the murderer will get away with not only eliminating your spiteful hide, but abscond with the money."

Angelina glowered at her, the flecks of gold in her amber eyes like burning embers.

"Who's your accomplice? Who tried to kill you?"

Angelina crinkled the bed linens in her good hand. "I don't know who it is. Ritka dealt with him."

Lelandi's heart missed a beat. "But it's a he?"

"Yes. He orchestrated the whole setup. At least I'm pretty sure it's a he." Angelina glowered. "Your sister was despicably weak. We all knew it. She should *never* have been the pack leader's bitch."

Lelandi opened her mouth to retort, but Darien entered the room and shook his head at her, his look dark, but sympathetic. "Let my men and me question her, Lelandi." He ran his hand over her shoulder and down her arm, taking hold of her hand and kissing it. "Silva wants to talk to you at the nurse's station."

Lelandi kissed Darien's cheek, and quickly wiped away a tear rolling down hers. "She admitted to black-mailing Larissa. Another orchestrated the whole sorry

affair. She said Joe stole the silver from the mine."
Before she gave in to her darker wolf instincts and broke
Angelina's other arm for good measure, Lelandi stormed
out of the room.

Standing beside Peter, Sam growled. "I was supposed
to be watching you."

"Peter had the job. I'm going to speak to Silva.
Right down there. All right?" She glanced down the
hall at Carol's room. Tom guarded her now. "Where
did Trevor go?"

"He's helping the sheriff with the train derailment,"
Sam said. "This town's never going to be the same."

"You didn't get any flak, did you?" Lelandi asked Peter.

"No, ma'am."

Sam ground his teeth. "I did, for not knowing where
you were when I called Darien."

Lelandi smiled at the rough and tumble bartender
and patted his shoulder. "You can handle it." Then she
joined Silva at the unmanned nurse's desk. "Did you
find out anything?"

"Nurse Grey said no one was brought in for
injuries sustained in a mudslide during the night of
the shootings."

"Which could mean none of the injuries were severe
enough to require hospital care."

"Right. So I checked with the *Silver Town Express*
staff. None were aware of the mudslide, but because of
the shootings they had concentrated on that news."

"What about the guys who have to clear the roads
during a storm?"

"My next thought exactly." Silva waved a slip of
paper, showing each of the points she'd checked off. "I

called the road-clearing crew supervisor. On the night
the gunman shot you, no mudslides had been reported,
but several of his crew were searching for you in the
woods. All were on call, so if a mudslide had occurred,
they would have been notified."

"What about when Trevor was supposed to be with
the sheriff at Hastings Bed and Breakfast and didn't
show up to help in the fight against my red pack?"

"One way to find out." Silva grabbed the phone off
the nurse's desk and punched in some numbers. She
handed the phone to Lelandi.

"Hastings Bed and Breakfast. This is Bertha Hastings.
How may I help you?"

"Mrs. Hastings? This is Lelandi. Was Trevor there
when the reds came to take me home?"

"The sheriff sent him on an errand. When he didn't
return, Sheridan left some men to watch the reds, and he
searched for the deputy. He found him and had him guard
the prisoner at the jailhouse." Mrs. Hastings paused, then
added, "Many thought Darien would take Trevor's sister
as his mate, but then he made it clear he was looking for
someone outside the pack. Rumors began to circulate
that Darien had a dream and the visions changed his
mind. Trevor's sister left Silver Town, joined another
pack, and mated with a beta male. Too loyal to the pack,
Trevor won't leave, but he resented Larissa because his
sister didn't share the bed of the alpha pack leader. His
position would have been elevated if Darien had taken
his sister as his mate. Trevor figured he'd be sheriff
when Sheridan retired."

"Do you think he could have masterminded blackmailing my sister?"

"I doubt it. He might not like that your sister stole Darien's affections, but he's not that underhanded. He huffs and puffs and can be disagreeable, but that's as far as it goes."

"When the gunman shot Tom, Sam, and me, there had been no mudslide, no injured victims. He said he was taking care of that mess instead of searching for me."

Mrs. Hastings took a deep breath and exhaled. "Obviously, he's guilty of a dereliction of his duties. Ask him. Whatever I can do to shed any light on this, please, anytime, call me."

"I will. Thanks." Lelandi hung up the phone. "If Trevor was not doing his duty and tried to cover it up, what *was* he doing?"

The sound of footfalls headed in their direction and they turned. Darien stalked toward them with Jake at his side. Neither looked happy.

Darien slipped his hand around Lelandi's arm, escorting her in the direction of the front doors while Jake shadowed them. "I'm taking you home."

"What did Angelina say?"

"She doesn't know who the mastermind is. Ritka knew, but wouldn't say. Since Hosstene was my accountant at the factory, she cleared Larissa's checks without a word to me."

"If Ritka was the only one dealing with this guy, do you think they had sexual relations?"

"Doc Featherston conducted an autopsy and confirmed she wasn't a virgin, yet officially, she'd never been mated."

Lelandi let out her breath. "So he might have been her lover, too. But no male seems to be unduly upset at her passing." She glanced back at Silva, looking abandoned. "Can Silva come with us?"

"Later. I want her to stay with Carol for now and keep her company. She needs someone to talk to until she can settle into her new life."

"*Hrumpf,*" Lelandi said. "She'll brainwash her."

Darien stared down at Lelandi as he walked her to his new SUV. "Brainwash her?"

"Sure, tell her that the grays were the first *lupus garous.*"

Darien laughed. "I'm staying out of this one."

"Can Trevor guard the house?"

"Carol thinks he's involved. She told Tom all that she suspected. I have Uncle Sheridan checking Trevor's story out, and in the meantime, he's got jailhouse duty."

"I think he's being set up. Why not have him guard me, and you can have someone watch him just in case. When you're not around."

"What are you up to, Lelandi?" He helped her into the SUV.

"I just want to talk to him."

Jake climbed into the backseat.

"I was seeing his sister," Darien said, sounding tired.

"I know." She took his hand and kissed it. "But then you had a vision. But not exactly a vision."

"The dream where I first found you. I knew then I had to have you, no other. Trevor was angry, his sister heartbroken. He didn't care so much about how his sister felt, but that he would have had more leverage with me had I mated her. When Larissa came to Silver Town and we were mated, Annie took off for Green Valley and mated with a gray there. I understand she's happy and due to have twins in the spring."

"Do you think Trevor could have been blackmailing Larissa?"

"Anything's possible."

Surprised Darien would permit it, Lelandi sat on one of the sofas, waiting for Trevor to join her in the sunroom, ready to question him about his mudslide story. The snow fell steadily outside the windows and a fire blazed in a rock fireplace centered in the room, giving it a homey, comfortable ambience—which didn't fit the mood of what she was about to do. Trevor's face couldn't have been any stonier and his icy glare held her gaze when he stalked into the room. But she steeled her resolve while Jake remained outside within earshot.

"Please, have a seat."

Not removing his jacket, Trevor shoved his hands in his pockets and ignored her.

Fine. "You lied about the mudslide when Tom and I were shot. You said you were taking care of accident victims."

Trevor continued to glower at her.

"Deputy, I don't believe you did anything malicious to contribute to my sister's death. I know you hated her. That you wanted Darien to marry your sister, hoping she could convince Darien to make you sheriff some day and not Peter."

"You have no authority questioning me. You're just Darien's bitch."

"Yes. And Larissa was my sister. You're right. You don't have to tell me anything. But how long do you think it'll be before Darien discovers you lied about the mudslide? Do you want to die for someone else's crime?"

"I was seeing someone," he mumbled under his breath, his gaze shifting to the fire.

Ohmigod, no wonder he hadn't been interested in Silva. He was already hung up on someone else. But why keep it a secret? "Someone Darien didn't approve of?"

Trevor refused to look at her.

"Someone who was already mated?"

He jerked his head around and cast her a chilling glare. "No, damn you. Just because your sister hooked up with three different mates, doesn't mean any of the rest of us do."

Needing his cooperation, Lelandi stamped down a hasty response. She hated the shameful way her sister had carried on with another male when she was mated to Darien, yet she couldn't help feeling Larissa was the victim of her circumstances. If her people had allowed for divorce, she would have been fine. "Then who?"

"You don't need to know who she is."

"You'll need her alibi."

"Why? Silva was the shooter. Ritka and her friends were the blackmailers."

"But Silva wasn't the shooter."

Trevor's eyes widened.

"Who was the mastermind who killed Hosstene?"

"You can't pin that on me. I had nothing to do with it."

"What happened to you when you were supposed to aid Darien in his fight against my red pack?"

"He had me replace Wilkerson pulling guard duty at the jailhouse. Later, I heard Darien said I was supposed to be at the house protecting you. But no one ever told me. Then here come two blasted reds, taller than any I've ever seen. They knock me out, tie me up, and free the prisoner. I'll tell you another thing, the sheriff told Darien he was looking for me as if he had no idea where I was. Hell, he sent me to the jailhouse."

Miscommunication? Or was Trevor lying again? "You said there were only six males from the pack who arrived. But there were several more."

"That's all I saw. Apparently, more sneaked in without our knowledge."

"Who told them about the guest room where I was staying? That's where they entered the second floor."

"I knew you were staying with Darien by then."

Lelandi was beginning to wonder about Darien's uncle. "Did the sheriff know I had moved to Darien's bedroom?"

"You'd have to ask him."

Trevor yanked his keys out of his pocket, but before he could leave, Lelandi asked, "What happened to you at the hospital when Ritka and Doc were shot? You were guarding Ural. Or supposed to be. Ritka screamed for you, but you never came."

The tips of Trevor's ears reddened. "I don't need to explain anything more to you." He stormed out of the sunroom.

Jake immediately peeked in on Lelandi. Assured she was all right, he lifted his phone from his belt and shut the door.

Lelandi took a deep breath. Next, she had to have a word with the sheriff. She was certain that would go over as well as the talk with his deputy. But she had to ask Darien if he knew what had happened to Trevor when Joe killed Doc and Ritka.

An hour later, Darien arrived home and Lelandi, anxious to get an audience with his uncle, dropped the salad fixings in the bowl and hurried to see her mate while Tom was preparing lasagna in the kitchen. She blurted, "Can you arrange for me to speak with Sheridan?"

Tom served up the lasagna and Jake finished the salad and set it on the table, both casting them a sideways glance. She assumed it was a sore subject.

Darien kissed Lelandi's mouth, then smiled and hugged her tight. "Let's eat."

She frowned at the dismissal. "What about your uncle? He might be the key to knowing what Trevor was doing the night he said he was working a mudslide."

Darien pulled out her chair. "We'll discuss it later. This afternoon, we'll have a memorial service for Doc."

"What about for Ritka?" Tom asked.

Darien cast him an annoyed look like he shouldn't have mentioned it. "Her family wants a private ceremony. Immediate family only."

Jake and Tom exchanged glances but neither said a word.

Lelandi hated it when the brothers knew something she didn't and were bent on keeping it from her. "Okay, so why do they want a private ceremony? Is this done regularly here?"

Back home pack members buried their kind. No one had a simple, family ceremony, although humans were excluded. She assumed humans would come to

Doc's funeral since his work had impacted so many in the community.

"That's what the family agreed upon," Darien said casually, giving her a look like he wanted her to leave it at that.

"But it's not normal. Which means something. Care to speculate?"

"No."

"It means," Lelandi said, clenching her teeth, "since Ritka was involved in my sister's death, her family's too ashamed to have the pack witness the burial."

None of them said anything.

"Right?"

"It means the family wanted it. Nothing more to it than that." Darien's voice had a warning edge to it.

"Sorry, if I don't agree."

Darien let out a harsh breath. "They feel your sister contributed to her death."

Lelandi's jaw tightened and she fought tears welling up deep inside.

"They know they can't exclude you from the funeral without offending me, but they look at you and are reminded of Larissa. So they are having a private funeral. Most likely she was involved in the blackmail. But we have no hard evidence to support this theory."

Lelandi got up abruptly from the table. "There's no need. You and the rest of the pack can go. I wouldn't want to deprive them of their leader's presence."

Darien seized her wrist and made her sit back down. "They made their decision. Under the circumstances, it's best for all concerned."

Because Ritka was involved in Larissa's death.

"All right," she said, "so tell me—when Ritka screamed for Trevor at the hospital, why didn't he stop Joe?"

Jake and Tom concentrated on their lasagna while Darien placed his fork on his plate and leaned away from the table. "When Joe saw Trevor was guarding Ural, he knocked him out."

"Really," Lelandi said, rolling her eyes.

"He had a concussion, Lelandi. So yes, really."

"And my brother and uncle conveniently got the better of him in the jail. Maybe Trevor needs a different job."

"Uncle Sheridan counseled him."

"*Hmpf.* He needs a heck of a lot more than counseling."

"As to another matter," Darien said, "we'll have a Thanksgiving feast for the pack."

She figured the feast was a tradition they'd always carried out like so many people did across the States until she saw the questioning glances on his brothers' faces. "Why?" she asked, because Jake and Tom wouldn't, and she figured something more had to be up.

"A feast to give thanks that I have a mate. Is that not reason enough?" Darien's expression was lighthearted, but the façade didn't hide the darkness brewing beneath the surface.

She offered a smile. "I'm sure everyone will enjoy a feast, no matter the reason. Free food puts everyone in good spirits."

"Where did you want to have this feast?" Jake asked, his voice shadowed. "The civic auditorium? School gym? The tavern, perhaps?"

"Here." Darien lifted his cup to his lips.

Lelandi suspected the worst. Darien knew who killed her sister, and he needed the majority of the pack together.

The feast was the battleground. Or at least the beginning. The battle would take place in the woods, secluded from town, perfect for a fight between wolves.

Her eyes filling with tears, she sat back in her chair. Ever since she'd learned her sister had died, she'd had this overwhelming ache to right the wrong, to avenge her sister's death. And now Darien knew who it was? But he would have told her right away if he'd planned to. Which meant he was keeping it a secret. Anger and upset bottled up inside threatened to spill out. She fought the emotions, trying to maintain a cool, alpha stance. "Who is it?"

"He'll reveal himself when the time comes."

She ground her teeth, attempting to stay calm, but her blood was running hot.

Jake scraped his empty wineglass across the oak table.

"What, Jake? You know how much doing that annoys me."

"Does he know you suspect him?"

"Who?" Lelandi asked in exasperation. She quickly brushed away insolent tears that dared streak down her cheeks. She was not a wilting damn flower.

Darien looked torn between comforting her and being the indomitable pack leader and setting up the rules. "I'm not sure, but I won't openly speculate. Too much of that has been going on of late. Several pack members have unduly ostracized Trevor because many think he had a hand in Larissa's death. At the feast, the murderer will reveal himself. That's all I'll say."

"I'll organize the men to cook the turkeys beforehand at the school," Jake offered.

"Tom, I want you to get the word out to the pack about the feast."

"Will do, Darien. I can coordinate the efforts of those making the vegetables."

"Good." Darien turned to Lelandi.

She couldn't stand his seeing how teary-eyed she'd become. Looking down at the table, she swallowed the lump in her throat.

"Lelandi," he said softly, "maybe you, Carol, and Silva can make some more of those apple pies that everyone loved so much?"

Her heart aching to the core, she glowered at him. "You know who it is, don't you?"

"Leave us," he said to his brothers.

"We'll make the arrangements at once," Jake said.

Tom inclined his head slightly to Lelandi, then the two brothers hastened to leave the dining room.

Darien didn't move from his chair, but just studied Lelandi.

Why did he have to keep her in the dark? Why?

He rose from his chair and walked around the table to join her, touching her cheek with his fingertips in a gentle caress. "If I tell you who I suspect and I'm wrong, you'll harbor a mistrust of the individual. But more than that, I know how you are. You'll confront him without regard to the danger you'd put yourself in. I won't have it. In two day's time, we'll know once and for all."

"Then you'll fight him to the death."

The phone rang and Tom hurried back into the room to get it. "Tom here." The look of shock on Tom's face made her suspect something awful must have happened. Jake poked his head in.

"Now what?" Lelandi asked.

Tom looked at Darien, waiting for him to allow him to speak in front of Lelandi.

He seemed indecisive about allowing it or keeping her further in the dark. Then he finally gave a slight nod, his gaze hard as he caught Lelandi's eye.

"Angelina's dead," Tom said.

"How?" Darien asked.

"Heart gave out."

"Natural causes or was she helped along?"

"Coroner won't be able to tell us for a few days."

Lelandi closed her eyes, not believing the killer could have struck again. She felt hands on her shoulders and looked up to see Darien rubbing them. He leaned down and kissed her cheek.

"Did he kill her, Darien? Did he get to her, too?" She choked back a sob.

Darien shook his head and said to Tom, "I want the report soonest. Jake, I need you and Tom to talk to everyone. Find out who was serving on guard duty when she expired and who went in to see her." He squeezed Lelandi's shoulder. "You've had enough excitement to last a lifetime and it's getting late. Let's go to bed."

But she couldn't brush her worry away, and when he led her upstairs, she felt drained, as if she wasn't even there. Would the killer truly be revealed at the feast? Or would he try for her again before then?

Two days later, Lelandi read over the coroner's report in Darien's office while he watched her. *Death due to asphyxiation.* "Murdered," Lelandi said under her breath, although she wasn't surprised.

"Her room was at the back of the hospital. Someone had unlocked the window, an inside job. Anyone could have slipped in, murdered her, and left without anyone being aware," Darien said.

"But it was a man who killed her, right?"

"Most likely, and she bit him."

Lelandi glanced up from the report. "It doesn't say that."

"Doc Featherston told me. He found remnants of blood around her teeth, but the blood wasn't hers. He didn't want the word to get out."

"Oh hell, Darien. By now the bite marks could have healed and disappeared."

"Maybe not. Mandatory dress is short-sleeved shirts for the men for the feast today. Only my brothers, Doc Featherston, and the killer will know the real reason."

"Couldn't he do a DNA test on the blood?"

"Not enough for the test."

"What if the murderer doesn't show up today?"

"He will. And the game will be over."

Later that afternoon, and with the tension running high, Darien welcomed Lelandi's family in the sunroom while Lelandi baked pies with Carol and Silva in the kitchen. He gave Lelandi's mother a hug, seeing the resemblance to Lelandi, the red hair, petite features, green eyes and riveting smile. He shook her father's hand as he sat in his wheelchair, looking proud, but with a weariness lingering in his features. His dark amber eyes assessed Darien with a wolf's guardedness.

Lelandi was unaware Darien had invited her family so that he had a chance to meet them first, and welcome them like a pack leader would before he switched roles to greet them as family. Darien shook Leidolf's hand next, then her Uncle Hrothgar's, and Ural's last.

"I'm sure you suspect the reason I've invited you here," Darien said.

"To ask permission to have my daughter after the fact," her father growled, banging his fist on the arm of his wheelchair. Lelandi's mother rested her hand on his shoulder.

Although it had never been his intention to ask for Lelandi since he'd already mated with her, Darien bowed his head with respect.

"You have my permission," her father said, his voice gruff, but admiration shown in his eyes.

Everyone else waited quietly for Darien's next words, tension filling the room. "The killer will be exposed today, the fight will follow, and the celebration feast afterward."

Her father inclined his head. "This is acceptable."

"We've heard rumors Lelandi may be with triplets," her mother said, her voice hopeful.

"Mrs. Wildhaven, it's too early to tell."

"Please, call me Eleanor."

"Certainly. But I wish to discuss another matter. We've lost our doctor and Lelandi has her heart set on Doc Weber of your pack joining us. Would this be agreeable?"

Hrothgar cleared his throat. "I, of course, would prefer he stay at Wildhaven with my pack."

"But," Eleanor said, "having triplets can be difficult for even *lupus garous*. Because Lelandi has a fondness for Doc Weber and he has for her…" She spread her hands, palms up.

Darien waited for Hrothgar's approval as Wildhaven's newest pack leader. Hrothgar gave a stiff nod.

Turning to Leidolf, Darien said, "I know you want to avenge Larissa's death. I ask that you allow me the honor since it is my pack, she was my mate—no matter how wrongly that came about—and the villain is one of my pack."

"As much as I'd love to tear the bastard from limb to limb, I acquiesce. Should you not succeed, I won't wait for either of your brothers to jump into the fray."

"Agreed." Darien looked at Jake and Tom, both who reluctantly nodded. "Settled then." He motioned to Tom, who opened the door and Mrs. Hastings and several other ladies hurried in with apple cider, shrimp, and cheese dips with crackers. "I'll tell Lelandi you're here."

He had every intention of delaying the inevitable, feeling an insatiable urge to prove to her that she wanted to remain with him and not return to her family no matter how much he told himself the notion was too ridiculous to consider.

Chapter 25

BUSINESS AS USUAL. THAT'S THE WAY EVERYONE PLAYED their roles as Sam organized the drinks in the dining room, Tom coordinated the side dishes, Jake managed the deliveries of the turkeys, while Lelandi, Carol, and Silva finished baking the pies. The aroma of roasted turkey and gravy filled the air, making Lelandi's stomach rumble, although she didn't think she'd be able to eat, she was so uptight.

Carol peered out the kitchen window where the table sat in an alcove. "Snow's still falling. This will be the best ski season Silver Town's had in five years."

Silva cast a questioning look in Lelandi's direction, but though she caught it, she didn't acknowledge her concern. Everyone was wearing polite smiles, the conversations centering around the weather, a hunt, some whispered speculation about Sam and Silva, but nothing about the reason for the feast. Lelandi was sure the conversations about that had already been held behind closed doors.

Darien walked into the kitchen, stretched his arms above his head, and smiled at Lelandi.

Silva stammered some excuse and hurried out of the kitchen. Carol took longer before it sank in that the alpha leader needed a moment alone with his mate. Her face suddenly flushed and she quickly made her excuses and hurried after Silva, shutting the door behind her.

"Why didn't you say something to me?" she scolded outside the kitchen.

Darien rested his hands on Lelandi's shoulders. "You smell of cinnamon, apples, and brown sugar. Good enough to eat." He kissed her lips, not waiting for her approval, slipping his tongue into her mouth. "Hmm, taste like brown sugar, apples, and cinnamon, too."

She melted like the dabs of butter she'd spread on top of the lattice-work pie crusts. "Have… have you seen anyone with bite marks?"

He groaned. "Lelandi…" He shook his head. "I'm afraid either Angelina didn't bite her attacker hard enough or the scar has already healed. No matter. We've got him where we want him. I've felt the distance between us when we've made love the last two days. I know you feel hurt that I wouldn't tell you who I most suspect. But I have to do this my way, knowing you the way I do."

She lifted her gaze from his chest to his eyes. "I love you, Darien, but I don't want to be kept in the dark."

He kissed her lips again, his fingers pushing a couple of buttons through the buttonholes on her silk blouse. He slipped his hands inside her blouse and fondled her breasts through the lacy bra.

"Ahh, Darien, you taste of apple cider, the good stuff." She tangled her tongue with his for another spicy taste.

Voices drew nearer the kitchen, but suddenly stopped and footfalls moved discretely away. Lelandi suspected Silva and Carol were warding everyone away in lieu of a "Don't Disturb" sign.

Darien tackled Lelandi's belt, but she stilled his hands. "What are you doing?"

"I'm feeling testy."

He captured her mouth with his, kissing her into submission and moved her hands away from her belt, then unbuckled it. "We'll enjoy the meal more after we relieve some of the tension between us."

She suspected there was more to his need to make love to her than he was admitting. She recognized his craving to prove she was his and couldn't understand what had triggered it again. Unless it was to confirm to his gathered pack that he had claimed her. No, it seemed to run deeper, like when he felt his pack members were hitting on her at the tavern, and he had to show she was his and only his.

He rubbed his hand between her legs, his fingers pressing the jeans and satin panties between her feminine folds, stealing her thoughts, eliciting a soft moan from her.

"Say you want to wait and we will," he whispered into her ear, his voice husky with desire. He leaned his hardened erection against her and rubbed. "Say you want me, Lelandi."

She could no more resist him now than she could in her dreams. Seizing the buttons on his shirt, she nearly ripped them off in haste. She ran her hands over his bare chest, her fingernails flickering over his already pebbled nipples. With a groan, he yanked down her jeans and panties in one fell swoop. Leaning her against the kitchen table covered in flour, granules of brown sugar, and speckles of cinnamon, he shoved away mixing spoons and a sieve that clattered to the tile floor.

He dipped his hand in a bag of brown sugar, then sprinkled it on her bare breasts and stomach. Lelandi smiled. "You're supposed to eat your meal, before you get dessert. Didn't your mother ever tell you that?"

"I was more of a red meat kind of guy—although all of that's changed."

He shrugged out of his jeans and pushed her legs apart. But before he penetrated her woman's core, he licked the sugar off her breasts and stomach, sending streaks of pleasure rifling through her. She needed this as much as he did. She wanted the closeness, the loving, the solidarity, before he had to fight. And if it gave him strength, all the better.

She combed her fingers through his hair, luxuriating in the feel of the satiny strands and of his velvet tongue lapping at her skin. His fingers slipped down her stomach, tracing the slight swell in her belly, lower, to her short curly hairs, combing through them to discover the dewy opening between her thighs. Stroking her nub, he triggered flames of desire to sweep through her, a delicious torment, begging to be appeased.

She dug her fingers into his back, the toned muscles of the *lupus garou* tensing with her touch, and she prodded him to penetrate her. She listened to the soothing sound of the thunder of his heartbeat, his heavy lusty breath, and her heartbeat pounding beneath his.

Darien plunged deep inside of her, his stiff cock thrusting with feverish intent, his pelvis rubbing her mound until every nerve was ready to explode.

"I love you," she mouthed against his lips, remembering the dreams when she couldn't hear her words or his. For the first time since he'd made the announcement about having the feast, she felt one with him again. Then an earth-shattering release compelled her to cry out, her body trembling with satisfaction, but Darien muffled her voice with another erotic deep kiss, his tongue probing her mouth.

Groaning, he filled her with his seed, but thrust twice more until she'd milked him dry, the orgasm rippling through her.

He closed his eyes and rested on top of her. "You are something else, honey."

"I could say the same about you." She combed her fingers through his hair. "Now you'll want a nap."

Chuckling, he licked her lips. "Now I want a feast. And then dessert again."

He rolled off her and a few granules of brown sugar sparkled on his chest. She licked them up, then he helped her off the table and wiped the flour from her back. "We're a mess," she whispered, her skin flushed with exertion.

He cast her a wolfish grin. "You got the brunt of it." He brushed flour out of her hair and she groaned. "At least the granules of cinnamon disappear in the color of your hair."

She gave him an annoyed look. "Next time, I'm on top. You can be covered in flour, sugar, and cinnamon."

Chuckling, he helped her into her clothes. "I'm game."

He touched her belly. "I understand Carol believes we'll have triplets."

"Conjecture."

"Right. But she won't tell me what sex they are."

Pleased that Carol thought she was pregnant, Lelandi still couldn't believe Carol could really know such a thing. She shook more flour and sugar out of her hair.

He kissed her forehead. "I invited your brother and uncle and parents to the feast. They dragged Ural along."

Lelandi stared at Darien, then slapped his shoulder. *That's* why he had been so intent on making love to her. It had nothing to do with his pack but all to do with worrying she might want to return to her family.

He grinned. "I thought you'd be pleased."

"You didn't have to prove anything to them. I would have stayed with you."

He took her hand and kissed it. "You're an alpha pack leader's mate, and you have the heart of a lion. Let's get the feast under way."

Lelandi was sure the fight would come first, but only after she dealt with her father, who wouldn't like it that she hadn't gotten his permission to mate Darien.

Darien escorted Lelandi into the sunroom where her parents were sitting, visiting with some of the members of his pack. Her brother and uncle were talking to Jake, and Ural sat in a corner looking unhappy. Probably still mad because of his incarceration and Darien's people's treatment of him. But he shouldn't have hung around.

"We'll leave you alone for a few minutes to get reacquainted," Darien said to Lelandi. Everyone remained stiff and formal until Darien gave Lelandi a searing kiss on the mouth, grinned, and then winked at her. He squeezed her hand and reiterated, "The entertainment begins in a few minutes."

The grays who were speaking with Lelandi's family rapidly left the sunroom while Lelandi kissed her mother and father, then her brother, uncle, and cousin.

"Triplets," her mother said, her face beaming. "I'll stay with you during the last trimester."

"Will… will you be living with Leidolf all the way out in Oregon?" Lelandi's voice betrayed her sadness.

"Heaven's no. Not with my grandkids coming and Hrothgar now in charge of the pack at Wildhaven." Her mother patted Uncle Hrothgar's arm. "Your father's little brother is now in charge and our land is saved." She glanced at Leidolf. "When are *you* going to give me some grandkids?"

Leidolf looked annoyed and folded his arms. "I need a mate and none are available, right now."

Eleanor tugged at Uncle Hrothgar's arm. "You'll need a mate, too. I did see a red female in the house earlier. What is she doing in a gray pack?"

"Carol? A red from Bruin's pack turned her. But she's an only child now and has aging parents here so I don't think she's interested in leaving."

Leidolf shook his head. "I wouldn't take a newly turned *lupus garou*. Too much of a responsibility. They don't know our ways and would need constant supervision."

"As if you can be that choosy, dear brother."

"And there's our line to think of."

"You mean because we're royals?" Lelandi rolled her eyes.

"It never meant much to you, but someone has to keep the line going. And not by mixing up with a gray either."

Their mother smiled. "Just like the old days. I forget how much you two fought." She sighed. "Your mate is motioning for this event to get under way. Save your teeth and claws for the one who deserves your wrath, if Darien should fail in his mission to avenge Larissa's death."

"He won't fail," Lelandi said with confidence. But

she sure as hell wanted to know who he was going to be pitted against—who had killed her sister.

In front of his gathered pack and their guests, Darien raised a glass of cider, his free arm around Lelandi's waist. "We're gathered here to celebrate the mating between our clans of Silver Town and Wildhaven. Lelandi is not only a royal," Darien said, pausing until the gasps died away, "but the daughter of pack leaders on both her paternal and maternal sides. So we are much honored to welcome Lelandi and her family into our embrace."

"Hear, hear," a chorus of grays and reds responded.

He raised his hand for silence. "Now for the grievous news. A pack bands together as a family, a united front against all others. But when one of our kind deviates from acceptable pack behavior, the individual must be dealt with swiftly and harshly. A death for a death, although in this case the murderer has killed more than one. But we can only mete out justice once.

"Normally, I would challenge the murderer and face him in our way, wolf to wolf. But I ask my Uncle Sheridan, sheriff of Silver Town, to fight on my behalf."

Low conversation filled the room and Lelandi glanced at Darien. He pressed her close and whispered in her ear, "I know what I'm doing."

Sheridan stood tall, a small smile curving his lips. He glanced at Trevor.

"He has agreed to fight Trevor."

The room was deadly silent.

Red-faced, Trevor stood his ground.

Lelandi looked up at Darien, tears in her eyes. Trevor wasn't the killer. How could Darien have made the mistake?

"Trevor admitted he lied about taking care of mudslide victims on the night of the shootings. Why? He wouldn't reveal the answer. But Uncle Sheridan knew. Trevor had hired the gunman who shot Lelandi, Tom, and Sam. He appeared on the ridge and killed the gunman before anyone could question him. The motive, you ask? He wanted to be sheriff. He thought his sister's mating with me would secure that position for him in the future. But some might have heard rumors Larissa's offspring were not my own and when Ritka revealed this to Trevor, he dreamed up this blackmail scheme. Through the sheriff's diligence, he discovered the money in a bank account in Green Valley in Trevor's name."

Trevor shot a dagger of a glare at the sheriff.

Darien motioned to Chester. "Acting on our behalf, P.I. Chester McKinley helped to uncover this treachery. All the puzzle pieces fit together. Trevor was a condemned man living on borrowed time." Darien's spine stiffened and his eyes held a feral gleam.

But Trevor didn't look like a condemned man, which made Lelandi suspicious that Darien and he had cooked up this whole charade.

"Except for one thing." Darien waved at Carol. "I wouldn't have revealed Carol's special gift because it's her choice, but she's agreed to save a man's life."

Carol nodded.

Lelandi stared at her. She knew, too? And didn't tell Lelandi? Inwardly, she growled.

"Carol has second sight."

Muffled conversation renewed.

"She saw not Trevor in the vision, but another man, who shoved the chair out from under Larissa's feet, allowing her to strangle until she was dead."

Darien held onto Lelandi when she felt ready to collapse, but she had to remain strong as the pack leader's mate, and she bit back the tears, willing them to stay at bay.

"Carol's visions aren't clear all the time, she explained to me. But one thing was—he wore a police uniform."

"Trevor," Sheridan said, his voice booming.

"At first, that's what Carol thought since all evidence pointed to him. But she touched the rope the murderer had tied into a noose. That man was you, Uncle Sheridan. You went on vacation, thinking you'd committed the perfect crime—murdered my mate, who was a disgrace to the pack because she was already mated and now having another gray's offspring. But you hadn't planned on Larissa having a family. A sister, who would come to avenge her. Ritka must have notified you when she was at the tavern that Lelandi had arrived, and you hurried home to take care of the mess."

"But Trevor's gun fired the fatal bullet that killed the gunman. He was the shooter," Sheridan said.

"My brothers and I investigated your house when you searched for evidence at Trevor's. We had already inspected his home first and found nothing to connect him with the crimes. However, at your home, we discovered the hunter's spray that makes an individual smell like decaying leaves. At Angelina's home, we found the kind that makes a person invisible to other animals. Why would either of you need hunter's sprays to hide your scent?"

Sheridan gave a coy smile. "I have no idea why Angelina would have such a thing, but the stuff I have was evidence."

"Hidden underneath your bathroom sink? And the GHB? Used to drug so many at the hospital? We found it in the same location."

"More evidence. I couldn't keep it at the jailhouse. Trevor might have destroyed it. Besides, I was drugged, too, remember?"

"Conveniently, yes. To counter suspicion. And you were the one in charge of so many of the investigations. You could 'find' whatever suited your purposes. If you had 'found' the GHB used in the crime at the hospital, why hadn't you reported it? We checked the area where we discovered Lelandi after she'd been shot. No decaying leaves like you'd said."

Lelandi shivered, realizing how close she'd come to death at Darien's uncle's hands.

"I must have gone to the wrong location. At the time of the shooting, I was at a hotel—"

"We investigated the hotel already. You checked in, but you disappeared in a hurry. One of the maids said you left several items in the bathroom and on the desk. You grabbed your bag, threw it in the truck, and roared out of there like the devil was after you. Even the manager said she noticed because you nearly hit another vehicle and the driver laid on the horn," Darien said.

"So I left in a hurry. Mason called me and said several shootings had occurred, and I needed to return at once."

"He called you on your cell phone well after you'd left the hotel. Time enough for you to have heard from Ritka, hired a gunman, and return so you could strangle Lelandi."

Uncle Sheridan turned his murderous glower on Trevor. "He has no alibi for the night of the shootings. He lied. And if I was strangling Lelandi, who shot the gunman?"

Darien offered a sinister smile. "You admit there had to be two of you? That the time was such that someone else had to have shot and killed the gunman? Only Jake and I knew this."

Sheridan's jaw ticked in restrained anger.

"True, Trevor lied about where he was. But he does have an alibi. He's been having an affair with an underage *lupus garou.*"

Ohmigod, was it Caitlin?

Sheridan looked smug. "Then the girl lied. To give him an alibi,"

"Her mother told me about her daughter's condition. She found them in bed together in a hotel on the outskirts of town. She was giving them the riot act for an hour at the same time when the shooting of the gunman occurred. Angelina used Trevor's gun to murder the gunman. *You* and she are without alibis."

"She's conveniently dead so she can't defend herself. But then again, she hated Larissa and Lelandi, so maybe she did hire the gunman. She *did* have the blackmail money."

Darien snorted. "You said Trevor had it." He waved a diary in the air. "Ritka was your lover. Doc Featherston examined the body and learned she'd been mated. Ritka wrote how you'd set up the blackmail scheme and when Larissa discovered you were the mastermind, you killed her. You were obsessed with keeping the pack line clean, and Ritka feared you, although you continued to come to her night after night. She was your partner in crime, along with Hosstene and Angelina, who you conveniently disposed of. But, you, damn it, you are my own flesh and blood."

"Your mate was a whore and brought shame to both the pack and our family's good name. It was only a matter of time before she took off with Joe. He'd been stealing from the silver mine so he and his lover could leave here. You would have gone after her, killed Joe, and brought her and her bastard children back to the pack as your own, while she remained the female pack leader, weak and disloyal. With her lover dead, do you think she would have changed her ways? Bah! She would have been more depressed, bringing the whole pack down with her. I couldn't allow it." Uncle Sheridan tore at his shirt. "You want me to fight Trevor, I will."

Lelandi hated Sheridan, but his words tore at her heart. He was probably right about everything he said. The pack would have suffered. But she couldn't agree her sister should have died because she had loved the wrong man.

Darien grunted. "No. I only wanted to draw the truth from you. You've shamed the family and our pack. You'll fight me."

Several of the pack members patted Trevor on the back, although some gave him dirty looks. Taking an underage *lupus garou* was unacceptable in their society, and Lelandi wondered again if it was Caitlin.

She glanced at Doc Mitchell and his gaze met hers. Caitlin's parents were absent. In fact, no underage *lupus garou* were present. When Bruin had such a gathering, everyone from the pack, regardless of age, was required to attend.

Darien kissed Lelandi's lips. "I'm sorry, Lelandi. I had to be sure."

"You've always done right by me. You will for Larissa as well."

Darien took a deep breath and nodded. "It ends here and now." He turned to face his pack. "To the field."

The battlefield.

Chapter 26

AS SOON AS LELANDI SAW SHERIDAN IN HIS WOLF COAT, SHE knew he was the one who'd stalked her in the woods. Too bad the pickup hadn't run him over on the road.

Nearly everyone loped out into the winter setting in their wolf forms where the upper crust of snow was crisp and giant snowflakes fluttered earthward. Wolves have the advantage over larger animals on deep-crusted snow, although Lelandi figured Sheridan wouldn't fall through the snow like a moose or elk might, slowing him down, despite his heftier size. Though she could hope.

Carol, not ready to join the wolf pack to watch another killing fight, didn't shapeshift. Maybe because she was afraid to turn wolf or the fear another wolf would attack her again. Lelandi's father, who remained in his wheelchair, watched out the sunroom window with Carol at his side. Since the accident, he hadn't been able to shapeshift, and she knew he felt like less of a *lupus garou* and battled depression, wishing often he had died with his people. Although she was certain he wanted desperately to be the one to avenge Larissa's death.

Both grays and reds alike formed a circle while Darien and his uncle faced off. Sheridan was taller by four inches and stockier built, but Darien had youth and strength on his side.

Leidolf crouched, ready to pounce, but Uncle Hrothgar growled at him, and her brother bowed his head slightly and straightened. For an eternity, it seemed Darien stared Sheridan down. Their wolf coats kept the chill out, the second dense coat keeping the snowflakes from touching their skin and melting. Everyone patiently watched for the showdown to begin while neither panted, just watched each other, their tails stretched stiff behind them, their thick hair standing at attention, ears perked, waiting for the other to move.

Lelandi's mind worked over the past events, and she realized how easy it had been for Sheridan to cover his tracks since he was always in charge of the investigations—even to confirm Larissa had committed suicide.

Darien turned and walked in a circle toward his uncle, who immediately moved away.

Sheridan continued to avoid Darien, but the pack leader was quickly closing the gap. Inwardly, Lelandi darkly smiled. The first test and Sheridan had failed. *The bastard.* Sheridan tried to turn, but he wasn't agile enough and Darien bit him in the flank.

If Lelandi hadn't been in her wolf form, she would have cheered Darien.

Sheridan yelped and dodged before Darien took another bite. He wouldn't kill him quickly, she figured. Not after Sheridan had murdered her sister, two pack members, and tried to murder Lelandi.

His people and hers would want justice—*lupus garou* justice, but drawn out enough to make it count.

Sheridan tried to hide his limp from the wound, but he continued to circle around the inside of the group, keeping away from Darien. By the way his tail drooped slightly, Sheridan was already showing signs of defeat.

When he neared Leidolf, her brother snarled at Sheridan, his teeth bared, his tail straight—readying for the attack.

Lelandi's fur stood on end. Let Darien take care of it, she prayed. But Sheridan snapped back at Leidolf, so close Lelandi nearly died. Leidolf's blood was running hot, the way the anger swelled deep inside him and she, being so connected with her triplet's emotions, felt swept into the maelstrom.

In the blink of an eye, Leidolf responded to Sheridan's taunt and attacked, sinking his teeth into the bigger gray's side.

Sheridan could kill her brother for being such a hotheaded fool as soon as the bigger gray shook him loose. But she didn't expect Sheridan to free himself from Leidolf's grip, then bite into Leidolf's neck, since Darien was more of a threat.

Instinctively, Lelandi went for Sheridan's throat and grabbed hold. She felt Darien brush against her side, trying to get to Sheridan, but she couldn't let go for fear the gray would kill her next. As fast as it took a bolt of lightning to strike the ground, Sheridan released Leidolf and seized Lelandi's throat. He would kill her like he murdered her sister, and if he did, he would destroy Darien's reason to live.

She didn't have time to panic, or feel Sheridan's jaws clamping down tighter, stopping the air from flowing, before Darien grappled his uncle's neck with his powerful jaws. Biting down hard, he crushed the bone and the life out of the gray.

Sheridan's mouth loosened on Lelandi's neck, and they both collapsed. When she fell on her side, she lay still, trying to catch her breath. But it was worse than that, and she couldn't help being totally humiliated. Darien quickly changed into his human form despite the cold and held his hand over the wound on her throat. "Carol!"

His own neck bleeding, Leidolf nuzzled her face.

Darien lifted Lelandi from the snow and hurried her into the house.

"Lay her there, Darien. I… I've never taken care of an injured wolf," Carol said, opening a first aid kit.

"They can be testier than in their human forms, but in Lelandi's case, I'm not sure that's always true," Darien said, a slight smile curving his lips.

Lelandi growled.

Doc Mitchell stalked into the house, zipping up his jeans and grabbed his bag. "Came prepared for any eventuality."

"Why isn't she changing back?" Carol asked.

Jake threw on a pair of jeans. "Too tired, loss of blood, trauma."

Carol's gaze strayed to Leidolf, yanking on a pair of olive drab khakis.

"I'll take care of Lelandi," Doc Mitchell said. "You look after Leidolf."

Leidolf buckled his belt. "I'm fine. I don't need looking after."

"Sit, son, and do it for your mother. She's already lost one of you, and she's looking a little pale," his father said.

Leidolf grumbled, then sat on a chair, his face scowling while Carol wiped away the blood on his throat, and then bandaged him.

Lelandi studied the way her brother treated Carol with such annoyance and the gentle way in which she ministered to his wounds. Possibility?

"Lelandi, honey," Darien said. "Can't you change back?"

Mitchell bandaged her neck. "Sheridan didn't have a chance to dig in deep enough so the bite marks aren't too bad. She'll be fine in a couple of hours." He gave her a shot for the pain, which she didn't want, and growled again. The medication spread through her veins, heating her blood.

Her mother wiped away tears from her own cheeks, then leaned over and patted Lelandi's head. "She'll be all right in a little bit, won't you, dear?"

Lelandi closed her eyes, hating that she would fall apart now. How did this look to the whole pack? She groaned.

Her mother sighed. "It's the shock of nearly losing her brother."

"She did not nearly lose me!" her brother snapped.

Her mother ran her hand over Lelandi's back. "She's been under a lot of strain. That was the last straw. Remember the time when you almost drowned?"

"Mother," Leidolf growled.

"Well, remember? She finally managed to get you by the neck and pull you to shore, but she was in shock over the ordeal. Took her three days before she could turn human again."

Leidolf gave an evil grin. "Yeah, I remember. She was awful to live with."

Lelandi growled low. She had no control over the connection she had with her siblings and their emotions. But she had been the only one who felt her siblings' emotions so severely she could put herself into such a state over them. She growled again.

"Fine." Darien lifted Lelandi off the floor. "Enjoy the feast. We will return when we return." He carried her toward the stairs.

"What about Uncle Sheridan?" Jake asked.

"Unmarked grave. The devil can take him."

Darien carried Lelandi up the stairs to their bedroom, then laid her down on the mattress. "You need peace and quiet, love."

She wanted to eat. To celebrate their union and the destruction of the gray who had murdered her sister. And she wanted to be human to do it! Damn it.

But because of the strain and extreme weariness creeping through her body from the pain killer, she drifted off to sleep and found her silver knight waiting for her.

"Lelandi, love."

She reached out her arms to him, and he took her into his hard embrace and willed him to love her.

The rush of adrenaline flowed through her, filling her with orgasmic pleasure, and Lelandi blinked her eyes and stared up at Darien. He smiled back at her, his cock buried deep inside her as hot lava filled her to the core.

"Hmm," she hummed. "When did I turn human?"

He arched a brow and slid off her, then pulled her onto his damp chest. "Before I ravished you." He chuckled. "You don't remember?"

"You came to me in a dream."

"Ah. You fell asleep and shapeshifted. I replaced your bandage, but as soon as I pulled you into my arms to snuggle, you had other notions. Started kissing me and stroking me. I thought you were awake."

She smiled and touched his taut nipple. "I am now." Then she frowned. "He's really dead, isn't he?"

"Yes, Lelandi. I'm so sorry he was the one." He stroked her hair. "My own flesh and blood."

"How… how did you know about Ritka's diary?"

"Carol had a vision that Ritka had hidden it in Doc's office, where no one would suspect it—buried behind deceased patient files. We didn't know if she had written anything incriminating, but she must have feared Sheridan might turn on her."

"I'm sorry for interfering in the fight."

He touched her throat below the bandage. "If you had tried to protect me and had gotten injured, I would have been perturbed. But I understand that you have this emotional tie to your siblings that can't be walled up. Although…" He kissed her eyelid, then the other. "… you got in my way when I tried to tackle Uncle Sheridan while he still had hold of your brother. I don't blame Leidolf for attacking him either. Both of you had every right."

"Your people aren't mad at me, are they?"

"They're eating and having a merry time of it. But they're looking forward to us joining them."

She nuzzled her cheek against his chest. "I'm hungry."

"Good. I'm starving and if I don't eat my main course, I won't get any more dessert." A sexy smile tugging at his mouth, he rolled out of bed, then jerked on his jeans. "And I'm hungry for dessert, again."

❖ ❖ ❖

Sitting before the fire in the living room, Sam's bearded face glowed in the light of the embers while he told another story of their ancestors' exploits of long ago. Darien wrapped his arm around Lelandi and pulled her close on the couch, and for the first time ever, she really felt part of the pack. Leidolf was sipping another beer in one of the chairs, studying Carol as she sat on the floor next to Tom, enraptured with Sam's tales, her blue eyes wide with awe. Silva served another tray of drinks, and Lelandi's father nodded off in his wheelchair.

Doc Mitchell and Chester McKinley played a game of chess nearby while Mason supervised. Eleanor and Nurse Grey made turkey sandwiches for everyone. The Hastings sat together on a love seat, cuddled together as if they were young lovers all over again. Jake took a seat on the other side of Carol and offered her a bag of chips. She smiled at him like she was in love, and Leidolf took another swig of his beer, his expression annoyed.

Peter looked happy and relaxed now that he was the new sheriff of Silver Town and gave Lelandi a satisfied smile. Trevor had vanished, and she wondered if he'd left to see Caitlin.

Darien rubbed her tummy absentmindedly and it made her warm and tingly inside.

She glanced at Carol. She didn't want her to leave Silver Town after they'd become friends, but what if she could be the one for her footloose brother? Lelandi frowned. Carol had wanted to be near her parents, and Leidolf now had a pack of his own to lead and couldn't abandon them.

She kissed Darien's cheek and snuggled closer. Leidolf could figure it out on his own.

Now that Lelandi was Darien's, life couldn't get any better. Although he still had to deal with Trevor's behavior concerning sixteen-year-old Caitlin. Her parents were agreeable the two were now mated, and she would move in with him, but his inappropriate actions had to be punished. Deviating from acceptable pack behavior couldn't be tolerated.

As for Leidolf, itching to return to his pack in Portland, Darien couldn't be more glad. The farther her brother was away from Lelandi, the better, considering how her emotional state was tied to his.

Carol was another issue. Dealing with a newly turned *lupus garou* was problematic. As soon as he could, he needed to have her mated so that her mate would keep her in line. He rubbed his chin as he considered Leidolf, who seemed aggravated over Darien's brothers' attention to Carol. Maybe Leidolf was the solution to Darien's problem.

He leaned back on the couch and pulled Lelandi closer. Larissa would never know how much of a nightmare she'd created, but in her death, she'd brought Lelandi into his life. Because of that, he could forgive Larissa.

But the families of those who'd died—Ritka, Angelina, Hosstene, and Uncle Sheridan—wouldn't be so easily appeased. For them, although they recognized their family members had committed grave injustices, many felt their actions somewhat justified. If Larissa hadn't been mated already, then had an affair with Joe, most likely none would have committed the crimes. Some had voiced their dissent, and he assumed they might leave the pack.

He glanced at his cousins, Uncle Sheridan's four grown sons. For some time now, they'd been conspicuously absent from any of the pack goings-on. Had they known about their father's complicity?

Connor, the most light-hearted one of the bunch, looked Darien's way. For the briefest of moments, he appeared sad, but he quickly hardened his expression and turned away.

Yep, ripples of dissent were already stirring, but Darien had dealt with problems like these for years. He'd deal with these, too.

Lelandi looked up at Darien and smiled, not in a sweetly innocent way, but in one that said she wanted some alone time with him. He rubbed her arm and leaned over and gave her a kiss.

Sam quit orating a story and Darien looked up and found every eye in the room on him.

"Lelandi's feeling tired."

Several smiled.

He rose from the couch with Lelandi. Loving every bit of her, the feral and the tame, he swept her up in his arms to whoops and cheers and headed to the stairs.

"You are so subtle, you know?" she said in a harsh, low voice.

He grinned. "You should be proud of me. I didn't say I was taking you to bed to ravish you."

She groaned and he laughed.

Several downstairs laughed and Sam began telling another story. And Darien, well, he was going to make sure Carol's prediction came true. In nine months, he'd be cradling an armful of triplets. God, how he loved Lelandi. His dream had finally been realized.

"About Carol," Lelandi said as Darien deposited her on the bed.

He growled low. "Now is not the time to discuss pack business." He straddled her, his rock-hard erection straining for release, and she gave him a coy smile.

"*This* is pack business," she reminded him.

"Believe me, from now on I'll be taking care of a lot more of *this* kind of business."

"Darien, I was thinking. I want to be a psychologist."

"No."

"You don't even know what I was going to say."

"You'd have to go away to college. So no." His dark eyes challenged her as he quickly divested her of her clothes.

"I can take it online. When Larissa needed help, a psychologist had to come from Green Valley." Lelandi ran her fingers through Darien's silky hair, but she could tell from his hard expression, he wasn't buying her pitch.

"I still say no." He jerked off his shirt.

"Why?"

He climbed off the bed and ditched his boots and jeans. "I don't want you talking to crazy people." Returning to bed, he leaned next to her, and massaged her breast. "They can become infatuated with their doctor, believing the doctor loves them because she listens to their concerns, she cares about them. And one as attractive as you…" He shook his head.

"I could help people deal with grief and all kinds of different anxieties. I need to have something to do."

His hand shifted to her belly, and he caressed her with a gentle touch. "You'll have plenty to do."

She growled.

He grunted. "All right. Get your degree online, and then you can see female patients, *only*."

She laughed. "I can just hear what your people will say."

"*Our* people. If a guy wants to see you, he'll have to request an audience with either me or one of my brothers first."

"That'll cut down the number of male patients I get."

He offered a devilish smile.

She touched his face, then leaned over to kiss his lips. "Hmm, Darien, my dream lover. Make the dream come true again."

"It already has, sweet Lelandi. It already has."

With that, he swept her into their own private world, vowing to take her for a romp in the woods in their wolf states later that evening to fulfill Carol's prediction that men and women dressed in wolf skins made love beneath the pale light of the moon.

The End

**Delve further into the world of the *lupus garou* with
another paranormal romance from Terry Spear:**

Heart
of the Wolf

Now available from Sourcebooks.

Prologue

1850
Colorado

AS SOON AS HE STRIPPED NAKED, HE'D BE HERS.

Unbraiding her hair, Bella's blood heated with desire while she observed the dark-haired boy. He looked about eighteen, two years older than she. He yanked off one boot, then another, at the lake's edge. It wasn't the first time she'd watched him peel out of his clothes, but it was the first time she'd join him. If he had a taste of her, wouldn't he crave her? Hunger to be like her? Wild and free?

She swallowed hard, longing to be Devlyn's mate—rather than some human's—but it would never be. Lifting her chin, she resolved to make the human hers. She untied her ankle-high boots, then slipped them off her feet.

The human boy's pet gray wolf rested at the shoreline, his ears perked up as he watched her. But the boy didn't see her—he was unobservant, as most humans were.

However, a boy who cared for his wolf such as he did would care for her, too, wouldn't he? He'd studied her when she swam here before, naked, splashing lazily across the water's surface, attempting to draw him to her. Though he'd tried to conceal himself in the woods, she'd seen him. And heard him with her sensitive hearing when he stepped on dried oak leaves and pine needles to draw closer, to see her more clearly. She'd smelled his heady man-scent on the breeze. He'd desired her then, setting her belly afire; he'd desire her now.

Tilting her nose up, she breathed in his masculinity. Masculine but not as wild as her own kind—*lupus garou*. A human who treated a woman with kindness, that's what she desired.

She tugged her pale blue dress over her head, struggling to shed her clothes as quickly as she could now. Wanting to get her plan into motion, before she changed her mind, or one of the pack tried to change it for her.

Adopted by the gray pack, she wasn't even a gray wolf. So why should it matter if she left them and chose the human boy for her own? Volan, the gray alpha pack leader, wanted her, that's why. Her stomach clenched with the thought that the man who'd nearly raped her would have her if she couldn't find a way out of the nightmare.

The human pulled off his breeches. A boy, still not well muscled, but well on his way. A survivor, living on his own, that's what intrigued her so much about him. A loner—like a rogue wolf—determined to endure.

Only in her heart, she desired the gray who'd saved her life when they were younger—Devlyn. Even now she had difficulty not comparing his rangy, taller body with this boy's. They had the same dark hair and eyes, which maybe explained why the human had attracted her. She wanted Devlyn with all her heart, but craving his attention would only result in Volan killing him. Best to leave the pack and mate with a human, cut her ties with the grays, and start her own pack.

She'd watched the human ride, run, hunt with his rifle, but she admired him most when he swam. Her gaze dropped lower to the patch of dark hair resting above his legs and…

She raised her brows. A thrill of expectation of having his manhood buried deep inside her sent a tingling of gooseflesh across her skin. If her drawers hadn't been crotchless, they'd have been wet in anticipation. She smiled at the sight of him. He'd produce fine offspring.

He dove into the water with a splash. With powerful strokes he glided across the placid surface of the small, summer-warmed lake. She slipped out of her last petticoat, then her drawers. Without a stitch of clothes on, she stood on the opposite shore, waiting for him to catch sight of her. Wouldn't he yearn for her like her own kind did?

She had to entice him to make love to her. Then she'd change into the wolf and bite him. And transfer the beauty of the wolf to him in the ancient way.

Running her fingers through her cinnamon curls, she fanned them over her shoulders, down to her hips.

They'd live together in his log cabin, taking jaunts through the woods in their wolf states under the bright moon forever. His mother, father, and little sister had died during the winter, and none of his kind lived within a fifteen-mile radius. He'd want her—he had to. Like her wolf pack, most humankind desired companionship.

She stepped into the water.

Then he caught sight of her.

His dark eyes widened and his mouth dropped open. But he didn't swim toward her as she expected. He didn't come for her, ravish her as she wanted. His eyes inspected every bit of her, but then he turned and swam away from her, back to the shore and his clothes. What was wrong with him?

Her mind warred between anger and confusion. Didn't he find her appealing?

She swam toward him, trying to reach the shore before he dressed and headed back to his cabin. But by the time she reached the lake halfway, he'd jerked on his breeches and boots, not even bothering with his shirt or vest, and vanished into the woods with his wolf at his heel.

In disbelief, she stared after him.

"Bella!" the leader of her pack hollered, his voice forbidding and warlike.

She snapped her head around. Her heart nearly stopped when she saw the gray leader.

Volan stood like a predator waiting for the right time to go after his prey. His ebony hair was bound tight, and his black eyes narrowed. As a wolf, he was heavyset, broad-shouldered and thick-necked, the leader by virtue of his size, powerful jaws, and wicked killer canines. But now he stood as a man, his thoughts darker than night, his face menacing as he considered her swimming naked in the lake.

Did the boy get away in time, before Volan caught sight of him? How could she be so naïve as to think that Volan would let her have a human male?

She paddled in place and glared at him. "What do you want, Volan?" she growled back, unable to hold a civil tongue whenever he stood near.

"Come out at once!"

He turned his head toward the woods.

Had he smelled the human? Her heart rate quickened. She swam back to her clothes, determined to draw his attention away from the boy.

Then she spied Devlyn, watching, half hidden in the shadows of the forest, as if he and the pack leader were maneuvering in for the kill. A pang of regret sliced through her that Devlyn might have seen her lusting after a human. Three years older than she, he still vied for his place within the pack. A strap of leather tied back his coffee-colored, shoulder-length hair, and she fought the urge to set it free, to soften his harsh look. His equally dark brown eyes glowered at her, while his sturdy jaw clenched.

He stepped closer, not menacingly, but as if he stalked a deer and feared scaring away his prey. She raised a brow. This time, he seemed to have Volan's permission to draw close.

She growled. "Stay away." Wading out of the water, she distracted Volan from considering the woods or who might have disappeared into them. Devlyn, too, eyed her with far too much interest.

She hurried to slip into her clothes, irritated to have the wrong audience. Still, the way Devlyn closed in on her, only keeping a few feet from her until she was dressed, while Volan remained a hundred yards away, sent a trickle of dread through her.

Volan never allowed males to get close to her when she was naked, and normally she wouldn't have permitted it either. So what were they up to? She left her wet hair loose, then Volan nodded.

As soon as he signaled to Devlyn, her heart skipped a beat, but she didn't react quickly enough. Devlyn surged forward and grabbed her wrist. In the same instant, Volan charged in the direction of the woods where the young man had disappeared.

"Volan!" she screamed.

He intended to murder the boy. Only *she* had really killed him, as surely as if she'd ripped out his throat herself. Wanting to save him, she struggled to free herself from Devlyn. "Let me go!"

He gripped her wrist tighter and hurried her toward their village.

"He didn't do anything!"

Devlyn glared at her, his eyes unforgiving, blacker than she'd ever seen them. Anger smoldered in the depths. An anger she couldn't understand.

"Please," she pleaded, trying to soften his heart.

She tried to break free, and he wrenched her back to his side. "You're a fool, Bella."

"I won't be Volan's mate!"

For an instant, Devlyn's grasp on her arm lessened. Then he tightened his grip again. "You have no choice. And after what you've done here, he won't wait any longer."

Was there regret in his voice? God, how she wanted him to save her from Volan… to be her mate.

A howl sounded in the distance, and she sank to her knees. Volan had murdered the young man and shouted his actions to the world with great pleasure.

Devlyn yanked her from the ground and hurried her on their way.

"You won't ever leave the pack, Devlyn. You'll always be nothing but a follower!" She hadn't meant to say the hurtful words, but the anger she harbored simmered red-hot, like molten lava beneath the surface. "Why can't you run with me? Why can't you take me for your own somewhere far from here?"

He glared at her. "They're my family. They'll always be my family. Something you don't comprehend, apparently."

"I—I thought you felt something for me."

Devlyn pulled her to a stop and grabbed her shoulders. "It can never be between us! Volan would hunt us down, both of us. What kind of a life would that be? He'd kill our offspring, too. Is that what you want? Maybe if I'd been older, stronger, but now he won't wait to have you." He shook his head. "Dammit, Bella, as far as the human was concerned, he wouldn't have wanted you! Can't you see that? If he'd seen you changed, he would have been repulsed. If he could have discovered a way, he'd have killed you." He held her tightly, staring into her eyes with a mixture of anger and hunger. "You know what I want from you."

He was hard and smelled of sex. She sensed that his hormones raged, urging him to mount her. Her breath came quickly as she desired his attentions, but feared them, too. Feared them because of what Volan would do to Devlyn if Volan caught him lusting after her. She'd never seen Devlyn so outwardly angry, so filled with venom—so sexually alive.

"You could smell his putrid fear, woman!" He pulled her against his body and kissed her hard on the mouth, no teasing or waiting for her approval—just pure lust, conquering and decisive. And she loved him, every bit of the dangerous and feral *lupus garou* that he was.

Her body melted to his touch, but Volan's musky, bloody scent drifted to her on the breeze. Panic sliced through her. Volan would claim her now. But if he caught Devlyn touching her...

Volan appeared in a couple of bounds in his ebony-pelted wolf form, his eyes narrowed with hate. He growled, and immediately Devlyn released her. She stepped back, assuming Volan would kill Devlyn for his actions, the thought wrenching at her gut.

Devlyn stood his ground. "I tried to convince her how stupid she was for feeling anything for the human."

Volan turned to Bella. He'd show her how a male wolf took a mate. The moisture from her throat evaporated. The image of him trying to take her when she was much younger still fed her nightmares. A streak of shudders racked her body.

Volan turned his attention back to Devlyn. The hair stood on end from the nape of his neck to the tip of his tail. He advanced aggressively, then stopped.

Torn between giving herself to Volan to protect Devlyn and fighting Volan herself, she knew neither would work. Devlyn would hate her either way—damn his male wolf pride.

Volan growled again. Devlyn yanked off his shirt. His muscles flexed as he tugged at his belt, his golden skin shimmering with sweat in the summer sun. Any other day, she loved to see every bit of his handsome physique—his muscled thighs, the dark patch of curly hair between his legs, and the erection she'd encouraged. But not now, not with Volan threatening to rip him to shreds.

As soon as Devlyn stood naked, he began to change, his body twisting into the form of a wolf, his snout elongated. A thick brown pelt as rich as a mink's covered his long legs and torso. He howled as the change took place. Volan waited patiently before he lunged.

She couldn't watch him rip Devlyn apart. She couldn't stomach seeing the bully hurt any other wolf of the pack. But certainly not Devlyn, with whom she'd played as a pup, not Devlyn who'd rescued her from the wildfire that took her red wolf pack's lives. She couldn't save him now… only maybe herself. Yet when Volan lunged for Devlyn, she dashed between them to protect him. Volan clamped his teeth down on her arm, having the ability to crush the bone with his powerful canines. She cried out when a streak of pain shot up her arm and blood dripped from the wound. Though his eyes reflected remorse at once and he released her, he growled at her to stay out of the way. And so did Devlyn.

Maybe if she ran, Volan would come after her. Maybe she could save Devlyn that way. But she would never return to the pack.

She bolted, with her legs stretched far out, her heart pounding, her breath steady, but her mind frantic— her only chance was to toss her clothes and run like the wolf.

Chapter 1

Present Day
Portland, Oregon

ONE HUNDRED AND FIFTY YEARS LATER—AGING ONE YEAR for every thirty that passed once a *lupus garou* reached puberty—Bella was the equivalent of a human twenty-one-year-old. She longed more than ever to have Devlyn for her mate, wishing she hadn't had to hide from the pack all these years. The burning desire for him flooded her veins whenever she came into the wolf's heat. Her body craved his touch, but her mind had given up hoping to ever have him for her own. If she could find a strong, agreeable human mate, she could change him into a *lupus garou*, and he would keep her safe from Volan.

She shook her head, trying to rid herself of the image of the brutish fiend, and continued to pack her overnight bag. Any man would be better than he—a good mate who would help her establish her own pack.

She turned to look at Devlyn's photo sitting on the bedside table, the most recent one that Argos, the old, retired pack leader, had sent her. Taking a deep breath, she threw another pair of jeans into her bag, determined to get her mind off Devlyn.

Knowing she couldn't put off mating much longer, she realized that one's second choice far outweighed living alone; even the sound of a dog's howl on the night's breeze triggered the gnawing craving to be with a pack.

She stalked into her office and left an email message for Argos, a routine she'd adopted because he insisted she keep him posted whenever she went into the woods. As a loner, she'd have no backup. *Off to the cabin for the weekend again, Argos. Give the pack my love, in secret. Yours always, love, Bella*

She didn't have to tell him to keep her correspondence a secret; he knew what would happen if Volan learned where she was....

Turning off her computer, she picked up her phone and called her next-door neighbor—a woman who had partially eased Bella's loneliness after losing her twin sister in a fire so many years ago. "Chrissie, I'm going to my cabin for the weekend again. Can you keep an eye on my place?"

"Sure thing, Bella. Pick up your mail on Saturday, too, if you'd like. And I'll water your greenhouse plants. Hey, I don't want to hold you up, but did you hear about the latest killing?"

"Yeah, the police have got to catch the bastard soon."

That was one of the reasons she was going to her cabin, to get away, to consider the facts of the murders, to search for clues in the woods. He had to be from Portland or the surrounding area, since it was there he'd killed all the women. And he had to take a jaunt in a forest from time to time. The call of the wild was too strong in them. She hadn't expected to smell red *lupus garou* in the place where she ran, as far away as it was from the city. For three years she hadn't smelled a hint of them. Not until last weekend. Was one of them the killer? She had to know.

Bella tossed a pink sweatshirt into the bag.

"You be careful, honey. The victims are all redheads in their twenties. And the last was killed not far from here."

"Don't worry, Chrissie. I've got a gun for protection." Well, two: one at her cabin, and one at home, but who was counting? Silver bullets, too; Bella had them made for Volan. It wasn't the *lupus garou* way, but she had no other way to fight him. She would never be his.

"A… a gun? Do you know how to shoot it?"

Yep, she'd learned how to shoot a gun a good century and a half ago, ever since the early days when she had lived in the wilderness, trying to survive in the lands west of Colorado.

"Yeah, don't worry. Give your kids hugs for me, will you? Tell Mary I want to see the painting she did for art class, and tell Jimmy that I want to see his science project when I return."

Chrissie sighed. "I'll tell them. You be careful up there all by yourself. That is, if you're going all by yourself."

Always checking. Chrissie was looking for husband number two, and she assumed Bella rendezvoused with some mountain man every time she returned to her cabin.

"See you Monday."

"Be careful, Bella. You never know where that maniac will end up."

"I'll be cautious. Got to go."

Bella hung up the phone and zipped her suitcase. Before it turned dark she had every intention of searching the woods for further clues concerning the red *lupus garou*—not a wild dog, a mixed wolf-dog breed, or as some thought, a pit bull that some bastard had trained to kill his victims—that might be killing the women.

Why had she caught the scent of red *lupus garou* in the area near her cabin now, when the woods had been free of their kind for the last three years? She envisioned a lone female wouldn't stand a chance at remaining that way. Her stomach curdled with the idea that she'd have to give up her cabin and find a new place to run. Just one more concern to add to her growing list of worries.

Acknowledgments

To my mother, daughter, and son who cheer me on and believe all my books should be made into movies. And to my editor, Deb Werksman, who inspires me every step of the way. Thanks to all the help my Rebel Romance Writers give as they encourage my writing daily. And to my fans who write to me and encourage me to continue creating more wolfish tales.

About the Author

Award-winning author of urban fantasy and medieval historicals, Terry Spear also writes true stories for adult and young adult audiences. She's a retired lieutenant colonel in the U.S. Army Reserves, a Distinguished Military Graduate of West Texas A&M, and an MBA from Monmouth College. Originally from the West Coast, she has lived in nine states and now resides in the heart of Texas. She is the author of *Heart of the Wolf, Winning the Highlander's Heart, Deadly Liaisons,* and *The Vampire... In My Dreams* (young adult).

$\mathcal{H}eart$
of the
$\mathcal{W}olf$

BY TERRY SPEAR

"A fast-paced, sexy read with lots of twists and turns!"

—Nicole North, author of *Devil in a Kilt*

THEIR FORBIDDEN LOVE MAY GET THEM BOTH KILLED

"Red werewolf Bella flees her adoptive pack of gray werewolves when the alpha male Volan tries forcibly to claim her as his mate. Her real love, beta male Devlyn, is willing to fight Volan to the death to claim her. That problem pales, however, as a pack of red werewolves takes to killing human females in a crazed quest to claim Bella for their own. Bella and Devlyn must defeat the rogue wolves before Devlyn's final confrontation with Volan. The vulpine couple's chemistry crackles off the page, but the real strength of the book lies in Spear's depiction of pack power dynamics… her wolf world feels at once palpable and even plausible."

—*Publisher's Weekly*

A *Publisher's Weekly* Best Book of the Year

978-1-4022-1157-7 • $6.99 U.S. / $8.99 CAN

DARK HIGHLAND FIRE

BY KENDRA LEIGH CASTLE

A werewolf from the Scottish Highlands and a fiery demi-goddess fleeing for her life…

Desired by women, kissed by luck, Gabriel MacInnes has always been able to put pleasure ahead of duty. But with the MacInnes wolves now squarely in the sights of an ancient enemy, everything is about to change…

Rowan *an* Morgaine, on the run from a dragon prince who will stop at nothing to have her as his own, must accept the protection of Gabriel and his clan. By force or by guile, Rowan and Gabriel must uncover the secrets of their intertwining fate and stop their common enemy.

"This fresh and exciting take on the werewolf legend held me captive."

—NINA BANGS, AUTHOR OF *ONE BITE STAND*

978-1-4022-1159-1 • $6.99 U.S. / $8.99 CAN

The WILD SIGHT

BY LOUCINDA McGARY

"A magical tale of romance and intrigue. I couldn't put it down!" —Pamela Palmer, author of *Dark Deceiver* and *The Dark Gate*

HE WAS CURSED WITH A "GIFT"

Born with the clairvoyance known to the Irish as "The Sight," Donovan O'Shea fled to America to escape his visions. On a return trip to Ireland to see his ailing father, staggering family secrets threaten to turn his world upside down. And then beautiful, sensual Rylie Powell shows up, claiming to be his half-sister…

SHE'S LOOKING FOR THE FAMILY SHE NEVER KNEW…

After her mother's death, Rylie finds tantalizing clues that send her to Ireland to find the man she suspects is her father. She needs the truth—but how can she and Donovan be brother and sister when the chemistry between them is nearly irresistible?

UNCOVERING THE PAST LEADS THEM DANGEROUSLY CLOSE TO MADNESS…

"A richly drawn love story and riveting romantic suspense!" —Karin Tabke, author of *What You Can't See*

978-1-4022-1394-6 • $6.99 U.S. / $8.99 CAN

BY LINDA WISDOM

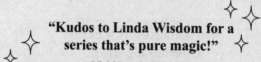

"Kudos to Linda Wisdom for a series that's pure magic!"

—Vicki Lewis Thompson,
New York Times bestselling author of *Wild & Hexy*

JAZZ AND NICK'S DREAM ROMANCE HAS TURNED INTO A NIGHTMARE...

FEISTY WITCH JASMINE TREMAINE AND DROP-DEAD GORGEOUS VAMPIRE cop Nikolai Gregorovich have a hot thing going, but it's tough to keep it together when nightmare visions turn their passion into bickering.

With a little help from their friends, Nick and Jazz are in a race against time to uncover whoever it is that's poisoning their dreams, and their relationship...

978-1-4022-1400-4 • $6.99 U.S. / $7.99 CAN

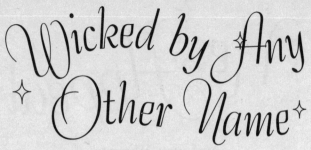

Wicked by Any Other Name

BY LINDA WISDOM

"Do not miss this wickedly entertaining treat."

—Annette Blair,
Sex and the Psychic Witch

STASI ROMANOV USES JUST A LITTLE WITCH MAGIC IN HER LINGERIE shop, running a brisk side business in love charms. A disgruntled customer threatening to sue over a failed love spell brings wizard attorney Trevor Barnes to town. Everyone knows that witches and wizards make a volatile combination—sure enough, the sparks fly and almost everyone's getting singed. The feisty witch and gorgeous wizard have more than simply a preternatural lawsuit on their hands. Can they overcome their objections and settle out of court—and in the bedroom?

978-1-4022-1773-9 • $6.99 U.S. / $7.99 CAN

SLAVE

BY CHERYL BROOKS

"I found him in the slave market on Orpheseus Prime, and even on such a god-forsaken planet as that one, their treatment of him seemed extreme."

He may be the last of a species whose sexual talents were the envy of the galaxy. Even filthy, chained, and beaten, his feline gene gives him a special aura.

Jacinth is on a rescue mission… and she needs a man she can trust with her life.

Praise for Cheryl Brooks' *Slave*:

"A sexy adventure with a hero you can't resist!"

—Candace Havens, author of *Charmed & Deadly*

"Fascinating world customs, a bit of mystery, and the relationship between the hero and heroine make this a very sensual romance."

—*Romantic Times*

978-1-4022-1192-8 • $6.99 U.S. / $8.99 CAN

WARRIOR

BY CHERYL BROOKS

*"He came to me in the dead of winter,
his body burning with fever."*

EVEN NEAR DEATH, HIS SENSUALITY IS AMAZING...

Leo arrives on Tisana's doorstep a beaten slave from a near extinct race with feline genes. As soon as Leo recovers his strength, he'll use his extraordinary sexual talents to bewitch Tisana and make a bolt for freedom...

Praise for The Cat Star Chronicles:

"A compelling tale of danger, intrigue, and sizzling romance!"

—Candace Havens, author of *Charmed & Deadly*

"A magical story of hope, love, and devotion."

—*Yankee Romance Reviews*

"Hot enough to start a fire. Add in a thrilling new world and my reading experience was complete."

—*Romance Junkies*

978-1-4022-1440-0 • $6.99 U.S. / $7.99 CAN